SPLINTERS OF SILENCE

Dancing while we may, 7

Kevin Corby Bowyer

Mysterious Strawberry

Copyright © 2023 Kevin Corby Bowyer

All rights reserved

The characters and events portrayed in this book are fictitious. Any similarity to real persons, living or dead, is coincidental and not intended by the author.

No part of this book may be reproduced, or stored in a retrieval system, or transmitted in any form or by any means, electronic, mechanical, photocopying, recording, or otherwise, without express written permission of the publisher.

Cover design by: Joseph Loganbill

Printed in Great Britain

CONTENTS

Title Page	
Copyright	
Introduction	1
The Origin of Vivianne Stamper	3
Natty Miller	76
Poor Nancy	112
Secret Girl	124
Stalker	175
The Apostate	187
The Mill	193
Faithfulness	224
In Her Sleep	230
Terrel's Women	234
Dilly and Emily	240
Dominoes	249
Character lists	259
The Origin of Vivianne Stamper	260
Natty Miller	263
Poor Nancy	268
Secret Girl	269
Stalker	272

The Apostate	273
The Mill	274
Faithfulness	276
In Her Sleep	277
Terrel's Women	278
Dilly and Emily	279
Dominoes	280
The Author	282

INTRODUCTION

This book has gone through many revisions over more than two years and has grown from a pair of novellas into a collection of twelve tales. My introduction, originally penned many months ago, now needs a rewrite.

The order of tales has changed. *The Origin of Vivianne Stamper* was always intended to occupy the first spot (it still does), and I'd originally thought to end with *The Apostate*, a kind of gentle postscript. But as the collection grew, it seemed to me that the stories should proceed in a more or less chronological sequence, arranged according to key events within them. Juggling the narratives in this way has resulted in some intriguing juxtapositions (for me, at least). Harmonies that were concords have taken on a dissonant aspect, while some clashes have been softened. It's not necessary to follow my ordering – take my pieces in any procession you like.

The tales draw their substance from the universe occupied by my earlier books. Strictly, the collection occupies the seventh place in the series begun with *The House on Boulby Cliff:*

1. The House on Boulby Cliff
2. In the Silence of Time, vol. 1
3. In the Silence of Time, vol. 2
4. Close to the Silence
5. Babylon House
6. Cadmun Gale
7. Splinters of Silence
8. In the Wake of Life (incomplete at the time of writing)

Despite the sequential numbering, the reader is invited to enter the story at any point. Take the present book as the first, if you like. The only recommendation is that the two parts of *In the Silence of Time* should be read in sequence – and it would be better to read *Babylon House* before *Cadmun Gale*, the two volumes telling the story of Leafy Crosthwaite in a single thread running forwards in time. I see the whole story as a maze with several possible entrance points. The way the reader receives the narrative will be subtly different depending on which portal has been selected as the way in. But every possibility will – I hope – be equally (dare I say?) rewarding.

The Origin of Vivianne Stamper, Natty Miller, Secret Girl, The Mill, In Her Sleep, and *Dilly and Emily* flesh out story threads encountered in the two volumes of *In the Silence of Time*. *Poor Nancy* and *Stalker* take their points of departure from *Cadmun Gale*. *Faithfulness* expands on events outlined in *Close to the Silence*. *Terrel's Women* enlarges on situations and relationships in *In the Silence of Time, vol. 1* and *Cadmun Gale*. *Dominoes* gives a picture of Jacob Crowan's father in old age. We first encounter him and his second wife, Alison, in the early pages of In the Silence of Time, 1, but meet him again here twenty-five years later. The incident described in this little story is viewed from another standpoint in *In the Wake of Life*. *The Apostate* takes *In the Silence of Time, 1* as its starting point (albeit tangentially).

The tales, all set in the mid-18th century, take place in Yorkshire, Cornwall, Bath, Ribchester, and Venice.

Character lists for each story can be found at the end of the book. Please use them; they'll make it easier to keep track of who's who. I make no apology for the size and complexity of my cast list. My stories are tales of life; everyone has a mother, a father, aunts, uncles, brothers, sisters, sons, daughters, grandparents, husbands, wives, ancestors, descendants, employers, lovers, enemies…

Happy reading.

      Kevin Corby Bowyer, Muirkirk, September 2023

THE ORIGIN OF VIVIANNE STAMPER

1. Olivia

Cadan and Isla

Words had been Cadan Tremayne's life for as long as he could remember. Words had always been in his family; words joined together like convoys of ships in the sunlight, bringing new delights – spices, fruits, textiles, jewels – to those who might sample them, so that their lives could grow, their experience expand. Words were the light of life: poems, essays, reflections, stories. The love of words had been handed down to him. His father wrote, and his grandfather had been a poet. And there were wordsmiths further back.

The Tremaynes had made their fortune in mining and fishing, and by the time Cadan was born they were well-respected, occupying the grand family estate near Lostwithiel in Cornwall. Cadan's mother, Eseld, counted among her friends Chesten Kello, the wife of one of the local clergymen. Mrs Kello's visits to the house came to mean a great deal to young Cadan because she always brought her daughter, Isla. And Isla loved words too.

Cadan and Isla fell in love as children, and their marriage in 1740 seemed as natural and right as the sunrise, as inevitable as the tides. They were happy, settled, and wanted for nothing.

But the months went by – a year – and there was no child. The two mothers, Eseld and Chesten, wondered if a change of scenery, a little excitement, might help, and suggested the pair take lodgings for a while in the metropolis of London. Perhaps the thrilling bustle of the capital might do some good.

So, in May 1742, Cadan and Isla took up residence in a house on

Tottenham Court Road, just at the point where the city petered out, not far from Capper's Farm. To the south lay the dizzy pleasures of urban life, open countryside stretching out to the north. On the opposite side of the road, about fifty yards down, lay a timber yard and a busy inn.

The young couple quickly found their milieu and became acquainted with writers, poets and playwrights, some successful, some hopeful. They settled into a happy life and found themselves ever more deeply in love.

By November, having suspected for weeks, Isla knew for certain that she was pregnant.

Ambrose and Cicely

Cicely Wood was one of those rare women who have a particular effect on men; one of those whose form, aura, glance triggers a certain primitive urge, stilling conversation, focusing raw physical desire. She'd spent most of the 1730s as the secret mistress of Joshua Foster, one of York's most respected and wealthy jewellers, more than twenty years her senior. He'd repeatedly promised to marry her when the time was right but spun an elaborate ongoing story explaining why it wasn't possible to tell his wife *just yet.* Cicely became pregnant six times during their relationship. On each occasion, Joshua convinced her to terminate, paying for every clandestine procedure. But she had a motherly instinct and craved a family. *Soon it'll be too late,* she thought. *I'll be too old.*

But a chance meeting one spring day in 1739 changed everything...

Ambrose Stamper hurried into the Minster, seeking shelter from the sudden downpour, and there she was – in the gloom of the interior, looking out at the sunlight cutting its arc through the swathes of rain. She was beautiful, with big, sad eyes, and he fell in love with her straight away.

Sensing herself observed, Cicely turned her gaze on him, sealing his fate forever.

"Hello," she murmured.

He could hardly speak. "Hello."

Her smile was cracked, a mask.

"You look sad..." he began, but stopped, shaking his head. "I mean, you look..."

She waited.

"Sorry." Ambrose felt stupid and embarrassed. The woman was clearly a good deal older than himself and must find him ridiculous. But something about her bewitched him – some intoxicating, erotic charge that defied him to turn his attention away.

"Do you work in the Minster?" she asked.

"No," he replied. "I'm a wine merchant. I happened to be passing when the heavens opened." She offered no reply, and Ambrose felt he should continue speaking – to maintain some kind of connection with her. "And you, if you don't mind me asking – you have work nearby? A home?"

She looked away from him into the darkening daylight and said, "No. I have no reason to be here, no reason at all."

She didn't move, and as the sky turned black and the rain hammered on the Minster roof, he knew he couldn't let her go, knew with absolute certainty that she would play a pivotal role in his life.

"If you have nothing better to do," he said, "perhaps I could offer you tea or something to eat. Soup perhaps? Or cake...?"

"Tea..." she echoed, barely audible above the din. Her face held the subtlest of smiles. "Cake..."

"I'd...I'd be honoured..." he stammered.

She walked to him, her heavy cloak of red velvet swaying as she moved, her proximity both intimidating and exciting. She said nothing for a moment but simply stood, smiling at him. The two made a curious spectacle; a few fellow visitors watched from a distance. She raised her hand, brushed his cheek, and whispered, "Boy..."

"Ambrose," he told her. "I'm twenty-seven."

"How old am I?" she asked.

"A woman as lovely as you has no age," he mumbled.
"I'm forty," she said.
Ambrose felt insignificant and more self-conscious than he'd ever been. The woman was overwhelming. He wanted to touch her. Her scent enfolded him, and he feared she might notice how exquisitely excited he was. He didn't know what to say, trembling with the thrill of her, his heart thundering.
"Is it really cake you want?" she muttered.
He shook his head. "No."

"You were nice," she said an hour later, lying in his bed. "The way you looked at me in the cathedral."
Ambrose traced his finger over her breast, dazed at the rapidity of events, overwhelmed with the wonder of her. "It was like a miracle. I saw you there, and I knew. It was like a message from God."
Cicely chuckled. "A message from God…"
"Yes," he replied. "You believe in God, surely?"
She shook her head. "No."
"I'm sorry you say that," he frowned.
"You're upset," she lamented. "I've disappointed you already."
Ambrose embraced her more closely. "No," he said. "I just wonder… Why? Why don't you believe?"
"I've waited years for God to smile on me, but if he has a face, he turns it away."
Ambrose listened to the noises in the street beneath his window. The rain had stopped, and the sun was shining once more. Cries of street sellers rang out, and carts trundled by.
"Cecily…" he began.
"Cicely," she corrected, smiling.
"Sorry."
She shook her head.
"God does exist," said Ambrose, "and today he brought me to you."
He paused, and she looked at him, curious.
"I want you to marry me," he said.

It took Cicely some time to recover from the fit of hilarity induced by Ambrose's statement. "You want me to *what*?" But she was crying with laughter and could hardly look at him.
Ambrose waited patiently, head propped on one arm, watching her.
After a while, she regained control and grinned at him. "You're a sweet boy." But his expression told her he was entirely earnest. She frowned. "Ambrose, you know nothing about me. You haven't even asked if I'm married already."
"Are you?"
"No. But…" She shook her head, trying to wake herself from this new world, this pocket of alternate reality.
"I love you." He said it as if it were an undeniable universal truth.
Cicely raised both hands, palms outward. "Wait. Wait wait wait." Ambrose lay quietly, allowing her to continue.
"Look," she said, "You've told me your first name…"
"Ambrose Stamper," he interjected. "Sorry. It's not a very delicate sound."
"I'm Cicely," she replied. "Cicely Wood. Pleased to meet you." She extended her hand, which Ambrose took. Then she fell to pieces once more, whooping with merriment. Again, he waited.
"Ambrose." She steadied herself, caught her breath, ran her hand into her coils of light brown hair and allowed it to remain there while she continued. "All I know of you is your name and the fact that you're a wine merchant…"
"There's nothing more to know," he interrupted. "My parents are both living. I have two brothers far away in Birmingham. As for me, I've occupied this little apartment for the last five years. My ancestors have been in service for generations, but I wanted to do something different. So here I am. I'm unattached, as well off as I need to be, and I'm in love with you. That's me. Now you know everything."
"Am I your first?" she asked.
"No," he replied straight away, adding with quiet emphasis, "That's how I know you're the one."
His words winded her. She sat up and pressed her fingers to

her mouth, irritated by her instinctive tears, squeezing her eyes tight shut till they were almost dry again.

"Ambrose," she began.

"Cecily."

"Cicely."

"Sorry."

She took a couple of deep breaths. "Listen. I've wasted a quarter of my life with someone who promised me everything but wanted nothing more than the use of my body. I'm cheap. I've been a fool for ten years – just someone's whore. Worthless, that's me."

He was shaking his head. "That ends today. Everything else begins."

She set her jaw hard for a few seconds, then said with increasing agitation, "I'm thirteen years older than you. I may look good, but it's a practised veneer, shined to perfection to keep the one I thought would be my partner for life. That's what you see now – that's what you lay with in this bed – some other man's cast-off. When I saw you there today – when I saw how much you wanted me – I thought, *Now I can spit in his face. I'll take this boy to bed. That'll teach him.*" She'd made herself angry but now paused, allowing her frustration to fade. "That's all I am. Just a failed doxy, crumbling into middle age."

Ambrose watched her. The Minster bells chimed two. "Then it's a new start for both of us."

She sighed. "Why? How? I don't love you. You're strange. I don't know who you are."

"We'll live together," he said. "We'll marry. And you'll be happy – you'll see. God will smile on you."

She stared at him, her expression rigid. "I want a child. I've always wanted a child."

"Then you'll have a child. I promise."

Cadan and Isla

Olivia Lucy Tremayne was born at half past three in the

afternoon of Friday, April 15th, 1743. The birth was drawn-out and sweaty but otherwise smooth enough, and the parents were overjoyed. Neither had admitted it to the other, but they'd both hoped for a girl. Eseld and Chesten, who'd travelled from Cornwall for the birth, fussed over the new mother and the tiny baby while Cadan's writer friends took him off to the alehouse to celebrate. Isla remained in bed for the rest of the day, cradling and feeding her daughter.
"You'll need a nurse," Eseld told her.
"We have a nurse," Isla replied.
"I mean in the long-term," said Eseld. "You'll know by now that husbands are demanding, and we elderly women have our own, waiting helplessly at home."
"I know," Isla answered. "There's a nurse ready. Bessie is her name. We invited girls for interview a few weeks ago. We're all fixed up."
"Oh!" Chesten exclaimed. "You're organised – you didn't need us."
Isla smiled. "Of course we needed you. And I'm sure you were glad enough to be here, mama and mama."
Eseld smiled, watching the child feed. "You two, you'll be wonderful parents."
"Cadan thinks of everything," said Isla. Gazing at her baby, she added, "And we're going to be so happy – all three of us."

Later that evening, when Isla was sleeping and Eseld and Cadan were talking in the kitchen, Chesten took the little girl to the bedroom window and looked at her face in the moonlight. "Olivia," she whispered. "Olivia Lucy. What does the world hold in store for you? What wonders will you perform?"

Ambrose and Cicely

Ambrose found a nest for Cicely – a large apartment above a bakery on Church Street, not far from the Shambles – and they moved in together just a few days after their initial meeting. Cicely adored the smell of fresh bread, and their home was full of daylight, high enough to escape the shadows of nearby buildings. She liked to keep the windows open whenever possible and delighted in the sounds of bustle that leaked in from the busy street below on the many afternoons when Ambrose returned home from his work to love her. She imagined the sounds of their lovemaking carrying into the hubbub, mixing with the jostle of life. She was alive at last.

For years Cicely had lived like a caged pet in a suite of rooms rented by Joshua Foster, maintained for his own secret pleasure, away from the knowledge of his wife and colleagues. It had been a delight to fly free, to smile gleefully at him as her things were moved out. She was no longer his – he'd never have her again.

"Where are you going?"

"Away from you."

"I've provided everything for you."

"You won't have to lie to your wife anymore."

"But – you're precious to me. I love you."

She'd been packing but stopped and glared at him. "You don't love me. I've been a convenience for you – a toy. Nothing more."

He was becoming angry. On another occasion she might have feared him, but there were men in the house, helping her move the few items of furniture she'd bought for herself, and she knew he wouldn't dare attack her.

"You have someone else," he stated.

Cicely looked him squarely in the eyes. "I do. A man who really loves me. A real man – strong, hard – not some despotic withered patriarch like you. I'll be able to have a family now, children of my own – *that you always took from me!*" She'd become heated, allowing her sustained resentment of him to boil into the light at last. "You selfish pig! You took away the years of motherhood I could have had. Well, despite your best efforts to suck out my life, it's *not* too late for me. Get out! I never want to see you again."

Cicely and Ambrose were married in September 1739 and were happy for a while. But the children (who'd queued so eagerly to be born when Cicely had been with Joshua) failed to appear, and her joy began to feel autumnal.

"What's wrong with me? It should be easy enough."

"Give it time," Ambrose encouraged her. "Be patient. I promised you a child – and you shall have a child."

But the months became years, and the lines in Cicely's beautiful face deepened. She grew increasingly irritable and began to blame Ambrose. Fearing it was too late, she sought solace in the bottle.

But Ambrose's love for her remained constant. Cicely was the centre of his life, as he'd known she'd be the day he first saw her sheltering from the rain.

"You'll have a child. You *will* have a child."

"It's too late, too late, too late…"

Cicely grew absentminded and spent hours gazing despondently into the fire. More than once she went out into the city and somehow got lost, relying on Ambrose to find her – which he always did, hurrying through the streets, full of concern. She became remote from him in bed, lying beneath him silently, eyes far away. He worried she was losing her sanity.

He asked in the poorhouse. Perhaps there was a baby that could be put into their care. But it was no good; there were plenty of children but no babies. He suggested to Cicely that they might advertise their willingness to take in an unwanted child.

"Are you mad?" she cried. "Can you imagine how Joshua would gloat? He took away all the children I could have had. How joyous he'd be if he saw how I've failed now! No – I couldn't bear it."

"Then we could seek a child elsewhere – Manchester, Bradford, Lincoln…"

But she was adamant. "No. He'd hear of it. He'd mock me."

One day in June 1744, Stuart Brown, a buyer in the wine warehouse, took Ambrose aside. "What's going on? Your mind's not on the job. Simon's asking what's wrong with you."

Ambrose shook his head. "Nothing new. I should be home with Cicely. I'm worried about her. She's getting worse – changing. She doesn't see things. I mean, she's… losing herself."

"Why? What's wrong. Can we do anything?"

Ambrose sighed, sniffed, and Stuart suddenly realised his friend was crying. He reached out, held Ambrose's arm and said, "Tell me."

"She wants a child. I promised her years ago I'd give her a child. It hasn't happened – and she's losing her grip – on everything. I'm worried I'm going to lose her."

"But she loves you, no?"

Ambrose paused. "I don't know. She used to. She's older than me – you probably know that."

"It's no secret," Stuart replied. "But she's still a fine-looking woman; all the men envy you."

"She's forty-five now," said Ambrose. "The opportunity may be gone for good."

Stuart stood silently for a few seconds. He removed his hand from Ambrose's arm and said, "Let me think. Perhaps we'll speak again later."

"Ambrose, I know someone who may be able to help – if you have money."

Two hours had passed since their previous conversation. Ambrose looked up, surprised and a little confused. "Money?"

"It'll be expensive."

"What? What will be expensive?"

"You know."

Ambrose frowned, shook his head.

Stuart went on. "Be in the Little John at five o'clock. Find a place inside, as close as you can to the door that exits into the coachyard, and be vigilant. You'll be waiting for an angel – a tall man."

Ambrose raised his eyebrows and tilted his head in a gesture that asked for more information.

"I've done enough," said Stuart. "I'll say no more. Good luck to you."

The Little John was a new inn on Castlegate, popular since its opening about ten years previously and only a short walk from the warehouse on Aldwark where Ambrose earned his living. He was in the taproom at five o'clock as instructed, purchased a flagon of ale at the bar and wandered over to the tables near the yard exit, where his attention was immediately captured by an odd-looking thin man in a visored black clerical hat. The stranger sat alone, in silence, and watched Ambrose approach.

"Pardon me, sir," said Ambrose, drawing to a halt close by. "I… have an appointment."

The strange man remained completely still. His eyes seemed very small, like points. "With…?"

Ambrose hesitated. "An angel, I believe."

The man raised his left hand and held it steady, indicating Ambrose should join him at the table. "Please sit."

"You're not drinking," Ambrose replied. "Can I buy you something?"

"I do not touch strong drink, sir. I cannot abide it."

"Something else then. Saloop, perhaps? I believe they have tea."

"Ambrosia?"

Ambrose leaned forward, believing the man had spoken his name. "I beg your pardon?"

"Ambrosia is what I'm used to, sir – the food of the gods. Or a dish of manna – manna from heaven – angels' bread."

Issued in any other tone of voice, it would have been a joke, but the man's expression was impassive, distant, like the face of a biblical prophet depicted in a painting. Ambrose didn't know how to answer. "I…"

The thin man interrupted immediately. "I thought not." His hand remained suspended in the gesture of invitation. Ambrose pulled out the wooden chair from beneath the table and seated himself. "Speak," said the stranger, quietly, flatly.

Ambrose related his story while the other sat motionless, unresponsive, seemingly lifeless. At its conclusion, receiving no response – no evidence that his tale had even been heard –

Ambrose leaned forward and muttered, "Sir?"
"You wish for a child," the man rumbled, eyes lighting.
"My wife will die without one. I fear for her."
The stranger was silent, staring.
"Can you help me? If you cannot, I must go home to her. She'll be worried now. I'm late."
"I can help you," the man purred.
Ambrose sat quietly for a few seconds, scalp tingling. The bar was busy, but the wash of voices receded into the distance. "You can?"
"I can."
"Who are you?"
"I am the Angel Gabriel."
Ambrose tried to control himself, managed for a brief moment, and then burst into laughter. The Angel Gabriel remained immobile, unsmiling, and watched until the younger man's hilarity faded.
"It will be expensive," he said.
"Angels need money?" Ambrose smirked.
"This world is full of those who crave wealth. If you have money, you will receive what you wish for. What you pay will be distributed among those who desire it. And they, in turn, will seek what they yearn, and sacrifice what they have to obtain it. It is the way of this world. And a way of measuring the balance in the hereafter."
Chill, taloned fingers clawed at Ambrose's heart; he feared he was on the precipice of a great evil. "How will it be done?"
"That is not your concern."
"Will people suffer?"
"People always suffer. Your wife is suffering now – and you suffer also."
Ambrose felt himself tumbling. "How much?"
The Angel Gabriel named a considerable sum.
"That's more than I have. I can't do it."
Gabriel gave a tiny shake of the head and said, "You can do it if you try. But you are under no obligation."

"When?" asked Ambrose, voice low.

"A month – two months. You will receive word."

"A baby..." said Ambrose.

"Yes," Gabriel confirmed. "A baby."

"Young enough to bond with my wife as its mother."

"Of course," said Gabriel. "Shall we say...younger than eighteen months? Old enough to have been weaned."

Panic was rising in Ambrose's soul. "My God, I'll go to Hell – I'll go to Hell for this."

"Many children in this world are not wanted," said Gabriel. "You will be giving a child a happy home – somewhere it will be loved."

Ambrose looked into the angel's eyes, his spirit rising a little. "You'll ensure it's so?"

"You need not worry," said Gabriel. "You will have your child, and your payment will be distributed among those who have need of it."

Ambrose saw Cicely's face in his mind's eye, dreamt of her happiness returning. "A healthy child," he said. "Boy or girl, it doesn't matter. From far away."

"Of course," Gabriel replied.

He had to decide. It was still possible to say no... But he didn't. "Alright."

Gabriel nodded. "You'll pay half the sum tomorrow; the balance on receipt of the child."

"Yes," Ambrose agreed. "I can get half tomorrow." He shook his head. "Please don't trick me. I cannot get a larger sum."

"I'm God's messenger, Mr Stamper. My word is good. Five o'clock tomorrow, in this place where we sit. When I have the child, I shall send word ahead. Check here every day, beginning a month from now. Do you agree?"

Ambrose nodded. "Shall we shake on it?"

"Of course," said Gabriel. He extended his hand, and the prospective parent took it.

"You feel like a man," Ambrose observed.

For the first time, the angel smiled. "So did our Lord."

The Angelic Host

When off duty, the Angel Gabriel went by the name of Guy Burrage. Forty-one years old, he was the leader of a trio who, far from being angelic, were more sinners than saints; opportunistic nomads who took money where they could and did whatever was necessary to obtain it. Robert Dixon had dubbed himself the Archangel Michael, and Patricia Muir went under the pseudonym of Mary Magdalene. They were not new to kidnapping children, having supplied them for God-knew-what purpose to those twisted individuals who would pay. The three never asked what the brats were destined for but merely struck a deal, obtained the goods, and delivered them.

Having decided to make London the poaching ground for their most recent commission, they drove their carriage south, briefly pausing at various locations en route to relieve a few fortuitously encountered folk of their earthly burdens, be it their gold, their virtue – often their lives. The early afternoon of Sunday, September 2nd, found them loitering around Tottenham Court Road and the fields and houses to the west. It was blind luck that Mary Magdalene spotted Bessie Graves carrying little Olivia Tremayne in the meadow between the rear of the houses and Capper's Farm.

"Hello there," she said, sauntering up, raising a hand in greeting.

"Hello," Bessie answered, surprised. "I don't often meet people in the fields."

"I'm enjoying the sun," Mary explained. "The main road is such a bustle. It's peaceful here."

Bessie felt uneasy.

Olivia turned her head and looked at the newcomer.

"Hello!" Mary beamed at the little one. She raised her hand as if to tickle the child's chin, but Olivia was shy and hid her face in her nurse's shoulder. "What a pretty little girl!" crooned Mary. "How old?"

"Not quite one and a half," Bessie replied. "Olivia is her name.

Born on April 15th last year."

"Not quite one and a half," Mary repeated, smiling. "Lovely. Is she a happy girl?" She repeated the question directly to Olivia (*happy girly?*), but the child kept her head turned firmly away.

Bessie smiled. "She's a lovely happy girl." Then, speaking to the child, "You're a happy, happy girly, aren't you, Livvy?"

Mary noticed a slight nod of the little head and asked, "Is she yours?"

"I'm her nurse," answered Bessie, and indicating to the right with her head, added, "She lives in the house just there."

Mary looked at the building and realised she could be seen from its windows. "I'm going to walk a little further," she said to Bessie. "You can come with me if you like."

Something was wrong. Bessie glanced at the house, hoping to find someone to whom she could signal, but there was no sign of movement. She was alone and very anxious.

"I'd better be getting back," she said, trying to smile. "Livvy's a heavy one, and I can't walk far."

"No, no," said Mary, smiling broadly. "You must come, you *must*."

Bessie shook her head. "Why? I want to go home."

Mary pointed to a tree a short distance away. "See that tree?"

Bessie followed the pointed finger. "Yes."

"If you look very carefully, you'll see a man behind it."

The woman was right. Bessie could see him standing there in the shade.

"He's a very good shot, and the gun he's holding is pointing at you. If you don't come with me, he'll shoot you – dead."

Bessie gasped and clutched Olivia tightly, fearing the woman might take her away.

Mary continued, her smile fixed in place. "After he's killed you, he'll come over here and shoot your baby." She gave a tiny, playful chuckle. "Come on, let's go for a walk."

Isla waited patiently for Bessie to return home with Olivia. She paced around the house, looking out of the windows, hoping to catch sight of them.

"I'm sure everything's fine," said Cadan. "She's met a friend, and they're talking – lost track of time." But despite his apparent calm, he was as worried as his wife and kept his eyes on the clock, following the minute hand as it traced the duration of his daughter's absence.

Isla knew the routes Bessie liked to take on her walks, having accompanied her on many occasions. The parents tried those first, running, calling out, but there was no sign of the nurse or the child.

Next, they divided the servants and sent them to look further afield. Cadan took his manservant and searched south into the city itself, along Oxford Street, around St. Giles, High Holborn and into the narrow lanes and passageways, asking passers-by if they'd seen anything – a girl carrying a child. Isla sent her maid to Bessie's parents' house to break the news of the disappearance and enlist their aid. Bessie's eighteen-year-old brother ran to find the constables, and the hunt continued until long after the sun had set.

About twenty miles north of the city, the Lord's messenger deemed Bessie redundant. She screamed as she was separated from the child, and Olivia panicked, threw herself about and refused to go into the arms of Mary Magdalene. It took the two male angels a little less than half an hour to fully dispose of the nurse in the way they preferred, during which time Mary shut the little girl in the lidded crib that occupied the central part of the carriage footwell; a wicker cage, cleverly designed with a lining that could be removed and cleaned. The padding had the added advantage of stifling the infant's squealing.

Olivia had been shut in her box for nearly a quarter of an hour when the men returned. Michael climbed in front to drive, and Gabriel sat opposite Mary in the interior. The two looked at each other but said nothing. Olivia screamed and raved distantly.

They covered almost thirty miles that first day, pressing the horses as far as they dared, and hid overnight in a wood south of Harpenden. By that time, the little girl had cried herself into an exhausted sleep. Gabriel built a fire and cooked a meal while Mary prepared food for Olivia, crushing some of their own supper into a paste and mixing in a small quantity of gin, hoping to keep her quiet overnight. She warmed it in the flames for a few minutes, then returned to the carriage and released the child. The screaming resumed almost instantly, but Mary sang to the girl, shrouded in the cool dimness, rocking her gently until she calmed.

The two angels, sitting opposite each other across the fire, exchanged glances as they listened to Mary's singing. Gabriel nodded, impressed, and Michael allowed himself a tiny smile. "A good day," he said. "Smooth."

"May it remain so," Gabriel returned quietly, the fire cracking, popping in the secret night.

Just enough light leaked into the carriage interior for Mary to change the child's soiled clothes and replace the bedding in the crib. Once those tasks were complete, she fed the girl. Olivia was hungry. She remained quiet and accepted food from Mary while sitting in her lap, falling asleep before her meal was done, a peaceful sleep at last. Mary laid the infant on her back in the crib, left the lid open, then went outside and found a place to relieve herself. Squatting in the dark, behind a tree, she remembered her own mother – a cruel, unloving hag – and sighed.

The city constables sent riders to alert all the parish officers around London, and they, in turn, sent deputies to those parishes further afield, north, south, east and west. The Tremaynes' friends appealed to the King, who issued instructions for the army to assist in the search.

Two farmers found Bessie's body face down in a pond in open country near Radlett four days after the kidnapping, but there was no sign of little Olivia. The search continued, extending ever further afield, but Mary and the angels continued steadily on their way north, about thirty miles each day, unnoticed and unchallenged.

A child

On Wednesday, September 12th, Ambrose Stamper found a sealed message waiting for him at the Little John. It read simply: *Wait beneath the Ouse Bridge at noon on Friday 14th, on the west bank. Bring what you owe and be prepared to receive your goods.*
His heart leapt to his mouth. It was time to tell Cicely.

"What do you mean?" she asked, tense, frowning in confusion.
"Exactly what I say," he replied. "My love, on Friday you shall be a mother."
She shook her head. "How? I...I don't understand."
"It's a child, an unwanted child that we shall take in and make our own."
"But I told you..." Cicely's eyes were rapidly filling with tears.
"It's from far away. No-one here will ever know."
"You're sure it has no home?"
"It was a stipulation of mine."
"Oh, God..." She sniffed, wiped her face. "Boy or girl?"
"I don't know," he replied. "I won't know till Friday."
"Ambrose," she blubbed. "Thank you."

Cicely prepared herself and waited in the house on Friday morning while Ambrose walked the short distance to the bridge. It was a sunny day, warm, autumn leaves not yet fallen. People wandered about, enjoying the heat.
He arrived at the appointed place a few minutes early and watched the river traffic as it passed. His heart pounded. Suppose it was a trick? How could he go home to his wife empty-handed if it was? Noon came, and there was no-one. Five past, and he felt dread clawing at his soul. Passers-by looked at him curiously, loitering there, ill at ease.
I'm drawing attention to myself.
He stepped forward and sat on the bank, feet dangling, trying to look inconspicuous.
"Mr Stamper."

Ambrose looked over his shoulder and saw the Angel Gabriel towering above him. He clambered to his feet and stood, ready to hear the news.
"You have the money?"
"I do," said Ambrose. He reached into his coat, took out a heavy leather bag and handed it to the angel. "Count it if you wish."
"There's no time for that – and here is not the place. If you fear the wrath of God, you will not have brought a lesser amount. And I sense that you *are* a god-fearing man."
"I am," said Ambrose.
Gabriel gave the tiniest of smiles. "Then I bring you glad tidings – you have a daughter."
The statement winded Ambrose. He felt faint; the air seemed to whirl and buzz. But the angel wasn't carrying a child. Where was she?
The Lord's messenger held out his left hand. "Behold."
Mary Magdalene emerged from the gloom beneath the bridge, carrying a large basket, smiling as she walked to join them.
"My God, my God! I don't believe it..." muttered Ambrose, eyes filling with tears.
"Take the child and go," said Gabriel. "This is no place for an exhibition. Go home to your wife – and to your future."
"Let me see," said Ambrose. He reached into the basket and pulled back the coverings to reveal the sleeping girl. "She's beautiful..."
"She's perfect," said the Magdalene. "And she's yours."
"What's her name?"
"She is nameless until you name her," said Gabriel. "It's better that way – to begin afresh."
"How old is she?" asked Ambrose, sniffing away his tears.
"Not quite a year and a half," said Mary. "Her birthday is April 15th."
Ambrose was too engrossed in the little girl to notice the glance of irritation that Gabriel shot Mary. *Too much information!*
Sorry, she mouthed.
"Away with you," Gabriel commanded the new father. "We are

gone."
Ambrose took the basket and watched the pair depart beneath the bridge and up the steps on the far side. He never saw them again.

The family

"Oh, Ambrose! She's beautiful, beautiful!"
The girl was still asleep, having been fed a sweet porridge laced with gin to keep her quiet.
"Fast asleep," Ambrose replied. "Our little angel."
"What's her name?"
"You must name her," said Ambrose, "as if she's completely new in the world. She's yours – your baby."
Cicely stroked the child's head. "She's so warm. Look at her lovely hair." She shook her head. "How could someone not love such a child as this? I could never give her away…"

Olivia was noisy enough when she finally woke to yet more unfamiliar faces, screaming and wriggling so hard that Cicely couldn't hold her.
"It's because she doesn't know us," said Ambrose. "Let me try." He took the little girl over his shoulder, walked around the apartment and sang gently until she began to quieten.
Cicely smiled. "*You* can do it!"
"She'll come to you," Ambrose reassured her. "Give her time. Everything here is new to her. She's confused – frightened perhaps. She's old enough to have grown familiar with whatever surroundings she had before."
Soon the girl's crying reduced to sniffs and sobs. Ambrose tried to pass her to her new mother, but the child didn't want to go and clung hard to the man.
He kissed the infant's head and asked, "Can you stand?" There was no response at first, so he tried again, and the girl nodded. "She understands," he said to Cicely, then knelt down and stood the child on her feet, holding her by the hands. She wobbled and began to cry again, so he took her up once more.

"I think she needs changing," said Cicely.
Ambrose wrinkled his nose. "I think you're right."

The days passed, and the child became more accepting of her new situation, even voicing a few words: *Mama, Dadda, Veffie, No*, and two or three more. Cicely wanted to know what her name had been, so she smiled and asked directly.
"What's your name? Do you have a name? Tell me what it is." She pointed to herself and said, "Mamma," then pointed at the child. Olivia said, "Vivvy." It was the closest she could manage to her own appellation and was the first genuine exchange between them. Cicely was overwhelmed with emotion. She tried again, to be sure, pointed to herself and said, tears dripping from her chin, "Mamma," before pointing to the girl.
"Vivvy," Olivia mumbled.
"Vivvy," Cicely sobbed, sniffing, wiping away the moisture. "Vivianne. Is that your name?"
"Vivvy," repeated Olivia.
"Ahhh…" gasped Cicely and bit her lip. "Vivvy. Vivianne. That's the name you had, and that's the name you'll keep. Vivianne. Vivianne Stamper."
Vivianne allowed Cicely to hold her, sing to her, and seemed pleased when Ambrose returned from work. She slept well and ate what she was given, creating the usual mess with food that young children always make.
"You're getting on well with her," said Ambrose.
"We love each other," said Cicely. "We're a family full of love."

Cadan and Isla

The intensive search for the missing girl threw up no leads. The days and weeks of desperation became months, the parents existing in a grey world of shock and stunned disbelief. Their precious child had been stolen, perhaps even murdered, and there was nothing they could do.
Unable to face the lonely despair of what would have been Olivia's second Christmas, they dismissed the servants, vacated

the house, moved back to Cornwall, and took up residence with Cadan's family.

There were no more smiles; there was no more joy – only a confused soulless emptiness. The light was gone out of their lives and would never return.

One day in spring the following year, Isla took a knife and walked up into the hills above Lostwithiel. There was a particular place where she and Cadan used to play together as children – a spot with a fine view over the valley. He'd made a swing for them, suspended from a high branch of one of the old trees, and she was surprised to find it still there after all these years, although the wooden seat had broken in two, the pieces hanging separately, never to be one again.

She sat in the shade of the tree, looked out over the land of her birth, and opened her wrists and ankles.

Cadan bore the shock as he'd borne the other. Alone once more, he shut himself in his rooms and rarely spoke. The years passed, and he remained a recluse, withdrawn into his own world, a world made of words, of poems – poems of loss, sadness and death.

2. Vivianne

Cicely's ten years as a caged bird had kept her apart from others. Her childhood playmates had drifted away, and her acquaintances in later life were superficial and few. Joshua had stifled her social existence until Ambrose came along. And Ambrose was naturally quiet and withdrawn. He called his work colleagues "friends", but they had their own allegiances, and he never became close to any of them, so few people were around to make a fuss of Vivianne as she grew up. Cicely took her out into the city now and then, mostly to shop or to feed the ducks on the river. Joshua happened upon her on one such occasion.

"Cicely!" he exclaimed.

She nodded. "Joshua."

He'd aged, become bent, walked with a stick.
"It's good to see you," he said. "You've kept your looks."
"Thank you," she replied.
He looked at Vivianne, dark-haired, four years old, holding Cicely's hand, huge brown eyes peering up at him curiously.
"Yours?" he asked.
"Of course," she replied, heart inflating with pride.
"She's beautiful. Like you."
Cicely set her jaw and drove the encroaching tears from her eyes; she'd loved him once.
"Vivianne," she told him. The girl looked up, hearing her name.
"Unusual," Joshua commented. "A lovely name." He smiled at Cicely. "Well – good luck to you. I wish you every happiness."
He set his weight on his cane and walked on. Cicely stood for a moment, gathering herself, sniffed once or twice, and continued in the opposite direction.

Ambrose schooled Vivianne himself, a process that was entirely new for him. He was astonished at how easily his daughter learnt to read and write, her natural talent flowering under his instruction.
"I don't believe it!" he said to Cicely. "She's so bright – and learns so quickly. Little more than a year ago she couldn't tell one letter from another. Now she writes her own little stories. She has a gift, an imagination."
"Of course she does," Cicely smiled. "It's because she has a happy home, a happy mother, and a proud father."
Ambrose liked to read. His modest collection of about thirty books was arranged on a pair of shelves in the parlour: John Bullokar's *English Expositor*; Henry Cockeram's *English Dictionary*; *Captain Singleton*; *Pamela*; *Paradise Lost*; *The Faerie Queene*; *Don Quixote*; *The Life and Adventures of Robinson Crusoe of York*, and various works by Shakespeare, Pope and others. He often found Vivianne lying on the floor, poring over them, lost in their pages, picking out the words, the sentences, and his heart filled with pride.

What an amazing, wonderful creature you are...
Life was good; all was well. Occasionally Ambrose caught himself whistling, even at work.
"You're making that noise again, Ambrose," said Stuart.
The piping ceased. "Sorry."
"Nice to know you're a happy man," said Stuart, "but the twittering drives Simon up the wall."
Cicely continued to drink, though not to excess. Her life was happy; she felt fulfilled and loved her husband.
"Read me a story, Mamma."
"Of course, my love. Jump up here on my lap..."

Ambrose died in November 1749. He was sent home from work one Tuesday noon – said he felt "strange, dizzy" – and slipped away quietly in his chair in front of the hearth on Wednesday morning, his ten-year marriage to Cicely and his five-year fatherhood of Vivianne at an end. He was thirty-seven years old. Cicely was distraught, and six-year-old Vivianne found herself tumbling into a dark, confused world, her father's light and love extinguished. Ambrose's work colleagues made the funeral arrangements and did what they could to comfort the mother and daughter. They ensured Cicely inherited all her husband possessed – which wasn't much. She was enclosed in loneliness, and the bottle welcomed her.
Vivianne burrowed into her world of fiction, escaping into her own universes, writing, writing, writing...

Cicely found it increasingly difficult to make ends meet. Ambrose's money might have kept them going until Vivianne was old enough to work, but Cicely squandered a large part of it on booze and allowed herself to get behind with the rent.
"You're always sad, mum. Dad's been gone a long time. You're pretty – you could be happy."
"Happy?" Cicely replied and looked away. "Happy. You're very wise for a little girl."
"I'm not little, ma – I'm nearly eight."

Cicely smiled and stroked her daughter's hair. "I know you are, my love – and I'm so proud of you. But time's going on, and I was never good at making friends."
"Didn't you ever have friends?"
"I had friends when I was your age." She paused, stared into her lap and added, "I'm sorry you never met your granny and grandad."
"Me too," said Viv. "It must be nice to have grandparents."
"Listen to you," Cicely murmured, gazing at the child in wonder. "Sometimes you frighten me; you think so deeply."
Ambrose's parents were still living (so far as Cicely was aware). She and Ambrose had taken Vivianne all the way to Birmingham when she was two years old, so she could meet them, but Ambrose's mother had disliked Cicely. *A fancy woman*, she called her. Cicely overheard the remark – and the next: *"She's a trollop – old enough to be your mother."* They hadn't visited again.

By June 1752, most of the money had gone, and Cicely was forced to confront her landlord.
"I'd help you if I could," he said. "Your husband was a kind man – always well-spoken, polite. His death was a terrible loss for you."
"I'm sorry, Joe," said Cicely, eyes cast down. "We've tried to make ends meet, but our resources are almost used up."
"I understand," Joe replied. "But business is business, and I have to make a living. I know you appreciate that." Cicely glanced up at him, and he went on. "I know a place with a vacancy – a cottage – if you don't mind living out of town. It's small – on a farm near Oulston. You know it?"
"I know where it is," she nodded. "Fifteen, sixteen miles north."
"That's right," he said. "The farmer's name is Haggard, Caspar Haggard – a friend of a friend – decent enough man as far as I know. Would you like me to inquire for you?"
"Would you do that? That's very kind of you."
"It's the least I can do, Mrs Stamper. I'll pay for the removal and transportation of your goods – if you'll allow me."
Cicely was moved by his kindness but also overcome with

emotion at the prospect of leaving the place she'd shared so joyfully with Ambrose. She swallowed, fighting back tears, but managed to nod her agreement and mumble her thanks.

3. Caspar Haggard

Vivianne and Cicely moved into their little farm cottage that short September. The accommodation was smaller than their apartment in York, having just one bedroom, but the rent was barely a quarter of what they'd been paying on Church Street, and the house was full of light, the air alive with the sounds and smells of farm animals. Caspar Haggard was a heavy man, squat, in his early forties. He didn't say much, although he shook Cicely's hand when she paid the first three months' rent in advance, nodded at Vivianne, and welcomed them both to his farm.
"Can I play with the animals?" asked Viv excitedly.
"Tha can do as tha likes," said Caspar, "so long as tha don't fret 'em and don't get thi sen 'urt. City girl, you – things in't t'same in t'real world."
"I'll be careful," she smiled.
"Course tha will," he chuckled, winking.
Oulston, a hamlet comprising an alehouse and a row of cottages facing a green, fell within the lordship of Oulston Manor. Haggard Farm, an expanse of flat open fields dotted with tenanted dwellings similar to Cicely's, occupied land half a mile south of the little village. Caspar, his wife and their two sons resided in a sprawling semi-derelict sixteenth-century house half a mile further south, just off the York road.
Cicely and Vivianne led a quiet life on the farm, lonely but content. The girl wrote endlessly: long, complex stories with well-developed characters; clever, moving poems that broke Cicely's heart; essays describing the farm, the animals, the sky, the wind.
"How do you write like this?" gasped her mother in astonishment. "Where did you come from?"

Vivianne shrugged. "I don't know. I only know I have to write. If I didn't write, I wouldn't be properly alive."

"You amaze me," said Cicely. "You're only ten, and you write a hundred times better than I ever could."

"You're my mum," said Viv. "You would say that."

But Cicely shook her head. "No. No, you're special. That's for sure."

The months went by, and the booze kept arriving from the city. Cicely saw the last of their money drain away. Less than a year after they'd moved in, she had to admit to Caspar Haggard that she was destitute.

"N'more money?" he echoed.

She felt ashamed. "I'm sorry."

They were sitting opposite each other at the kitchen table. She'd sent Vivianne outside to play with the animals so the child wouldn't have to hear her interview with their landlord.

Caspar watched her in silence, then asked, "'Ow old are you, Mrs Stamper?"

"Fifty-four," she said. "Fifty-five in February."

The farmer raised his eyebrows in surprise. "I'm impressed. I'm forty-three, and I'd'a said you were younger'n me."

He looked at her intently. Cicely swallowed, guessing what was in his mind.

"You could live 'ere wi'out payin' rent."

She clenched her teeth and waited, heart pounding.

"Let's see you," he said. "Stand up – step away from t'table."

She did so, watching him.

"Lift your skirts."

She raised them to just below the knee.

"You know what I mean," he said.

She did as he wanted, trying to fight off the humiliation as he inspected her. He gestured she should approach him. She did so, and he sampled her with his hand. Finally, he nodded and allowed her to drop her clothes back into place. Cicely resumed her seat, sickened.

"Sound. Top class," he muttered, unable to resist the urge to sniff his fingers. "Tight 'n' fresh. No-one'd guess you were in your fifties."
She said nothing.
"You'll live 'ere rent-free," he continued. "Tha'll want for nothin'. I'll supply thee wi' goods from t'farm at no cost. In return, you'll accommodate me wi'out question whenever I say. 'Ow's that strike thee? Agree?"
She couldn't speak but nodded, eyes fixed on the tabletop.
"Good," he said, standing. "Then I'll 'ave next month's rent now."
Cicely swallowed, her mind screaming, *No, no, no...*
"There's one more thing," she said, voice trembling.
"And that is?"
"You'll pay for my gin."
He laughed. "I will not. Specially now, wi' t'new taxes. Tha'll cancel tha gin. I'll keep thee supplied wi' booze from our own still. It's good stuff – an' strong. Tha'll like it. Good enough?"
She nodded, staring at the floor.
"Come on then," he urged. "I don't 'ave all day."
Cicely stood, her body swaying with the thundering of her heart.
"Bedroom," said Caspar. "Don't be fearful. I won't 'urt thee."

The sun was shining. Vivianne sat patiently on the wall by the first field, wondering why her mother was taking so long. She watched the house, but nothing moved there, and she could make out little through the windows. A magpie settled on the roof, strutted about for a while, then flew cackling away.
Viv wanted her mother to be happy. She'd watched the gin increase its hold in recent months, sensed Cicely's tension, and knew there was going to be trouble of some kind.
The afternoon lengthened, and the girl became increasingly uneasy. What could they be talking about for so long? Were they arguing? Was her mother in danger? Should she go back even though she'd been told to stay away?
More than an hour passed, and she made up her mind to go home, but Caspar emerged from the cottage just as she hopped

down from the wall. He closed the door behind him and adjusted the buttons on his breeches as she approached him.

"Mr Haggard," she called. He looked at her but said nothing, so she repeated herself: "Mr Haggard. I want to work on the farm."

"What dost tha mean?" he asked, squinting.

"I want to work for you. I'll milk the cows, muck out the pigs, anything you like. You don't have to pay me much."

He shook his head. "I 'ave all the 'elp I need. Tha can do whatever tha likes, but thee'll get no payment from me."

The door opened, and Cicely stepped outside, summoning Vivianne with her hand. "Come indoors now, Viv." As the girl approached her mother, Cicely addressed Caspar Haggard. "Bottle. Now, please."

Haggard turned and replied, "I'll send one o' t'boys wi' it." He looked at the woman quietly for a few seconds and added, "Thank thee kindly, Mrs Stamper. I'm reet chuffed wi' our arrangement."

Cicely didn't reply. Caspar went on his way.

Vivianne looked up at her mother, frowning. Cicely was shaking. "What happened?" asked the girl.

"I need a bath, love. Help me? Take the pitchers and fill them at the pump. Quick as you can."

"What's wrong? You're upset."

"Just do it, please. Right now."

"Mum?"

But Cicely was sobbing, lips quivering, tears flowing, dripping off her chin, her nose. "Water! Need it *now!* Please, please…"

Seventeen-year-old Bennet Haggard, the younger of Caspar's two sons, knocked ninety minutes later and thrust a bottle towards Vivianne.

"For your ma. Dad says there'll be more in t'mornin'."

Viv took the flask, thanked him, and shut the door. She turned the dark green bottle up and down, watching its sluggish oily contents as she stepped into the parlour where her mother was soaking, recovering in her bath by the fire.

"Caspar sent this for you."
Cicely nodded and extended an arm. "Give it here." Vivianne handed the thing over, and Cicely drew out the stopper. "Homemade," she mumbled and put it to her nose. "Jesus!" (recoiling – holding the bottle at arm's length). "What on earth is in there?" But she sniffed again – tentatively – upended it to her lips and drank. Next second she was choking, doubled up in the bathwater, struggling for breath.
Vivianne sighed, eyebrows knit. "I wish you wouldn't do that, mum."
"I'll be alright," Cicely spluttered. "Just got to get used to it. I don't have to pay for it – it'll save us money."
"What happened?" asked Viv. "Did he hurt you?"
Her mother reclined in the tub, right hand dangling the bottle over the side, left still cleansing where he'd been. She took a deep breath and forced a half-smile. "No, love. He didn't hurt me."
"But you're upset," Viv pined. She knelt on the floor next to the bath, took the bottle from Cicely and held her hand.
"We've still got each other, you and me," said the woman. She raised her eyebrows and nodded. "And we've still got the house. We'll be alright. You don't need to worry about me."
Vivianne murmured, "Did he...?" The incomplete question melted in the air between them. Cicely didn't reply but squeezed the girl's hand, and Viv saw the moisture in her mother's eyes, saw the jaw clench, heard the laboured breathing.
Oh no; Oh my God...
Cicely whispered, "Never give up. Never lose yourself."
The tear hanging in the corner of Vivianne's eye fattened and broke loose, trailing down her cheek. "I love you, mum."

Caspar returned the next day. Cicely had been expecting it – knew he'd want her again, want to pleasure himself with his new toy.
"Viv," she said. "Outside till I call you."
"Mum?"
"Just go. I'll call you."

The girl left, and Caspar began to unbutton himself.
"I thought about thee all night," he rasped. "I was achin', 'ard as iron – thinkin' o' you, on your back. I bin ready all mornin'."
She stared at him, pulse racing, steeling herself.
"Upstairs," he growled, brushing her cheek with the back of his fingers. "Don't make me wait."

He lay beside her in bed when he was done, leaning on an elbow, lazily playing with her breasts.
"Tha tits are good," he said. "Bigger'n Joan's – firmer. And thy rear's nice – round, womanly."
"Does she know you're here?" asked Cicely.
"My wife? Joan?" He guffawed. "Jokin' are thee? She'd slice off me rod and feed it to t'dogs."
He slid his open palm over her body, steadily lower, and found her with two fingers. Cicely closed her eyes and tried to imagine she was far away.
"Dost tha like it like I do?" he breathed.
She said nothing.
"Tell me," he whispered, pressing himself closer and adding a third explorer to join the other two. Cicely gasped, and Caspar took it as a sign of pleasure.
"I thought so," he muttered, lips close to her ear.
I'm not here, you're not here, I'm not here, you're not here, I'm not here...
He was on top of her again.
Oh, God, God, God, help me. It'll stop soon; it'll be over.
It took longer the second time, and he was fiercer, thrusting, mauling, roaring when he came.
Afterwards, he lay by her side, fingertips roving, kissing her shoulder, her neck.
"I won't be 'ere tomorrow. I 'ave to go to York."
She didn't reply but drew the covers around her and lay on her side, facing away from him.
Caspar sighed, sat on the edge of the mattress and began to dress.
"I've 'ad a good afternoon." He reached across the bed and laid

his hand on her form, obscured beneath the covers. "I'm glad to 'ave you 'ere. Means a lot to me. 'Tain't just…fuckin' – you know…"

She had to make an effort – had to give the impression that she wasn't disgusted by his attention.

"Bye then," she said. "Have a good day tomorrow."

Cicely grew used to him as the weeks passed, her revulsion turning to acceptance. He was eager, and it was a rare day that he didn't visit the cottage. Coupling with him was a mechanical necessity, a thing that had to be endured so that she and her daughter might continue with a roof over their heads.

Seeing her mother's misery diminish day by day, Vivianne found a kind of equilibrium in the situation, a balance that posed as normality. Turning her back on what happened in the house, she made the fields, the hills and the hedgerows her own and wrote about them when she returned home.

The bottles continued to arrive at the cottage in a steady supply, and although Cicely got used to the sharp, raw booze, she never found out what it was made of.

"What's in this?" she asked Caspar on one occasion, lying next to him post-coitus, propped against the bedhead, drinking from the bottle.

"I doubt thee'd want to know!" he laughed. "Good stuff though, in't it? Does t'trick."

"It does," she replied. "It was vile at first, but I practised and got it right."

"My father made it, an' 'is father before 'im. Family recipe."

"Does Joan drink it?"

"Joan?" Caspar snorted. "Joan don't drink nothin' 'cept tea and milk." He gazed blankly at the bedsheets covering their naked bodies and became uncharacteristically reflective. "Joan's a good woman in 'er way. She in't no beauty, like you," (he flicked his eyes at her face), "and she's ordinary, not…ripe, bewitchin', like you are. But she's a good woman, thoughtful, takes care of 'ouse, sees food's tasty, place is clean." He paused for a few seconds.

"Sometimes I imagine I'm married to you, not 'er, and wonder 'ow different things might've been. It's special, bein' 'ere wi' you. No-one knows I come 'ere. Part o' t'thrill is *because* no-one knows. You know what I mean?"
"Of course," she answered. "It's the daring – the knowing you could get caught and lose everything. It's a gamble."
He squinted at her. "You've done this before."
She nodded. "For years. Before I met my husband. It doesn't go anywhere."
"Ah," he purred. "But while it's goin' – *while it's goin' – what a ride it is!*"

The weather soon became too cold for Vivianne to be sent outside, and Cicely was forced to allow her to remain in the parlour while she and Caspar went aloft.
"Try to be quiet," she told him as he undressed. "For the girl's sake."
But Vivianne listened to the sounds – the creaks, the groans, gasps, soft voices – trying to picture exactly what was happening.

The two beds were arranged in opposite corners of the room, Viv occupying the smaller. One night in winter, with the heavy snowflakes drifting down in the light of the full moon, the girl whispered, "What does he do with you?"
There was a long silence; she thought her mother must be sleeping. When Cicely answered, her voice sounded far away. "He does what men do."
Vivianne was quiet for a while, pondering if she should ask more. But her imagination was in turmoil, and she had to understand. "I want to know exactly what happens. I only know that you…join up somehow, down there – that he gets inside you. But I don't really know how. Tell me."
So her mother explained it to her; how it worked; what the pieces were like; how they changed so the thing could occur; how they went together; the activity that led to the conclusion,

and the conclusion itself. Vivianne listened, absorbing every detail until her mother came to an end.

The moon cast its bright silver into the room; the girl watched the shadows of the dancing snowflakes.

"Is it nice?"

"If you love the person you're with, it expresses your love for them. It's like giving yourself to them, everything that makes you who you are. And they give themselves to you. It's the most honest thing there is. It's when two people become one, body and soul."

"That sounds amazing," Vivianne whispered.

"That's how it was with your father," Cicely murmured.

"So, do you love Caspar?"

"No, of course not!"

"Then why...?"

Cicely interrupted the question. "You'll understand one day. Don't worry about it. It doesn't upset me so much anymore. He's thoughtful enough, and he doesn't hurt me. There are men in this world who are far worse than Caspar. We're lucky, really."

"Do you kiss him?"

"No." A pause. "Viv?"

"Mum?"

"You must never tell anyone he comes here. You know that, don't you?"

"Yes – you told me before."

"I know – but it's important. If people found out..."

"I'm not an idiot, mum."

The comment stopped Cicely in mid-flow. It was typical Viv – sharp, bright, perceptive and direct. She began to laugh.

"What's funny?" asked Vivianne.

"I am," Cicely chuckled. "Sometimes I think of you as a little girl who needs protecting – then I remember you're my Viv."

Vivianne let her mother's merriment disperse, then said, "One day, we'll be rich. I'll do something that makes you proud of me and earns us a fortune. Then we'll have a big house with servants, dogs, gardens. And you'll dress like a queen and be happy. You won't be sad anymore. You'll have everything you want."

"Nothing would surprise me about you, my love, my sweet girl. But I *am* happy. I'm happy because I've got you. You're the best thing in my life – you always have been. And you always will be."

Caspar liked to remain in bed with Cicely after their unions, holding her, being warm with her, skin to skin. He told her about himself – his life, his marriage, his boys, the farm, his plans – and she listened, showing an interest. She told him about herself. It was nice to have someone to talk to besides Vivianne – even him. He listened quietly, and his hugs felt genuine. She even wept once or twice, and he held her and tried to comfort her.

"Am I a bad man?" he asked one day, cradling her head against his chest. "You'll know because you're a good woman, a good mother to your girl."

"You're not so bad," she whispered.

"Am I bad to you?"

She waited a while before answering. "No. You're not bad to me."

Things came to a precipice one night in September 1754. Caspar had led his wife to believe he was spending the evening in Ampleforth at a business meeting with a few local farmers and would be home late. In reality, he wanted to spend a long evening in bed with his lover.

Vivianne was downstairs, writing by rushlight – an essay about harvesting and trying to befriend the newly weaned lambs. But she wrote with an ear cocked in fascination as always, catching the sounds from above.

The bedroom was lit by a single lamp, burning low, and Caspar was unusually tender in his lovemaking. As he moved, slowly, gently, Cicely felt a new fondness for him. He nuzzled her affectionately with his nose as he loved her – something he often did, hoping for a kiss, which she rarely gave him. But on this occasion, she allowed his lips to find hers and kissed him passionately, clawing at his buttocks as he peaked.

Ending, calming, heart slowing. He lay on top of her, supporting his weight on his forearms, his head buried in her neck, silent, breathing deeply.

What was that? she thought. *What happened?*

The wind blew hard, howling round the cottage while she held him in the near darkness. A minute, two. He kissed her neck and began to raise himself on his hands.

"Stay," she whispered.

"Stay?"

"Mm," under her breath.

"Cicely..."

She could see the faint lamplight reflected in his eyes. He stiffened, began to move again, long, measured, easy, and she was kissing him, squeezing, encouraging, telling him yes. Her breath came in gasps, and she was amazed to find she was approaching the top – if he could keep going, she'd come, the first time with him.

Her excitement thrilled Caspar. Body tensed on the point of climax, he confessed what he'd known for weeks: "I love you! Cicely, I love you!"

She kissed him and ignited, gasping, as he burst inside her a second time.

They lay as before, bathed in sweat, hearts slowing, breath settling.

"Jesus!" he muttered. "I never knew it could be s'good."

Cicely clutched him and kissed him on the cheek. He turned his face to hers, and their mouths met. "I meant it," he murmured.

"I know you did," she replied.

"I love you."

"I know."

"What should I do?"

"I don't know."

He turned onto his side, holding her in his arms. "I never expected..."

"Neither did I," she replied.

He said nothing for a long time but stroked her and gazed at her

face in the gloom.
"Joan'll know. I can't 'ide it. She'll know."
"What will she do?"
"She'll cut me in pieces. Then she'll cut *you* in pieces."
"Better not say anything then."
"I'm not sure I can keep it from 'er."
"Things might seem different in the morning."
He listened to the howling wind. "I 'ave to go – walk about. Need to think." He sat on the edge of the bed and began to dress.
Cicely watched him as he stood to button his breeches. "Where will you walk?"
"Round about, on t'farm, in t'lane, in t'wind."
"I'll come if you like."
"I 'ave to be alone. Things to mull over."
She nodded. "It was nice tonight."
Caspar glanced at her, then looked away, stepped to the door, and left. She heard him clump down the stairs and address Vivianne. "G'night, girl."
"Bye, Mr Haggard."
Cicely touched herself, his stickiness, as the cottage door slammed shut.
Vivianne hurtled upstairs and crashed into the bedroom. Cicely instinctively pulled the covers over her breasts.
"Bloody hell! You were noisy tonight!"
"Don't swear! You shouldn't be listening."
"It's never been like that before! What happened?"
"Was he noisier than usual?"
"No, mum! *You! You* were noisy!"
"What did you hear?" Vivianne was about to describe it, but Cicely raised a hand, forestalling the reenaction. "No! Stop! I don't want to know – and you'd better forget it! Next time, out you go, whatever the weather!"

But that was the last time either of them saw Caspar. When the knock came at four the following afternoon, Vivianne opened the door to find Joan Haggard, tense, red-faced, swaying with fury, armed with a whip.

"Show us thy mother," she snarled.

Cicely came running, yanked Vivianne back into the cottage, and tried to slam the door. But Joan had her foot in it and forced her way in, driving Cicely ahead of her. She spoke rapidly, low, hissing. "You filthy 'ore! Come 'ere and think you can take my man? You're just a bit o' laced mutton! *Older'n me!* What's he see in you?"

Cicely backed away, eyes on Joan's whip, keeping Vivianne behind her.

"Think you're special, don't you? You're nowt but a fancy soft box for 'im to spill 'is seed in."

"Mrs Haggard…" Cicely began.

Joan raised her voice, crushing Cicely's interruption. "Don't you *Mrs 'Aggard* me, you 'ore! You and your brat – you're out 'ere today! Reet now! Get out! Or I'll flay you both till you're dead!" She brandished the weapon, insane with rage, eyes burning lamps of hate.

"Let us get some clothes," Cicely begged. "Some things. Then we'll be gone."

"Ten minutes," Joan spat. "If you in't out b'then, I'll lock y'in and burn 'ouse to t'ground!"

"Alright," Cicely agreed. She turned to Viv. "Gather your clothes and a few things. Do it quick."

Vivianne was distraught – in tears. "What about dad's books?"

"We'll send for them. Let's just go."

Breathless with shock, they squashed a few items into bags, shambled into their coats and shoes, and abandoned the house, Joan shooing them into the lane.

The outraged woman faced them, finger pointing, cottage key dangling.

"You show your faces 'ere again, m'boys'll shoot you for trespass. You'll 'ave no further warnin'."

Then she was gone.

Viv faced her mother and wailed, *"MUM?"*

Cicely's face crumbled, tears spilling. She knelt and held her

daughter. "We'll find somewhere. We'll be alright."
Someone was running towards them from the direction of the village – Bennet Haggard. Cicely stood and waited. The young man halted and offered a small leather bag.
"Mi father wants thee to 'ave this. 'Tain't much – fifteen guineas. To pay for tha things. 'E says don't come back." Cicely took it and stared at him. "'E says sorry."
"How is he?" she asked. "Is he alright?"
"Mi mother whipped 'im – whipped 'im raw. I'm sorry. Me and me brother, there were nowt we could do." He shook his head. "There's somewhere thee can stay tonight. I've arranged it for thee. You'll 'ave time to think – go on tomorrow – to wherever…"
"Where?" Cicely asked.
"In t'village," he pointed behind him. "In Oulston. Third cottage along, north o' t'Bull ale'ouse. Greta and Milo Grimes. Milo works in t'manor garden. 'E's not 'ome now, but Greta's expectin' thee. 'Tain't much – thee'll have to sleep in t'kitchen. It's best I could do. Sorry." He paused and sighed, shook his head. "Thee'd better be on tha way."
Cicely thanked him and watched him go, then turned to her daughter and drew a deep breath – slow, calming – smiled, and offered her hand.

Sixty-two-year-old bulky, grey-haired Greta Grimes opened her cottage door to Cicely's knock and scanned her visitors at length, rubbing her hands in her apron.
"You can't stay 'ere."
"But Bennet…" Cicely began.
Greta shook her head. "I din't think tha'd look like this. Sorry. Walk on." She began to close the door.
"We've nowhere to go," Cicely pleaded. "Have pity on my daughter at least."
"*Mum!*" Vivianne cried, alarmed at the sudden prospect of separation.
Greta peered at the girl, then back at Cicely. "And you, where will you go?"

"There's someone in York who might help."
"I want to come with *you,* mum," Vivianne wept, grasping her mother's arm.
Cicely rubbed her hand reassuringly. "I'll be back, I promise. I'll sort things out – then I'll come and get you." She looked at Greta. "She can stay? For a few days? Two, three, four days?"
"Your girl can stay, but not you – not wi' my 'usband int' 'ouse. I won't 'ave you 'ere."
Cicely nodded and knelt before Viv. "There's someone I know in York from the old days. He has money – I don't think he'll turn me away."
"*Don't* leave me here! *Please, please, please,* mum!"
Cicely's lips began to tremble. "I'll come back," she sniffed. "In a few days, I'll be here again."
"But it'll be dark soon," Viv pleaded, voice breaking, "and you'll be outside on your own."
"I can look after myself," said Cicely. "It's not cold. I'll be fine."
Vivianne was crying hard, and Cicely could no longer hold back her own tears. She leaned forward and embraced her daughter, kissing her. "Just a few days, and I'll see you again."
Vivianne flung her arms round her mother's neck. "Don't forget me, mum!"
Cicely squeezed her eyes shut, tears rolling down her cheeks. "How could I forget you, love?"
"Promise you'll come back," Vivianne pleaded, desperate.
"I promise, I promise, I promise I'll come back." Cicely tried to stand, but the girl wouldn't let her go. She looked up at Greta, seeking assistance.
"Come wi' me, child," said the woman, taking Viv's hand.
Cicely stood, sniffed again and wiped her face. "I'll be back before you know it. Be good." Then she turned and hurried away.
Vivianne watched her receding figure for a few seconds, desolate. "Mum…?"
"Thee'll see tha ma again soon enough," said Greta. "Come on, child – pull thi sen together. I'll get thee summat to eat." She drew the girl into the cottage and closed the door.

4. Greta and Milo

Vivianne sat in stunned silence at the kitchen table while Greta produced bread and cheese. "Eat," she ordered, setting the plate in front of her visitor. "Tha mother won't be pleased if she comes back and finds thee starved to death."
But Vivianne hardly saw the food, eyes staring at nothing, mind broiling like a storm. Greta tutted, shook her head and fussed around the kitchen.
"How far is York?"
"How far?" Greta responded. "About sixteen miles."
"How long will it take her to walk?"
"It takes five or six hours to walk to York if you're fit and keep goin'."
"That means she won't be there till late tonight. No-one'll let her in."
"Tha mother got money?"
Vivianne remembered Bennet's leather pouch, relieved. "Yes."
"Then she'll be able to get a room at an inn when she arrives."
The girl's mind lit up with an image of the village alehouse they'd passed, just yards from Greta's cottage. She leapt from the bench in excitement. "She could stay here! We passed the tavern. We could both stay there!"
She hurried towards the kitchen door, but Greta stopped her. "There are no rooms at t'Bull. It's a tiny ale'ouse, not an inn. You can't stay there."
Viv's despair flared to anger. "You've given me food, but you didn't offer my mum anything. She's walking all that way with nothing. If I run, I can catch her and give her what you've given me."
"Calm down," said Greta. "Tha mother's a grown woman and can look after 'er sen. I can't 'ave someone like 'er in this 'ouse – not for any reason."
"Why not?" Viv protested.
"Because o' the kind o' woman she is. She's the kind of woman

that men drool over. There's a certain type – and your mother's that type. I can't 'ave 'er 'ere – not wi' my man about to come 'ome."

"My mother's lovely!" cried Vivianne. "She'd welcome *you* into *her* house! She wouldn't let *you* go hungry!"

"Shut your mouth, child, and sit down, or I'll wallop you! Dare to show me disrespect, who's welcomed you into 'er kitchen!"

Vivianne didn't reply but stood her ground by the door, glaring. Greta levelled a finger. "I've promised tha mother I'll look after thee till she returns – and that's promisin' a lot! Be grateful, child! She'll be back 'ere t'day after tomorrow, or t'day after that. Until then, be civil."

Viv clenched her jaw and forced herself to calm. "Can I at least run after her with some food?"

"No. Leave 'er be. It's still light. If she's 'ungry, she'll stop and buy food. There's 'ouses and farms on t'way. If you go runnin' after 'er, you'll prob'ly get lost, and I'll 'ave failed in me obligation." She pointed at the table. "Now sit and eat."

Vivianne reluctantly resumed her seat, but she was upset and could only pick at the food, pulling the bread apart and poking her finger into the cheese.

"Do I have a room?"

"There's no bedroom for you," said Greta. "There's only one bedroom in this cottage. You'll 'ave to sleep in 'ere, under t'settle wi' t'dog."

Viv hadn't noticed the dog. She looked around and caught sight of it, an old black water spaniel with tired eyes, watching her nervously from its nest beneath a long settle on the far side of the kitchen.

"What's his name?" she asked.

"Her," said Greta. "'Er name's Blousy."

"We never had a dog," said Vivianne. "I've never lived with a dog before."

"Well, she don't know what to make o' *you*, that's for sure," said Greta. "What's tha name, child?"

"Vivianne."

"Vivianne," Greta repeated. "Unusual." She stepped to the door. "I'll get thee some blankets. While I'm gone, see if you can make friends wi' Blousy – and get some o' that grub in thee."

Vivianne was still sitting at the kitchen table when the front door banged at half past six. Greta glanced at her and said, "That'll be Milo, 'ome from t'manor. Be'ave thi sen now."
The kitchen door opened, and a rotund man entered, ruddy-faced, grey-whiskered, about sixty-five, brandishing a walking stick. He saw the newcomer straight away, glanced across the room at Greta, and back at the girl. "What? Who's this?" His voice was gravelly.
Viv stood, and Greta introduced her. "Vivianne's 'er name. I've said she can stay a few days. I'll tell you why later."
Milo addressed Vivianne directly. "By yourself?" She nodded. "Where's your ma and pa?"
"Pa's dead," said Vivianne. "Ma's walking to York."
Milo raised his eyebrows. "Walking to York? Why?"
"I said I'd tell you later," Greta insisted. "Leave t'child be."
"Step away from t'table, girl," Milo instructed. "Let's 'ave a look at you."
Vivianne obeyed. Greta stared sharply at her husband and said, "She's eleven, Milo. Just a girl."
"Hm," grunted the man. "Gonna be a looker, though – in't you, girly? With your black 'air and your big eyes. Tell us tha name again?"
"Vivianne."
"Vivianne," he repeated, nodding.
"What's *your* name," asked the girl boldly.
He raised his eyebrows again. "Me? I'm Milo. I eat little girls."
"I'm not little," said Viv.
"I bet you're not," said Milo.
"Milo Grimes!" warned Greta. "Don't you get ideas. 'Er mother'll be back in a few days, and she'll be gone. She's in our care in t'meantime – and she'll be safe 'ere. Understand?"
The man strode forward into the room. "Away wi' you, woman.

You know I'm only teasin'. Where's me dinner?"
"It's stew," said his wife.
"That'll do." He sat down opposite Vivianne and indicated she should reseat herself. "You eatin' with us?"
Greta raised her eyebrows at the girl, the expression suggesting she should answer in the affirmative.
"Yes please, if that's alright."
"Course it's alright, my dear," said Greta. "Keep your strength up. You'll look nice and rosy when your ma comes back."
"So what's 'appened?" asked Milo.
His wife answered, her voice steadily louder, "I said I'd tell you later – and I shall tell you – later…"

It was dark in the kitchen at night, but warm. Vivianne's bedding was soft and comfortable, although it felt strange to be sleeping on the floor. She wondered if there were many spiders, not relishing the thought.
Has she arrived in York yet? She must be exhausted. Poor mum. She'll be worrying about me.
Blousy wandered over, sniffed around the new creature and settled beside her. The dog smelt odd, old. Vivianne petted her. "Hello, girl," she whispered. "I'm Viv. Nice to be friends." Blousy licked her hand. "I've never been friends with a dog before. Aren't you lovely?"

Milo went off to work next morning, and Greta took Viv into the yard to milk the cow, pulling the animal out of a small shed she called "the dairy" attached to the cottage's rear wall.
"Watch me first; then you try. See she don't kick. Your ma won't want to see you wi' a black eye."
It took the girl just a few minutes to master the technique, and she was soon laughing delightedly as the milk squirted into the pail.
A few yards from the cottage's back door stood the peat bunker. The far side of the little building housed a pigpen at ground level, with a henhouse raised above, accessed by a steep ramp.

Vivianne clambered up, searched around inside and excitedly pulled out eight eggs.

"Look, Greta! Eight!" She held out two full hands.

"Eight," the woman replied. "Aye, 'bout reet number." She smiled at the girl. "Did they make a fuss?"

"A bit," Vivianne replied. "They ran around, squawking."

"Daft creatures they are, wi' their fuss and gossip."

"Can I take Blousy for a walk?"

"No, girl," Greta answered. "Blousy's too old for walkies. Yard's all she can manage."

The day ended, and Viv was in the dark again with the dog, hoping for her mother's imminent return.

But Cicely didn't appear the next day. Or the following day, or the day after that.

"She'll come," said Greta. "Give 'er time. She'll be workin' things out."

A week went by, ten days. Vivianne's dread deepened steadily. She began to fear she'd never see her mother again. She was alone – alone in the world.

"Something's happened to her," she murmured.

"There's nowt we can do but wait," Greta replied, uneasy. It seemed likely that something had indeed befallen the woman, and Greta was beginning to feel an acute responsibility for it.

"We have to search," said Viv.

"Who? Us? It's sixteen miles from 'ere to York, and I'm sixty-two years old. I can't go 'unting about t'countryside."

"Maybe not," said Viv. "But I know who can." She was determined – marching to the hall where her coat hung on a peg.

"Where are you goin'?" called Greta.

"To Haggard Farm. I want them to know what they've done."

"You cannot go there," cried Greta, rising from her seat, stepping after the girl. "Joan 'Aggard'll rip you to bits."

"I may only be eleven, but I can teach Joan Haggard a thing or two," Viv called over her shoulder.

Greta caught her at the door, gripped her by the arm and

commanded, "Calm down, child!"
Viv rounded on Greta, finger raised in warning and threw off the woman's grip. "Don't tell me to calm down! And don't keep calling me *child!*"
Greta paused, chastened, and sighed. "Alreet. I better come too."

Joan answered Vivianne's knock, glared at the girl and exclaimed, "What the 'ell d'you mean by it, comin' back 'ere?"
"My mother's gone," Viv retorted, "and it's your fault."
"My fault?"
"You drove us away without a second's thought – in the evening, with no idea where we might go. Now she's gone."
Joan looked beyond Vivianne at Greta, who nodded, eyebrows raised. "It's true. 'Er mother set out to York a week an' 'alf ago and ain't come back."
"Well, why was she goin' to York?" asked Joan.
"Because we had nowhere else to go," said Viv. "We weren't given time to make any arrangements."
A voice from within: "Who is it?"
Joan turned and shouted, "Back to your room, you. Ye don't venture forth till I tell 'ee." She turned to face her visitors again and asked, "Well, what do you want *me* to do about it?"
"Search the road from here to York – and all the houses and farms," Viv replied.
"I can't spare t'manpower for such a thing," said Joan.
Greta replied, "Joan, I think you should – for t'girl's sake."
Joan glanced at Vivianne, then at her hands, then at Vivianne again. Finally, she said, "Alreet. I'll get Bennet and Joel to set about lookin' f'r'er. We'll scour t'road. It'll tek days I shouldn't wonder." She paused, raised her hands, palms upward and said, "I'm sorry. I din't intend this. Go 'ome. It's gettin' dark. We'll start first thing in t'mornin'."

Bennet, Joel and eight farm labourers searched the road, the ditches, fields, woods, ponds and lakes for almost two weeks. After the first few days, Joan allowed Caspar to join the search.

They asked at the houses and farms all the way into the city, but no-one had seen the missing woman. It was a hopeless task. There were no leads, and they had to give up.

Cicely's journey had been doomed to failure anyway. Old Joshua Foster, whom she would have begged for aid, had died the previous year. But she never discovered that fact. She never reached York.

5. Day One

In early October, Greta visited Haggard Farm on Vivianne's behalf to negotiate the salvage of the goods that had been in the cottage. She returned with ten guineas and the news that Joan had had everything burned in the days immediately following the Stampers' expulsion. Vivianne's papers – her stories, poems, essays, diaries, and all her father's books – had gone up in smoke. There was nothing left except the clothes she'd brought with her, and her memories.

Greta wasn't entirely without a heart, and the loss of the girl's things amplified the guilt she already felt at having driven Cicely away. "I'm sorry, dear. There's nothin' to be done."

Vivianne didn't want Greta to see her tears, so she went outside, sat on the wall of the pigpen and cried silently. The day was warm for October, bright and sunny. She listened to the birds, watched the stir of the gentle breeze in the meadow grass behind the cottage, and thought of her mother.

I'll have to start again, alone – a new life, beginning at this moment. Day One.

She gathered herself, returned to the house and found Greta in the kitchen.

"*Paper?*" Greta repeated in response to Viv's question. "We don't have no paper."

"Something to write with then?"

"There's only chalk and t'blackboard, so I can keep track of what's needed int' 'ouse."

"Then I need to buy some things," said Viv. "Paper, quills, ink."

Greta thought. "Ask Milo tonight. 'E might be able to get such things at t'manor."

It wasn't much, but it gave Vivianne a means of focusing ahead. Writing had always shaped her life, and now writing seemed like life itself.

Within a few days, having acquired the items she needed, Vivianne settled into a corner of the kitchen to surround herself with words.

"Scribble, scribble," said Milo, watching her in puzzlement. "Never could make 'ead nor tail o' letters and scribblin'."

"No," said Greta. "You're nothin' more than an ignorant lump of meat that smokes at one end and farts at t'other."

"Who brings a livin' into this house?" he countered. "You, woman?"

"Away wi' you," she said. "Let t'girl do as she will."

"I wasn't goin' to stop 'er," he replied. "I like to see 'er there, all studious."

Greta paused in her work, took a couple of steps towards him and brandished the pan she was polishing. "I know what's in thy mind, Milo Grimes," she warned.

"Ach, woman!" he cursed. "Always thinkin' the worst o' me."

She raised a wagging finger. "I *know* the worst o' you. Don't you forget it."

"Ach!" he repeated. "That were years ago and far away."

She shook her head. "Men don't change…"

The kitchen was warm at night. Greta always kept the fire in with a damp turf before she went to bed, so the place remained cosy. Vivianne was snug enough in her nest of bedding to wear only her nightgown – and Blousy curled up with her as if she were another dog.

The cottage's ground floor consisted only of the kitchen (which was very large), a little entrance passage, and a tiny parlour that had its own small hearth. The parlour was Milo's room, and he liked to withdraw there and smoke his pipe, sitting before his own fire, often remaining there until late at night, long after Greta had retired.

"If 'e comes troublin' you when you're abed," Greta told her, "you 'oller for me."

Christmas came, the first without her mother. It went more or less unmarked in the cottage, except Greta made a special cake and spiced biscuits. On Friday, December 27th, they walked to The Bull and drank with some of their neighbours. Milo was no stranger to the place, but it was rare for Greta to be seen there.

"Mrs Grimes!" cried Jack, the landlord, when they pushed through the door into the tiny taproom.

"Jack," she called. "'Ow's tha wife?"

"Troublesome as ever," Jack threw back. "This your girl?"

Greta propelled Vivianne to the bar. "This is Vivianne."

Jack sized her up. "Pretty one," he said, then spoke directly to her. "Fancy a job? You could serve be'ind t'bar. Men like a pretty face."

But Greta vetoed the proposal. "Don't you tell 'er that. She's too young for bar work – not twelve yet."

"You only eleven?" asked Jack, surprised.

"I'll be twelve in April," Viv replied.

One of the drinkers at the bar, overhearing the conversation, craned forward and submitted his opinion that twelve was "old enough."

"Old enough for what, you devil?" Greta growled at him, setting off a few guffaws close by.

But the remark made an impression on Milo, and when Viv looked up, she caught him looking at her with a new kind of interest.

Once each month, Greta prepared a bath for Vivianne with water from the handpump heated on the stove, and the girl bathed before the kitchen hearth. Early in January, as she stepped out of the tub into Greta's waiting towel, the woman tutted and shook her head.

"Tha buds are comin' quick," she sighed. "And there'll soon be a proper thatch below. That's when t'trouble starts – bleedin', and men sniffin'."

"I can look after myself," said Viv.

"Maybe you can, and maybe you can't," Greta replied. "If they want somethin' enough – a certain thing – they usually get it, one way or t'other."

Vivianne took hold of the towel and dried herself vigorously while Greta applied a second towel to her hair.

"You're goin' to be…a fair one." She'd been on the point of saying *You're going to be like your mother,* but stopped herself before it was too late. "You noticed Milo lookin' at you?"

"Yes," Viv replied simply.

Greta nodded. "That's good. You know. Watch 'im…"

As Greta had predicted, the blood came just a few weeks later – suddenly, like a slimy sweat between Vivianne's legs as she was writing in the kitchen. There'd been no warning, none of the cramps or aches Greta said she should be vigilant for. It had just crept up on her – and leaked. Her shocked realisation sent ripples through the kitchen like a modest soundless charge. Milo, drinking gin at the table, sensed the tremor and looked up in surprise, although the girl had made no sound. Vivianne stared at him, dropped her quill and pressed her thighs together, squeezing the stickiness.

He knows, she thought. *How? Can he smell me?*

"Greta…"

The woman, cleaning dishes at the sink on the far side of the kitchen, sensed the urgency in the girl's quiet call and stepped towards her, catching Milo's glance as she passed him. Vivianne put both hands on her belly and looked at the older woman, communicating with her eyes. Greta understood immediately, motioned to Milo and said, "You – go and smoke your pipe."

Milo guessed what was happening and rose to obey his wife's command, chair scraping on the floor. He was undeniably curious about this girl ripening in his house but had no wish to invite confrontation with Greta by displaying any visible interest in the young woman's physical functions. He took up the gin bottle and hurried away, the door clicking shut in his wake. Vivianne got to her feet and found a dark stain on her chair. Her dress and shift were sodden with blood.

"What did I tell you?" said Greta. "So – you're a woman. And they'll all know."

Milo liked to keep himself to himself. He worked all day, often on Sundays too, and shut himself in the parlour when he came home, although the three of them usually ate together, and he wasn't entirely taciturn. He was a labourer in the grounds of the manor house, one of a group. Occasionally he'd speak of the other men, but he never brought any of them home. He spent two or three nights a week in The Bull, and although there was often booze on his breath, he never came home drunk.

One evening in early April, after their meal, he asked Vivianne if she'd like a proper drink.

"Milo…" warned Greta from across the kitchen.

"She's old enough," he protested. "Don't cosset t'girl. Let 'er try if she wants."

"My mother drank," said Viv. "I'd like to taste it. Only one."

Milo cast a glance at Greta, eyebrows raised in a little *told-you-so* victory. "There, you see? She wants to try. And she's nearly twelve – some folk get wed at twelve."

Greta warned, "'E's out to trap you. It's t'way o' men."

"Get away with your nonsense, woman. It's only a drink." He produced two small glasses from the dresser, uncorked his bottle, and poured them both a measure. "There you go," he said to the girl. "See what you think."

Vivianne lifted it to her nose. "I remember the smell."

Milo downed his own drink in one and nodded encouragingly at her. "Go on."

She poked the tip of her tongue in the liquid, withdrew it and shivered. "Ugh! It's really sharp!" But she was determined, and took the entire contents of the glass into her mouth, swilled it round and swallowed. Her whole body shuddered in reaction, and she gasped.

Milo laughed, slapping his knee. "That's the way! That's the way!"

Greta turned her back on the pair and continued with her work, voicing her displeasure in a string of chastisements.

"Take another, girl," Milo prompted with gleeful enthusiasm.

"Alright," said Viv. "Another." She pushed her glass forward and waited for Milo to fill it, but Greta came hurrying to the table and wrenched the bottle from her husband's hands.

"I said no!" She was furious. "Thee'll do no 'arm to t'girl! Away wi' you! Find your mates in t'boozer! Clear off!"

He shot out of his chair, cursing, and Greta chased him out of the kitchen. The front door slammed.

"It's just a drink!" cried Vivianne.

Greta levelled her finger at the door through which Milo had fled, and replied, "*Thee* sees a drink; *'e* sees *thee* on tha back."

Vivianne was irritated and wanted to be somewhere else. She stood and grumbled, "I'm going to shut up the hens."

"Go on then," Greta answered, more quietly. "If tha wants to do somethin' grown-up, learn to smoke – that'll do thee no 'arm."

"I just wanted to see if I could smell my mum in the drink."

The comment stung Greta; it was as if she'd been slapped. She clamped her jaw shut, clenched her fists, forced the threat of tears from her eyes, and paused, balancing herself to respond. "I know." She sighed and dropped her gaze to the floor. "An' did you?"

"Yes – a bit."

Greta nodded, swallowed, and said gently, "Away with you then. See to t'girls."

It was dusk, and the stars were coming out. The hens had already put themselves away; Vivianne merely had to shut them in, safe from the fox. She sat on the wall of the pigpen – one of her favourite thinking places – clasped her hands in her lap, thought of her mother, and found herself crying again. The pigs were out of their pen, and a couple of them came grunting around her dangling feet. She greeted them by name and reached down to fondle them.

Cicely had often read Viv's work, as had her father. They'd been the people she'd bounced ideas off, her sounding boards, her audience. It was different now; there was no-one to appreciate what she wrote, no-one to understand. Milo couldn't read at all, and Greta only a little. There was no-one with whom to communicate. It was like being Robinson Crusoe – marooned, cut off from human contact. She'd come to like the two elderly people, but it wasn't the same as having someone who genuinely understood.

She thought of Greta, carrying the burden of what had happened to Cicely. If she hadn't rejected her… Viv sensed Greta's remorse even though the woman had never apologised for her actions. The child knew it must be a terrible weight to bear – saw it in the old woman's eyes. And she was aware that Greta's protectiveness towards her was partly the result of her guilt.

The night closed in while Vivianne pondered her uncharted future, mopping the sadness from her face, nursing the ache in her heart.

Greta made a sweet lamb pie for Vivianne's twelfth birthday, with ingredients donated by or purchased from the manor house. It was not something Mrs Grimes was used to preparing, and it took a good deal of planning, care and effort, all of which paid off. The dish was a resounding success with the girl, and Greta's heart warmed to see how much she enjoyed it.

"This is lovely, Greta! Thank you!"

"I thought thee'd like it," the delighted chef replied. She put her arms round Viv and gave her a hug. "'Appy birthday, sweet girl."

"'Appy birthday," Milo echoed. "All t'stuff in that pie – it come from t'manor. T'meat fresh killed."

Greta cut in. "Milo brought 'ome most o' t'spices too. I 'ad some nutmeg and currants, but 'e got t'mace and t'cloves – and t'grapes an' all. An' candied orange peel."

"I've never eaten anything like this before. It's *so* tasty."

Greta beamed. "Mmm. Makes me glad to see thee sup it so!"

Vivianne took the woman's arms and kissed her on the cheek; then she rose, hurried round the table and embraced Milo.
It was the happiest day she spent with them.

Things soured in the early hours of Saturday, April 19th.
It was as Greta had warned. Milo's shuffling footsteps brought Vivianne up from sleep. She looked past the slumbering dog and saw the man's boots dimly illuminated in the soft lamplight. A chair creaked as he sat down. He was silent for a while, summoning the courage to speak, knowing there'd be no going back from this. Viv knew why he was there, and her anxiety clawed inside her. Milo wanted from her what Caspar Haggard had desired from her mother.
"Greta's asleep," he whispered. "I brought some gin. I don't want nothin'. I just thought thee might care for a drop."
She didn't move – pretended to be asleep. She knew he couldn't see her under the settle, behind the dog.
"I know you're awake," he said. "I can 'ear it in tha breathin'."
"I'm not thirsty," she replied.
"Come on," he insisted, tapping the settle with his boot. "Keep me company. Just for a bit."
"I'm in my nightdress. I can't come out."
"I shan't look at thee," he replied.
"Fetch me something? A blanket?"
"In't you got blankets down there?"
"They're all tucked in. You'll see me while I take the bed to pieces."
"A blanket…" he said to himself, and Vivianne sensed him looking around. He got up, wandered off and returned a few seconds later.
"'Ere's a blanket."
He handed it down, and she extended her arm and took it.
"Out you come then. I'll do t'gin while you crawl out. I won't look."
He fetched two glasses and poured the fluid. When he was done, he turned to find the girl standing behind him, wound tight in

the covering he'd provided.

"That's better," he said. "Take a seat."

She obeyed, and he sat close and pushed the glass towards her, his breath already thick with booze.

"There you go," he said. "'Ere's gladness to you." He drained his glass. Vivianne matched him, grimacing, and Milo quickly refilled both receptacles. "Another," he said, and emptied his own again.

Vivianne shook her head. "I don't want any more."

He chuckled. "I shan't eat you."

"You'll hurt me," she said.

Milo looked stung, and Vivianne regretted her words. He knit his brows. "I don't want to 'urt you. I wouldn't ever 'urt you."

"You…" She'd intended to say, *You promise?* but immediately remembered her mother's last words and bit her tongue. She reached for the glass and drank the gin in a single draught.

"That's the way," he said. "Good girl." He repeated the phrase, watching her closely, savouring the words: "Good girl."

Vivianne stared back, ready to fight him off if it came to that.

Milo studied her in silence, eyes screwed small, sizing her up. "One more," he muttered and refilled the two glasses.

"Mm-mm," Viv refused, shaking her head.

Milo was silent again. The girl kept her eyes fixed on him. They'd come to an impasse.

He stared at her middle – towards the thing he wanted. "Let me see."

"No," Vivianne replied, voice quiet. "Go away, or I'll call Greta."

"I'm not gonna 'urt you," he said. "I won't touch – I just wanna look, then I'll go."

"You're frightening me," said Vivianne.

Milo held up his big hands, palms open. "I don't mean no 'arm. I'm just a weak man, wi' t'common weaknesses of all men. I won't lay a finger on you, I swear."

Vivianne knew that if she screamed for Greta, the dynamic between the three of them would alter forever.

Nevertheless…

She drew a deep breath and yelled, "GRETA!"

"Jesus!" Milo cursed, shooting to his feet, shaking his head. He tried to stagger out of the kitchen, but his wife was there before he could reach the door. She glowered at him, then at Vivianne, standing by the table in a sheet. Milo lifted his hands, about to utter some excuse in an attempt to fend off the whirlwind that was about to strike.

"YOU FILTHY BASTARD!" Greta cried, leaping forward and pounding him with her fists.

"I din't 'urt 'er!" he shouted, head down, arms raised to defend himself. Greta reached into the dresser and produced a large, heavy frying pan. "No, no, no!" yelled her husband as she battered him with it.

"DISGUSTIN', WORTHLESS, SOULLESS BASTARD!" striking him a fresh blow with every word. "DISGUSTIN'! DISGUSTIN'!"

"'Ave mercy, woman!"

"GET OUT! OUT, OUT, OUT!"

Milo stumbled from the kitchen, and Vivianne heard the front door crash. Greta shot her another glance, face rigid with fury, before following in the wake of the beaten man. The bolts on the front door slammed home savagely, one, two, three, then she was back in the room, glaring at the girl.

Vivianne's third glass of gin remained untouched on the tabletop. "That yours?" snarled Greta. Viv nodded. The woman strode to the table, frying pan in hand, lifted the glass and swallowed the contents. Then she took up Milo's bottle, upended it into her mouth and drank at length, banging the flask down when she'd done. Her eyes pierced Vivianne for a few seconds while her breathing calmed. Finally, she said, "To bed. He's not comin' back int' 'ouse tonight. And tomorrow, we'll 'ave to make other arrangements for you."

So Vivianne found herself sleeping in the attic space above the peat bunker, next to the hens and pigs. It was smelly in there, colder than the kitchen, and she no longer had Blousy at night. Greta spent most of the first day making it as comfortable as possible, brushing out the masses of cobwebs and pinning sheets over the roof timbers to keep the spiders off her. She moved Viv's bed inside and added lots more sheets and towels. Finally, she unscrewed two bolts from the front and back doors of the cottage and fixed them to the inside of the loft hatch.

"There," she said, "you're safe in 'ere. 'E won't be able to get thee wi'out tearin' t'place down. And if he tries that, I'll batter 'im to pulp."

"There's no light," said Viv. "It'll be dark."

"I'll give thee a lantern and striker," said Greta. "Mind thi sen wi' it in 'ere. Be vigilant, or thee'll go up in smoke. See it burns low."

"Sorry," Vivianne muttered, not for the first time.

"'Tin't thy fault, girl," sighed Greta. "Men are no better than animals; only one thing on their mind. We women – you and me – we 'ave to put up wi' 'em." She nodded to herself. "One day, women will rule this world. Then we'll show 'em a thing or two."

"I'll be cold out here," said Viv.

"I know," Greta replied. "But summer's comin'. Come winter, we may 'ave to think again, but tha'll be alreet for now."

Vivianne rarely saw Milo after that. Greta allowed her into the cottage only after her husband left for work in the morning. In the evening, he ate in the kitchen with his wife while Viv sat on the pigpen wall, played with the animals or wandered in the meadow behind the house. When the disgraced man had finished eating, Greta sent him off to his parlour or to the alehouse. He wouldn't speak to Vivianne on the few occasions they bumped into each other, acknowledging her greeting with nothing more than a curt nod. She couldn't decide whether he was sorry or embarrassed for his actions, or was merely dismissive of her.

"Don't speak to 'im," said Greta. "It'll be safer that way."

Vivianne's loft was prone to dampness at night, her breath condensing in the chill while she slept. The roof leaked, and the moisture soon brought down the sheets Greta had pinned up to keep the insects away. She had to air her bedding most mornings. Despite the bolts on the door, she didn't really feel safe at night, with the pigs fussing and other animals prowling around, especially the foxes screaming in the distance and snarling as they tried to get into the henhouse. The wind was often loud around the little building, pulling at the roof just a few feet above her head, and heavy rain produced a deafening roar. Through it all was the reek of the pigs, although familiarity steadily lessened its potency.

I probably stink of pigs all the time, she thought, *but I can't tell anymore. If I met the King and dressed up in fine clothes to bow to him, thinking I looked splendid enough, he'd probably just think, "She stinks like a pig."*

6. Daphne

A morning in late July. The sun cast rays of bright gold through the kitchen windows, setting the flagstones aglow. Blousy lay on her back in the pool of light, eyes blissfully closed, mouth wide open, tongue flapping loose to one side, paws lifted, lazily angled. Vivianne smiled, contemplating the dog, quill poised to set down the next line of her sonnet about the daylight and the rain.

Daft creature, she thought; *lovely, daft creature. God's old woofer: "This is my dog, with whom I am well pleased..."*

"Vivianne." Greta's voice summoned the girl from her daydream. She looked up. The woman stood a few feet away, hands on hips, wearing her *I-have-something-important-to-tell-you* face.
"Mm?"
"Thee 'as to bathe. Someone's comin' to see thee this afternoon."
Eyebrows raised in surprise: "To see me?"
"Aye, to see thee," Greta confirmed.
"Who?" asked Viv. "Who wants to see me?"
"People are stayin' at t'manor. They're comin' 'ere. Milo told me, and I said 'e should tell 'em about thee."
"Why? What do they want?"
"They're lookin' for girls."

Vivianne pondered this for a moment, wondering what it might mean. "Why? Why are they looking for girls? What do they want with girls?"

"It's for a new school, they say."

"Where? You mean I'd go away?"

"I don't know where. But aye, it would get thee away from 'ere."

Vivianne set the quill down, eyes wide, mind whirling. "But…"

Greta shook her head questioningly. "What…but…?"

The ground beneath Vivianne's self-perception began to crumble, and an image of her mother, dressed in cape and hat, fixed itself in her mind. The last time she'd seen her was at the door of this house. Viv felt like a dog who'd been perpetually watching the place where its master had disappeared, and who was now faced with the prospect of never being able to see that place again. It was like a withdrawal of hope. She felt dizzy; her head spun.

"I'm preparin' tha bath now. This is important. They 'ave girls int' 'ouse already. They bin travellin' 'round collectin' girls from work'ouses."

"What kind of girls?" asked Viv. She felt breathless; her voice was hoarse.

"Girls like thee."

"What do you mean, like me?"

"Special girls, bright girls."

Viv began to bluster. She didn't know what to say or do.

"Calm down, child," said Greta. "Just get thi sen ready, and let's see what's what. We 'ave an hour or two."

The scouts had been touring Yorkshire for almost a month, looking for suitable girls in the poorhouses. They'd begun in the south, in Sheffield, and worked their way round, most recently in York, Harrogate, Wetherby and Ripon. Darlington and Middlesbrough remained – almost a week's work – then they'd be on their way with their cargo of blessed children.

Sir Nicholas Yearsley, Oulston's Lord of the Manor, a friend of their employer, had granted them the use of one of the larger houses on his estate so that the girls could live in comfort while they were being gathered. So far, six young ladies were in residence, together with the four scouts.

Jasper Denholm, forty-two years old and keen to get the job done so he could return to his family in Durham, asked, "Is it likely we'll find one so close by?"

"It'll only hold us up for a day," Daphne Harlan replied. "We could do with a break anyway. Look, it means a pause, and you three can spend the afternoon boozing. What's to be lost?"

Daphne was thirty-three, unremarkable in appearance, but kindly, with shoulder-length yellow hair and dull blue eyes. She lived with her mother in Yarm and was glad to earn a good living from her job, travelling the country searching for likely young females. Her employers valued her and trusted her judgement. She knew precisely what they were looking for.

"Who's going with you?" Edmund Carlton enquired. At twenty-five, Edmund was the youngest of the group (and the least suitable for the job, in Daphne's opinion).

She thrust her chin at Martin Brixton. "You, Martin."

Martin was the eldest, almost fifty. Daphne appreciated his calmness and steady judgment. He was also her lover.

"Suits me," he said.

The girls were playing some kind of game in the garden, their excited voices drifting into the house through the open window. "I'll sit outside and keep an eye on them," said Edmund, rising, walking to the door. Jasper went back to his reading, and the room became quiet except for the cries and laughter of the young ones.

"Listen to them," said Martin to Daphne. "Happy children. Maybe the happiest they've been for a long time." Daphne watched his face. He was a softie, really too kind and thoughtful for this job – but that was why she loved him. He had a golden heart.

"You. You silly old thing," she chastised him affectionately.

"I often wonder about what we do," he replied. "Where they're heading."

"They're going to have a wonderful few years," said Daphne.

"Privileged, petted, surrounded by friends. What would they have had if not for us? A miserable life, nothing but poverty, filth – a bleak, hopeless existence."

"We each have to find the precious thing," he replied. "The thing that defines who we are, that gives our life its contour, shape and worth. And that can be found in muck and squalor – perhaps even misery – just as well as in riches and a life filled with love. Maybe, in taking away the opportunity to suffer – even for a brief while – we're skewing the course of their lives..."

"Martin," Daphne interrupted.

"What?"

"Don't."

"Don't what?"

"Don't talk like that. You can't possibly know what their lives are supposed to be. Perhaps we were always meant to find them."

Martin sounded a little irritated. "You misunderstand. I wasn't talking about fate."

"I know," said Daphne. "I know what you mean. Look... Martin, you're just too nice for this job. Look at me." He did so, and she asked, "Am I cold-blooded?"

"Yes," he answered.

She smiled and gave a half snort. "Alright. But I'm not unkind. I look at the girls the same as you, and my heart warms for them. Who's to know what the future holds? Maybe there'll be rough waters ahead, but perhaps they're heading for long, happy lives. I hope so. In any case, they'll be out of harm's way for years now. Perhaps things will alter in that time. Just think of today – forget the rest." She paused, and he gazed at her, smiling. Daphne was thoughtful. He loved her. She continued, "If you can't disconnect a little, I really think you should become a farmer, or a printer." Her smile broadened. "Or a parson."

Daphne and Martin strolled to the cottage in the early afternoon. The squat, thatched dwelling was a few doors up from the alehouse, unremarkable, identical to the others in the little hamlet. Cows grazed on the green opposite.

"After you," said Martin, holding open the gate so Daphne could take the four or five steps required to reach the front door. Her knock was answered by a plump, elderly woman, grey hair arranged in a ball beneath her bonnet.
"Mrs Grimes?"
The matron nodded, wiping her hands in her apron. "Greta Grimes. Yes, that's me."
"We're here to see…" But Daphne halted, catching sight of the child, unsmiling and suspicious in the little passage, half hiding behind the woman. She was tall, with long dark hair and big brown eyes, dressed in a pink gown that didn't quite fit her. (Vivianne had grown out of all her good clothes, so Greta had scrounged an old but serviceable dress from one of her neighbours, altered it to fit – in a way – and presented the girl in it as best she could.) Daphne nodded to herself. The child was beautiful, one of the best they'd found. "My word!" she said. "Aren't you a pretty one…"
"She's a good girl," said Greta proudly. "Clever – writes more than I could ever read. Studious."
"You sound ideal," said Daphne to the girl. She looked at Martin and found him smiling. Concerns about whether the child had been worth the extra day dropped away.
"What's going to happen to me?" asked Vivianne.
"Nothing at all if you don't want it to," Daphne replied. "Can we come in and talk?"

The four of them sat round the kitchen table, Viv still tense, worried.
"I'm Daphne. This is Martin. We're scouts, looking for suitable girls for a new school on the coast a couple of days' journey from here."
"What kind of girls?" asked Viv.
"Exactly the kind of girl *you* appear to be: clever, attractive…" She nodded, smiling, trying to be nice. The man was smiley too, and Vivianne sensed genuine kindness in him. Daphne went on. "Can I use your name?"

"Vivianne," said Viv.

"I think names should be used only with permission. You can use my name. You've told me yours. May I use it to address you?"

Viv thought the question strange but was oddly flattered to be asked permission. "Yes," she said. "Call me Viv if you like."

"Viv," said Daphne. "I like that."

A tiny smile glimmered in Vivianne's face, mostly in her eyes, and Daphne knew the ice was broken. "Let me tell you about the school," she said. "It's called The Lookout, and it's set on the coast between Whitby and Scarborough – a huge house and grounds. It has its own beach, its own woods. You'll learn to play music, to sing, to dance; you'll learn foreign languages – all sorts of things. I've heard you like to read."

"I do," Viv admitted.

"That's good," said Daphne. "There's a library with books stacked so high you need a ladder to reach them. Thousands and thousands of books."

Vivianne swallowed. She'd dreamt about such places but had never dared imagine she'd have the use of one. "Will I be able to write?"

"As much as you want," Daphne replied.

"What must I do?"

Daphne shrugged. "Just be you."

"Why? Why me?"

"Like I said. Because you're clever and beautiful."

"Beautiful?" whispered Viv.

"Yes," said Daphne. "You're beautiful. You're a very beautiful girl."

Vivianne pressed her lips tight together, biting the inside, on the verge of crying, although she didn't quite understand why. Relief mixed with joy, excitement, and a host of other emotions. She knew she'd burst into tears if she attempted to say anything, so she stared at Daphne and tried to blink away the moisture.

"The school is for orphan girls – girls who've wound up in the poorhouses, in the workhouses." She flicked a glance at Greta and quickly added, "Not that this is one of those places. I know you've been well cared for here."

"We've looked after 'er, Milo and me," Greta nodded.

"Of course you have," Daphne reassured her. "Mr Grimes told us what happened."

"My mum…" Vivianne began.

Daphne raised a reassuring hand. "I know. I know how hard it must have been for you." She paused. "Viv, if you come, you can expect to spend six or seven years at the school. You'll have your own maid, your own space. You'll make lots of friends and have the most amazing time. When it's done, you'll be a lady, with your own means of living." She lifted her eyebrows, tilted her head. "How does that sound?"

"Too good to be true," Viv responded.

Martin spoke for the first time. "But it *is* true." Vivianne instinctively liked the man. His expression, his voice, made her feel warm and calm. He continued. "It's indescribable – one of the loveliest places you'll ever see."

They fell into silence for a few seconds. Vivianne looked across the room and found Blousy under the settle. The tired old dog was lying in her bed with head raised, rheumy grey eyes fixed on her as if she knew the girl would soon be gone.

Daphne asked, "Will you come with us, Viv?"

Vivianne felt the tears coming again. She turned to Greta, face puckering. "Can I take Blousy?"

Greta extended her hand and stroked Viv's hair. "No, love. She's too old."

Viv sniffed and faced Daphne again. "Alright."

"Good," said the woman. She reached across the table and took Vivianne's hands. "I need to examine you – for the medical records. Is it alright?"

Vivianne frowned. "You mean…?"

Daphne gave an affirmative murmur, mouth closed, and added. "We can go somewhere private." She glanced at Greta. "Upstairs?"

"Yes," said Greta. "The bedroom's tidy – if you want to use that."

"Can Greta come?" Viv asked.

"Yes," Daphne answered. "If you like."

Martin waited at the table while the women went upstairs with Vivianne. The house creaked in the day's heat; a fly buzzed persistently, settling here, settling there. He swatted it away a couple of times. Floorboards creaked above. He clicked his tongue, smiled at the dog, hummed a few notes. After a few minutes, Mrs Grimes, Daphne and Vivianne returned. The girl looked flushed, self-conscious. Daphne's glance told him all was well.

"So," he said, "you can go whenever you like. Now, tomorrow, or in a few days when we're ready to leave the manor."

Before the girl could answer, Greta interjected, "No point ditherin', child. A new life awaits thee. Grasp it now."

Vivianne felt cut off from shore, drifting from everything she knew. "My papers...I'd better change."

"Tha can keep t'frock, Viv. It'll be no use to Mrs Limb now."

"Alright. I'll get my clothes."

"Go on then, girl. I'll find a sack for thy things."

Vivianne withdrew to her little fortress to gather her few possessions while Greta supplied the visitors with refreshment and repeated the girl's story, so far as she knew it. "My 'usband can't be trusted 'round women," she told them. "'E was looking at t'girl – sniffin' round her. She 'ad to sleep in t'peat loft to stay safe."

Vivianne was ready to leave twenty minutes later, having said goodbye to all the animals one by one, and hugged Blousy for the last time. She embraced Greta tearfully at the front door. "Thank you for looking after me. Say goodbye to Milo."

Greta's guilt welled up within her, and she struggled to keep her emotions hidden. "Go, girl. Make a life for thi sen and be 'appy. Away wi' you!"

Daphne thanked Greta, and Martin shook her hand. Then they were on their way, Vivianne leaving the house forever. After a few yards, she looked back to wave, but the door was closed. Greta lay huddled on the hall floor, sobbing.

7. A New life

It was the first time Vivianne had seen a landscaped estate. She trailed behind Daphne and Martin, admiring the wide-open parklands, grazing sheep, ancient trees, follies, lake and summerhouse.
I wonder if Eden was like this, she thought. *A garden in the east...*
"That's where we're going," Martin pointed. "You can see the girls playing."
"That house?" asked Viv, amazed. "I'm going to live there?"
"Just for a few days," Martin laughed, "until we're ready to leave."
It was the largest, most magnificent house Vivianne had ever laid eyes on – two stories tall, gleaming white and red stone, ornate, with seemingly endless rows of windows.
"It's incredible!" she breathed.
Daphne smiled. "It's just the garden house. The manor house is much bigger." She raised her eyebrows and added, "And if you think the manor house is big, wait till you see the Lookout. It'll dwarf anything you ever imagined."
The circle of girls paused in their game and watched Viv as she passed. Two or three raised their hands in shy greeting.
"This is Vivianne," Martin called to them. "We'll get her settled in, then she'll come and join you." He turned to her and asked, "Is that alright?"
She said it was and murmured her thanks.
Vivianne's room was more sumptuous than any she'd slept in before – lofty, airy – tall windows welcoming the daylight. There were three beds.
"You're sharing with Orla and Nana," Daphne told her. "You don't mind sharing, do you?"
"No, no," Viv responded, still dazed at her change of circumstances and the rapidity of events. "I...don't know what to say. I'm..." (she knit her brows, appreciating the deepest meaning of the word her lips were about to frame) "...astonished."

She set down her things, washed her hands and face, and followed Daphne into the garden, where she was introduced to her new companions. There were six of them. Penny Dyson was the eldest – thirteen years old, blonde, a little taller than Viv. The others were all ten or eleven, very pretty: Orla Stapleton, Nana Hall, Carol Witherington, Betty Elliot, Harriet Dixon. Orla had been travelling with the scouts the longest. She'd been collected in Sheffield from the workhouse, where her mother had died a few months earlier.

"You're all so beautiful," said Viv. "Nana, I love your hair. It's so pale; it's almost white."

"Where did they find you?" asked Nana.

"I've been living with people near here. My mother disappeared last year."

"Dead?"

Viv shook her head. "I don't know. Probably."

"It's dreadful, not knowing."

"Mm…"

Nana took Viv's hand and held it between her own. "We're on a big adventure by the sound of things – all of us."

"I know," Vivianne replied. "Feels strange."

"Are you leaving any friends behind?"

"No. I've never really had friends. I used to see children when we lived in York, but that was a long time ago. What about you?"

"I was in Ripon, in the workhouse. My mum died years ago, and my dad got lost in the bottle – died of it last August. But I wasn't alone – there were other children." She was quiet, remembering them. "But Daphne and the others only wanted me – they only took me."

"Why so few?" asked Vivianne. "There are only seven of us here, and they say they've nearly finished searching."

"I don't know. Daphne says it's because they're looking for *ladies*, whatever that means."

"You're all beautiful," said Viv. "That's what you have in common."

"You too," said Nana. "Maybe they have a certain idea of what a *lady* should look like."

Daphne and Martin set out early the next morning on their final foray north, Edmund driving the coach, leaving Jasper alone to look after the girls. It was another sunny, warm day, and they spent most of it in the garden, chasing around, playing games, talking. Vivianne felt sad, drifting like a leaf in a brook, carried further away from the tree of its birth towards some unknown landing place. She sat close to the house at midday, with paper and ink, putting together a poem. Jasper watched her from a distance, the voices of the other girls ringing in his ears, and decided to speak to her.
"Daphne says you're a writer."
"I've always written. My dad taught me when I was small." She looked up at him. "I saw you reading. What was the book?"
"Don Quixote," he said. "It's Spanish, translated…"
"I know what it is," she answered.
He was surprised. "You've read it?"
"A long time ago. My father had a copy."
"You understood it?"
She smiled at him. "I'm not completely uneducated."
"Sorry," he apologised, spontaneously returning her smile, shaking his head. He glanced at her paper. "What are you writing now?"
"Poem," she said.
"Can I see?"
She handed him the page, and he read it, his smile fading. The girl watched him as his eyes followed the words. When he got to the end, he remained still, distantly aware of the other girls at play, the paper nipped between thumb and forefinger. Vivianne noticed the moisture in his eyes as he returned the poem to her. He sniffed, wiped something away from his right cheek, looked directly at her and quietly enunciated her name. "Vivianne Stamper."
"That's me," she breathed.
"Your heart's bigger than Yorkshire."

"Thank you," she replied softly. "No-one's read my stuff since my mum went away."
"You're amazing," Jasper murmured. "How old are you? Twelve?"
She nodded.
"My God," he said. "You're going to change the world."

A few days later, Vivianne, writing alone in the garden once more, looked up and saw Milo Grimes watching her from the shade of an oak tree. She put down her paper, secured it with a stone so the breeze wouldn't carry it off, and walked towards him. Seeing her approach, his shame overwhelmed him, and he began to retreat, but she called to him, "Don't go." His face was ruddier than usual, darkened with embarrassment, but he stood his ground as bidden, and she came to a standstill before him.
"Thank you for everything you did," she said. "I didn't get a chance to say goodbye."
His eyes shone, and he sighed. "I'm sorry."
"I know," she replied.
He fidgeted, unable to find the words he wanted.
"Can I give you a hug?" asked Viv.
Milo bent forward in relief, arms extended. "You can," he sobbed and embraced her. She felt the emotion in his chest as he crushed her to him, and saw the tears on his face as he let her go. "Good luck to you then, girl."
"Goodbye, Milo. Give my love to Greta. And save some for yourself."

The carriage returned after a further two days, with a final pair of acquisitions. Twelve-year-old Dearbhla Blackwood had been discovered in Darlington, and Iris Little, aged ten, in Middlesbrough.
Supper that night was a happy occasion, all nine girls and the four scouts invited to the manor house as guests of Sir Nicholas Yearsley and his wife, Lady Anne. It was the first time any of the girls had been waited on by servants, and they were awed by the grandeur of it all. Towards the end of the evening, His Lordship

stood and toasted them.

"To nine of the prettiest girls I've ever entertained in my house." Over the stifled giggles, Sir Nicholas raised his glass to Daphne and added, "And the tenth, it's true to say, is your good self, Miss Harlan." He was about to sit, but his wife jabbed him with a finger, and he scrambled to his feet again. "Oh, sorry my love. And you, of course, my own dearest." He half raised his glass, chastised, and the girls laughed out loud.

They left the following morning after breakfast, Martin and Edmund driving the two coaches, the girls divided between the vehicles.

"We're on our way," said Orla to Vivianne. "On our way to new lives."

Viv was concerned that the carriages would turn left out of the estate and drive past Haggard Farm. She hadn't ventured that way since the failed search for her mother and was frightened that seeing the place again might overwhelm her with memories. Mercifully, they pulled to the right and followed the road north, then east. She sat back in her seat, closed her eyes and felt the past drop away.

Dearbhla soon became ill and was sick, so they stopped at the Worsley Arms in Hovingham for an early lunch while the carriage was cleaned and Daphne took care of the upset girl.

"She was worried about the journey," said Betty Elliot. "Told me she doesn't travel well. It's the swaying of the coach. Poor thing." They were on their way again in little more than an hour, Dearbhla under instruction to call for a halt whenever she felt queasy. Consequently, it took rather longer than expected to achieve the end of their day's journey.

They took lodgings for the night at The Dove in Pickering, three girls to a room, Daphne and Martin together, Jaspar and Edmund sharing. The landlord allocated a private chamber for their evening meal so the young girls could avoid the attention of the men in the taproom.

"They're good-lookin' things," he told Martin. "And some of 'em look old enough."

Vivianne shared a large bed with Iris Little, while Penny Dyson slept in a smaller one near the window. It rained in the night, and Viv lay on her back in the near darkness listening to the water splashing in the street.

"Are you awake?" Iris whispered.

"Yes."

"I can't sleep," said Iris. "I'm so excited."

"Me too," Viv replied.

"You're really pretty," Iris muttered.

"Shh," Penny whispered from the other bed. "Listen to the rain."

Hear the rain, thought Viv. *On my back in a field under the warm rain. Washing, washing away my mother, carrying the last of her – her smell, her touch, her love – into the earth, leaving me small and new, drying in the sun.*

A late breakfast, and they were on their way once more, following the road east, the moor's southern edge on their left.

"Look at the view!" cried Harriet, gazing out the window. "It's so bleak and barren, romantic. Look! Sheep all around!"

They passed through Thornton-le-Dale and stopped at Snainton to eat before travelling on through Wykeham and the Aytons to Scarborough, where they took rooms for the night at The George Inn, overlooking the water. None of the girls had ever seen the sea before, and they were beside themselves with excitement. Daphne and Martin took them down onto the sands before supper, and they spent an hour paddling and teasing each other.

"This is *amazing!*" shouted Carol.

"It's wonderful to see them so happy," said Martin to Daphne, watching them splash about.

"They're lovely, aren't they?" she replied. "I wonder if any of them has ever been as happy. Look at Vivianne, running along the shore in the surf."

Martin followed her gaze and saw the girl, arms flung wide, crying out with joy, Dearbhla following in her wake. Orla, Iris and Harriet were digging a huge hole in the sand, while Nana,

Carol, Betty and Penny stood close together on the shore, arms around each other, watching the boats and the gulls.

Vivianne sprinted across the sand to Daphne. "You said there was a beach at the school. Is it like this?"

"It is," Daphne replied. "Smaller, and with more shingle than sand, but yes, you'll have the sea and the wind and the gulls. You'll be *so* happy."

They met late again for breakfast, and Daphne said they should be ready to leave by eleven. "It's only a short journey from here," she told them. "Less than two hours. We want to get you there early so you can settle in and explore. Mr Crowan, the headmaster, will meet us when we arrive, and you'll be shown to your rooms. Then we'll have lunch together in the dining hall. That's when we'll say goodbye to you – me, Martin, Edmund and Jasper. We all have our own homes to go to."

"Will we see you again?" asked Orla.

"Maybe," Daphne replied. "We still have to travel around looking for new girls, so you'll probably see us from time to time as we bring them home."

"We'll miss you," said Harriet.

Daphne felt a pull at her heart. "We'll miss you too. We get very fond of you all." She paused. "But you're going to have the most amazing years at the Lookout. I envy you – we all do."

The coaches pulled away shortly after eleven, the streets and buildings of the town soon falling behind. They drove north into open countryside and then onto a tree-lined road, the sea out of sight to the east. Vivianne sat opposite Nana, and they watched the thrill in each other's eyes all the way along the route.

They lost a little time, stopping once for Dearbhla to recover herself, but at one o'clock, drew to a halt before a pair of iron gates with the words, *The Lookout* fashioned into the scrollwork. Jasper, who'd been driving the lead carriage, jumped down and yanked the bell rope, setting the shiny brass bell jangling atop its gatepost. A man approached from within a few seconds later, squat, about sixty, pipe clenched in his teeth.

"Mr Denholm," he greeted Jasper. "We meet again. Escorting the ladies as usual?"

"Hello, Jack. Cargo of nine."

"Nine!" Jack repeated, swinging back the gates. "Bring 'em in."

Jasper thanked the man, reseated himself on the box, and clicked the horses forward. The girls waved at the gatekeeper as they passed, and he waved back at them, grinning, winking, and puffing smoke.

"We've arrived," said Daphne. "Girls, you're home. Welcome to the Lookout."

They continued along the drive, and a few minutes later the house itself came into view: vast, like a palace, four stories high, long wings set at right angles to the central span, turrets on each corner. The girls gasped in awe.

"Is this it?" asked Penny.

"The school, yes," Daphne answered.

"*Oh, my God!*" Viv exclaimed. "Nana, look! Look at *that!* We're going to live *there!*"

The coaches halted at the turning circle, and the girls spilled out into the sunshine. After a moment, the building's front door opened, and a young man emerged, slender, smartly dressed, clean-shaven, with dark brown hair and piercing eyes. He was smiling at them, walking towards them.

He's so handsome! thought Vivianne. The man looked right at her. She felt strange, dizzy, and told herself she wasn't falling in love with him.

Then he spoke, surveying each in turn. "Absolutely lovely, every one of you! I'm Jacob Crowan, headmaster. Welcome to The Lookout. Welcome to your new home."

NATTY MILLER

1. Natty – Barbara – Nicholas

It was the smile. The fixed smile and the sustained gaze, big brown eyes, piercing. Expression aside, she was an unremarkable girl: average height for her age, dark hair tied in bunches, plain grey dress, grubby white apron, bonnet battered and off-centre. But the smile suggested she knew everything about you: your secrets, your guilt, all the troubles you daren't tell another living soul. And after you'd passed her by on the street and continued on your way, the smile lingered in your mind, unsettling, as if the universe you inhabited had brushed against another, alien, elusive, in which a stranger might know more about you than you did yourself.
Natty Flint's consciousness intersected the world at a different angle from that of most people. She possessed a naïve and immovable self-confidence that ploughed through this life with the unflagging momentum of a sailing ship ahead of a favourable wind, her sunny gaze its figurehead.
"Good morning Natty!" Henry Swallow, balding, red-faced, forty-six-year-old parson of St. Peter's, raised his hat.
"Good morning sir."
"You've brought the sunshine! Sorry I missed your birthday. Did you have a happy time?"
"I did, thank you, sir."
"And you're – how old now?"
"Eleven sir."
"Eleven!" (Natty nodded enthusiastically.) "You're growing up fast. I'll be along to see your mother later."
Barbara, Natty's mother, was not a child of the village but had travelled north from her native Warwickshire, settling in

Lealholm in 1701 when she was twenty-two. Taking rooms in a boarding house overlooking the village green, she rapidly gained a reputation as a healer, a craft inherited from her mother. She was popular, successful, and within three years had built an income reliable enough to rent a secluded cottage west of the village, on the north bank of the Esk. Here, Barbara was able to fully develop another of her skills. She'd been fond of the little apartment in Lealholm, but the crack of her whips and the cries of her clients had, from time to time, drawn undesired attention. Parson Swallow had been instrumental in securing the cottage for "Mistress Barbara", not primarily out of any pastoral desire to protect his flock from sin but so that he himself might take advantage more discreetly of the lady's services.

Barbara Flint was a powerful woman – unusually tall, lithe yet muscular, dark hair cropped short, an armoury of gold rings in her pierced ears. There was a coldness about her; she smiled only with her mouth, not with her eyes. Attired in leathers, straps, harnesses, spiked armbands and collar, she took on the aspect of a goddess, a fantasy for those submissive, cowering souls who craved her lash. Her callers (both men and women) were permitted to achieve physical gratification in her presence, but only by their own hand. Madam Barbara's ministry did not embrace her own participation in any manner of congress; she did not allow intimate physical contact.

Barbara had no particular fondness for men as a race and forged no close friendship at any point in her life. Natty came about simply as a result of her mother's desire to continue the family line. In 1709, thirty years old and still a virgin, she drove her cart to Whitby, took a room at The Abbey Inn and wandered around the May Fair searching for a likely candidate.

Tom Britton, a bear-like Eighteen-year-old dockhand, drinking with his mates outside the Cross Keys, fell silent as the strange woman approached, sinuous, snake-like, pale-skinned, eyes fierce, staring, dressed in a tight-laced pink linen gown. The boy was on his feet even before her beckoning finger commanded him erect. Her lacertine smile – and gold sovereign elevated between finger and thumb – told him all he needed to know. Leaving behind the whistles, exclamations and obscene encouragement of his peers, Tom followed Barbara to her room and copulated with her.

Mechanical, empty, it was over in minutes.

"What's your name?" he asked, pulling on his breeches.

"What difference does it make?" she answered.

"Easiest coin I ever made!" he declared.

"How would you like to earn thirty guineas?"

He paused in his dressing and frowned at her. "What d'you mean?"

"I'll pay you thirty guineas to come back to my house…"

"Where's that?" he interrupted.

"Not far. Listen – thirty guineas to stay in my house for a month and do this every day. What do you say?"

Tom stared, confused, fingers fiddling with his breeches buttons. "What, you mean…?"

"Just this," she confirmed. "You'll be confined to a single room for a month. I'll feed you, give you all the booze you want…"

"What – and just…" He gawped, wagging a finger between Barbara and himself. "You and me? Every day?"

She nodded. "Every day – for a month. Then I'll drive you back."

He laughed. "Are you serious?"

"Yes. It's just a job – a commission."

"Thirty fuckin' guineas?" he crowed. "For pokin'? I don't believe it!"

"You'll be blindfold there and back."

"Whatever, milady! Fuckin' twisted!"

Barbara stayed overnight in Whitby, giving the boy time to make arrangements, then blindfolded him and returned to Lealholm.

"What's this all about then?" he grinned, perched next to her on the box, unable to believe his luck.

"Not your concern," Barbara replied. "Just do what you're paid to do."

Tom's arrival in the house was no great surprise for the maids,

used as they were to seeing hooded and bound men about the place. The only difference with this one was his length of residence – a month rather than a day or two.
"No-one's to go into his room but me," she told the servants.
So Barbara brought his meals, his drink, took away his waste, freshened his bed, and coupled with him thrice daily. She hated this fleshly intercourse, scarcely comprehending how humanity had propagated itself through such a ridiculous, ugly, clumsy process. As if the method itself were not bad enough, the priapic immature stud's grunting, sweating, groping, thrusting abuse of her body resolved her against a repeat. If this experiment were to result in success, its fruit would remain without a sibling.

Natalia Flint emerged into the light of this world at twenty-five minutes to three in the afternoon of February 23rd, 1710, an average, screaming, wrinkled little girl. Scarlet Sykes, the "wise woman" from Cappleman Farm, performed the task of midwife, assisted by her fourteen-year-old daughter, Hazel.
"Congratulations, Babs," Scarlet smiled, teary, handing over the new blob of life. "You've got a daughter."
So, here's Natty, thought Barbara, taking the bundle. She was pleased; she'd wanted a girl – hadn't even thought of a boy's name. She was a mother for the first and only time at the age of thirty-one.

How two such parents – the mother intelligent, quick-witted and determined; the father boneheaded, bovine and coarse – managed between them to produce kind, sunny, innocent, untroubled Natalia is a puzzle difficult to solve. She watched the callers come and go as she grew up: the people seeking salves, ointments, medicines, massages for aches and pains; and the others (mostly men) who attended for more exotic relief. Barbara didn't allow her daughter to observe these latter ministrations, but Natty was curious enough to watch through the keyhole: the whippings, the birch, the slapping, beating, begging, and more. Some of the faces she knew from the village:

Parson Swallow, of course – but also Mr Taggart the chandler; Mr Forley the thatcher; wealthy, gracious, well-spoken Mr Davies; and pretty Mrs Noble, the undertaker's wife. These visitors, Natty noted, surrendered themselves for their discipline in a state of partial or complete undress, so she became familiar with a range of male and female anatomy at an early age. At no point did it occur to her that the proceedings might be at all unusual; she guessed what she saw was normal and probably took place in every household. Her friendly smile and happy demeanour remained unruffled, her perception of the world serene as the surface of a lake on a calm day.

Barbara strove to teach her daughter the secrets of the hedgerow, the art of selecting, preparing and combining what nature provided, producing oils, potions, creams and infusions to cure illness and ease suffering. Sometimes Natty listened, sometimes she daydreamed, picking up a few things but never becoming truly adept. Twice a week from age seven, she attended Mrs Shepherd's little school in the village and learned to read and write moderately well. Her amiable nature ensured she was well-liked by the other children, both the girls and the boys. When Natty felt at ease (in the company of her friends, for example), she spoke in broad Yorkshire; for more formal discourse, she adopted her mother's smooth, rolling Warwickshire.

Natty met Bruce Miller by chance at Lealholm market in July 1725. She was fifteen, he was twenty-one. It was a warm sunny day, and Bruce, recently appointed warrener at Cappleman Farm, thrummed with self-confidence. He had a good job, money, a beautifully situated cottage of his own by the woods on the bank of the Esk above Glaisdale – and here was a pretty girl, young, ripe, smiling at him. He smiled back, introduced himself, and took her to lunch in The Black Stallion.

"What's up," asked Barbara that evening. "What's this spring in your step?"

"Met someone," the girl replied.

"Hm," Barbara snorted. "Boy?"

"Aye," Natty admitted, tipping her head side to side, the familiar smile unruffled.
"Never understood them," Barbara returned. "Never saw the attraction. Watch yourself."
Natty's friends giggled at the developing relationship, embarrassed and envious, whispering, speculating how far it had gone.
"Do you think they've done it yet?"
"Aye, I do…"
"Nay. She'd have told us…"
"We'd know – we'd see it in 'er face…"
Bruce invited Natty to the tavern during the Michaelmas Fair for a meal of roast goose. She dressed in her best frock and got her friends to plait her hair so she looked like a lady.
She's ready, thought Bruce. *Tonight…*
After the meal, he took her into the meadow, down to the riverbank, and kissed her. She didn't stop him but let him do what he wanted. It felt strange, having his hands on her skin and smelling him so close. But she kept smiling; it didn't trouble her. And the thing itself – it tickled when it went in, and she laughed – just a little.
"Is it nice?" he rumbled.
Natty bit her lip. "Mm."

"Oh Natty," sighed her mother four months later when the result of the girl's indulgence could no longer be denied. "What are we going to do with you?"
"He wants to marry me."
"To marry you? You're not even sixteen."
"Peggy got wed at fourteen – Peggy Silkin. She's got two now."
Barbara sighed again, shook her head. "And is that what you want?"
"Aye, I s'pose so – if Brucie wants it."
"And where would you live? Would you live here?"
"In t'warrener's cottage – at Cappleman."
"So, I'd lose you…"

"It's only just down t'road, mum. I'd see thee every day…"

It was around this time that Barbara's health began to fail. First, there were stomach cramps in the night, lasting hours, keeping her awake; then fatigue during the day, heart racing, dizzy spells, shortness of breath. For one who'd been fit and robust all her life, the experience was frustrating. She tried medicating with her own substances; it did no good. Natty sent one of the maids to fetch Doctor William Clover from Easington.

"Difficult to know what to do – other than wait," he said, perched on the edge of Barbara's bed following an examination.

"Is this what took Scarlet?" the patient asked.

William frowned. "Scarlet's been gone a long time – five years, six. And your illness has come on more rapidly than hers – but… Peculiar though, that it should affect you and she – both healers. Perhaps it's the result of something you handle – or because of a particular process. Chemical substances alter, you know, depending on how they're prepared – heated, mixed. What do you think?"

She shook her head. "I don't know."

"Your mother – you learned your craft from her, didn't you? How did she…?"

"No, no," Barbara stopped him. "My mother died from a bullet wound."

"What?"

"She was shot by an officer of the Church, convinced he was carrying out the will of God."

Doctor Clover was horrified. "What on earth…? I thought that nonsense ended decades ago."

"It's why I came here," she told him. "There was nothing left for me at home."

"Why didn't you tell me about this before? Does anyone here know? Does Natty know?"

She shook her head. "No-one knows. It's behind me – gone." She stared at him. "Please keep it to yourself."

"Of course, of course," he blustered. "Barbara, I'm so sorry…"

"They caught him," she said. "Put him on trial, hanged him for murder."

"Well, that's some consolation, I suppose…" William's breath had been knocked out of him.

Barbara watched him for a second or two, then picked up the thread. "So this – sickness – whatever it is – it's not hereditary, if that's what you're asking. At least, I don't think it is. How would I know?"

"How old was she – your mother?"

"Thirty-eight."

William put his hand on hers, sympathy almost overwhelming him. "Oh Barbara, I don't know what to say…"

"What's done is done," she dismissed. "It can't be brought back."

"Your father…?"

"Left when I was six. Not sure I ever knew his name."

The doctor met his patient's eyes for a moment, then asked, "Has Hazel seen you?"

"She's been here," Barbara replied. "Does what she can – which isn't much – not much more than I could do myself."

"No," William nodded, helpless. "Then we'll have to observe developments. I suggest you stop work for a couple of weeks – three weeks. If there's an improvement, we'll know the cause of your ailment is related to your occupation. Will you do that for me, Barbara?"

"I will," she replied. "For my daughter's sake."

Natty Flint, great with child, became Mrs Miller at Glaisdale church on May 28th, 1726, the ceremony performed by the fresh young parson, Cornelius East. Barbara attended in a plain blue gown, doing her best to look well, determined that her disease should not spoil her daughter's wedding day.

"I'm much better," she said. "Look at me. I feel healthier than I have for months. You don't need to worry."

Many of Natty's childhood acquaintances walked the two miles from Lealholm to cheer their friend into married life. Bruce's mother had been dead more than ten years by then, but his

father travelled across the county from Thimbleby to stand at his son's side. The party from Cappleman Farm included Douglas and Maria Buckley, Bernard Swift, Tozer Robinson, Bridie Lyle (in whose house Bruce had lodged prior to his appointment as warrener), Hazel Priestly (née Sykes) and her husband, Oswin. Benjamin Flesher, the loved and revered owner of Cappleman Farm, was also in attendance, together with his son, Hugh.
It was a happy day; Natty's smile was broader than ever.

Natty gave birth to Nicholas in the warrener's cottage soon after dawn on July 5th, Hazel fulfilling the role of midwife, Florence Swift assisting.
"It's a boy," Hazel blubbed, emotional, lifting the child clear and wrapping him in a towel. "You've got a little boy."
"Let me 'ave 'im," Natty reached out, sweaty, exhausted, smiling as ever. "And get Brucie in."
Her husband had been cowering in the parlour, safe from the horrors of birth, but now hurried obediently to his wife's side.
"Look, Brucie," she said, cuddling her boy. "It's little Nicholas."
The warrener was speechless, gawping. "Bloody 'ell…"
Barbara arrived later in the day in the company of Doctor Clover, who'd collected her from Lealholm on his way from Easington. She'd hoped to be present for the birth, but her frailty prevented it.
"Shall we go in?" asked William, standing with her in the parlour, supporting her so she wouldn't fall. "Would you like to sit a moment?"
"No," she replied. "Let's see the new Flint."
The doctor smiled, amused as ever by the woman's steely-edged obstinacy. "The Flint line," he murmured.
"Of course," she answered. "What else?"
She stood a moment, swaying in the birth chamber's doorframe, gazing at Natty, lying in bed, the baby at her breast.
"Great God, child! What have you got there?"
"One o' me own, mum," Natty beamed. "Me boy – Nicholas."
Bruce, perched at his wife's side, nodded a greeting to his

mother-in-law, who hadn't appeared to see him till then. "Mrs Flint."
She flicked a glance. "Yes. Er…you."
Natty presented the baby. "Do you want to hold 'im?"
The new grandmother staggered forward, shaking her head. "I'd drop him. You hold him; I'll look…"

Barbara Flint died two months later at the age of forty-seven. Natty held her hand as she passed away, her kindly smile framed by slow tears.

2. Cappleman Farm, 1728-40

The marriage lasted only two years. It wasn't that Bruce fell out of love with Natty; rather that love – real love – hadn't been there in the first place. At least, that's what he told himself. There'd been lust, and there'd been convenience. She was a pretty girl and he'd wanted her body – and she'd given it to him. He'd mistaken that for love. His pride at having achieved a position of authority on a respected Yorkshire farm at the age of twenty had blinded him to his true feelings. He should never have led the girl on. He didn't explain this to her, fearing his words might hurt her. *Better sharp and quick,* he thought.
"Natty, I'm going."
"Going?" She'd been putting the dishes away but stopped, fixed in a ray of slanting sunlight, a plate in each hand.
"Yes. I'm sorry. I can't stay."
She'd guessed something was coming; he'd quietened over the last few weeks, changed, become withdrawn.
"Well," she said, the smile flickering. "There we are then. Have you got someone else?"
He shook his head. "No, no, it's nothing like that. It's me."
Natty nodded. She sensed Bruce's guilt and tried to ease it by broadening her smile, but the attempt failed and her lips trembled.
It was the first time Bruce had seen sadness on Natty's face, and he couldn't bear it. He hung his head and turned away. "I'm

sorry. I won't come back."

His wife nodded again, drove grief from her features and forced a degree of resolve into its place. "Well, what must be must be. Take care of yourself, Bruce."

He half raised his hand in acknowledgement but didn't meet her gaze, conscious that his emotions would overwhelm him if he did so. Instead, he turned and hurried away, collecting his bag before leaving the cottage – and the farm – for good.

So Natty was abandoned in her secluded dwelling, faced with the task of bringing up Nicholas unaided. Fortunately, Barbara had left an inheritance substantial enough for her daughter to live without toil and to pay the rent for a good few years; and the Fleshers, her landlords, were compassionate enough to allow her tenancy to continue. Toby Hawxwell, who lived across the river in Glaisdale, replaced Bruce as warrener, and life went on, stability restored.

The cottage's remote location meant that visitors were few. The journey from Glaisdale involved crossing the bridge into the farm before tracing the Esk north to the woods, and the trek from Lealholm meant following the river south through dense woodland. The house was situated in the northwest extremity of sprawling Cappleman Farm. Even the journey from the labourer's cottages occupied an hour or so on foot. Nevertheless, childhood friends did occasionally turn up on Natty's doorstep, and a few others looked in now and then. But days passed – weeks even – when not a single soul ventured by. It was peaceful, but lonely.

Natty schooled Nicholas as best she could. He was bright, independent. She took him to Lealholm and Glaisdale every so often, ensuring acquaintances were maintained. They walked on the moor when the weather was fine. The boy wandered widely on the farm, making friends with the other youngsters, greeting the labourers, tradesmen – even the masters – by name.

"Ho there, Nicky," called Hugh Flesher, pulling his waggon to a halt.

"Good day, squire."
"All well at home?"
"All good, Mr Flesher. Thanks for asking."
"How's your mother?"
"Fine sir."
"Still smiling?"
"Always sir."
"You're growing up. How old are you now?"
"Ten sir."
"Ten." (nodding) "I bet you know the farm through and through."
"Every inch, sir."
"You're a fine lad. Your mother should be proud of you."

Hazel Priestly visited once in a while, driving her carriage across the farm from Vine Cottage, her little daughter Nara at her side.
"Here's your Auntie Natty," she said one summer day in 1737, lifting the child down from her harness on the box.
"Hello girly," Natty grinned, pleased to have company on such a lovely day.
"Can I play in the water?" the child babbled.
"Go on then," said her mother. Then, to Natty, "You don't mind, do you? We'll sit out here and keep an eye on her."
"Course not," Natty answered, watching the little girl charge excitedly to the riverbank.
"Stay where I can see you," Hazel called, settling on the ground.
Natty eased herself down next to the older woman. "I could make some tea. We could 'ave it out 'ere."
"I'll do it," Hazel offered. "You relax and guard my little pet."
Natty grinned. "She's sweet. 'Ow old is she?"
"Four," Hazel replied. "My happy little bundle."
"I'll 'ave a daughter one day," said Natty, smiling as always.
"You will?"
"For sure."
"That'll be nice."
"Aye, it will."

They watched Nara splashing at the water's edge, neither speaking for a moment.

"Your Nicky's a lovely lad."

"Aye, 'e is. I know reet enough."

"Everyone loves him."

"So they should. 'E's a good boy."

"He's best friends with my Will," said Hazel. "Dickie Swift too…"

"Dickie Swift?"

"You know – Richard – up at the manor."

Natty nodded. "Yes, course. Florence's boy."

Nara had fallen suspiciously silent.

"What have you got?" called Hazel.

"Frog," the child replied.

"Don't hurt him."

"Watching."

"That's a good girl."

"She's very clear in 'er speech," Natty observed.

"Mm," Hazel agreed. "That's Oswin – all the bedtime stories." She changed tack, eyes on her companion. "Natty, you should get down to the farm more often."

"It's a bit of a trek from up 'ere," Natty defended.

"I know, but…"

"We've no carriage, you see…"

"But you could get one, surely – a little one. Or walk. It's not *so* far."

"Aye, I know. I do it now and then…"

"I know you do. But people are fond of you. They'd like to see you more often – *I'd* like to see you more often. You're always welcome at the cottage. The boys would love to have you there – and Oswin."

Natty sighed. "You're lovely people, all o' you. It's a privilege, livin' 'ere."

"There might be a cottage closer to us – further east – in the centre of the farm…"

"I wouldn't want to move," Natty countered. "I love it 'ere – in t'quiet. I don't mind bein' alone. 'T'ain't the same as bein' lonely…"

"I know," Hazel nodded. "But it would be nice to see more of you. You're one of life's happy folk – make people feel good. You're a bit different…"

"Different?"

"Yes," Hazel nodded. "You *are* different – refreshing. You're a little bit – eccentric. You don't mind me saying that, do you?"

Natty lifted her eyebrows, inviting her friend to elaborate.

"It's your face," Hazel continued, "the bounce in your step, the little tunes you hum. Everything about you – the words you use, the way you express things. It's bright, sharp, lively. It makes people feel more alive. You're one of life's gifts, Natty."

The Wise Woman's words had almost brought a tear to Natty's eye. She looked away, swallowed, sniffed. "Aw…you make me feel reet guilty. P'raps I'm just lazy. I've got used to t'solitude. I'll make an effort – do me good, prob'ly, trudgin' on t'farm. An' I ain't bin to Lealholm for a year or two. Should do that, I s'pose. Aye, you're right."

"I'm glad to hear it," Hazel smiled.

Natty grinned. "An' when I get me daughter, I'll bring 'er to your place, like you brung your's 'ere today."

"That'll be good," Hazel chuckled. "And when will this be?"

"I couldn't tell 'ee that," Natty replied. "Not too long, I 'ope."

Hazel paused. "Have you got a man, Natty?"

"A man?" the other responded. "No, ain't got no man. But I see 'er in me dreams."

Hazel knew a little about dreams. People sometimes brought them to her, craving interpretation. "Tell me?"

Natty glanced at her visitor. "What? The dream?"

"Mm."

"An angel sings to me. Least, I *think* it's an angel. Shinin' light anyway – wi' wings – I think."

"What does the angel sing?"

Natty adopted an abashed expression. "I've not got much of a singin' voice, 'Azel."

"Have a go."

Natty pondered briefly, then decided to do it. "Alright then. Brace thasel'." She cleared her throat, glanced once more at Nara's mum, took a breath, and sang in a passable alto…

"Lovely little daughter
Buffy in the water
See the pretty lady lead the
Precious lambs to slaughter."

Natty smiled warmly at her audient, mildly embarrassed, waiting for a response, but the Wise Woman wore a frown.
"What does that mean?"
"Well, Buffy's me daughter, I s'pose."
"And the 'pretty lady'? And the 'lambs'?"
Natty shook her head. "I don't know. You're the clever one; you tell me."
Hazel stared at the ground, brows knit, chilled, as if someone had walked over her grave. She shook her head. "Strange. Is it a children's rhyme?"
Nara came running, something clutched in her hands. "Look, mummy. A poor fish. Make it better?"
"Yuck!" Hazel exclaimed. "It's dead, love. Someone's tried to fish it and got it all cut up, poor thing. Throw it away."
"Mummy!"
"Throw it away, love. We'd better wash your hands."
The girl obeyed, dropping the corpse. Hazel got to her feet and rubbed the child's hands in her apron. "I'll go and make that tea," she said. "And Natty, you won't have a daughter unless you find a man. And your best chance of finding a man is to search one out – amongst people."
Natty laughed. "Right you are, 'Azel. I'll 'eed your words."
"I'm glad to hear it!" Then, to Nara: "Come on, you mucky tyke, let's get you brushed up."

Nicholas was appointed assistant warrener when he was thirteen. The position demanded very little: watching out for foxes and poachers, feeding the rabbits when necessary. It was created largely as a reward for a boy who'd become a valued and familiar face. Natty was no longer required to pay rent for the cottage.

Nicky spent even more time away – at his tasks, with his friends, wandering, exploring – leaving his mother alone, except for the birds, the wind, and the gentle purling of the Esk on its long journey to the sea.

3. The Grand Gentleman

Friday, cold but bright; fresh crisp snow lying an inch deep; less than a week to Christmas. Nicholas has been out since before dawn, and Natty potters about the cottage, fussing, busying. The fires are all lit; it's cosy; fingers of sharp winter sunlight cast dappled shadows through the south-facing windows either side of the door. Her mother's tall clock tells her it's an hour past noon.

Then comes the knock, the knock she never forgets. She wipes her hands on a cloth, lifts the latch, opens up, and stares dumbfounded at her visitor. In all Natty's fourteen and a half years in the warrener's cottage, it's the first time he's appeared at her threshold...

(Her hand instinctively shoots to her mouth.) "Oh! Oh my! Sir!"

"Hello Natty. Sorry to appear suddenly, unannounced..."

"Ooh!" (gasp) "You're very welcome, sir! Very welcome indeed!"

(He waits, hat in hand, but she seems frozen, staring. He gestures towards the cottage interior.) "Do you think I might...?"

(His words jab her into action.) "Oh, pardon me. Please, come in out of the cold."

(She moves aside, and he steps in, appears discomfited; she closes the door.)

"Make yourself comfortable, sir. Let me take your coat."

(He does as bid, adding hat and gloves to the pile.)

"I won't take up much of your time, Natty."

"Well, you're very welcome, sir – as I say." (She's putting on her best voice for him, awed in his presence.) "Please make yourself welcome, sir." (She lifts some things from a chair and bids him sit – which he does.)

"You're very kind, receiving me like this…"

"Ooh, not at all, sir. What an honour! What an honour! Would you care for some tea? I've got some nice fresh-baked cake…"

"No, no. Thank you, Natty. You really are very welcoming, but I won't stay long."

(Natty settles opposite, displays her best smile, and waits. Her visitor looks ill at ease, sighs, pulls his beard repeatedly.)

"Well…"

"Yes sir? How can I be of service?"

"Natty…"

"Sir…"

"Natty, this must be only between us – you understand? No-one must know anything…about…anything about…"

"Of course, sir, of course. You can trust me completely, sir."

"Yes…"

(She shakes her head, refreshes her smile – feels she's an observer in a dream.) "Ooh, what an honour! I can't believe it!"

"Natty…"

"Sir…"

"I have a problem, Natty – a certain…embarrassing problem…"

(She's nodding, gazing at him, encouraging.)

"I'm an old man, Natty…"

"Oh sir! No! You're not old at all – fine-looking handsome man, you are…"

(He elevates a hand.) "Hear me out."

"Of course, sir."

"Natty, I'm…not as strong as I once was…" (He stares at her, willing her to understand without him having to say it. But she clearly doesn't. He sighs.) "My wife…is fifteen years younger than I…" (Realisation breaks across Natty's face, and her visitor experiences an almost overwhelming sense of relief; he won't have to spell it out after all.)

"Oh, I see… And…how can I help you with that?"

"Wasn't your mother a healer?"

"She was. But…"
"Couldn't you…? Didn't she pass on her craft to you? There are stories…"
(She's shaking her head.) "Well, she tried, but I've forgot most of it."
"Really? Wasn't this kind of problem exactly what she was renowned for?"
"No, no, sir. I'm afraid you've got things mixed up. It weren't quite like that."
(He stares, waiting for more, hope fading.)
"People came – men mostly – wanting…punishment."
"Punishment?"
"The whip, sir. Or worse…sometimes…"
"………"
"Sorry…sir…"
"Oh dear. I'd hoped…"
"Couldn't you see Mrs Priestly? She could help, I'm sure…"
"No, no, no, I can't go to Hazel with this – it's too…personal… humiliating. I watched her grow up; her father John was my closest friend – Scarlet too, of course. I can't go to Hazel. It's just too…awful…"
"Doctor Clover then?"
(He sighs, shakes his head.) "No. I'd pinned my hopes… I don't know why." (He stands.) "Forgive me, Natty. I'd better go." (Holding up a finger…) "Not a word of this."
(She stands, reaches for his coat.) "Of course, sir. God bless you."

But he was back four days later. The air felt different that morning – crackling, charged – and the winter light had a vivid, shocking whiteness. Natty felt strange, alert, primed. Thinking back later, she told herself she knew he was coming that day, and deep down, understood her role…
(…he and she, sitting opposite each other in her parlour…)
"I've been thinking about what you told me – about your mother."
"Yes sir?"

"And the men who came – to be lashed."
"Yes…"
"Do you think this was for their…gratification?"
"Gratification?"
"Pleasure – relief. You understand?"
"Well, I s'pose it must have been – otherwise, why would they have come?"
"You must have vivid recollections."
(She shakes her head vehemently.) "Oh no, sir. She never let me in the room…"
"Then, how do you know?"
(Her face reddens with embarrassment like a child caught fibbing.) "I…saw through the keyhole."
"So…you *did* see?"
"A bit. Not much."
"Do you think anything you saw could help me?"
"I can't whip you, sir. The weapons have all gone – lost or mouldered away. And I never handled one. I wouldn't know…"
"No, no, I don't mean that." (He sighs, stares at the floor.) "Didn't your mother…? I mean, did your mother ever…?"
"My mother wasn't a doxy, sir."
"Oh, no, no, no." (He sighs, curses himself.) "This is all going the wrong way…"
"Let me see it, sir." *There. I've said it…*
"What?"
"Let me see it. I've been a married woman – I have a little experience. Let me see it."
(He narrows his eyes, shakes his head, unsure if he fully understands what she's suggesting.) "You mean…?"
(She nods.) "If you think it might help."
(He hesitates…) "Alright." (…stands, unbuttons his breeches, folds back his stockings, and pushes all to his knees.) "There."
(She peers at it.) "Is there any pain?"
"No."
"And what happens when you're with your wife?"
"Nothing at all. It used to be so easy. But now…"

"How long have you been married, sir?"
"Forty years. Emmeline's sixty-two – and a very fine-looking woman. There's really no excuse…"
"So that makes you…?"
"I'm seventy-seven." (Pause.) "It's extraordinary! I feel quite comfortable standing here in this ridiculous position with you staring at my fellow!" (Laughs.) "Whatever would my wife say?"
"You've been faithful? Always?"
"Of course. Absolutely. I've lain with only two women my entire life. The other was a mistake – when I was a very young man – long before I met Emmeline."
"Can I handle it?"
(He snatches a short sharp breath through his nose.) "Touch it, you mean…?"
"If you don't mind."
(Pause.) "Do what you feel's necessary."
(She leans forward, takes it in her hand, squeezes, rubs with her thumb – and he's surprised to feel a tingling, then…more.)
"My God…!"
"How does that feel?"
"It feels…exquisite." (His breathing has become more rapid.) "I promise you, it hasn't done that for years. Oh, my goodness! You must think I'm some perverted old man come to your cottage to take advantage of you."
"Not at all, sir. I'm happy to help. It's quite a handsome one, I think. Your good lady's fortunate."
"Aren't they all the same?"
"I've not seen many, sir. Not up close anyway…"
"Certainly not *this* close…" (He instantly regrets the remark but smiles nevertheless, enjoying the intimacy.)
(She withdraws her hand and studies the object.) "It's standing, but not fully filled." (She traces its outline, stiff at the base and tip but weak in the middle, like a slender hourglass.)
"But even this…is new. I wonder why it springs to life here, but not…"
"Could it be to do with anxiety? You're worried you'll disappoint

your wife – but you're not worried here?"
"Surely it can't be that simple?"
"Maybe it is. If you've worried about it a long time – and failed repeatedly – you might have fallen into a kind of continual… dread…that prevents…"
"So, what can I…?"
(She stands, unbuttons her dress, slips her arms free and pushes down the material, exposing her breasts and shoulders.)
(He stares, lips parted, desire surging like a flood.) "Oh, Natty…"
"My Brucie liked these."
"Oh, Natty…"
(She steps forward and takes his flesh again.) "There. Stiff as a broom."
(Breathless…) "Let me see all of you."
(She obeys, pushing down her dress and shift.)
"Oh Natty. You're really quite lovely…"
"Shall we see if it works?"
(He's already pulling at his shirt buttons.) "I've never betrayed Emmeline…"
"This isn't betrayal, is it? You came to me for help – I'm ready to give it."

(Her room is quiet except for the bed's creaking, covers thrown aside, she naked beneath him, knees elevated, thighs spread, he on top, thrusting, that which was dead alive again, Lazarus resurrected.)
"Oh, Natty, Natty!"
(Whispers…) "Is it good?"
"Oh yes! So good! Let me kiss you."
(Another minute, his hands on her body, her buttocks, breasts, owning, claiming, crushing, his lips on her lips.)
"Oh, Natty! *Natty, Natty, Natty!*"

Natty felt changed, lying alone in her bed that night – renewed somehow. She wasn't entirely sure what had happened. The physical aspect – of course, she understood that; she'd lain with a

man, the first since Bruce left her. But *how* it happened – that she didn't comprehend. Had she found him attractive? She didn't know; she was certainly dazzled by him. The whole thing had seemed to follow a course that was already decided. Something had taken hold of her the moment she answered the door. Deep down – deep, deep down in an inner world beyond words, she'd known their paths were locked together.
Ah well, it's happened. Can't be undone.

The great man visited many times as winter gave way to spring and spring to summer. It was a healing process for him, Natty told herself, although there was more than a twinge of guilt. She enjoyed his attentions and looked forward to his visits, proud she was able to excite him so deeply. She – cast aside, rejected by her husband – was now the object of desire, the scarlet woman, delicious enough to tempt such a man to deceive his wife after forty years of constancy.

Recalling how Bruce used to enjoy seeing her provocatively dressed, Natty dug out an old item she'd made long ago to inflame him: a pale blue sleeveless linen tunic, open at the neck, plunging to her navel, loosely laced. The waist was drawn tight, waspish, her hips rounding the material to the hem – which was very high, extending only a couple of inches past her bottom, leaving her legs entirely exposed. Thirteen years had passed since she'd last worn it, and she was both surprised and delighted to find it still fitted.

"Oh, my sweet soul, Natty!" said the great man when he laid eyes on his mistress in such attire. "Look at you!"

"You like it then?" she grinned.

"I'm breathless – speechless. Come sit on my lap."

She obeyed, and he kissed her, slipping his hand first into her bodice, then sliding it back and forth along her thigh, finally up between her legs.

A growl, molten: "My fellow wants your maid."

"Then he shall have her," Natty whispered close to his ear. "My maid's obedient and wants only to please her master."

In bed later...
"Have you tried with your wife yet?"
"No."
"Why?"
"I'm not sure I could sleep with two women. I'm concerned she might...know...somehow – sense it."
"Dost that make thee feel bad?"
"Bad? I suppose it does – in a way. It's despicable, I suppose, what I'm doing – treacherous. But I love the secrecy. Lying here with you, so quiet, so remote. It's exotic, fantastic – a dream. Me, seventy-eight; you, thirty-one, beautiful, skin smooth, body firm. It's an old man's fantasy."
(She smiles, explores with her fingers and finds him rigid.)
"We're very close now, thee and me. Maybe I should call you B..." (He stops her.) "No. Please don't. Keep 'sir' – if you don't mind. It makes things a little easier for me. Do you mind?"
"No sir, course not."
"It's difficult to explain. 'Sir' feels safer. I can almost pretend I'm someone else – when I'm with you. If you were to use my name, I fear that defence might crumble." (pause...) "I'm not a strong man, you know – particularly when hiding from myself."

A sudden shock brought the relationship to its termination. The lovers were in each other's arms in bed one August afternoon when Nicholas came home unexpectedly.
"Mum?" The lad's voice carried clearly from the parlour.
"Oh God!" the great man hissed. "I can't be found here!"
"In t'closet," Natty replied, easing out from beneath him. "Don't worry. I'll see what's up."
She slipped into her housecoat and left the room, leaving the great man in a panic, struggling into his clothes.
Nicholas was in the kitchen, pouring himself some lemon water.
"Your home early," said his mother, settling onto a chair. "Summat wrong?"
He glanced at her. "Nope. Come 'ome to change. Goin' to Whitby."

"Whitby?"
"Aye. Party – dancing."
"Party? Sounds nice. Who you going with?"
"Willow – and a few others."
Natty knit her brow, curious. "Willow Robinson? Apple's girl?"
"Yep," he grinned. "Got to wash, freshen meself up."
"How long's this been going on?"
"Nothing's going on – not yet anyway. But she likes me – and I like her."
"Well, well. She's a nice girl. Who's driving?"
"Adam Priestly. Will's coming too. So's Alice Foley."
"Zach Foley's daughter? Why do you say that with such a leer?"
"Alice is with Adam. Keep it to yourself."
Natty gasped in surprise. "Keep it to meself? She's barely fifteen. Adam must be near twenty-five! What's 'er ma gonna think?"
"Adam's twenty-one, mum. Anyway, what's a few years' age gap?"
What indeed? she thought.
"You not dressed?" asked Nick, scanning his mother while unbuttoning his clothes.
"I was tired," she lied. "Been asleep."
He was pulling off his breeches. "Should bugger off if I were you – or you'll see me bum and bits."
Natty shook her head, tutting. "What kind o' child 'ave I brought up?" she complained, withdrawing, shutting the door.
She'd expected to find the grand gentleman cowering in the closet, but he was gone. He'd pulled a chair close to the window, opened the casement and squeezed through – a daring feat for a man within sight of eighty.
Natty stood in the silent bedroom, pressed her hand to her belly, and knew she was pregnant.
The great man didn't visit her again, didn't dare take the risk. That was the last she saw of him.

4. Buffy

Nicholas began his questioning as soon as Natty's pregnancy became apparent.
"Who, ma?"
"A nice man."
The boy shook his head in frustration. "But who?"
"I can't tell thee – can't tell anyone."
"Is it someone I know?"
"I don't know who you know." She continued to potter about aimlessly in the kitchen, moving things from place to place so she wouldn't have to sit and be interrogated.
As far as Nicholas knew, the only visitors to the house were females – old friends from Lealholm, Mrs Priestly, Miriam Exley – and even they were infrequent callers. Parson East came about once a month…
"It's not the parson…?" he asked, suspicious, brows furrowed.
Natty was scandalised, almost dropped the plate she held. "What? How could thee…?" She shook her head in disbelief. "Anyway – parson's bin after me to tell an' all. But before you ask – I haven't told 'im. No-one is to know."
"Did someone attack you?"
"No, Nicholas."
He paused. "Do you still see him?"
"No."
"Did you see him for long? I mean, was it months? Years? Was it just once?"
"Goodness' sakes, boy! If tha must know, it were a few months."
"But he's gone now?"
"Yes, he's gone now."
Another pause. "Did you love him?"
She pondered, uncertain she really knew the answer. "I'm not sure. I think so."
"Must hurt then, not seeing him anymore."
"Enough, Nicky. No more."
"Why won't you say who he is?"
She stared at her son. "Nicky. Have you lain with a girl yet?"

He flushed, clenched his jaw.

"Do you want to tell me?" pressed his mother.

Nicholas remained silent.

"I didn't think so," Natty continued. "I'm thirty-one years old, Nicholas, and 'ave me own life. I'm happy – that's all you need to know. And you'll soon 'ave a sister."

He glanced at her, puzzled. "Sister? How do you know?"

"It's a girl, Nicky. I've seen 'er in me dreams."

Natty was increasingly troubled by visions as the birth drew nearer. She daydreamed, imagining her angel stood in the room with her. She fancied herself surrounded by water, waist high, cold; she was plagued with dizziness and had to clutch at things to prevent herself falling. Nicholas remained at home, apprehensive, awaiting the appointed hour.

On February 25th, fearing his mother's puffing signalled the onset of labour, he mounted his horse and rode to Vine Cottage to fetch Hazel Priestly. But his knock was answered by Apple Robinson.

"Hazel's taken the boys and Nara to Northallerton – to look after Oswin's mother. I'm just cleaning the house."

"The baby's coming. What should I do?"

"You sure?"

"I think so."

"Alright. I'll ride back with you."

But it was a false alarm. Apple found Natty relaxed, her usual smily self, preparing bread for the oven.

She felt odd throughout Saturday, March 6th. Her senses were heightened, the slightest sound amplified; the light seemed abnormally sharp and crisp. Surfaces – fabric, dishes, glass, her own skin – became exquisitely detailed to the touch, contact so vivid as to be almost heartbreaking. The angel was in the room, shining, motionless, silent, watching.

She retired at nine, leaving Nicholas smoking his pipe on the riverbank.

The angel woke her shortly before two, his voice echoing in her mind:

It's time, Natty. Walk to Egton, to the mill. The child must be born in the water. Rise, and go now.

The house was quiet, dark, except for the embers in the kitchen fire. Nicholas had gone to bed. Natty donned her coat and hat, opened the door and set out…

She remembered little of her nocturnal trek to the millpond. As far as she was aware, she passed no-one, and no-one noticed her passage – even when she trudged through the close-packed labourers' dwellings at the heart of the farm. Vine Cottage was in darkness – she remembered that. And she remembered pondering whether she should knock. Perhaps Hazel had returned, her vigil at Eleanor Priestly's deathbed concluded. But she didn't stop; she passed by, turned right onto Watermill Lane, followed the river towards Beggar's Bridge, then down into the mill meadow.

It was still dark when she arrived at the pond. She removed her boots and coat and took a few steps into the icy water.

Don't fear the cold, the angel whispered. *Be brave. Show that even here, so close to the mill, life's light does not fear the dark. Do you trust me?*

Natty looked up into the sky and saw the angel there. "Course I trust thee!" she called, loud enough to startle a few unseen ducks that had been dozing nearby.

"Who's that?" The voice came from the lane. Natty heard the cry but didn't try to locate its source. Instead, she squatted in the frigid black, gave herself a moment to absorb the shock, then sat on her bottom, not quite waist-deep in the water.

Whoever it was had raced down the slope and now stood on the bank, staring at her.

"What you doin'? Tha'll bloody kill thasel'! It's perishin'!"

"Fook off! I'm avin' me baby."

There was silence for a long time; the cold bit deep. And then the people began to appear – three or four at first, watching, as if Natty were some form of curious entertainment, then more – many more. Some she recognised, others she didn't. They were trying to coax her from the water. A few brave souls waded in to attempt a forcible eviction, but she struggled, swore at them, even landed a few blows. High up – in the sky – the angel was watching. Natty knew all would be well.

A new face on the bank – a young man she'd never seen before. And behind him, her Nicky.

"Mum!"

"Natty, I'm Doctor Levinson. What on earth are you doing?"

"I'm 'avin' baby, doctor. What dost think I'm doin'? What do it look like?"

"Yes, but why here, in the pond?"

"Angel said so. Shinin' angel from God on 'igh. Get thee cross t'farm, 'e said. Get thee in t'millpond so t'baby be born. So I done what 'e said – an' 'ere I be."

"But this water is very cold, Natty. I don't think it'll do the child any good. Besides, how clean is it?"

"I'm 'avin' it 'ere."

Rapid conversation ensued between the doctor and a group of onlookers. Natty couldn't hear what they were saying, but next second, a squad of determined men left port and splashed towards her. It was a bad move, and all the would-be rescuers were savagely driven off, hulls and fittings in need of repair.

The doctor sighed. "For God's sake then! Let's get it done as quickly as we can."

Seconds later he was in the shallow water, on his knees, sleeves rolled up. Natty rested back on her elbows and let him play his part. The angel smiled down, filling her with warmth despite the bitter chill.

Buffy was born the moment dawn lit the sky – Buffy Miller, known for the rest of her life as "Pond Girl".

So Natty's cottage by the woods, the Esk running nearby, became home to three occupants. Apple moved in to help out for a while, and Miriam Exley looked in every few days, bringing provisions from the farm. In the last week of March, Hazel Priestly, fresh returned from her mother-in-law's funeral, arrived to lend a hand. Even Peggy Silkin braved the wilds from Lealholm a couple of times. But Natty thought they were all fussing unduly anyway and eventually shooed them off, smiling as ever, thankful to have friends.

Shortly thereafter, Nicholas was promoted to Warrener, Toby Hauxwell having become too infirm to continue in the job. Nicky's remuneration was increased accordingly, and the three of them were able to live in reasonable comfort.

In November 1744, Nicholas came home with the news that old Benjamin Flesher had passed away. Natty withdrew to her bedroom and cried.

5. Living with a secret

Buffy grew up an attractive, loving girl with freckly skin and light brown hair, doted on by her brother.

Hmm, Natty dreamt. *One day, you'll have kiddies of your own, you and Nicky both – and I'll have a flock of little grandchildren. That'll be nice...*

Like Nicholas, Buffy became popular, made lots of friends and was often away, playing, visiting, adventuring.

Natty treasured the stillness of her home, but she was not a complete recluse. She liked to chat with Apple Robinson, visited Bridie Lyle once in a while, and trekked across the farm to Vine Cottage now and then to spend an hour or two with Hazel. At harvest 1748 she joined the huge crowd assembled in the meadow to watch Nara handfasted to Alder Swithenbank, an emotional event for everyone, especially Hazel, who officiated, giving away her own daughter.

Fifteen years old, thought Natty, *and wed to a man three times her age. Still, they're in love – that's obvious. Was the same with me though – I was the same age...*

Hugh Flesher acted as Nara's witness that day. He made a striking figure, immaculately dressed, standing close to his charge in the early evening sunshine, compact, handsome, dark hair and beard peppered with grey. Natty wondered if Emmeline, *his* wife, was somewhere in the throng. Despite having lived on the farm for so many years, she'd never met the matriarch, never seen her.

She turned to Miriam, standing nearby, and asked, "Is Mrs Flesher here?"

"Amelia?" Miriam returned. "Yes, she's just over there, talking to Florence."

"No – I mean…old Mrs Flesher."

"Emmeline?"

Natty nodded.

Miriam shaded her eyes and scanned around. "I thought she was here somewhere. Can't see her now…"

The whole day had been breathtaking, overwhelming: the harvest processions, the chanting, singing, the ancient rituals, the handfasting – and finally the torchlit party in the meadow, the feasting, and the music.

"Natty!" It was Cornelius East, open-necked, out of uniform, offering his hand. "Dance with me."

"Parson East!" she exclaimed. "Me! With you?"

He grinned. "If you'd do me the honour."

So, she'd danced with him – danced with the parson! But a minute or two into their whirling, Natty noticed Hugh Flesher nearby, dancing with Apple Robinson. He was smiling, happy – and briefly met her eye.

Oh no, she thought. *He's going to ask me next.*

Fearful of how she might feel if such a thing were to occur, Natty thanked Parson East, fled into the crowd, located an unlit exit from the meadow and made her way home, cursing herself for a coward.

"Where's my daddy, mum?"

Natty had imagined the moment over and over, wondering when Buffy would ask the question, but its abrupt arrival still caught her off guard.

"Mm?"

They were in the parlour, all three of them. Nicholas, sitting near the fire fashioning some object out of wood, stopped what he was doing and looked at his mother, curious to hear her response. Natty shot him a glance.

"All my friends have got mums *and* dads," Buffy went on. "Amy and Beatrice, Meadow, Louise – they've all got dads."

Natty took Buffy's hands. "You had a dad too – lovely man, 'e was."

"Where is he then?"

"He died, love – years ago."

"What was his name?"

"I can't tell you, pet."

"Why?"

"Because I can't tell no-one. I made a promise, and I 'ave to keep it. Keepin' promises is important in't it?"

Buffy nodded. "How did he die?"

"He just died, love. People die."

"Like Nara's dad?"

"Yes love, like Nara's dad."

"Did Nicky know him?"

In truth, Natty had no idea whether Nicholas had known the Great Man. She glanced again at her son and gave an answer that may or may not have been true. "No love, 'e didn't."

"Will you tell me one day?"

Natty was suddenly close to tears. She sniffed. "Maybe, petal. Maybe one day."

When the note arrived inviting them to Henry Flesher's fourteenth birthday party, Natty felt the world slip out from beneath her feet.

"What? Why? Why me?"

"Because you're my mum – and I'm Amy Swift's best friend," Buffy grinned.

"Amy Swift," Natty echoed. "That's…Emma's daughter?"

Buffy nodded. "Emma works up at the big house – remember?"

Natty scowled. "Course I remember! I may be more decayed than thee, but I ain't beef-'eaded yet."
But to be in the house – in *his* house... Natty pondered, frowning, unsure whether she'd be able to handle the emotions – even though he'd been dead so long.
"Come on, mum! You'll love it. Mrs Priestly's going – Alder, Nara. You can cuddle Kate."
"Kate?"
"Kate Swithenbank. You know! She's sweet!"
"Oh aye – Kate – 'Azel's granddaughter. I remember." (She did indeed remember; Hazel and Nara had brought the child to the cottage a couple of years previously, precisely so that Natty could dote on her.) "But...what shall I wear? I've got no fine things."
"Haven't you got your mum's dresses? You said you kept them."
Natty shook her head. "I did keep 'em – I didn't want to chuck 'em away. But she were much taller'n me. They're prob'ly mouldy anyroad. I ain't 'ad sight of 'em since before you was born."
"Well, let's 'ave a look then," Buffy retorted, standing. "We've got a week to sort you out."

(The manor house – *his* domain: grand, imposing, gleaming plaster, dark timbers. She's never been this close. *"Oh, Natty! Natty, Natty, Natty!"*)
I can still run – it's not too late – I could just turn round and go back to Miriam's house...
(Her blood's pounding, legs wobbly. She feels acutely self-conscious in her mother's green silk gown, miraculously adapted by Buffy, her hair equally impressive, tied up with ribbons beneath the pretty bonnet pressed upon her by Bridie.)
Oh God. I can't...
(But it's too late. There's Elys Buckley emerging to meet her, immaculate in his dark livery, gleaming silver buttons and splendid white wig.)
"Natty! Welcome! It's been a while!"
"Thank you, Mr Buckley."

"Elys – please. It's so good to see you. When were you last here?"
"I've never bin 'ere."
"Good Lord! Seriously? All the years you've lived on the farm?"
"Well, it's a long way from t'cottage…"
(He smiles warmly and squeezes her hand.) "In that case, it's long overdue. Buffy and Nick are here already…"
"I know. I let 'em hurry ahead. It's such a lovely day – I wanted to enjoy the stroll."
"Quite right. Well, come on in and mingle."
(So she does, breathless, tense.) *They must know – surely, they must know. He must have told them – must have confessed to her…*
"Mum!" (It's Buffy, scything towards her through the crowd with the ease and grace of a bird.) "You're the last! Where've you been? Come and wish happy birthday to Henry." (Cupping her hands round her mouth, whispering…) "He's so handsome!"
(Buffy takes her mother's hand and steers her throughout the multitude. People smile and greet her as she goes. And there he is – there he is – *his* grandson.)
"Henry, this is my mum."
(He extends a hand.) "Mrs Miller."
"Hello Henry." (She takes his hand, searches for resemblance.) "So, you're fourteen."
"I am. Thanks for the present." (Nicholas had made him a catapult. Natty hadn't been sure it was a good idea, but after her son's dismissive remarks she'd concluded that 'boys will be boys'.) "That's my sister – and Meadow." (He calls across the room, and Louise Flesher, sixteen, slender, dark-haired, dressed in pale blue, smiles and waves at the newcomer. Her companion, an extremely beautiful dark-haired girl, stares unsmiling.)
(Buffy's pulling her hand again.) "Kate's over here with Nara. Come and see Kate."
(There she is, eyes fixed on Natty as she approaches – a strange, intense child, four years old, astonishingly red hair, piercing hazel eyes – as if she knows everything there is to know about the world – everything there ever was and ever will be. It's unsettling.)

She knows about me; she's like the angel. She could tell everyone...
(Nara, lovely as ever, stands as Natty draws near and rubs her daughter's head.) "Remember Auntie Natty, Kate?"
(The child smiles, and, for some reason, Natty feels all the weight, all the worry, lifted from her shoulders. The sensation is so overwhelming, so unexpected, she almost collapses.)
"Hello Auntie Natty."
Oh! Oh, my goodness!
(Natty plants her hand on her heart and draws breath.) "Kate – you come to me 'ouse. D'you remember?"
"Yes. I had strawberry jam. It was lovely."
"That's right!" (then, to Nara...) "She's wondrous."
(Nara smiles.) "I know. She's my girly."
(A group of young girls pulls Buffy away, demanding to play with "Pond Girl".)
"Hello Natty." (It's Hazel, appearing from behind.)
"Ooh, hello, Hazel." (Everything's fine – everything will be well. There was never anything to worry about.)
"Lovely to see you here, Natty. You know most folk, I expect?"
(Natty turns and surveys the faces, no longer fearful of what they might make of her.) "I ain't very good at rememberin' folk. I know a fair few..."
(Hazel gestures with hand and eyes, pointing out a few figures.) "There's Hugh, of course, Henry's dad – and Amelia, Henry's mum. Isn't she pretty?"
(Natty nods.) "Aye, she's a fair one."
(Hazel lowers her voice.) "Forty, but you'd never know it – still looks twenty-eight. There's Stephen Flathers, blacksmith, talking to Cornelius." (Parson East catches Natty's eye and waves cheerily. Natty grins in response, happy now to be here.) "That's Robert Forest talking to Apple – new parson at Easington – bit of a sour one, I'm afraid. Tozer's around somewhere too – probably outside, smoking with Alder – telling filthy jokes, I shouldn't wonder. There's Cedar and Holly. And over there, that's..."
(But Natty recognises her and interjects, nodding.) "Hazel – t'other 'Azel..."

"That's right – Hazel Robinson. But do you know her gentleman?"
"Gentleman?"
"Hm. We'll see a wedding soon, I think. There he is – Tudor Green – carpenter. Good-looking, no?"
(Natty assesses the man with her eyes and agrees.) "Mm. Not bad!"
(Hazel laughs.) "You and me – pair of filthy-minded middle-aged women!" (sigh…) "Ah, I miss Oswin."
(Natty's tears are threatening again.) "I know. It's 'ard, losin' someone you love."
(Hazel gazes at Natty, trying to plumb her depths, searching for what she keeps hidden.) "You know…"
(Natty nods.) "Aye, I do."
(Hazel's asked before – offered to bear some of the weight – to share the secret. But Natty won't allow it.)
(A door opens at the far side of the room, and an elderly woman enters, tall, graceful, grey-headed, dressed in black silk trimmed with white. She intercepts the many greetings, smiling, raising a hand.)
"Ah. Dear Emmeline. She's quite frail now. Maybe you know her?"
(Natty gazes at the woman, shakes her head.) "No. Never met 'er."
"Let me introduce you."
There she is – his wife – the reason Buffy…
"Emmeline, you're looking well."
"Thank you, Hazel. You too – radiant as ever."
"Emmeline, this is Natty Miller."
(Natty curtsies awkwardly. She's practised the operation at home in front of the mirror in readiness for precisely this moment, but hasn't quite mastered it.) "I'm honoured to meet thee, Mrs Flesher."
(The aged woman protests…) "Oh please – no formalities. Call me Emmeline…" (she reaches out and takes Natty's hand, sending a thrill through the latter's body, a thrill of reconnection – even though by proxy – after all these years.) "I don't think we've met before. But you're Nicky's mother, I think – Nicholas,

who looks after the warrens?"
(Natty is unable to speak, but nods, and blinks away moisture.)
"It's lovely to meet you after all this time. We often see Buffy here. She's so full of energy – makes me recall my girlhood. She and Amy Swift, such happy girls."
(Natty almost curtsies again but catches herself.) "Thank you…" *(I can't say her name…)* "She's my light."
(Emmeline pauses, looks thoughtful.) "Your light. What a lovely way to put it."
"Mama!" (A man's voice, baritone, energetic. Natty turns her head and watches as Hugh Flesher joins their group.)
(Emmeline gestures with her hand.) "My son, Hugh – Henry's papa."
(Natty smiles at him.) "Mr Flesher."
"Natty. I know you, of course. I'm the man who trundles past in the cart – always in a hurry!"
"Of course, sir. It's an honour to be invited to your house."
"You're very welcome, Natty – at any time. We'd be delighted to see more of you. You're well-loved, you know."
(There are those tears again, surging perilously close…)
(Someone else is approaching. It's Buffy, radiant, rosy. She stands between Hugh and her mother and takes the latter's hand.)
"See ma? I knew you'd have a happy time."
(Natty glances from Buffy to Hugh.) *Oh, I wish I could tell you! If only it were possible. But it can never be.*

POOR NANCY

Bath, October 1748

"Don't ever do that to me, Tom – please," begged Brenda.

Tom Cox was a devoted husband and couldn't imagine himself embroiled in the kind of mess that had swallowed his old friend Raymond Harding. It wasn't uncommon to keep a mistress (two or more were not unknown), but there was a way of going about these things. Tom himself had never got involved with a secondary woman, and now, at the age of sixty, was (he believed) safely beyond temptation. Brenda had been his life anyway, and he'd never dreamt of behaving in a way that might have made her anxious or upset.

"Such a thing would never occur to me, my little chicken," he crooned, hugging her. "You know that."

"I know," she smiled, teary. "I never thought Ray would do something like this. Poor, poor Nancy."

She'd been best friends with Nancy Harding for more than forty years, ever since they were girls. They'd played together, grown up together, travelled together. Each had been best maid at the other's wedding. They were devoted, lifelong companions.

Tom sighed and held her tighter. The problem wasn't that Ray had openly transferred his affections from his wife to a mistress (although that would have been hurtful enough); the problem was that the young woman involved had been Nancy's own maid, an impressionable twenty-year-old girl who'd jumped at the chance of raising her social standing through the attentions of a wealthy gentleman thirty-five years her senior. Ray was utterly besotted with the creature and had set her up as his consort, entirely replacing poor Nancy, his wife of thirty years. Wherever he was seen in public, Fanny was on his arm. Even the gentlemen at the Grove coffee house accepted it (more or less), any objections they might have harboured parting like the Red Sea in response to his confident advancement of the fragile young thing.

"How's Nancy?" one or other asked.

"Well enough," he replied, "last time I saw her."

Thursday, October 20th

"What have I done wrong?" sobbed Nancy. "I've been a good wife – obedient even."

"Poor you," Brenda answered, squeezing her friend's hand in both her own. They sat in Nancy's drawing room on Trim Street, in the house she and Ray had shared their entire married life.

"I don't understand why this is happening," Nancy blubbed. "I used to make him happy – he told me. 'You're the light of my life,' he used to say, 'my greatest joy.' What's happened, Brenda? Why is he doing this to me?"

"It's not you, sweet one," Brenda assured her. "Men can be such thoughtless, selfish brutes."

Nancy lifted her dripping red eyes to her companion's. "He doesn't love me anymore."

"I'm sure he does, dear," said Brenda. "I expect this will pass. He'll come to his senses."

But Nancy was vehemently shaking her head. "No, no. He doesn't love me. I asked him. I said, 'Don't you love me anymore?' and he couldn't look at me, couldn't answer. He left the house straight away – went to her, I expect, in the plush little apartment he's set her up in – with her frilly clothes and nice soft bed…" Nancy's grief flooded free at the thought. "OH, GOD! I CAN'T BEAR IT!"

"There, there, Nancy, my dearest, dearest friend," purled Brenda, herself close to tears in sympathy for the wronged one.

"I can't bear to think what they do together; it fills my mind. We used to be so joyous, so intimate. I loved him, *loved* him! And now he's forgotten me – left me in this dreadful, loveless swamp.

OH, GOD!"

"Oh Nancy, don't cry so!" Brenda pleaded. "It breaks my heart to see you so sad. I'm sure all this will be over soon. Look, why don't we go to The Saracen and have a meal together? You'll like that."

"It'll remind me of him," Nancy answered.

"Alright then," said her friend. "Pack a bag. We'll go away for a few days. A change of scenery will do you good."

"It won't be the same without him," Nancy pined. She began to weep again, so forlornly that Brenda felt utterly helpless.

"Well, let's go and see a play then," she tried. "When was the last time you did that?"

Nancy shook her head, indicating either that she'd never done it or that she couldn't remember, or wasn't interested.

"They're doing King John at Lindsey's – Shakespeare. What about that?"

Nancy sniffed and mopped her eyes.

"Come on, dear," Brenda begged. "Let me try to do *something* for you."

The forsaken one wiped her face and gazed pathetically at her supporter.

Brenda offered a sideways smile intended to be encouraging. "A year from now, this will all be in the past. Ray will be home again, sheepish, doing his best to get you to forgive him. It'll be a distant memory – and you'll be happy again."

They arrived fifteen minutes early and selected seats six rows from the front, slightly right of centre. Brenda sat at Nancy's right and took her hand.

"This is going to be good. It's been nearly a year since I saw a play."

"Two," Nancy answered, "if the last was Romeo and Juliet…"

Oh dear, thought Brenda, *that'll set her off again.* And she was right.

"Ray was there – and Tom," Nancy continued, staring into her lap. "It was a happy evening – made me think of when Ray asked me to marry him. Of course, he'd already got Papa's permission, but he leapt over the garden wall and got down on his knees beneath my bedroom window..." (tears were rising). "We were so much in love..." (sob).

Brenda passed a handkerchief and glanced round at the assembling spectators.

"There, there, dear. Try not to think about it. Remember, you're at the very bottom of this. Things will only get better from now on. This is nothing more than a little hiccup. Put it aside for a while. We're best friends, you and me, and I'll be here to support you. Tom too."

"I shouldn't have got fat," Nancy hissed.

"You're not fat," Brenda assured her. "Neither of us is fat. We may have put on a little...padding – most women do at our age – but neither of us can be said to be fat. Anyway, you're taller than me. You're statuesque – a noble, statuesque, attractive woman. You're better-looking than me. Don't blame yourself."

"I've always done everything he asked." Nancy shot a sideways glance at her friend. "Everything. You know?"

Brenda raised her eyebrows and rocked her head slightly side-to-side in a gesture subconsciously intended to communicate, *Well, yes, I suppose so, dear, but I'd rather you didn't spell it out.*

"There's nothing Fanny Harris can give him that I haven't already – nothing."

"Shh," Brenda whispered. "People will overhear."

"Then why...?" Nancy hissed, outrage close to the surface.

"It's because she's young – you know that," Brenda returned, hoping to stem her friend's fury before it grew out of control. "There's no other reason. Raymond is fifty-five and sees old age looming – same as all of us. What he's doing is a kind of panic. Running after a twenty-year-old girl – he's trying to prove to himself that he's not done. She's a badge to him, a badge that he can show off, parade in front of his friends."

"What about me?" Nancy countered. "I dress well, I look good (I hope), and we have lots of friends together. What must they be thinking of me? How would you feel if Tom abandoned you like this?"

Brenda patted Nancy's hand. "I know. I'd feel the same. But...you know, that's not likely to happen. Tom isn't as...adventurous as Ray. Ray stands out in a crowd – you know he does. He has a striking appearance."

"Oh, Brenda," said Nancy, more calmly than before. "Tom's lovely. You're so lucky."

"I know," Brenda returned. "But...he's Mr Ordinary in a way, isn't he? I mean, if he went after someone like Fanny Harris, I imagine she'd laugh at him." Brenda felt guilty describing her own husband in such unflattering terms but hoped the sacrifice might have some consoling effect on the betrayed woman.

Chairs scraped in the row behind a few feet away to the left, and the voice of a man carried clearly to Nancy's ear; a distinctive, aristocratic voice, with a charming Cornish inflexion: "These'll do. Sorry we can't get places nearer the front. I suppose I should've guessed it would be full."

Nancy glanced over her left shoulder and watched the couple take their seats: an elderly man and a young woman several decades his junior. She'd never seen either before. Both were finely dressed: he in a spotless, dark jacket braided with gold; she in an expensive scarlet silk gown that fell free and loose from the waist down. Her décolletage was fashionably low, her pretty breasts offered for eager male fingers. Nancy hated her immediately. She turned her face forward and hissed to Brenda, "Look at that whore! Dressed for the flesh market."

Brenda glanced behind. "She's just like any young woman," she protested. "Looks innocent enough to me. Her father's brought her to see a play, that's all. It's nothing more. Calm down."

Nancy turned her head again and stared at the couple. The man had his hand on the woman's knee and was rubbing it back and forth, enjoying the feel of her limb. She faced front again, eyes wide.

Is this how Ray behaves with her? Does he flaunt her in public like that? His bauble? Does he touch her, feel her, map her charms shamelessly in public? Does he publicly insult me with another woman in this same scornful manner?

"He's got his hands on her," she breathed to her friend.
Brenda glanced behind and saw that it was true. She was about to offer something along the lines of, "Just pretend they're not there," but the actors had taken their places, and the play began before she could form the words.

King John: Now, say, Chatillion, what would France with us?
Chatillion: Thus, after greeting, speaks the King of France…

Part way through the first act, Nancy ventured another glance to the rear and observed the elderly gentleman rubbing his hand against the inside of his partner's thigh, a few inches above the knee. As if that wasn't enough, she found the impudent trollop smiling directly at her when she peeked behind a second time. The tart had evidently noted Nancy's discomfort and had arranged herself to meet the next glance head-on, mocking her offence.
Nancy's agitation had not gone unnoticed by Brenda. "Pay no attention to them," she whispered, clutching her companion's wrist. "We're here to enjoy the play."
But Nancy's mind was filled with images of Raymond and Fanny, things she didn't want to imagine. She was trembling with anger and had already lost the story's thread.
Brenda endured her friend's fidgeting and sub-vocalised disgust until the first interval, at which time she took the lead, gripped Nancy by the hand, and suggested they take the opportunity to enjoy a glass of wine in the cool evening air.

But standing beneath the darkening sky, savouring their fine white wine, Nancy could speak of nothing else.
"Did you *see* them? Did you *see* them? Such effrontery! In a *public* space!"
"Please, dear," Brenda replied. "Don't let them spoil our evening."
"What's he going to do next? Lift her skirts and service her while she obligingly bends over the back row? Perhaps they'll charge threepence a view!"
Brenda sighed. "Nancy, fretting is not going to make things

better. You must be calm. Take a couple of deep breaths."
Nancy stared at her companion and realised she meant it.
"Go on," Brenda insisted, raised eyebrows backing up the command.
Nancy filled her lungs, held the fresh autumn, and breathed out, surprised to find she did indeed feel calmer.
Brenda smiled. "That did you good – I could see it. Another."
The operation was carried out, Nancy exhaling at length, a drawn-out sigh, eyes closed. "Why am I worrying?" she murmured. "I can't do anything anyway, and being upset doesn't help."
"Wise words," Brenda purred.
Nancy took a swallow of wine. "Others are outraged too. I saw them looking, saw their faces. It isn't just me."
Brenda feared her companion might be about to lose equilibrium once more and was relieved when she took another deep breath and a second substantial gulp of refreshment.

The tart was ready with another welcoming smile when Nancy and Brenda resumed their seats. For once, the elderly gentleman wasn't mauling her but seemed to be adjusting something in his boot. Nancy rewarded the girl's happy expression with a neutral stare.
Act III commenced almost immediately, and the first words uttered by Constance, innocent though they were, darkened Nancy's heart, conjuring images wholly unrelated to the play:

Constance (to Salisbury): Gone to be married? Gone to swear a peace? False blood to false blood joined?

Glancing behind once more, she saw the gentleman's hand again on his partner's knee. The girl didn't look directly at her, but some awareness in the corner of her eye told Nancy her curiosity had not gone unnoticed.
Eyes forward, she told herself. *Forget them; you never saw them; they're not here.*
But despite her best efforts, she found herself unable to keep her

eyes off the couple for more than a few minutes at a time, and as the act neared its conclusion, watched in disbelief as the man fondled the girl high up inside her thigh, just an inch or two shy of her…

Another interval. Many people were hurrying away again, seeking liquid sustenance. Nancy distinctly heard the old groper address his wanton hussy: "I'm away for a piss. I'll bring us some wine. Back before you know it."

"You're upset again, my dear," Brenda observed, taking her friend's hand.

Sadly, Nancy had allowed herself to become incandescent. She glowered at Brenda and spat, "It's *unnatural.* Did you see him? *Fondling* her! *He must be forty years older than she!*"

The girl heard the remark, leaned forward, smiled, and said, "Fifty actually. Fifty-three, to be precise."

Nancy was outraged. The bare-faced cheek! To be so forward as to invite confrontation! Red-hot with anger, she turned in her seat and addressed the wanton little slut.

"He shouldn't touch you in public! If he hadn't *handled* you, we'd have thought he was your father. Or your grandfather!"

"He's my husband," the girl replied. "He may touch me as he pleases."

"Evidently," Nancy answered, features contorted with disgust. "Fifty-three years between you? What was your mother thinking?"

"My mother died before I knew her," the girl replied.

Brenda was sweating with embarrassment, energetically flapping her fan, unsure what to do.

Nancy pressed ahead. "Your father then."

"No-one knew his identity. I was raised by my grandmother and given to missionaries."

"Who sold you for a pretty penny, no doubt, to the grasping gentleman who owns you now." Nancy's raised voice had attracted the attention of several spectators, who now gathered closer, eager for entertainment. One elderly gentleman sitting about eight seats to Nancy's left tried to intervene.

"Please, ladies. Calm yourselves."

"I'm quite calm," said the girl.

Nancy was exasperated. She glared at the man and threw up her hands. "This doxy's customer was *feeling* her while the play was proceeding. I didn't come to the theatre tonight to watch whores at work."

The girl's face registered surprise, followed instantly by anger. She craned forward and spoke emphatically. "I am not a prostitute, madam!"

"No husband treats his wife so grossly in public," Nancy hissed.

"Ladies, ladies!" said the elderly gentleman, extending his hand as if to calm a troubled sea.

Nancy, aware she was beginning to appear like the lying woman in the Judgement of Solomon, appealed to the pacifier. "There's more than half a century between them!"

"That is no crime, madam," the man replied.

"It's not *natural!*" Nancy insisted. "And with his hands *all over her...*"

"His hands weren't *all over* me!" the girl cried. "You exaggerate."

The kindly gentleman pressed on. "Madam, who's to say what is natural and what is not?"

"Sir, that is not the issue!" cried Nancy, red-faced, furious. "His *hands* were on her! And this is a public place – where people go for polite entertainment."

"Then, with respect, madam, you should not have made an issue of their ages."

"I am *incensed,* sir – *outraged* by this lewd behaviour; a display deliberately arranged to cause upset!" She was fuming, shouting, her moral superiority under siege. This man, reasonable of voice, was taking sides with the evildoer. Poor Nancy's frustration was about to overwhelm her; she was going to cry.

The girl looked dismayed, sat back in her seat, and said, "I'm sorry. I didn't mean to upset you." But Nancy was hardly aware of it, engaged as she was in battle with the doxy's supporter, neither she nor he willing to give ground.

The tart's owner appeared a couple of minutes later, carrying two glasses of wine, frowning at the conflict.

"What on earth's going on?" he asked, taking his seat at the young strumpet's side.

"She didn't like you touching me," the girl explained. "She also didn't like the fact that I appear so much younger than you."

"Daft old harridan," muttered the man, loud enough for Nancy to hear.

She turned on him. "How *dare* you, sir! I heard that remark!"

"I will not have you upset my wife, madam," he retorted calmly but with an edge of threat, taking the young woman's hand in his.

The absurdity of it struck home. His wife? What nonsense. Where was his real wife? At home, neglected, betrayed, abandoned? Like she herself?

"So, she's your wife, is she?" Nancy spat, mocking him.

"She is," the man answered. "My tenth wife."

This was a joke! Nancy's jaw dropped at the audacity. "Your tenth…? And what happened to the other nine?"

"That is no concern of yours," he replied.

The elderly man with whom Nancy had done battle caught the whore-owner's attention and complimented, "You're very fortunate to have such a beautiful young bride, sir."

"I am, it's true," returned the other. "I never forget it."

Nancy faced the front, humiliated, puffing. Brenda laid a hand on her friend's shoulder and lullabied, "Shh…calm down." But things had gone too far; Nancy's defence of decency had been repelled, and the powers of filth had won – again! She was assaulted on all sides; her husband had deemed her useless, and now the entire world seemed to have declared immorality the natural order. She clenched her fists – her jaw too – and wondered if she might actually explode. Brenda's mollification went entirely unnoticed. Nancy took up her bag, fired herself erect, barged along the row of seats with scarcely a thought for the people she collided with on the way, and exited the theatre.

Brenda sighed, closed her eyes and relaxed her shoulders, realising for the first time how tense she'd been. Turning in her seat, she briefly caught the attention of the elderly man and the young woman and wondered if she should say something. Apologise? Explain? The man looked impassive, neutral, but the woman's expression showed compassion, sympathy, and… what? Guilt, regret? Whatever – it was too late; the damage was done, and there was nothing for it but to run after poor Nancy.

The actors were returning. Brenda watched them for a few seconds, issued a resigned breath through her mouth, then rose and walked out.

It was late, the coal-black sky prickling with stars, and there was little light in the street. Brenda looked all around, but Nancy was nowhere to be seen.

Someone was hurrying towards her, a man.

"Brenda, is that you?"

It was Raymond, Nancy's husband. Brenda was surprised, and for a moment was concerned that something dreadful had happened.

"Ray?"

"Polly told me you'd brought Nancy here."

"She's gone," Brenda replied. "What's happened?"

"I've been stupid, stupid," said Ray, evidently distressed.

Brenda shook her head, confused. "Where's Fanny?"

"At her mother's. Please. Where's Nancy?"

Brenda sniffed, her emotion catching in her nose – or perhaps it was the night's chill. "On the way home – probably. Only a couple of minutes ago."

"Walking?"

"I don't know."

"Did something happen?"

"She's upset, Ray, heartbroken."

"Oh, God," Raymond answered, eyes cast down. "What have I done?"

"She was distraught," said Brenda. "I don't think she'd have taken wheels; I imagine she's storming home on foot."

"I'll follow her," Raymond muttered and hurried off into the dark.

Carriages were lining up, ready to take people home from the play. Brenda signalled one over.

"Milady?" said the driver, tugging his forelock as he stepped down. "Been to the performance?"

"I have," she replied, climbing into the vehicle.

"Where are we goin'?"

Brenda gave the coachman her address.

"Be nice to be 'ome again in the warm, I reckon?" said the driver, closing the door.

Brenda smiled, thought of Tom – steadfast, reliable Tom. "Yes," she smiled. "Yes, it will be."

SECRET GIRL

1. Halifax, Yorkshire, 1749. Ivy and Jerome

The news of Ivy's pregnancy hit the Reverend Jerome Ottershaw like a bolt of lightning. His failure to produce a child with his wife or with any of his three earlier conquests had convinced him he lacked potency. How was it possible that four women should remain childless, only for Ivy Stavely to conceive at their one and only intimacy?
"But it can't be," he said, trembling with disbelief, staring at her across the little table in her drawing room.
"There's no mistake," she assured him.
"But, are you sure it's mine?"
"What do you mean? Of course it's yours. My husband is on the other side of the world."
It was true. Alasdair Stavely had been in the Chesapeake Bay since autumn, assisting Ivy's father, Sir Percival Finch, on his tobacco plantation.
"You haven't…?" Jerome began.
But Ivy silenced him. "How dare you ask me that!"
She'd trusted him, confided in him, told him how sad she was, trapped in a cold marriage with a brute of a man she didn't love. She missed her mother, Anne, dead ten years, and felt remote from her father not only because of the distance that separated them but because he'd remarried and transferred his affections entirely to his brides. His second wife, Rebecca, had been kind enough but had died in childbed three years earlier. Sir Percival's third wife was an American Indian woman, Dyani, about the same age as Ivy herself. Ivy felt alone, unwanted and trapped, her existence bleak and pointless.
Jerome found her deeply attractive, the fifth woman he'd lain

with. His first had been Agnes Pickering, married and ten years his senior, a parishioner of his father's in Skipton. He'd been about twenty, studying in Oxford, but they met whenever he returned home. It had been secret, delicious, a young man's fantasy.

Next, there was Caroline Thackley, who led the singers in his first parish in Todmorden – two years older than he; the town clerk's wife. She'd broken off their relationship after two years, concerned that her husband was beginning to suspect.

Maude Risby had been his third, a woman he'd met at a hunting party in Westmorland in 1745, a year after taking up his current position as Rector of St John's, Halifax. She'd been twenty-seven at the time, seven years younger than he, and unmarried (as far as he knew – although a friend told him she had a partner, a woman). She was secretive, divulged little about herself. They'd seen each other three times the following year, but Jerome gave her up soon after meeting Celia, who became his wife in November 1746.

Jerome had been faithful to Celia – until that one fateful afternoon with Ivy. And now, when it seemed impossible, his seed had found a foothold.

"What's to be done?" she asked.

The rector stared at her, still so deep in shock he didn't know what to say.

"Alasdair will want to know who the father is," Ivy pressed.

Jerome was horrified. "You can't tell him."

Mrs Stavely had hoped for a more positive response. "You have no children with your wife. We could be married, you and I."

"You and I?" he echoed incredulously. "I'm an officer of the Church of England. I cannot surrender my spouse and take up with another woman."

"But you *have* taken up with another woman," she protested.

"One defenceless instant..." he began.

"But a lifetime's responsibility for me," she concluded.

Jerome sighed. "Surely, you...you cannot have the child."

But Ivy had made up her mind. "I'm keeping him – her," she said.

"It'll be a reason for me to go on despite everything; a reason to look forward to the next day. I'll have some purpose, some function. I'll have something to love."

Jerome swallowed. "Please – you must not name me as the father. If you do, I'll lose my position – and the integrity of my marriage."

She rose from her seat, face flushed with anger. "Mr Ottershaw, I mistook you for a man."

Jerome took up his hat and stood facing her. "I will arrange a trust fund for the child so that it's well provided for, whatever happens." He paused and added, "I'm sorry. If you identify me as the father, I'll deny it. It'll be your word against mine."

King Street, Halifax
Tuesday, March 14th, 1749

My Darling Husband,
I have some shameful news that I have been unable to share with anyone for fear of dishonour and ridicule. This will sound absurd, but I swear it is the truth.
A few days before Christmas, I woke to find a man creeping about in the bedroom, looking for valuables. It was a bright night, the moon full. I tried hard to stay quiet despite my terror, hoping he'd think me asleep, but I must have made a sound – or perhaps he saw some movement. In any case, I was discovered. He commanded me to be silent or pay with my life. First, he pressed for the location of the jewellery. When I told him it was in the strongbox, guarded by Sullivan, he became angry and demanded to know what I would give him in recompense. I was very frightened. He said he would sheath his blade in me – not the steel one he clutched, but the other.
And so it was. Forgive me. I was so ashamed, I told no one. But now the price is made manifest – and I am with child...

Alasdair returned from his travels in June, seething, and confronted his wife, by then six months pregnant. Holding her letter in a trembling hand, he shouted, "You expect me to believe this absurdity?"

"It's true," she quaked. "I swear it's true, every word."
"You are a liar, woman. Who's the father?"
"I do not know." She clasped her hands and bowed her head. "Please, have mercy."
"I will know the identity of the man who used my wife as a whore! I will have his blood!"
"Please pity me," she begged. "I am your faithful wife. I swear it."
"You took advantage of my absence to pleasure yourself with a man," he insisted. "I will not have the child under my roof."
"Oh no!" she wailed. "Please, no! The child is not to blame."
But he was adamant. "I'll find parents for the little bastard. You won't keep it."

Alasdair interviewed the staff at length, fancying one or more must be in league with his faithless wife, but despite his veiled threats to their employment and employability, none suggested any likely suspect. Dutiful Frank Sullivan shrugged, threw up his hands and said, "I'm sorry, sir. I honestly cannot explain it. Lady Ivy has always been a paragon of virtue: modest, quiet, withdrawn, demure. If I thought there might be some credibility in the idea, I might suggest a visitation from the Holy Spirit."
Alasdair grimaced. "Is that a joke?"
"No, sir," replied the butler. "It's just that the whole thing seems so out of character. I've always known Lady Ivy to be upright in heart. If you don't mind my saying, it seems to me that her explanation of an intruder in the night is actually the most likely possibility. In fact, I can well imagine her being so distraught and shamed by such an occurrence that she might indeed have hoped to keep it secret."
Alasdair sighed. "Alright, Sullivan. You can go. Thank you."
Stavely was aware of Frank Sullivan's long history with the family. The man had been butler in the house for nearly forty years, joining the staff when Sir George Finch and Lady Sophia had occupied the place, their son Percival (later to become Ivy's father), a young man of seventeen. Sullivan was dependable. His inability to explain Lady Ivy's condition troubled Alasdair and

made him wonder if his wife was, in fact, telling the truth.

Linda Drewitt, housekeeper, was equally at a loss, as was her husband Kenneth, who, in his duties as gardener, might have noticed something amiss if an intruder had scaled into the house from the rear. Even Ivy's personal maid, Bronagh Duffy, knew nothing. Alasdair offered her five guineas for information – a vast sum for a twenty-year-old girl fresh from Ireland.

"Ooh, sir!" she said. "For such a sum, a girl might make something up – just for the cash, you know. My lady's a sweet soul, a faithful wife. She'd never cheat on you."

So – a robust ring of support for the good Mrs Stavely.

But Alasdair didn't believe it.

2. The Rectory. Sunday, June 25th

Sam Dunn listened. He always listened – listened hard, alert for the next opportunity. He'd landed the position of rectory butler three years earlier – the result of listening and of following up chatter, chasing up opportunities. A few forged references, the endorsement of one or two hastily acquired mutual friends, and his acceptance into the Ottershaw household had been easily managed. Reverend Ottershaw listened with interest to Sam's entirely fictitious, carefully rehearsed life story, eloquently performed at his employment interview, and welcomed him onto the staff with open arms.

Sam had a passion for women. Nothing unusual in that, especially for an unmarried man of fifty-two. But Sam's passion for women manifested in a unique way, its fulfilment demanding elaborate ritual. He moved from place to place, a few years here, a few there, taking his chances where he found them. Sometimes the opportunity arrived unexpectedly, unannounced, and he acted instantly, instinctively. But he preferred to draw out the stalking if he could, savouring the anticipation, watching the woman of his choice for weeks or months until the exquisite yearning became almost unbearable. Sometimes the prey was entirely unaware of him (or almost so), but occasionally he liked to groom his quarry as a friend, gaining her confidence, rendering the ultimate pleasure so much more delicious. He'd been seventeen years old when he first fully consummated his desires, and had satisfied himself with twenty-two women since then.

Now Sam was hungry, having restrained his inclinations during his entire career as the rector's butler. He thought Celia Ottershaw a very fine specimen: young, impressively breasted, thin of waist and round of hip. He relished serving the master and his wife at dinner, standing silent, watchful, listening.

"Ivy Stavely looked miserable in church this morning," Celia observed, spearing a carrot with her fork.

"Really?" Jerome answered. "I didn't see her there."

"Oh yes," Celia replied. "She sat at the back with her maid. You must surely have noticed; she's hard to miss, being so rotund."

Jerome flicked his wife a glance. "Rotund?"

"Pregnant dear, pregnant. You must have noticed her. You stand so high, delivering your sermon, scanning your flock, ensuring you have their attention."

"My attention is focused inwards, my love – on my text, my message."

"Even so," Celia began. "She must be six months, seven months... Hasn't her husband spent nearly a year away in the New World? I wonder..."

"Tut-tut, dear!" Jerome interjected. "Such scandalous thoughts. He must have been home for a spell."

"Wouldn't we have heard?" asked his wife.

"Alasdair Stavely isn't exactly a pillar of Halifax society, is he? I hardly know the man – I believe few can say they do. He came to me four years ago to make preparations for his marriage, and that was the only conversation I've had with him."

"Poor girl," Celia mused. "She was so young. What did she see in him?"

"Lady Ivy was nineteen when she wed," Jerome pointed out. "It's not particularly young for a woman."

"Yes," Celia conceded. "But to such a gloomy, joyless ogre of a man. He must be twice her age."

"You're about right, I think," Jerome replied. "He's more than twenty years older than she."

"Dreadful," said Celia. "To be dominated by a spouse old enough to be one's father." She looked across the table at her husband. "But what was your point?"

Jerome had lost track. "My point?"

Dunn came forward discreetly, refreshed their wine glasses, and withdrew to his corner.

"Yes. You said he wasn't well-known in town," Celia pressed.

"Oh yes, yes. My point... My point is that because he's not well-known about town – not popular – it's possible he could have spent time at home without anyone noting it. I imagine that's what happened. Or were you about to suggest the child mightn't be his?"

"Well, it's not impossible, is it? I mean, you told me I was not your first..."

Jerome chewed a piece of mutton, gazed at his wife and waited for the rest.

"You also said," she continued, "that you had liaisons with women who were already married..."

"For which I begged God's forgiveness," he interjected.

"Of course," Celia acknowledged. "I'm simply pointing out the fact that respectable men do have relationships with women who are fully bound in matrimony."

"It's true – I suppose," Jerome admitted. "But until I'm reliably informed otherwise, I shall suppose that Mrs Stavely was impregnated by Mr Stavely."

Celia smiled at him. "Quite right, dear. Good for you! I hope you didn't think I was gossiping."

"Of course not, my one-and-only," he returned. "Heaven forbid I should be chained to a two-tongued wench."

Celia chuckled. She loved her husband, and these little flashes of wit bound her still more tightly to him. She'd been a virgin when they wed, twenty-six years old. Jerome had seemed like a god to her, manly, confident, nine years her senior. He thrilled her in bed, made her feel joyful and complete, enshrined in his love. She'd hoped for children, but he'd warned her before their marriage that he believed himself infertile. "If God wills it, we'll have a family," she'd whispered, held in his arms. "Whatever happens, we'll be happy together."

And they *were* happy. But it didn't prevent what took place that fateful December afternoon in the Stavelys' parlour. Jerome's guilt was so intense it felt like a physical weight. Ivy had been so unhappy. He'd sat with her in front of the little hearth, close, gripping her hands in his, assuring her that God remembered her, that she wasn't alone. She'd seemed so pitiful, and he'd so fiercely wanted to help her. Her moist eyes were so big, so deep, her hands so smooth, so fragile. He'd known it was going to happen in the seconds before it actually did – and he'd seen that she knew it also. Something passed between them, through their joined hands. They drew closer, his touch found her cheek, and they were kissing...

Jerome was not a man who abused his position, and what happened that day was wholly out of character. He saw Ivy again on several subsequent occasions but ensured that circumstances never allowed a second union.

"I love you," she told him. "Don't you feel it too?"

"I'm infinitely fond of you," he replied, "but what happened was a weakness. I have Celia and the parish to think of. I'll care for you and support you as much as I can, but what occurred between us must not be repeated. Please understand."

3. A Plan. Wednesday, August 2nd

Jerome was in his study preparing his sermon when Muriel knocked and announced Ivy Stavely. The rector swallowed, sighed, and gave permission for her to enter.

"Reverend Ottershaw," she greeted him, crossing the room slowly, beautiful, heavily pregnant with his baby.

Jerome got to his feet. "Mrs Stavely, how nice to see you. Shall we have tea?"

"No, thank you," she replied. "I don't intend to remain long."

The rector dismissed Muriel and motioned Ivy to a seat. "Ivy," he said quietly, sitting opposite. "How are you?"

"I'm as well as might be expected," she replied. "I'm not to keep the baby."

Jerome squeezed his eyes shut, regret, self-loathing and compassion welling up within him. "I feared that might happen."

"Alasdair says he'll find a good home for it."

"Well, that's something, my dear, dear lady," Jerome replied, taking her hand.

"You don't understand," Ivy replied. "He'll only find a good home if I tell him the identity of the father."

"Oh no," Jerome muttered. "Please – you mustn't. It would put me in an impossible situation. I'd have to deny it, and I wouldn't wish to hurt you so cruelly."

She dipped her head and stared into her lap. "I haven't told him. He'd never guess it was you – even in a thousand years."

Jerome watched her in silence for a moment. "And if you don't tell him?"

"He doesn't say precisely – only that the child won't be so fortunate. I don't know what that means."

"You don't think he intends…?"

She lifted her head and met his eyes. "To kill it? No. I don't imagine he's quite that cruel."

"Alright," Jerome nodded. He'd spent a lot of time thinking about possibilities and now brought one forth. "Here's my plan: I will arrange for the child to be adopted by worthy parents – and I will pay for its upbringing. I'll see that you have access to it."

She leaned forward and clutched his wrists, tears springing to her eyes. "You'd do that? For me?"

"Gladly," he answered. "It won't be easy. I'll have to plan it carefully. But I'm sure it can be made to work."

"Oh, Jerome!" she sobbed. "How can I ever thank you?"

Halifax

August 3rd

My dear Claudius,
Greetings from Halifax! I hope this finds you well. Celia and I have fond memories of you from our wedding. We must meet again before too long.
I shall come straight to the matter as it is of some urgency. There is in my parish a woman in distress, soon to give birth to a child not fathered by her husband. As you can understand, there is a good deal of unrest in the house, and the father has threatened to have the newborn removed. The woman has begged me, as her consoler, to intervene and find a home for the child, one that she herself might visit from time to time as its mother. You and I have known each other a long time, and I know you to be a man of great insight and sympathy. Your parish is populous. Might you be aware of a suitable home for this poor youngling?
Your good friend,
Jerome Ottershaw

When Claudius Daubuz, vicar of St Peter's, Huddersfield, received Jerome's note, he divined immediately and correctly the origin of the dilemma. It wasn't the first time in his twenty years as a man of the cloth that he'd been asked to conceal the illegitimate child of a clergyman. He sighed as he charged his quill.

My dear Jerome,
I am in receipt of your letter and will act upon it straight away. As luck would have it, I do know a couple, both in their forties, whose six-month son passed away in his sleep a few weeks ago. I think they may be prevailed upon to help. They are good people. I shall arrange to see them as soon as possible. You may expect to hear from me again shortly.
It's kind of you to ask after my health. I'm no worse, thank you, and I give thanks that I am still able to labour for our Lord's greater glory despite my infirmities.
Give my love to dear Celia.

Your own,
Claudius

The arrangements were a success. Revd Daubuz secured the consent of the surrogate couple, and at the end of August, Jerome travelled the ten miles to Huddersfield to meet them. The one remaining obstacle was to devise a way of removing the child from the Stavelys' house.

But it was all a waste; the plan never came to fruition.

4. Alasdair and Ivy. Monday, September 4th

"After your mongrel is born, we shall sell the house and travel to Virginia," said Alasdair.

They ate at opposite ends of their long dining table, relations between them remaining hostile. He'd sent the servants out so he could inform Ivy of his decision without fear of her creating a public spectacle.

She watched him in silence for a few seconds as he chewed his food. "You mean forever?"

"Yes," he replied. "Your father's successful. We shall become part of his enterprise."

"But I don't *want* to go," said Ivy. "I like it here – I want to stay here."

Alasdair spoke across her. "Nonsense. We'll get your sordid little mishap out of the way, then start a new life for ourselves out there. Who knows? Perhaps you'll even honour me with offspring of my own."

Ivy hated him. Their marriage had been arranged by her father, who admired the man for the ruthlessness of his business dealings, and Ivy had been too young and obedient to protest; an innocent lamb led to the butcher's block. But Alasdair's real love was for her father's money, not for her. He'd been brutal on their wedding night, savage with her untried body, and she'd feared him from then on. He formed occasional attachments with the young footmen, none of whom remained in service for any length of time, and Ivy came to realise that women held little interest for him. Their subsequent rare couplings in the marital bed had been cold, business-like procedures, carried out purely in the hope of fathering progeny to fully cement Alasdair's position in the family. Ivy briefly wondered why he didn't just pretend her child was his; it would have relieved him of the tedious process of attempting to fecundate her. But she knew him to be too proud to tolerate the presence of a bastard child; he was determined to create one of his own, however distasteful the process might be.

"Have you told Papa about…about…"

"Of course not!" Alasdair spat. "And neither have you – at least, I hope you've retained at least that much common sense. There's no reason he should ever know. We can put the issue behind us."

Ivy was becoming distraught, her hands trembling. "But, my baby…"

"We've had all this," Alasdair dismissed. "You know what our arrangements are…"

"*Your* arrangements," she interrupted.

He ignored her and went straight on. "You will identify the child's father. I will then see that your little embarrassment has a reasonable start in life. If you don't tell me, you'll be condemning the thing to a far more ignominious fate." He cut a potato and popped it in his mouth. "Eat up; you'll need your strength."

"What are you planning?" she quavered. "You're not going to…"

He grinned across the table at her, a little juice escaping his lips. "What? You think I intend to take it to the Hebble and throw it in?"

"You wouldn't…" she whimpered.

Alasdair snorted. "The thought did occur to me."

An image of a cold, drowned baby appeared in Ivy's mind. "No…" she muttered.

"You think I'm a murderer?" He waited for her answer, but none came; she merely stared at him, open-mouthed. "I'm not so merciless," he breathed.

"Let me keep it," she begged. "Please. I'll do anything."

He sighed. "That will not happen. There's a price to pay; you

have a choice to make. I will not be shamed in my house by the presence of a brat fathered on my wife by some stiffcock Romeo. There's an end of it. Don't disgust me with your pitiful whining."
"I'll have the midwife take the child away," Ivy threatened. "I'll tell her what you're planning. She'll support me – she'll stand up to you."
Alasdair chuckled and shook his head. "Not so. I've already engaged the services of a suitable midwife – one drawn from afar. She'll receive a good fee for her work – and she'll have little to say to you."
"You devil!" Ivy snarled.
"If you upset yourself, you may miscarry," he mocked, amused at her distress. "Go on, fire away, do your worst. It'll save us all a lot of trouble."

5. Flowers. Sunday, September 10th

Bronagh sat with her mistress as the church cleared after Mattins. It was a lovely sunny day, the huge old building crisp with the scent of bright new flowers.
"Are you alright, my lady?"
Ivy seemed tense, clutching her hands, staring into her lap. Bronagh was surprised she'd wanted to come out that day, so close to her delivery.
"Yes," Ivy replied, granting her maid a little smile. "I need to speak with the rector."
"Of course, my lady," Bronagh nodded, returning the smile. She felt sorry for her mistress, married to such a horrid man. Poor thing.
Jerome swept down the aisle, fresh from sending off his congregation. He slowed as he passed them and raised his hand in greeting, casting his eyes first at Ivy, then at her maid. "Mrs Stavely."
Ivy's voice was weak, with a pleading quality that Bronagh picked up instantly. "Jerome…"
"In the flower room," he murmured, glancing anxiously at

Bronagh, something in her eyes telling him she knew.

Ivy struggled to her feet, gestured that Bronagh should remain seated, and followed the rector away. The maid watched them, realisation flooding in.

Oh, my God...

"Tell me you've found somewhere," Ivy begged, lowering herself into the seat Jerome offered her.

"I have," he replied. "All's arranged."

"Where?"

"Perhaps it's best you don't know yet," he replied, sitting opposite, leaning forward, holding her hands. "It's ten miles from here. You can journey there and back in a day – not too far."

"Oh, thank you, thank you! The people – they're…?"

"They're good people," he assured her. "And they'll be expecting you. You can be the child's mother."

"He wants to take me away," said Ivy, desperation in her eyes.

"Away?"

"To the New World – to my father's estate in Virginia."

Jerome stared at her, the poor woman's distress surging over him like waves. "You don't want to go."

"Of course I don't want to go," she replied. "Not without my little one."

He sighed, thoughts tumbling over each other. "Then we need to get you away." He pressed his hand to his forehead and shut his eyes, trying to map a route through the problem. "You'll be casting yourself adrift from your husband, from your family, your father."

"I don't care." She pierced him with her eyes, waiting to hear his solution.

He stared back at her and murmured, "Your maid."

Ivy shook her head. "She doesn't know."

But Jerome had seen it. He nodded. "She knows."

"Bronagh's good…" Ivy began.

"Will she go with you? If I get you away, will she go with you?"

Ivy looked down, breaking eye contact, thinking. "I don't know.

Perhaps. Why?"

Jerome realised he was worrying at least partly about himself. The maid would have to go with Ivy. If she remained in the Stavelys' house, she might be pressed to identify him as the father. To Ivy, he said only, "You'll need a friend, someone to help."

"But *you'll* be my friend, won't you?" she begged. "You won't desert me?"

He squeezed her hands. They felt soft, precious, vulnerable, and he felt suddenly close to her, as he had that day.

"Oh, Jerome," she muttered, and he took her in his arms and kissed her.

"I love you." The words were out before he knew what he'd said.

"I know," she replied. "And I you, my lovely man – with all my heart."

Jerome was surprised to find his eyes filling with tears. "Go," he said. "Leave the arrangements to me. I won't let you down."

"Oh, my love, my love!" Celia gasped, legs wrapped around her stiff hard, vigorous husband in the secrecy of their bed that night, his ardour driving her to ecstasy, then a second blushing, melting into the waves of the first.

Ivy! his instinct cried. *Ivy, Ivy!* achieving fruition in his wife's flesh.

He lay on his side when it was over, Celia exhausted in his arms, her body warm, smooth. Her heart had beat so fast and hard, and she'd panted so hoarsely and rapidly, he'd worried she might expire.

"Oh, Jerome," she muttered. "That was the best. You're amazing. Oh God, how lucky I am to have such a man."

He caressed her, his touch sliding smoothly over her flank. "Good wife."

"Do you love me?" Celia murmured.

"I do."

"Tell me."

"I love you." It was easy to say, and he meant it. The fact that he'd said it to another woman just hours earlier didn't make it any less true.

Celia slid her hand across his chest, tugging at the little curls of black hair. "I wish we could spend all our lives in bed, just doing this."

He kissed her forehead.

"Do I excite you?" she whispered.

"You know you do," he replied.

Jerome felt her smile as she kissed him on the lips. She took that part of him, still sticky from their congress, in her hand and repeated, "I love you."

Jerome thought of Ivy again, his flesh quickening in Celia's grip. *Perhaps it's possible,* he thought. *Why not? Could I do it? Could I split my life in two? She could be my mistress, far enough away so that no-one would ever find out. I could remain in post here, with Celia, but have Ivy and the child – perhaps more children – elsewhere. Two entirely separate lives; two Jeromes.*

Rigid again, he mounted his wife once more, Ivy's face shining in his mind, her body open beneath him.

"Oh, Jerome..." gasped Celia.

6. Anne

Jane Stephenson needed money to escape the clutches of her manipulative landlord. Her husband had run off eight years earlier with a Bradford prostitute, leaving her alone in Leeds, the single occupant of a tiny room, earning a meagre income from midwifery, a competitive profession in such a densely populated urban centre. She was often short of money – particularly short of money for the rent. So Albert Bridewell, landlord, accepted payment by other means.

Jane was no beauty – she knew it well enough. She had poor skin, numerous warts on her face, and thin, sickly-looking fair hair. But it didn't seem to worry sixty-one-year-old Albert. Jane was seventeen years younger than him, and the parts of her body that he required for the periodic settlement of her debt were still in reasonably good order.

But he disgusted Jane – and Jane disgusted herself. So, when the advertisement appeared in the press *(Reliable midwife required. Discretion essential. Good money paid for single engagement)*, she wrote to the address in Halifax straight away.

A Mr Sullivan responded, arranging to visit her in Leeds. It was an unfortunate matter, he said, a great sadness to a noble family. She would need strong nerves and would be asked to sign a document binding her to silence. She would be paid twenty-five guineas for her services. Could she agree to those terms?

She grinned, pictured herself sticking the finger to Albert Bridewell, and said, "Yes sir, absolutely, you can rely on me!"

Jane arrived at the Stavelys' house on Monday, September 11th, and was taken directly for a brief interview with Alasdair.

"You are here solely to carry out this one assignment. If things go well, that is good. If there are complications, my wife's life is of greater importance than that of the infant. Do you understand?"

"Yes sir, of course," Jane replied.

"Good," said Alasdair. "Do not form any attachment to my wife, and do not succumb to her pleading. She may ask you to take custody of the child. You will not do so. Your duties extend only to the delivery of the baby; they include nothing else – nothing. You will be paid upon your departure. You will not speak of your task. Do you understand?"

"I fully understand, sir. I'm grateful to have been honoured with this employment and will carry it out precisely to your requirements."

Alasdair nodded. "Good."

Jane was concerned she might feel some compassion towards the mother but realised at their first meeting that there would be none. Ivy reminded her strongly of the pasty, pathetic whore with whom her husband had run off. She despised her straight away.

"My husband hired you," said Ivy as Jane examined her.

"He did."

"Where are you from?"
"Far away."
"What am I to call you?"
"Mrs Stephenson."
"You're married then."
"Was."
Pause.
"Is your husband…?"
"Dead? No. Buggered off with a doxy."
Another pause.
"I suppose you're being well paid for this?"
"Handsomely."
Ivy clenched her jaw. "And you'll have been issued instructions, no doubt."
"No doubt," Jane repeated.
"Do you have any children?"
"No, thank God."

Jane lived in the house from that day. She had a room to herself, ate with the servants and reported to the master each evening. Mind on the gold, she was ruthless enough to obey his instructions to the letter.

The child was born at a quarter past three in the afternoon of Thursday, September 21st. The labour was long and difficult, leaving Ivy shattered. Alasdair went about his business as usual while it proceeded, only Jane and Bronagh present as the mother gave birth to her little one. For some reason, Ivy had convinced herself she'd produce a boy – a boy, like Jerome. The child would be named George, after Ivy's grandfather.

But it wasn't a boy.

"Anne," Ivy wept as Jane wrapped the newborn and handed it to her. "My little Anne."

"After your ma," Bronagh smiled.

"Yes," Ivy wept, happy despite everything. "I've got a daughter!"

Jane left the room hurriedly, returning moments later with Alasdair.

"So, it's here," he said.

"My baby," Ivy muttered, holding it close, fearing he'd wrest it from her.

Alasdair addressed Jane. "You'll stay a week longer – see everything's in good order. Then our arrangement will be complete."

"Of course, sir," the midwife replied.

Alasdair left without inspecting the child or speaking another word to his wife.

7. The New Father

Baby Anne was healthy, skin bright, suckling well at the breast. Bronagh remained in the room much of the time, but Jane withdrew for lengthy periods, returning to check all was well every few hours. Ivy knew the only way she could get word to Jerome was through Bronagh, but she'd never confessed the truth to anyone, not even her trusted young maid.

I'll have to do it, she thought. *I'll have to tell her.*

So, on Friday afternoon, heart in her mouth, she beckoned the young woman to draw close.

"Bronagh," she whispered. "My husband's going to take my baby away."

"Oh no, my lady," the maid whispered back. "He says he will, right enough – but I'm sure he won't do it."

"He will," Ivy nodded. She clenched her jaw and gazed into the other's eyes. "Bronagh."

"Yes, my lady?"

"Anne's father…"

The maid settled on the edge of the mattress and hugged her mistress. "I know."

The relief had Ivy on the verge of crying, but she quickly sniffed her tears away. "You do?"

"Yes, I do, poor love. It's the rector of St John's."

The tears welled up; Ivy covered her mouth with her hand, trying to stop them. "How did you know?"

"I saw it in his eyes – and yours."
"Does anyone else know?"
"No, my lady. Only me."
"Oh, Bronagh. Can I trust you?"
The maid leaned forward and held Ivy again. "Of course you can, my lady. You can trust me to the end o' the world – and beyond."
"Thank you," the mother sobbed.
"You want me to tell him the little one's here, don't you?"
"I do," Ivy replied. "Listen, Bronagh." She paused, bracing herself for what she was about to say. "Jerome's going to take me away – me and Anne – so we can be together."
"Together…" Bronagh frowned. "What about his wife?"
"I don't know," Ivy answered. "First, we must get safely away from here."
Bronagh sat still, mouth an inch open, staring.
"Do you understand?"
"I do," the maid replied.
"Will you come with us?"
"With you…and…the rector?"
"Yes," Ivy confirmed. "To help me look after the baby. Please."
"What about my mother?" asked Bronagh. "I send my money to her. She has none of her own – she relies on me…"
Ivy nodded and squeezed her maid's arm. "Jerome will see to it. You'll have no concerns."
"You promise?"
"I do," said Ivy. "I promise."
Bronagh was quiet a moment longer, then said, "Very well – I'll come."
"Good. Thank you!" Ivy embraced her, relieved. "Now, please, if you will – go and tell him."

"Miss Duffy is here, sir," said Dunn. "Mrs Stavely's maid."
Jerome folded his newspaper, dropped it on his desk, and stood. The woman's visit could mean only one thing.
"Alright, Sam. Show her in."
Bronagh Duffy was dressed entirely in black, hatted, wearing a

veil which she folded back on entering the room. Her manner and dress seemed so strange and at odds with what Jerome might have anticipated that he felt suddenly transmuted into another existence and was lost for words. The maid appeared to be in mourning. Despite his fondness for Ivy, the rector was ashamed to find himself briefly eased *(she's dead, the problem removed)* before catching himself (eyes squeezed, shake of the head) and realising that Bronagh was attired thus simply out of respect for him. She probably thought her appearance was that of a well-to-do unaccompanied lady attending a Sunday service in the parish church.

Dunn had withdrawn. The door was closed, and the two stood facing each other.

"Miss Duffy," Jerome began. "To what do I owe this pleasure?"

Bronagh curtseyed as best she could in her elaborate dress and said, "Your Grace."

Jerome chuckled in spite of himself. "Hardly, Miss Duffy. Reverend Ottershaw will do."

The woman blushed with embarrassment. "Sorry. I..."

Jerome indicated she should sit, which she did, her hands in her lap. He settled opposite her, conscious of how tense she was.

"It's Bronagh, isn't it?"

"Yes, sir," she nodded.

"And you've come with a message?"

"I have."

He waited a couple of seconds. "Tell me?"

She looked squarely into his face. "Your daughter is born, sir."

The directness of her delivery winded the rector. He sat back in his seat and let the reality hit him.

I have a child. After all this time.

He was trembling. For a moment, he couldn't speak. "Name?"

"Anne, sir."

"Anne," he repeated.

Bronagh smiled, and Jerome suddenly realised he was in danger of bursting into tears. He cupped his face in his hands and breathed deeply, once, twice.

"How much do you know?" he asked, wiping a little moisture from his eyes.

"I know you're going to look after my lady," Bronagh replied. After a short pause, she added, "I'm to come too."

In truth, Jerome was unprepared. He'd tussled with a variety of hypothetical plans. The Huddersfield couple would no longer suffice, as they'd been expecting only a child, not a mother – and certainly not a retinue involving the rector of a parish church. He'd need to get them away to an inn, where they could stay in safety until he organised something more permanent. He was gripped simultaneously with joy (the joy of becoming a father), great excitement (Ivy was going to be his, his!), and a dreadful horror: he was going to betray his loving wife in the most calculated, scheming, irreversible way.

"How long have we got?" he asked.

"About a week," Bronagh replied.

"A week..." Jerome echoed.

"The master will dismiss the midwife on Thursday," Bronagh explained. "Then he'll take the baby away. At least, that's what my lady says."

"Thursday," Jerome muttered, mind racing. He looked at the maid. "I'll need your help."

"I thought you might," she replied.

"We'll have to get her out of the house. At night. Is it possible?"

Bronagh dropped her gaze, imagining it – smuggling Lady Ivy and the child down the stairs in the dead of night, floorboards creaking, terrified that any moment...

"Maybe," she mumbled.

"Let's say...Wednesday." Jerome caught her eyes again. "Half past two in the morning. Does that sound possible?"

Bronagh nodded. "You mean after Tuesday night?"

"Yes. You can do it?"

"I'll try."

"I'll have a carriage waiting along the street," he said. "By sunrise on Wednesday, you'll all be safe."

(Sam Dunn sensed something was going on. There was some

secret. He stood silent just outside the door, listening, ready to move away should one of the servants appear, or Mrs Ottershaw. Dunn's ears were sharp, but the rector and his visitor spoke in hushed, clandestine tones, and he picked up only a few scattered incomprehensible words. What was going on? Was Ottershaw having an affair with this girl?)

The rector's bell rang, signifying the end of the interview. Dunn waited a few seconds to give the impression he was approaching from some distance, then opened the door and stood ready.

"Would you see Miss Duffy out, please?" asked Jerome.

The butler nodded and escorted the girl to the front entrance, where she descended the steps to the street. *Pretty little thing,* he thought as she bustled away.

8. Attack

Alasdair Stavely changed his mind. The child had been brought safely into the world, and there seemed no reason it should linger in his house. He summoned Jane Stephenson to the study and asked if all was well with his wife and the brat. Receiving the answer yes, he commanded the midwife to be gone by dusk and paid her the agreed sum plus a small bonus so she could get lodgings for the night at The Cross and find transport home the next day.

On Monday morning, his resolve hard as steel, Alasdair visited his wife's bedroom, intending to bring matters to a conclusion. He found her in bed, feeding the child. Bronagh sat patiently in the window.

"It's time," he said, staring, impassive.

"Time for what?" Ivy muttered.

"Time for the infant to be gone."

Ivy clutched her baby tighter. "No…"

Bronagh rose from her seat, eyes on the master. "My lady…?"

Alasdair shot her a glance and pointed to the door. "Out."

The maid flicked her eyes from the master to the mistress and back again.

"*Out!*" Alasdair insisted, and she left the room, rustling past him. He shut the door and glared at his wife. "The father?"
Ivy shook her head and mewled, "I've already told you."
"This is your last chance," he said. "I won't ask again."
"Please..." Ivy begged, tears flowing. "Please don't take her."
"*The father?*"
"No, no..." she wailed.
Alasdair strode forward and opened the little basket set up as a cot. Next, he wrenched the baby from Ivy's grasp and laid it within, where it began to cry immediately. Ivy struggled out of bed, shrieking, striking her husband, but he slapped her and threw her back onto the mattress.
"NAME THE FATHER!"
"NO!" she cried. "PLEASE! *PLEASE!*"
"Then it's gone," he said, lifting the receptacle and striding to the door. "You'll never see it again."
Ivy knelt upright on the bed and pulled wildly at her hair. "ALRIGHT! ALRIGHT! IT'S JEROME OTTERSHAW!" Having uttered it, she collapsed, howling.
Alasdair froze, eyes wide. "The rector of St John's? Our fine spiritual pastor? Father of your child?" He sputtered, stifling a laugh. "What utter nonsense! One absurd lie after another."
"It's true."
"Really?" His tone was mocking.
"I swear it."
"Like you swore last time?"
"I swear it on my baby's life," Ivy murmured. "She's Jerome's daughter."
Alasdair pondered in silence for several seconds, the basket clutched in his hand, the baby wailing pathetically.
"I shall go to the rectory this minute," he said.
"Go," Ivy sobbed.
Alasdair waited a moment longer, then planted the basket on the bed. "I shall."
The next second he was gone, door closed behind him.
Ivy pulled baby Anne from the cot and clutched her to her breast,

both she and the little girl weeping piteously. Bronagh returned straight away without knocking.
"My lady, we must go now – right now."
"I told him," Ivy whimpered. "He's gone to confront Jerome."
"I know – I heard it all. He'll be back here in a few minutes, and we must be gone by then. Let's get you dressed."

Stavely was furious – that much was clear. And this time Sam Dunn heard every word.
"How dare you come to my house and accuse me of such a thing!" Jerome hissed, feigning outrage. He felt like a rat cornered by a savage dog.
"You're the father! She swore it on the child's life!"
"I will not enter into discussion with you, Mr Stavely. And I will not have you address me in such a tone!"
"You deny it then?"
"Of course I deny it. Withdraw your accusation."
Alasdair paused a second. "Why would she tell me it was you?"
"How can I say? I know nothing of the matter."
Stavely suddenly realised he might have been outwitted. He was out of the house; he'd given his wife a chance to escape…

They'd almost managed it. Ivy and Bronagh were in their coats, ready to go, when he stormed into the bedroom, face dark as thunder.
"LIAR!"
Ivy was dumb with terror. She raised her hands in defence and positioned herself between her husband and the child's basket.
"Sir, please," begged Bronagh.
Alasdair rounded on the maid and gestured at the door. "OUT, YOU!"
Bronagh glanced at her mistress, dread clutching at her heart. "My lady?"
But Alasdair attacked the girl, striking her about the face and body. "You knew about this! Ungrateful slut!"
"Have mercy, sir!" she wailed, breaking free, escaping through

the door.

"As for you," Alasdair growled at Ivy, "this is done!" He thrust her aside and grabbed the basket by the handle.

Ivy went mad, pummelling him with her fists. When that had no effect, she picked up a candlestick and beat him with such fury he might have been killed had he not managed to cover his head with his arm. Hurriedly setting down the basket, he turned and retaliated, punching her once, squarely in the face. Ivy fell back, stumbled against the bed, and collapsed to the floor, her nose a mess of blood.

"Bitch," Stavely spat. He retrieved the basket and left, locking the door and slipping the key into his pocket.

Bronagh, Sullivan and Mrs Drewitt stood on the landing outside the bedroom. None of them spoke, but all stared at Alasdair with shocked expressions. There was complete silence for a second, then Ivy began to shriek and hammer on the bedroom door, screaming as if she were on fire.

"You may leave my employ if you wish," Alasdair told his spectators. "But you'll regret it if you stand in my way." He pointed to the locked door. "No-one enters here until I return. My wife needs to learn from her errors. If I find this door has been opened, dismissal will follow – with no reference or pay." He hurried past them down the stairs and out of sight.

"Oh my God!" Mrs Drewitt muttered, hand covering her mouth. "We can't let him... What's he going to do?"

"I'll follow him," said Bronagh. She descended the stairs, carefully scanning ahead, wary of attack. The master wasn't in the hall; his coat was gone. She turned and glanced up at the landing to where Mrs Drewitt stood watching her. Ivy's screams rang through the house. Bronagh could hear Sullivan trying to console her, speaking through the door, but couldn't make out his words. She turned to the exit, opened the door and stepped down into the street.

It was starting to rain. Bronagh cast her eyes left and right, hoping to catch sight of Alasdair, but carriages, people walking, children playing obscured her view. He wasn't in sight; she had to choose which way to go. King Street was close to the town's western edge, so it seemed likely he'd walked east – but it was a guess. She hurried on her way, hoping to follow close enough to see where he'd take the baby.

A dead horse lay rotting on its side at the end of the road, just before the junction with Crown Street, abandoned where it had died, left to decompose sufficiently to be hacked up and carted away. Bronagh crossed the street, trying not to gag at the stink.

It was raining harder. People hurried by, splashing through the gathering puddles.

Turn right onto Crown Street, or left onto Copper Street?

Suddenly, she saw him, striding away from her on Crown Street, nearly at the Market Place.

He's going to the church, she thought. *He's taking Anne to the rectory.*

Bronagh hurried on for about fifty yards until she was close enough to follow without fear of losing him but sufficiently distant to remain unseen. He was walking purposefully, the basket with the child hanging from his right hand. People passed him in the street, and no-one gave a second glance, the swaying motion having lulled the little one to silence. Passers-by probably thought he was carrying fruit, eggs, bread, or something else that didn't need the love of a mother.

Two or three minutes later, it became clear that the rectory wasn't his destination after all, as he passed by the church on the north side rather than the south.

It's the workhouse, thought Bronagh. *The horrible brute's taking a four-day-old baby to the workhouse.*

And so it was. He approached the great oak door, set the basket down in the wet, and pulled the bell chain. Bronagh watched from an alleyway about thirty yards distant and was horrified to see him withdraw, leaving the basket unattended so that any stray dog might take an interest, sniffing out something tasty to gnaw.

My God! I don't believe it! she thought. *That's inhuman!*

She was fixed to the spot, wide eyes on the basket, praying for someone to open the door and take it in. Too late, she realised he'd seen her – and was striding towards her. She backed away in fright, mouth agape, hands raised to defend herself.

"You little trollop!" He gripped her by the arms, forcing her back into the alley. "You deceitful, worthless scrap of flesh!" Slapping her hands aside, he struck her across the face.

"Please!" she begged, desperate. There was no-one in sight, no-one to help. He could kill her.

"How dare you spy on me!"

Stavely caught her under the chin and banged her head against the alley wall so hard she thought her skull cracked.

"It's the end of you!" he growled, slamming her head into the stonework again. A thousand stars burst in Bronagh's vision. Her muscles weakened, and she weed herself, droplets of warmth spattering her legs.

"Your position in my household is rescinded," he snarled. "If I catch you there again, I'll have you arrested. Do you hear me?"

"Yes sir, yes," she sobbed, collapsing against the wall, sinking, squatting, humiliated.

"I mean it," he spat. "You will not see my wife again."

"Yes sir," she repeated, head cradled in her hands. She listened to his footsteps echoing away, then slumped forward in the drenching rain, sobbing, wretched.

A hole swirled in Bronagh's consciousness, a whirlpool that, for a few minutes at least, entirely swallowed her self-awareness. Her mind spiralled into the dark, out of harm's way, and she lay still, terror dissolving, tears emptying, calming, calming…

Down, stay down, safe…

Her breathing steadied. Shattered thoughts began to reform. After a while, she was able to sit upright, staring at her knees, water drops suspended on the tip of her nose, rain channelling through her hair.

Anne, she thought. *I have to see what's happened to the baby.*

She pressed herself upright against the wall and began to gather her strength. There was blood in her mouth, her teeth having ruptured her lip when he'd struck her. She tested the wound with her tongue, silently damning him to hell. Someone walked past in the nearby street, and Bronagh's concern about the baby returned with full force. Anyone could take the child.

The basket was gone. Bronagh pulled the bell chain and waited. People were moving inside; she could hear their voices. A moment later, the door opened, and a grimy, overweight, middle-aged woman stood there. "What?" she asked, frowning at the bleeding, bedraggled visitor.

"There was a baby here a few minutes ago," Bronagh managed through her thickening lips.

"Is it yours?" asked the woman.

She felt a rush of relief; they'd retrieved the basket, taken the child in. "No," she said. "Not mine."

"Whose then?"

Bronagh thought quickly. If she revealed the mother's identity, they'd return Anne to the house. Alasdair's next method of disposal might be even more drastic.

"I can't tell you," she replied. "I just wanted to know she's safe."

"Sure she's not yours?" asked the grubby woman, suspicious, narrowing her eyes.

"She's not mine, I promise," Bronagh replied. She looked intently into the woman's eyes, silent for a moment. "Her name's Anne."

"And how do you know that?"

"Anne," Bronagh repeated, withdrawing. "Take care of her."

She turned and hurried away past the church. The grimy woman watched her for a few seconds, then shut the door.

Linda Drewitt and her husband faced each other in the Stavelys' kitchen. She was fifty-nine, Kenneth three years older. Both had served in the house for nearly twenty years, Linda as housekeeper for most of that time.

"I don't want to stay here," she said.

"Where would we go?" Kenneth protested. "We'd find no work elsewhere – not at our age. This is our 'ome."

"I can't believe how bad things are," said Linda. "You should have seen him – he was savage! And taking the baby, too. The child's not even a week old."

"'E'll 'ave took it somewhere safe," Ken replied. "'E ain't no monster."

Linda stared at her husband. "Isn't he? Are you sure?"

He tried to reason with her. "Look, I don't know what 'appened – none of us know what 'appened. A man 'as a right to be upset if…"

"You don't believe her then?" Linda cut across him. Ken threw up his hands, gesturing, *who knows?* Linda continued, "We've known her since she was a little girl. She's a sweet, kind little thing. She wouldn't lie – 'specially to her husband."

"You really believe there were an intruder?"

"I do."

Ken sighed. "Well, look. We can't go; we'd be livin' on t'streets."

"It's poison to stay here!" she responded.

"Even so," her husband argued. "We *cannot* go. We 'ave to stay and 'ope things get better. Look at it this way: you might be able to 'elp 'er if you stay. You and Bronagh – you're prob'ly t'closest she's got to friends…"

Alasdair produced the key, inserted it into the lock and let himself into the room.

Ivy sat on the bed, staring at him, her huge eyes sulphurous, her face an angry red, blood-smeared, bruises forming.

"What have you done?" she asked, voice low.

"The child's gone," he said. "You'll never see her again."

Ivy gazed into her lap, lips trembling. "I hate you."

"You'll remain in your room until we leave for our new home," Alasdair replied. "The arrangements are made, passage booked."

"I won't go."

"You're my wife," he said. "You'll do as I say."

"I want Bronagh."

"She's been dismissed," said Alasdair.

"You've killed me," Ivy muttered, eyes sightless, head dipped. "All my dreams…"

"Things will get better," he replied. "Don't try to leave this room."

Then she was alone again, dead inside, scooped out, her soul torn to pieces.

Frank Sullivan stood in the doorframe, barring Bronagh's way. "I can't let you in. The master's denied you entrance to the house. I'm sorry."
"What about my things?" she pleaded.
"Give me an address. I'll have them sent on."
"But I don't have anywhere to go."
Sullivan squinted at her face. "Did he hit you?"
"Yes," Bronagh replied. "I thought he was going to kill me."
Sullivan sighed, lifted his eyebrows and shook his head.
"The baby? Anne?" Bronagh began.
"What about her?"
"She's in the workhouse. He's taken her to the poorhouse."
Frank felt relieved; he'd thought the master might actually have killed the child. "Alright," he said quietly. "We'll let it remain there for now."
"Will you tell Lady Ivy?"
Frank wasn't sure that was a good idea but replied, "Yes, of course. What will you do now?"
Bronagh held his gaze, then lowered her eyes and said, "I have someone to see."

The girl was in considerable distress; it was obvious. Her coat and hands were filthy as if she'd fallen in the mud, and her face bore the marks of assault.
"Miss Duffy," Sam Dunn frowned.
"I need to see the rector," she replied.
"I'll ask if he'll accept your visit," said Dunn. "Step in out of the rain."
She did so, wringing her hands in anxiety as he went off to announce her; anxiety for the child, for her mistress, for herself. Dunn reappeared a moment later, indicated she should follow him and led her to the study. He smiled at her as she passed inside, then closed the door and listened. The girl was more

desperate this time, her voice carrying clearly. The rector's voice too, a little elevated as he tried to calm the young woman. Dunn heard almost everything.

"Your daughter's in the workhouse, Reverend Ottershaw – *in the workhouse!*"

"But I thought we had nearly a week…"

"It was a trick!" Bronagh replied tearfully. "He wanted her to believe she had a few days – to get my lady's guard down so he could take Anne away."

"How is she? I mean Ivy," asked Jerome.

"Dreadful," the maid sobbed. "More broken than I can say."

Jerome sank into a chair, head in his hands. Bronagh settled opposite.

"What will you do?" she asked. "Will you rescue her?"

"The baby?" asked Jerome.

"Yes," Bronagh replied. "Your daughter – for which you have responsibility."

The rector's mind tumbled rapidly through the options. He could take the child to the kind couple in Huddersfield. But then the workhouse matrons would want to know why this particular girl. Would they suspect? It might be risky. But if he could somehow get Ivy free so she could identify herself as the mother, he could then take them away, all three including Bronagh, and preserve his fantasy of keeping a secret family.

He looked at the young woman. "Is it still possible for you to free Ivy?"

She shook her head. "No, sir. I've been dismissed and barred from the house."

"The butler then?" asked Jerome. "Sullivan, isn't it? What about Mrs Drewitt?"

The maid shook her head again. "I don't think so."

"Then how?" asked Jerome.

"It'll have to be you, sir," said Bronagh. "You'll have to go and confront the master."

The thought horrified him. "Me?" He jabbed a finger at his chest. "It'll be an admission of guilt. I'll be opening the church to scandal. No. I can't do that."

She leaned forward and implored him. "You can. You can say you've heard of his cruelty – that you believe her life's in danger. You can say you intend to take her away to protect her…"

He broke in as she was speaking: "He's her husband. He has authority. Nothing I can say will force him to give her up."

Bronagh stood. She wasn't getting anywhere; he was a coward. "Then her blood's on your hands, Mr Ottershaw – the baby's too. Shame on you."

Jerome got to his feet. "Wait, wait… Look… Miss Duffy. If there was anything I could do…"

"I'll tell you what you can do," said Bronagh vehemently. "You can give me a hundred guineas, so I can pose as Anne's mother and take her away."

Jerome's eyes popped wide open. "You?"

"I'll take the baby and set her up in a good life with me – until you find a way to free my lady."

His thoughts whirled. "So, you'd take her…where exactly?"

"A hundred guineas will buy security for a long time."

"You'd let me see the child?"

"Of course."

He pondered, nodding. "It's a good idea. Ivy must know – somehow, Ivy must know."

But Bronagh was shaking her head. "No-one knows you're Anne's father except me. I can't get a message to my lady, and there's no-one I can trust."

"Alright," said Jerome. "We must get Anne first and worry about her mother later."

"You'll give me a hundred guineas?"

"I will," Jerome answered. "But I don't have such an amount in the house. I'll need to obtain it from my solicitor tomorrow. You have somewhere to stay tonight?"

She replied that she didn't, so Jerome went to his desk, produced two guineas from a cashbox in his drawer and handed the money to her.

"Take this," he said. "Get a room at The Rose. We'll meet

tomorrow, and I'll give you the money."
She looked at the two coins in her hand. "Alright. I'll come again tomorrow. Same time."
"A little later," he said. "So I can be sure to have what you need. Come to the church – not here."
"You won't trick me?"
"No. I want this as much as you do. Let's say six o'clock tomorrow."
"I won't try to get Anne until I'm sure of you," she said.
"Yes," Jerome replied. "It's the first step. You'll live at The Rose until I've arranged somewhere more permanent."
Bronagh was relieved; there was a path through this horror after all. "Six o'clock tomorrow," she nodded.
"Six o'clock," Jerome echoed, ringing for the butler.
The rain had stopped, but the sky remained overcast. Sam Dunn stood at the rectory door and watched Bronagh till she was almost out of sight.

9. Cold

Ivy sat on her bed all day, silent, motionless, ignoring Mrs Drewitt's pleas that she should eat something or at least drink a cup of sweet tea. Her breasts hurt, swollen with unsuckled milk. She was still dressed in her coat as if her attempt to escape was only paused rather than utterly confounded. Hope had gone; there was no-one left. Jerome, Bronagh, Anne; all were lost to her. She was haunted by images of her mother and father, the former dead, the latter far away, leaving her abandoned, building a new family for himself across the ocean with his dusky young bride. Ivy was alone. There was no point in continuing. She'd reached the cliff at life's edge and was looking out into Eternity's dark sea.
Night came, and still she sat there. Midnight, one o'clock. At two, she rose, undressed to her shift and opened the little casement window, letting in the chill nocturnal air and welcoming the stillness of the slumbering town into the stillness of her mind.

The day's rainclouds had cleared away, and the stars, ruled by a bright half-moon, pierced night's vast canopy. Ivy looked down into the yard at the rear of the house, a drop of about thirty feet. Gripping the window frame, she hauled herself up and squeezed through the narrow opening, bare feet on the ledge. No-one was in sight. A few faint lights burned in distant windows, but nothing moved. She looked up at the sky and wondered if God knew she was squatting there in the last seconds of her life. But there was only coldness. The stars would remain unchanged after she died. The extinguishing of her tiny spark would mean nothing, her sadness as if it had never been.

She let go.

Her left shoulder and head hit the ground first, body like a discarded rag doll. Internal organs ruptured and bones cracked, the bitter red wave of agony igniting, flooding her senses – but life persisted.

After a while, vision clearing, she pressed herself up on her hands and managed to get to her knees, then to her feet, trembling, steadying herself against the house wall, head hanging forward. Nausea took over; she collapsed once more and retched, vomiting blood.

Ivy remained on her hands and knees for several minutes, pain searing her insides, long threads of bloody saliva dangling from her lips. *I'm out of the house,* she thought. *I'll go to Jerome. He'll help me.*

So she struggled to her feet and stood for a while, left arm outstretched, supporting herself against the stonework. Breathing was painful, but after a moment, she felt strong enough to stand unaided. The rectory was on the other side of town. Not far for a healthy body. But for her? She took a step. It was possible. Another. And another...

In her shattered state, the journey took more than forty minutes. A few people lingered in the open despite the lateness of the hour – men mostly, and prostitutes. They stared with curiosity at the bloodied, broken young woman, dressed in almost nothing, inching through the filthy streets in her bare feet. But none offered help. It would have been easy for one of the observers to drag her into a passageway and abuse her, but none did. Ivy was only subliminally aware of them; it took all her strength and determination to keep going. She hardly noticed the stench of the dead horse at the top of King Street as she trod through the slime of its decay before turning onto Crown Street and up towards the Market Place. A knot of drunks on Wool Shops ceased their hilarity as she passed, watching her in silence. When she was well east of them, one called, "Come and have a drink with us, Missus."

"And the rest!" another shouted, and the group burst into laughter, their good humour revived.

On to Causey Top, then Causey. Skirting the churchyard on her left, she finally arrived at Vicarage Lane, the rectory coming into view on her right.

She halted, chilled to the core, shivering, pale, and looked up at the house where her lover lay with his wife, warm in their bed. The windows were dark. Which was theirs? Perhaps she'd catch him looking out at her…

But there was no face. The house seemed like a hand raised against her, to keep her away. She dropped her gaze, eyes unfocused, stood motionless for a minute or so, then continued to the end of the road, down Bury Lane, across the bridge and out into the open countryside.

10. The Transaction

Jerome drew his hundred guineas on Tuesday morning.

"Quite a weight of coins," said Carl Lipscombe, solicitor, himself a man of considerable mass. They'd become acquainted soon after Jerome took up his position at the parish church, and in that time, Carl had increased in size by about a third. The rector reckoned his friend must weigh more than thirty stone.

"I expect it is," Jerome nodded. "Bag?"

"No," Carl replied, glancing across his desk at the clergyman. "I thought I'd put them in your hat."

Jerome chuckled.

"Got some girl in trouble, have you?" the solicitor grinned.

"Tut-tut," Jerome replied. "Your question betrays your own preoccupations."

"I pity you men of the cloth," said Carl. "Having to beg forgiveness every time you catch sight of a plump pair of…"

"Yes, yes, yes," Jerome cut him short. "Hand over the gold, and I'll be on my way."

"As you wish," Carl replied, wholly unchastened. He produced a stout leather bag from a drawer in his desk, swept the coins into it and hefted it across the table to the rector. "There you go. Don't fasten it to your wrist if you intend to jump off a ship."

"Thank you, Carl," said Jerome, standing, lifting the bag by the neck. "You must come for dinner again."

The solicitor raised his eyebrows; a rectory banquet was a delicious proposition. "Dinner with your good self and the lovely Celia. Yes, yes, that would be most agreeable." He pursed his lips and shook his head. "You're a lucky man, Ottershaw, to have a woman like that."

"Bring a friend," Jerome smiled.

"I will," Carl answered. "I'll select a lady from my hareem."

The sky darkened in the late afternoon, and a storm settled over the town, thunder firing like heaven's artillery, jagged lightning tearing the sky apart. Jerome waited in the church's gloom, rain pounding on the roof.

Bronagh arrived a few minutes before six, sodden, shaking water off her coat.

"Did you get it?" she asked.

"Of course." He handed her the bag.

"Oh my goodness," she muttered, almost dropping it. "I didn't realise it would be such a weight."

"Sorry," Jerome murmured. They stared at each other in silence for a second or two. "So, you'll get the baby?"

"Yes. Will you come with me?"

"I will," he said. "We'll go in the morning. With luck, the weather will have cleared by then. We'll arrive calmly, in the light of day, unhurried. I'll tell them you left the baby because you were upset – you'd been thrown out of your home. But now a friend has taken you in, so you and your child can be safe together. I'll endorse you; they'll trust me."

"Thank you," Bronagh whispered.

"You have a room?"

"Yes," she replied. "At The Rose, like you said."

Jerome nodded. "Good. You'll keep Anne there until we can get Ivy safely away."

"God bless you," said Bronagh. Without warning, she stepped forward on tiptoes and kissed him on the cheek. "God bless you."

"You're a good girl," he breathed. "Faithful, resourceful."

She smiled. A tear ran down her face, dully glistening in the low light.

"Half past ten," said Jerome. "We'll meet at the workhouse door."

"Half past ten," she repeated. "Can I stay here a while? To pray – to give thanks for you and for what you've done for my lady, for the child, and for me."

Jerome was touched. He wanted to embrace her but restrained himself. "Of course you can," he murmured. "Stay as long as you like."

Then he was gone, striding down the nave and out through the south porch. Bronagh selected a pew, knelt, and joined her hands in prayer, eyes closed.

Sam Dunn waited in the dark at the west end, heart hammering in anticipation.

11. The Child and the Mother

The storm passed during the night, and Wednesday dawned bright and clear. Jerome breakfasted with his wife and was in the street near the workhouse before half past ten. A few parishioners walked by, singly or in pairs, greeting him as they went.

"Good morning, Rector. Nice day after yesterday's flood."

He raised his hat. "Indeed so, Mrs Fulham. How's your husband?"
"Miserable as ever."
A quarter to eleven; no Bronagh. Eleven o'clock. Jerome felt self-conscious and began to pace back and forth. Half past eleven. Could it be that the girl had simply absconded with the money?
At noon, exasperated, he took matters into his own hands and rang the workhouse bell. Nearly half a minute passed as he stood, sighing, impatiently tapping his foot, before chubby middle-aged Celestine Pringle, one of the nannies, opened the door.
"Reverend Ottershaw," she beamed. "Should we 'ave been expectin' thee today."
"No," he replied. "There was a child abandoned here a few days ago – a newborn. I'd arranged to meet the mother this morning, so we could take her off your hands. But she's...not here. I don't know why. She seemed so keen when I saw her yesterday..."
Celestine nodded, eyeing him carefully. "Would that be Anne? Little girl in t'basket?"
"Anne," Jerome acknowledged. "I believe so, yes."
"Would you care to wait inside?"
Jerome hesitated, wondering if he should remain in the street, or perhaps go down to The Rose and see if she'd overslept. He looked once more in the direction from which he imagined she would come. "Er..."
"I'll leave someone on t'door to watch out for 'er," the woman suggested.
"Very well," Jerome agreed, stepping inside. "I think that would be appropriate."
Celestine leaned back and shouted along the corridor, "Doll! Mind t'door."
A scrawny woman in her thirties scurried towards them from a chamber some distance away and dropped a rapid curtsey to the rector.
"We're expectin' a woman," Mrs Pringle told her. "Mother o' baby Anne. Keep your eyes peeled."
Doll acknowledged the command, launched herself into the

street and took up her position as lookout.
"Would you care for a glass of ale?" asked Celestine, leading the rector along the passage. "It's that time o' day, and you've been waitin' in t'sun a while, I think."
"Yes," Jerome nodded. "That sounds like a good idea. Thank you."
"You can sit wi' t'child while I get glass," said Celestine, leading him into a room containing eight cribs. She put her finger to her lips, but Jerome was already quiet, trembling, conscious of the fact that he was about to see his daughter for the first time.
The nursery was hushed. Most of the cribs were bare, only three appearing occupied. Celestine led the rector to a cot in the far corner and whispered, "Here she is, sweet little thing. Can't be more than a week old."
And there she was, lying on her back, covered up to her chin, confused grey-blue eyes darting here and there. Jerome pressed his hand to his mouth, eyes swimming. He couldn't speak without betraying his emotion.
Celestine watched him and guessed. "Take a seat, Rector. I'll leave the two o' you alone. Give us a few minutes for your ale."
Then she was gone, the door closed.
Jerome's lips quivered. "Anne. My little girl..." He reached out a finger and touched her face, soft and warm. The baby seemed to look at him. "I'm your daddy," he sobbed. Reaching beneath the covers, he found a tiny hand and pulled it free, amazed at how tightly the fragile digits gripped his forefinger. "Oh, my goodness," he breathed, a tear breaking free and coursing down his cheek. "Oh, my goodness..."
The door opened, and Celestine reappeared, tense and anxious. "Rector."
Jerome gently peeled the child's fingers free and dried his eyes. "Yes?"
"They're askin' for you at church. There's a body – a woman."
Dread took hold of him. "What? Her mother?"
The woman shook her head. "I don't know."
"Oh no," Jerome muttered, hurrying towards the door. "Please, God, no."

She'd been found in a field half a mile south of the town, cold, stiff with death, lying face down in the mud, arms raised either side of her head. It was Dan Morris who discovered her – his foxhound, Crafty, actually, barking, tail wagging; something worth sniffing at.

It was Dan's second corpse, the first having been that of his sixty-four-year-old grandmother eight years previously. But this woman (he turned her over) was young and pretty. She'd been injured. Her filthy shift was spotted with blood, and her face was dark with bruising. Her limbs were blue where the blood had pooled. Dan guessed she'd been attacked – dragged into the field and murdered. He scanned around for the rest of her clothes but found nothing.

It was a ten-minute sprint to Mo Grayson's farmhouse, the dog racing ahead. Half an hour later, Mo, Dan, and Vic Entwhistle returned with the cart.

"Bugger me!" bulky red-faced middle-aged Mo offered, removing his cap in the presence of the deceased.

"Reco'nise 'er?" asked Dan. Having discovered the woman, Dan felt a little proprietorial, the more so as she appeared to be in her early twenties – the same age as him.

"No," Mo replied, staring at her face. "Can't say I do. She's been 'ere a while, I reckon – day or two, mebbe more."

Dan nodded, then noticed that Vic was lifting the hem of the woman's shift, trying to get a look underneath. He took a step to the right and kicked the bastard hard. "Stop that, tha filthy get! Give t'poor woman some dignity! For t'love o' God!"

Vic got to his feet and lifted his fists, ready to attack. "She's dead!" he cried. "Who's to know? She don't care."

"Pig!" Dan spat, fists raised, feet planted for combat. Vic was twice his age and probably twice his strength, but Dan was a knight, bravely defending the honour of his lady. Crafty barked in circles around them, eager to be part of the game.

"Look at t'pair o' you!" Mo cried in disgust. "Act like men. There'll be people lookin' for this poor woman; mebbe children somewhere, cryin' for their mother – or a father, wonderin' why 'is daughter ain't come 'ome. And all you can do is scrap over 'er. Come on! Get 'er onto t'cart. We'll take 'er to town."

They instinctively selected the church as the appropriate place to carry the young woman, and that's where Jerome found her, lying on an old door the men had set across the rear pews. They parted to let him through, their faces grim, silent. He'd expected it to be Bronagh, but it was Ivy. His heart cracked wide open *("Oh, no, no, no!"),* and he knelt, sobbing, taking her cold hand in his. "Oh, forgive me..."

Vic, Mo and Dan glanced at each other. Mo mumbled, "You know 'er then?"

Jerome sniffed hard, wiped his eyes, and put his head in his hands. "Yes." He swallowed, sniffed again. "It's Mrs Stavely."

Mo was puzzled at the rector's grief; surely, the man must have seen dead bodies before. It was a terrible thing, certainly, an attractive young woman killed, but the clergyman's sorrow seemed excessive. He glanced again at his two companions and sensed they were equally uncomfortable. After a moment, he asked, "Should we get t'constable, sir?"

Jerome nodded but didn't look at them. "Yes. I think that would be the right thing to do."

Mo pointed his finger at the youngest of their party. "Dan, fetch Peter Creston. 'E'll be in 'is shop on Petticoat Lane."

The young man nodded and was gone, Crafty hurrying after him.

Jerome sat on a pew by the body and brushed Ivy's cheek with his fingers. "Where was she?"

"In t'field, sir," Mo explained. "Been dead a while, I reckon. Dan found 'er." He paused. "Was she dear to you, sir? Pardon me if I'm too forward."

Jerome sighed and wiped his eyes again. "All God's children are dear, Mr Grayson."

"O' course, sir." He waited a second or two, then asked, "'Ow d'you think she got there? I mean to t'field. We 'unted round for clothes but din't find nothin'."

"I have no idea," Jerome answered.

"D'you reckon she were attacked?" asked Vic. "Murdered? Prob'ly raped, I reckon, dressed like that."

"'Ave a 'eart, Vic," Mo beseeched in an undertone.

"She'd been…unhappy," Jerome murmured. "At least she's at peace now."

He watched his dreams, his plans, pour down a black well in his mind. *This is a punishment for me. A punishment from God. This woman has paid for my sins with her life.*

"What should we do, sir?" asked Mo.

"Sit, if you would," Jerome replied. "Wait for Peter. He'll want you to tell him exactly how you discovered her."

They sat quietly and awaited the arrival of the constable. Victor stared at Mrs Stavely, his imagination alive with wild thoughts. He wished he'd found her before the others. Even though she was cold and dead…

Less than half an hour later, Dan returned with Peter Creston and Alasdair Stavely. Jerome got to his feet as the newcomers entered the church.

"My wife…" Alasdair muttered, staring at the body.

"She was found in a field," said Jerome, fury rising; "dressed in next to nothing."

"You know there's been trouble," Alasdair glared at him.

"Trouble of your making," Jerome snarled.

"My making?" Alasdair mocked. "Hardly."

Peter Creston had been inspecting the body but now stood and addressed Mo. "Tell me exactly 'ow you found 'er, please."

The story occupied only a minute or two, after which Peter faced Alasdair. "So. *'Trouble'*, Mr Stavely. You better tell me everythin'."

"There's not much to tell," Alasdair replied, eyes flicking between the constable and the corpse. "We were at variance. She had a child by another man. I would not have it in the house, so I made arrangements for its accommodation elsewhere."

Jerome stood tense, listening, fingernails digging into his palms, wanting to fly at this callous excuse for a man. Could he reveal that he knew the child's location, or would that risk rumour? Would it be safe if he told them Bronagh had come to him? He'd have to think fast if he were to fill in the holes in the narrative brought about by her current absence. Where was she anyway? Had Stavely killed both the women?

"You better tell me where t'baby is, Mr Stavely," said the constable.

Alasdair nodded. "I will tell you in private. It's perfectly safe and in good hands."

"So, what 'appened to your wife?"

Alasdair shook his head sorrowfully. "I'd hoped we could put this behind us. She crept out of the house the night before last. We found her window open..."

"*She leapt out of the window?*" Jerome spluttered, horrified.

"Clearly," Alasdair answered.

"Why'd she do that?" asked Peter. "I mean, why t'winder?"

Jerome snorted. "You locked her in the bedroom, you demon."

"I wanted to keep her safe," Alasdair snapped, "safe, until she came to her senses."

"She were found dressed in next to nothin'," said Peter. "It looks to me like she were attacked. We ain't found 'er clothes yet..."

"She wasn't attacked," Jerome interjected. "She wanted to die. She thought the fall from the house would kill her. And when it didn't, she wandered around in the cold until grief finished her off. Or exposure – or injuries she suffered falling from her window." He paused, stared at Alasdair, and hissed, "You unspeakable, merciless ogre."

"I have done nothing wrong, sir," Alasdair returned frostily. He faced Peter. "I hope you're not suggesting I deliberately did away with my wife, Mr Creston."

The constable raised his eyebrows. "If you don't mind me sayin', Mr Stavely – you don't appear to be particularly grief-stricken."

"I am one who does not show his emotions as easily as our good rector." He glared at Jerome. "I wonder why our grand churchman is so upset. Do you behave in this accusatory way to all bereaved spouses?" He stepped very close to Jerome and muttered so the others didn't hear, "She's yours, isn't she, the brat?"

Jerome's nostrils flared; if he'd had a dagger, he'd have gutted Stavely on the spot.

Receiving no answer, Alasdair grinned and murmured, "Coward."

12. Endings

After a day or two of interviews, Peter Creston concluded that no crime had been committed. The whole thing was a sad business, but it appeared Lady Ivy had brought about her own end. He instinctively disliked Alasdair Stavely – a cold, unsavoury fellow – but the town would shortly be rid of him as he was emigrating to the New World to assist on his father-in-law's tobacco plantation. Good riddance. As for the newborn, she'd joined the handful of abandoned children in the workhouse, Stavely having provided funds to care for her there. Hardly generous, thought Peter, but at least the little girl was safe.

Mrs Stavely's burial was a modest affair. She had few friends, it appeared, other than the staff in her own home. Stavely himself attended, of course, but it would be a few more weeks before Sir Percival received news of his daughter's death. The rector clearly found the short service extremely difficult, repeatedly pausing, struggling to keep his voice steady. It was all a pitiful tragedy. Why couldn't people treat each other better? Peter didn't understand why there should be such sadness in the world.

Another horror came to light less than a week later, a horror that had the whole town in fear. A severed arm was found in the Hebble in a secluded spot a few hundred yards before it joined the Calder; the next day, the other arm was discovered – and a leg, hacked off at the thigh. The limbs were swollen with decay, having been in the water several days. Despite a thorough search along the river and in the countryside on both banks, no other body parts were recovered. The town surgeon declared the remains were those of a woman, probably young.

Jerome guessed it was Bronagh. He enquired at The Rose and was told she hadn't been seen recently – hadn't used her room. That meant she'd either run off with the money or had been abducted or killed. He suspected Stavely, but there was no proof. If he made accusations, there'd be more questions: *why* did he think it was her? Had she been in contact with him? Was he hiding something? It all seemed too risky and was likely to focus attention on him.

Sam Dunn was calm, his compulsion satisfied. And he was richer to the tune of a hundred guineas.

Alasdair Stavely dismissed his staff, left the house in the hands of his solicitor with instructions that it should be sold, and took ship for America, where he was later to have his throat slit by one of the plantation slaves, whose young son he'd abused for his pleasure.

Jerome prayed for strength, quickly pulling himself together after Ivy's burial. He had to go on; there was Celia to care for and his flock to lead. *Time heals,* he thought. *But does it?* It had been a mistake to give in to his instincts; someone precious to him had lost all because of it. And there was the child, Anne, growing up in the workhouse with the other orphans. He visited in the first few weeks, months, years, the kindly clergyman suffering the little children to come unto him.

Celestine welcomed him on his visits and observed as he carefully treated Anne no differently from the others – as if she wasn't his daughter. But he couldn't easily hide the longing in his eyes or the sorrow and love in his face. Celestine knew. And once or twice, catching his glance, she guessed he was aware that she knew.

"You're a kind, sensitive woman," he told her once, quietly, as he was leaving.

"I am, Rector," she smiled. "You can be sure of it."

Lovely, kind man, she thought. *A sad, loving father carrying a secret he can never reveal. What a weight that must be.*

And the poor woman who'd been found dead in a field, having

had her baby taken away… So the little one's name was Stavely, or Ottershaw. But she couldn't be so named; that would be scandalous.

"You can 'ave my name," said Celestine, bouncing the little girl on her knee. "Anne Pringle. That's you, my love."

Jerome's visits became less frequent as time passed. It was painful to watch his little girl grow up; he wanted to hug her, to hold her, to rejoice he had a child, to tell everyone she was his. But it could never happen; he'd lose everything – he'd lose Celia. So he began to withdraw, entrusting the pastoral care of the workhouse to his curate.

I must visit her, he thought. *At least once in a while. Just to see…*
But the years drew on, and he delayed again and again…

Sam Dunn disappeared without warning in July 1753. The household woke to find their butler gone, his clothes and belongings vanished. There was no note, no explanation.

Bronagh's mother, Maeve, never heard from her daughter again. She lived alone, frail and sick, in poor conditions in Belfast, and died in December 1750 at the age of forty-nine, heartbroken and confused, wondering what had become of her lovely, kindly child.

13. Bip

Anne Pringle and Pamela Heron squatted opposite each other, building a rickety castle of wooden bricks. Anne was making that sound again, over and over, popping her lips: *bipbipbipbipbipbipbipbip…*

"You're funny," Pammy laughed.
Anne grinned. "Why?"
"You make that noise all the time."
"What noise?"
"*That* noise…" (she copied the action with a degree of success). "That noise. With your mouth."
Anne did it again, then burst into giggles.

"You're funny," Pammy repeated, sniggering. "Bip – that's your name."

Celestine Pringle died in 1754, shortly before Anne's fifth birthday. Jerome had come to think of her as Anne's stepmother and felt her loss deeply.

"Dominic," he said to his curate, "you've bonded with the workhouse women – and the children. It should be you taking the burial."

Jerome knew he couldn't trust himself – couldn't trust his emotions. The staff would be there, and many of the inmates. But what if the nurses brought the children? They'd all loved Celestine, and it was likely they'd all want to attend. How would he cope if Anne was there?

Best keep in the background.

In fact, Anne was not present. The women had decided that only those old enough to understand should be at the graveside. Jerome was both relieved and disappointed.

In the first days of January 1760, filled with the goodwill and joy of Christmas, the rector finally summoned the resolve to visit his daughter again, hoping to find a happy ten-year-old surrounded by friends.

But she was gone – gone to a better life, they said.

"Oh dear," one of the nurses consoled him. "She'd 'ave loved to see thee, I'm sure. She asked after thee a few times…" (Jerome's heart nearly burst at the words) "…but she's been gone a while – last summer, July, August, 'round then."

"What happened?" (blinking moisture from his eyes).

"Two of them went – Pammy Heron and Anne. You remember Pammy? Pretty girl, very pretty, nut-brown 'air, lovely big blue eyes…"

Jerome nodded. "Yes, I believe so."

"They were taken by people from a school…"

"A school?"

"Aye. A new school – for young ladies. On t'coast somewhere

– Scarborough, I think. Sounded lovely – and they were nice people. Come wi' letters of endorsement, assurances. The girls would have new lives, they said – become real ladies…"

So that was it. He would never see her again. Perhaps he could have pressed for the address, but Anne's removal seemed to Jerome like the Will of God:
This is your punishment, your sadness, your suffering. Know that your child is well, but know also that you will play no part in her life. There will always be an ache in your soul, the unresolvable pain of loss, the consequence of your weakness.

14. August 1761

Celia's two remaining guests stared at each other, both quivering with the desire to bicker but neither willing to be the instigator. Lorraine Philips had left the house seconds earlier, explaining she had "an appointment."
"You first," blurted sixty-year-old, impressively attired Portia Ralston.
"It's scandalous!" sixty-five-year-old, equally splendid Agnes Fairchild responded.
Celia had been watching the interaction of her three visitors for about a quarter of an hour. She was as well acquainted with the tittle-tattle as anyone and found the response to the supposed scandal highly entertaining. It was simple enough: Lorraine Philips, an attractive sixty-one-year-old Halifax widow, had taken thirty-five-year-old Desmond Ellerby as her lover. There was nothing wrong with it, as far as Celia could see. Desmond was unmarried, a kind man who'd spent years looking after his bedridden father. The "scandal" arose simply because of the unorthodox age difference between them.
"He must have forced himself upon her," Portia proposed. "Why else would she submit to him?"
I can think of a pretty good reason, thought Celia, hiding her smile behind her teacup.
"A woman of her age," Agnes responded. "Of *our* age!"

"I hardly dare think of it!" said Portia; "what it must be like."

"Yet she shines!" Agnes proclaimed, stretching out the word. "Did you see her face? As if she was actually looking forward to it."

"To what, dear?" asked Celia, brows knit in mock puzzlement, keen to stir her entertainers to further outrage.

Agnes gazed at her, wide-eyed. "To what? Why, to… Oh, my! I feel quite faint just thinking about it."

Celia pretended she'd suddenly grasped what they were talking about. "Oh! You mean…"

"Yes, dear, yes," crooned Agnes, nodding, glad they had arrived at mutual comprehension.

"I am so glad my husband no longer expects such things," said saintly Portia.

"Oh," Celia interjected in her most understanding tone. "Don't you…?"

"Certainly not," said Portia. "We laboured for our three children when I was in my twenties and thirties. After that, we…well, we…laboured for a fourth…" (pause, during which she moved her head in a circular motion, demonstrating how obedient and longsuffering she'd been as a wife) "…but it was not to be. The ordeal became less frequent, and by the time I was fifty or so, George had…set aside his lusts."

Bizarre, thought Celia. *Am I then so abnormal? As for Lorraine and her young man – the very best of luck to both of them!*

"You're not bored with me, are you?" Celia murmured to her husband, warm in bed that night.

"Bored with you, my little peach?" Jerome replied. "How could I ever be bored with you?"

"We've been married fifteen years," she said. "I'm forty-one; no longer the pretty little thing I once was."

"What are you talking about?" asked Jerome, puzzled. "You're still the best-looking woman in Halifax – you know you are. And even if you weren't…"

She waited a moment. "You've heard about Lorraine?"

"Mrs Philips?"

"Yes."

Jerome smiled, tried to restrain his laughter – and couldn't.

"What are you chortling at?" asked his wife.

Jerome brought his mirth under control. "That you should worry about such a thing."

"Aren't you sad we never had children?" she asked.

It suddenly hit him again; this secret he had to keep for the rest of his life, even from the person he loved most of all. His heart swelled, and he clenched his jaw to steady his emotion. "It wasn't to be, my love. Let's give thanks for what we have, and for the good we may – with luck – bring to the lives of others."

"I love you," she said. "I love you as much now as when we first married."

"And I you, my dearest, dearest one. You'll always be as fresh as the morning to me; as crisp and bright as the stars on a clear night. You're my love, and always will be."

That night, against all the odds and despite the many years of failure, Giles Ottershaw was conceived.

STALKER

Early August 1751

Daniel Higgins felt elevated in the Love of God. He'd been rewarded. After all this time. Revenge had been delicious – Felix Poole, defenceless, the target for Dan's righteous fists, the heaven-sanctioned bull's-eye for his boots.

Then the girl, the unexpected prize. It was as if the Almighty smiled on him. *This is your day, Dan. Take her; she's yours; you deserve her.* And Dan had been merciful; he could have snuffed out her life but had shown restraint. Even so, he was, with hindsight, disappointed not to have taken the opportunity. To have killed her, an attractive young woman. What would that have felt like? How easy, how...sublime...the act would have been, his blade opening her smooth pale skin.

It was a lovely night, the stars shining like blessings in the velvet heavens. Dan strode across country towards Gweek, his heart full of love for his wife and children. In a while, when his excitement had calmed, he'd find a comfortable place for a few hours' sleep, but right now his senses burned with life. It had all been so effortless. Neither Poole nor the nameless girl had dared offer resistance.

Dan's job as manager of the Falmouth Royal Mail packet station was a straightforward one, his assistants undertaking all the work – which was lucky, as Dan was also the town's constable (another easy job, run almost entirely by lackeys). Thirty-seven, he'd enjoyed a decade of blissful Holy Matrimony with lovely, plump Grace, eight years his junior. Their union was blessed with three children: Vincent, now ten; Jenny, seven; and happy little Tim, nearly three. While the family was not wealthy in the generally understood sense of the term, they were able to live in reasonable comfort, enjoying the services of a butler, a pair of maids and a cook. The maids were pretty things, young. They stayed awhile and moved on when they wed. Dan liked to interview the new ones, choosing them for their smiles (or other attributes) rather than their references. But he'd never taken advantage of them, never strayed. He'd thought about it, certainly, imagined it in some detail, but he'd never risk his family's happiness or compromise Grace's love. So, what had taken place less than an hour ago was an entirely new departure for him, the realisation of a dark fantasy. And he was completely safe. Grace would never know, and the anonymous girl had no way of discovering the identity of her attacker.

But the girl was only the pudding. The main course had been the opportunity to kick the excreta out of Felix Poole (if that was his real name), a highwayman who'd terrorised western Cornwall for years, a black-hearted bastard for whom Dan had a personal hatred:

In the summer of 1749, Poole had stopped a coach carrying Isaiah and Deborah Collins, friends of Dan and Grace. The robber took a liking to Deb, twenty-seven years old and five months pregnant, and declared his intention to "grace her with his seed" in the carriage while his accomplice covered the driver, guard, and Isaiah with a pair of pistols. Things went badly wrong. Isaiah rose to the defence of his wife and got himself shot and killed attempting to disarm Poole's man. Poole himself then killed the driver, and his partner shot the guard in the back as he was fleeing. Finally, Poole raped the undefended woman.

"Tell everyone you met Felix Poole and lived."

Deb lost her baby.

Poole's notoriety grew to almost mythical proportions: robber, rapist, murderer. His attacks were merciless. He did not hesitate to kill when it suited him, and took whatever he wanted – valuables or virtue.

But it was all over now. The news of Poole's arrest had been delivered by courier the previous Saturday – a note from Jason Matthews, Penzance constable, informing Daniel that the scoundrel was in his custody. "You'll want to see him, I know, because of your loss. I'll tell him to expect you…"

Dan conveyed the news to Deborah Collins, who received it with tears of joy.

"At last! Revenge for my husband, and for me. I'll stand at the foot of the gallows when he meets his end, and laugh at him! Justice has been granted me!"

On Monday morning, Daniel mounted his horse and rode the twenty-three miles from Falmouth to Penzance, keen to cast the first stone.

Jason Matthews sat at his desk in the office adjoining the gaolhouse. Dan settled opposite and waited for the details.

"Zachary Stannard brought him in – coach guard. The driver was killed, sadly – shot in the face."

"Hm," Dan grunted. "Do I know him?"

"The driver?" Jason asked. "Don't think so. Hal Brown?" Daniel shook his head, and Jason continued, "Good man. Left a wife and three kids. Poole fired on him. Stupid – he should have put both bullets in Zach."

Dan was impressed, his eyebrows bearing witness to the fact. "So, your coach guard was shot but caught Poole anyway?"

"Flesh wound – he's alright."

"And the other bastard? Poole's man?"

"Nathaniel Humphreys, thirty-one, from Whitecross. His mother's only son. Been riding with Poole for three years, apparently…"

"Poole told you that?"

Jason nodded. "He did."

"So, this man, Humphreys – he's dead?"

"He is," Jason replied. "Zach's bullet blew a hole in his skull."

"And Poole?"

"Shot in the knee. Tried to get away, but Zach took the driver's pistol and shot the horse."

"Quick thinking," Dan laughed.

"Zach Stannard's the hero now – the man who caught Felix

Poole."

"Is that his real name?"

Jason shook his head. "Who knows? He's not saying; won't speak about himself."

Dan drew a deep breath and exhaled slowly. "I guess he'll be going to Bodmin?"

"To be tried, yes," Jason confirmed. "And hanged, almost certainly. Thank God."

Felix Poole was older than Daniel had imagined; about fifty, swarthy, wrinkled, bald, save for a few lingering tufts of wool-like grey. He sat alone in the gaol room, hands secured behind him, sweating from the pain in his wounded knee, and glared at the two constables as they approached.

"Felix," Jason announced, "visitor for you."

Poole stared tensely at the newcomer, jaw clenched.

Dan pulled up a chair, perched before the prisoner, and pinned him with his eyes.

"Couple o' years ago you held up the stage from Exeter to Penzance."

Felix exhibited no response.

"Friend of mine was on that coach," Dan continued, quiet, calm. "You put a bullet in him. Remember that?"

"Not me," Poole muttered. "Nate killed him – self-defence."

"Self-defence…," Dan grinned.

Felix snarled. "'E'd still be breathin' if 'e 'adn't tried to be a 'ero!"

"Hero!" Dan cried. "He was trying to defend his wife!"

Poole's face registered disgust. "Why you 'ere? Say what you wanna say and fuck off."

Dan nodded. "The assizes are months away. The bruises you're about to get – they'll have healed by then."

Felix hawked and gobbed on the floor. "That it? You gonna untie me, or are you a fuckin' coward?"

"Pardon me," Jason purred, turning on his heel. "Things to do – you know…." Next second he was gone, the door shut behind him.

Dan scowled at Felix. "On your feet, you godless shit..."

It felt good, visiting the wrath of the Almighty on the malefactor. Twenty minutes later, when Poole lay unconscious on the floor, pulped to oblivion, Dan brought forth his old man and urinated on him, giggling with glee.

"There you go! You're no more than the slime on my boots. I baptise thee in the name of my piss – too damn good for you though it is."

Jason was waiting in the office. "Take this," he said, handing Daniel the highwayman's mask. "Memento."

"Thanks," Dan chuckled. "Fond memories forever!"

Then there'd been the strange incident with the horse – a good beast, though not remarkable. Dan was enjoying dinner at his inn when the stable boy approached him with the news that a visitor – a stranger passing through town – wished to acquire the animal.

"Sell my horse?" asked Dan, puzzled. "Why?" He'd owned the creature only a couple of months, so didn't feel particularly attached to it, but he was curious to know why someone would want to purchase this particular mount.

"Dunno, sir," the boy replied. "There's a man – weird-lookin' – been sniffin' round the stalls."

Dan (who'd paid only eighty shillings for his steed) stared at the boy for a few seconds. "Ten guineas."

The lad went away and returned a few minutes later with ten gold coins, which he laid on the table one at a time.

"I don't believe it!" cried the bringer of justice, bursting into laughter.

The stable boy grinned. "I can get a new one if you like – nice one – easy."

Dan shook his head. "No, I'll walk – it'll do me good."

So he strode out early on Wednesday morning, whistling, ten guineas richer, the air heating as the sun ascended. Everything was going excellently – Poole, the horse. Dan felt invigorated, joyful to be alive, filling his lungs with the crisp morning air. Things couldn't get any better. Thoughts of his wife filled his head as he marched along, the distance between them diminishing step by step. He wanted her. When he got home he'd take her straight upstairs and bed her. He could hardly wait.

Three miles, four, striding on. Then he saw the lone girl, crossing his path a little way ahead, travelling south on a pale horse. If he'd been riding, he would probably have set out later and missed her. He thought of the maids at home, the ones he didn't dare touch.

This girl, he thought, *is she another gift, a reward for me?*

He let her pull a few hundred yards ahead, then followed, careful to stay out of sight.

She dismounted at Cudden Point and sat hugging her knees, looking out to sea. Dan took out his spyglass and studied her. She looked thoughtful, introspective, sad. He liked that. She had light brown hair, quite long, brushed out, a little like Grace's. Her frame was slighter than his wife's, more delicate. There was something exciting about the situation; she sitting there unaware of him; he spying on her. The girl shouldn't be travelling alone like this; it wasn't safe, especially in such remote terrain. Better not let her stray out of sight, just to be safe…

She stood after a while and led the horse on foot for about an hour, pausing again at Trewavas Head, where she sat once more. Dan passed behind her, unseen, anticipating she'd continue down the coast. Concealing himself behind some rocks, he used his glass to examine her as she ate lunch.

She's not bad looking, he thought, *not bad looking at all.*

His fantasy distracted him for a moment, his body stiffening in his breeches, and he suddenly realised she was staring at him.

Shit!

He ducked down, cursing himself for his carelessness, and scurried away out of sight, hiding in the undergrowth. A few minutes later she passed by on horseback, casting her eyes left and right, anxious. Dan gave her a couple of hundred yards' start, then followed.

After a mile or two, he began to think of turning back. *(What am I doing anyway?)* He was way off his route home, and although the mounted girl wasn't hurrying, she was travelling faster than he could comfortably walk, and he was frequently forced to run in order to decrease the distance between them.

Where's she going? She has to stop somewhere, or she'll wind up in the water.

Five miles, six, seven. He was getting tired. Eventually, the girl came to a halt at the edge of a wood overlooking a sheep-dotted hillside descending towards the sea. She dismounted, set the animal on a long tether, and surveyed the downward gradient, hands on hips.

She's indecisive – troubled by something…

The girl took a step forward, paused as if she'd changed her mind, then proceeded down the incline. Dan gave her about a minute before approaching the horse.

"Hello," he greeted the animal. "Aren't you a beautiful girl?" The creature was nervous of him and edged away, snorting, ears flicking, but Dan persevered and in just a little time had the beast settled and calm. "Brave girl. Good girl," he crooned, petting it.

If she finds me, I'll just say I'm admiring the horse. He gave the animal a couple more minutes, then moved to the top of the slope and scanned the hillside. A ramshackle cottage was visible about a hundred and fifty yards down, a little to his right. The girl was nowhere in sight, and he guessed she was either inside the building or had walked on to the seashore. Should he follow or wait? He stood with arms folded as the minutes passed and was about to venture forward when she appeared from within the cottage. Dan crouched and watched as she roved about, looking here, looking there.

She's searching for something – or someone, he thought. The girl cupped her hands around her mouth and shouted, "BRITTA!"

The name stirred a memory. *Britta? The so-called witch? This is her house?* Alarmed, he hurriedly looked around, fearful the legend should discover him peeping. But there was no-one.

The girl continued downwards and soon passed beyond his

view. He followed till he was overlooking the shore, then watched as she strode north along the rocky beach and into the mouth of a cave.

Can't follow her in there – not without the risk of being caught.

Dan suddenly realised he was extremely hungry. He'd been so engrossed with the pursuit that he hadn't thought about it until now. Fortunately, he'd armed himself with some bread and cheese before setting out that morning, so he produced the food from his jacket pocket and ate, eyes on the cave mouth the whole time.

The girl reappeared after a few minutes, striding purposefully in his direction. Guessing she was returning to her horse, Dan scrambled up the slope and took cover in the wood.

He'd been right. There she was, greeting her steed. "Come on, Teg. Away to the farm." She untethered the animal, mounted, and set off into the trees.

The farm, thought Dan. *That's where she lives?*

He followed her through the trees and out into the grassland on the far side, but the cover was not so good there, and he had to stay further back, eventually losing sight of her.

Bugger! I've lost her. Damn waste of time – all this way, and I've let her go. Shit!

Buildings were visible in the distance – barns and houses. Dan hurried this way and that, trying to re-establish visual contact with his prey, but it was no good; she'd gone. The farmhouse she'd spoken of could be any of several dwellings.

Damn it!

His bowels were complaining, so he dropped his breeches and squatted in the low undergrowth.

Walking's done me a lot of good; got the guts moving.

He cleaned himself with grass, then uncorked his flask, washed his hands and face, and took a substantial swig of water. He was about to stand when he caught sight of the girl returning from wherever it was she'd been. Ducking out of sight, Dan waited till she'd passed, followed her through the wood and watched as she retethered her animal at the top of the slope, in precisely the same spot she'd left it earlier.

The daylight was fading; it was late, and she was clearly uncertain what to do, standing still, looking down the hill as before. Dan put on Felix Poole's mask and loosed a few buttons on his breeches. He'd need to be ready to take his chance when it came.

But she was moving again, striding down towards the water. Dan removed the mask and followed.

At the shore once more, she turned north towards the cave but passed beyond it, halting about a hundred yards further on. The sun was sliding into the sea by that time, painting the sky pink. She stood motionless for a few seconds, looking around her, checking there were no observers. Dan ducked down, took out his spyglass, set it to his eye, and watched the girl kick off her boots, lift her skirts and step into the water, squatting, allowing the cold to lap at her. Excitement stiffened his loins anew, watching her there, visualising her cleaning herself, the brushing of her hands…

But his entertainment was only beginning. Half a minute later, she stepped out of the water and undressed completely. The daylight had all but gone, but the crescent moon was bright, and the stars were coming out. Dan kept his glass steady in the few seconds she stood naked, and decided precisely how he was going to do it. When she was safely back in the water, he hurried up the slope to her horse, loosed it, and led the beast into the wood where she wouldn't find it. Then he undressed from the waist down and became one with the shadows.

The girl returned about twenty minutes later, and Dan relished her panic as she dashed right and left, hunting for her animal, her fright so tangible he could almost smell it. He grinned; she was trapped, confused, ready to be picked off.

"Teg?" she whimpered. "No… Please have mercy on me."

Dan removed his jacket, set it down by his breeches, and readied the mask.

The girl tried to hide herself in the trees, as he'd known she would. She made herself small and pressed low against a trunk, hoping to hide in the dark, to wait until the sun brought safety. Dan crouched in his spot for about a quarter of an hour, enjoying the tension, relishing the kiss of the cool night air on his exposed flesh. Then he donned his mask, slipped his dagger from its scabbard, crept up close behind her tree, inches from her ear, and whispered, "Don't move."

The girl gasped with fright and leapt forward, but he grabbed her shoulder and pressed his blade against her face almost hard enough to cut the skin. She was panting with terror.

"I'll kill you if you make a sound," said Dan. "Calm down. I'll only hurt you if I have to."

"Please..." she managed.

"You were scared when you couldn't find your horse," he murmured, savouring her fear. "The horse is fine. Nice animal. You'll have her back."

The girl whimpered incoherently as if she were trying to say something. Dan ignored her.

"I followed you," he said. "I saw you down at the water. You're a pretty girl. I've been following you all day – thinking about you."

"Please..."

"I won't hurt you."

"Please, don't," she begged.

"You know what I want," said Dan. "Do as I say, and there'll be no trouble."

The girl began to sob. "Please. No."

"Lift your skirts and lie on your back," Dan ordered, hardly believing it was happening.

She cowered against the tree, clutching the trunk tight. "No."

"I'll cut you if you don't do exactly as I say. I won't tell you again."

"Please have mercy on me, sir."

"On your back," he repeated, "skirts up round your waist."

She turned and looked at him. It was the first time he'd seen her face close up. She was quite pretty – big eyes. "Don't hurt me," she breathed.

"You'll come to no harm so long as you do what I tell you. Do it now."

She knelt, lifting her clothes; then she lay down.

God! She's mine, he thought. *Mine for the taking!* He gazed at her white body, shining in the pale silver light, crept forward and put his hand on her, fingers claiming, penetrating. She flinched but didn't resist.

"That's nice," said Dan, "very nice."

God! I don't believe it! I don't believe it. She's going to let me!

"Pretty girl," he said. "How old are you?"

"Twenty."

He nodded and repeated, "Twenty." She was like the maids at home. If he could have this one, maybe them too?

Now. It was now.

"Oh God…" she muttered and turned her head away.

"Don't struggle," he told her, holding his knife close to her eye. "If you struggle, scream or kick, I'll have your face off."

He spat into his hand, moistened her. And then, incredibly, it was happening – the thing he'd dreamt of all day. He'd worried it might end in disaster, but it was easy. The girl cried while the assault took place, and mouthed something – a single unidentifiable syllable.

Dan had hoped he might last a good length of time, but his excitement got the better of him, and he was done in little more than a minute, gasping.

He lay still afterwards, breathless, deflated. "Thank you," he whispered. The girl opened her eyes and looked up at him but didn't reply. "I'm sorry," Dan murmured. "I'm not a bad man."

"Don't kill me," the girl muttered.

The thought of taking her life hadn't occurred to him until she said it, but now it seemed as if it might be another gift awarded him by God, another element of his reward. Why not? Why not kill her? He'd never killed anyone; this was his chance. He could simply drive his blade into her neck and watch her life ebb away. But something in him pitied her. "I'm not going to hurt you," he said, withdrawing, kneeling upright. "You must have been very frightened. I'm sorry for that."

"Can I have my horse?" she asked.

"Of course," Dan answered. "Stay here ten minutes. I'll tether your horse where you left her." He stood and looked down at the girl, pathetic, broken. "Forgive me," he said, then strode away to where he'd left his things and got dressed. Finally, he fetched the animal, returned it to its place, and set off across country, invigorated, chest inflated with pride.

After a well-deserved sleep under a tree north of Gweek, the conqueror set out cheerfully, arriving home at three o'clock on Thursday afternoon.
"Dan!" cried Grace. "Where's your horse?"
"Sold him!" beamed her husband, "for a mighty profit!"
"Daddy!" yelled Vince and Jenny, running to greet their father.
Dan knelt and took them both into his embrace. "Hello, my lovelies! Been good?"
"We're always good," Jenny replied.
Little Timmy appeared from the parlour and came stumbling forward on unsteady feet, giggling, arms outstretched. "Dadda!"
"My little piglet!" Dan laughed, expanding his embrace to include the boy. "Aren't I lucky to have such happy children?"
Grace beamed at him. "Did you have a good time, my sweet?"
"Oh yes," Dan answered. "Yes, yes, indeed. I had a *great* time…"

THE APOSTATE

York, 1752/53

James Bevington was a fine violinist. In fact, he was the best violinist he knew, having received a firm grounding in the art from his father, who had been an equally fine player, as had his father before him. James's mother, Margaret, recently deceased at the age of ninety-two (God rest her soul), had been a portrait painter of local fame, although failing vision in her final twenty years had rendered her talent useless.

James's wife, Mary (the love of his life), had kept his house in fine order, cooked for him, mended his clothes, managed his diary, and brought up his two sons, Matthew and John (violinists), until they found wives of their own and went on their way.

The family was happy enough, though always on the brink of penury, able to afford a maid only two days a week. Mary considered herself blest, despite the scarceness of money. The house was filled with music. When the boys were young, and James's father (James) was still alive, the singing of four fiddles could be heard in the parlour almost every day. Gentlemen from the minster choir visited frequently to play the spinet and add their voices to the supplication of the strings. Mary smiled, warmed, to spend her days enfolded by such beauty.

But time was moving on. James was gaining years but not wealth. He looked around him and observed how other musicians, other fiddle players, were managing. Some dropped out of the profession early, but others climbed high, became celebrated and wealthy. They were the ones who shouted loudest, who preened themselves most impressively, who had a talent for inflating themselves in the public awareness. Many of these violinists were friends of James. Though they possessed only a fraction of his talent, they knew better how to embed themselves in polite society.

All through his marriage, James had dreamt of a special life for Mary, his love. He'd dreamt of giving her a grand house, a big garden (she was a keen gardener), and servants, so she could have time to read, walk, visit her friends, or do as she pleased. But he was approaching his seventieth year, and Mary was only two years younger. It wasn't going to happen; his dreams were not going to come true. They'd die in poverty as they'd lived. Things were never going to get easier.

His playing began to suffer as he realised ever more keenly the profundity of his failure. The tone remained the same – perfect, lyrical, firmly projected; his intonation never flagged; the notes were rarely anything less than wholly accurate. But a coldness was creeping in. His listeners seemed not to hear it, but James knew it was there – a deadening. There was a hole in his spirit. It had always been there, he realised, ever since he admitted for the first time that he did not possess quite the character that would have ensured success.

"I wanted you to have a nice life," he said to Mary, not once but on several occasions.

"James," she reassured him. "I do have a nice life. I have a lovely life! A life full of music. I have you, and we've brought up two sons to be proud of. We have loving grandchildren."

But James knew she deserved more; he knew he'd let her down. Thinking back over his life, he began to wonder at what point, if any, he could have taken a different route, a route that might have led to a happier outcome. His mother was often on his mind; her thoughtfulness, care and compassion. James's parents had been no better off than James himself, although Margaret's portrait painting sometimes provided a little extra security. They'd always had tea in the house in those days – a luxury James could rarely afford. He remembered those who'd visited to sit for their likeness, and recalled his mother going away from time to time to paint elsewhere. She'd had her own vocation, her own reason to live, that was independent of her husband's music.

Poor Mary had no such gift.

One day, James climbed to the attic of their little house and retrieved Margaret's painting equipment. Most of it was useless; the paints and bladders had dried, and the brushes had mouldered away. But the palette might be serviceable, he thought, and the easel. He set up the easel in the parlour and hefted the useless brushes in his hand, trying to get a little deeper into her mind. His mother had done her best in his boyhood years to teach him the rudiments of painting, but he'd never been more than marginally interested in it. Violin playing had seemed to him the most important thing in the world, the thing that occupied him hour after hour, week after week. This daubing of paints held scant fascination. But standing in his parlour that day, staring at the vacant easel, he heard the first whisper of something honest, something that might save him from the sense of fraud that had (for him at least) developed in his music. He went out into the city streets and purchased what he needed to make a start.

James sat in the parlour every morning after that, staring at vegetables, fruits, pots, flowers, trying to represent them in paint. And not just that; not just to fashion images, but to find something beyond the image, as he'd been able to find something beyond the notes of his music; some spiritual, communicative, living thing. It was a struggle, sometimes infinitely slow, but with the passing of time, he began to feel it might be closer, closer to his grasp.

In the warmer weather he took his easel and canvasses on his back, his bladders of paint slung round his waist, brushes in his pockets, and set himself up to paint the cathedral, or the market, the river. Occasionally, he tramped out into the countryside and painted the landscape, trees, hills, sheep, cows, birds, the sky, the clouds. The holes in his spirit began to mend. He smiled more often and practised the violin less.

One day, he woke and realised he no longer thought of himself as a musician but rather as one who created. Music remained a part of his new sense of self, though it was a small part and no longer the central thread of his life. He politely refused applications from new students and didn't replace those who moved on. He took only simpler playing engagements, turning down those that would have intruded too dearly on the time he spent painting. He fell increasingly out of the public eye (not that he'd made any significant impact when he was in it). He'd been reborn, his life renewed.

Mary seemed as content as ever, although she knit her brows and shook her head.

"Why give up something for which you were respected?"

"Because I no longer respected myself," he replied. "What is the point of living if the ultimate goal is to be only that which others perceive us to be?"

Tuesday, September 4th, 1753, York

"James, what on earth are you playing at?" spluttered James Nares, organist at the minster (we shall call James Nares simply *Nares*, on account of the fact that the two gentlemen share a Christian name. However, our Mr Bevington will call Mr Nares James...).

"I know it's difficult to understand," James (Bevington) replied. "Particularly difficult for *musicians* to understand."

They shared a table at The Starre, flagons of tar-black ale arranged between them like chess pieces, set up for battle.

"You're one of the best fiddle players in Yorkshire," Nares protested. "Probably in the country. You have a duty to your art."

"A duty, you say? I buried my head in music for more than fifty years. I taught, I played publicly, I played in divine worship – I played for you."

"Of course you did. That's why I'm so infuriated with your behaviour."

"I never imagined I'd ever do anything else," said James. "But you know, it's quite possible to be committed to something all your life, then wake up one morning and not be committed to it anymore."

"That is beyond my comprehension," Nares replied, speaking rapidly and with a dismissive shake of the head. "The fiddle *belongs* under your chin. You're well respected, held in the highest esteem. Younger players look up to you; they seek your guidance. How does it benefit them if you declare that the art to which they've committed themselves is something they can forget on a whim?"

James paused, considering the great man's words. "I've been on a journey in this life, a journey of self-discovery. Music took me this far. It was a frustrating journey – hostile at times – with many pitfalls, a lot of hardship, mistakes along the way, even people who actively sought my failure. But I struggled on through it. There were highs and lows, joys and sorrows. Failures and – yes – successes (I suppose, in a way). My music was the vehicle that got me here – all this way, mile after mile, year after year – to this point, the point at which I leave it and travel onwards in a different carriage. This carriage is called *painting.* The journey goes on as it always has, but the means are different."

Nares stared at him. "So you're never going to play again?"

"Of course I'll play…"

"I'm glad to hear it."

"…but it's no longer my first love – and I'll only give it a little time, not the hours of dedication that I previously sacrificed."

"Would you be this fickle with a wife?"

"I'm not married to the fiddle, James; I never was. In any case, you mistake my love. My love is for my muse, not my music. I know now that she has two faces – perhaps there are more."

"Many people will be disappointed with your decision."

"That may be. But I'm happier than I ever was. I never quite fitted this mould, and I'm ever more certain with every passing day that my decision was the right one."

"Never fitted the mould? That's absurd – and a bit insulting, frankly. You're a far finer fiddle player than I am a keyboardist. So where does your *never fitted the mould* leave me?"

"Life isn't a race, James."

Nares was quiet for a moment. "I've seen some of your paintings. They're not bad. But you'll never be as good a painter as you are a musician."

James raised his eyebrows. "That's not the point, is it? Ah, the struggle to be the best – doesn't it make you tired? It frightened me – always aspiring to something that was destined to fail – in however small a measure. There was always the disappointment at the end of the performance – always. And the disappointments built up over the years, one after another, the weight eventually unbearable."

Nares scowled. "Are you God, James? Perfection is reserved for God alone."

"But man is given the opportunity to choose," James replied. "And I bless the Lord for granting me the gift of a new pilgrimage, a pilgrimage I intend to pursue with all my heart."

Nares's frustration burst forth. "You're a *violinist,* for God's sake!"

James smiled, his conviction solid. "No," he said. "I *was* a violinist."

THE MILL

Annabel Epplewith saw ghosts. Every day, all around – a world full of lost souls, of those who'd gone before. She grinned at them, giggled, called out to some, sang, lifted her bottle and drank their health in whatever kind of hereafter they inhabited. Any sharpness of perception she might once have possessed had been dissolved in years of gin.

Annabel had been sold by her mother at the age of eleven to work as a doxy in Betty Drabb's bawdy house on Whitby harbour. Fully embracing her fate, she'd slummed through life without hope or dream, on her back, a convenience for sailors, fishermen, market traders, whoever paid the silver. Annabel gave birth to Rosepetal at the age of fifteen. God alone knew who the father was. Two stillborn boys followed in the next few years.

Rosepetal was raised by the other prostitutes, who passed her round from one to the next for the sake of convenience. Even old Betty herself had a hand in the girl's upbringing, keeping the child close when the women were occupied, wagging her finger at Annabel, demanding the young woman control her boozing, the customers preferring the tarts to be alert. "We're all slaves of the bottle, Annie, but you're the only one that's fell right in."

The child watched her mother as the years passed, never really knowing the parent who was present in body but absent in spirit. Rosepetal was a quiet girl, patient, intelligent, long-suffering. She smoked and drank with the rest of the women as she grew up, joining them in the profession at the age of thirteen. "Only the hand – for now," Betty insisted, dangling the threat of permanent exclusion before the men who wished more from the young girl. "Two more years, then you can do as you please."

Annabel didn't live long enough to see her daughter fully

initiated as a harbour whore. One morning in April 1743, she was discovered face down in the Esk, arms splayed, mouth agape. Was she attacked? Was it an accident? Who knew? No-one had seen her go into the water. Pissed once too often, they said. She was twenty-eight.

Rosepetal hated her name; it was childish and absurd, a frilly nonsense foisted on her by a weak-minded parent. In fact, she hated both her names. Epplewith sounded clumsy, awkward – and Rosepetal felt herself neither of those things. So she banished it and decided to be known simply by the monosyllable, Roz.

She became attractive: slender, dark hair long, eyes green, skin smooth, breasts full, hips round. At the age of fifteen, she was broken fully into The Order by the Lord Mayor's secretary, fifty-four-year-old Will Pratt, who paid handsomely for the delight. Men liked her – even a few women, the more timid of whom attended in men's apparel lest they be found out and made the subject of scandal. Roz was the fantasy of them all and rapidly became as expert as her peers.

Disease was a rarity in Betty's establishment, the clientele familiar (mostly), the girls observant, but pregnancy was an ever-present possibility, despite the use of contraceptive powders and other precautions. Nurse Matilda Little took care of most of that, with her needles, flushes and years of experience, assisted when necessary by Doctor Frank Butterworth (neither Nurse Little nor Doctor Butterworth were quite as respectably qualified as they claimed, although both were reasonably successful in their ministry). Even so, children did occasionally slip through, adding to the little band of bawdy-house infants. By the time she was twenty-two, Roz had endured three terminations.

Diminutive Betty Drabb, a product of the seventeenth century's eighth decade, had been a staunch churchgoer all her life and insisted her girls pay their respects to the Lord God every

Sunday morning at the very least ("For the good of your souls"). So each week, the band of fallen women climbed the hundred-and-ninety-nine steps to St Mary's and nestled at the back, sinners, frowned upon by the vicar. Many of their customers perched further down the nave, their families around them, and the doxies were occasionally rewarded with a surreptitious grin or wink as they passed on the way out. Now and then, a disapproving wife issued a glare.

The girls remembered their clients first by sight (the ginger one, the spotty one, the ugly one, the hairy one, the bent crabby toothless one who should have been in his grave twenty years ago), learning their names only with repeated familiarity. Roz became aware of "the miller" in her middle teenage years. The man – muscular, wiry-haired and unsmiling – would visit in his cart and take away one (sometimes two) of the girls, returning them several days later. Callers usually visited, had their way, and went home – or off to a tavern. But this one, coming and going with a degree of regularity every two or three months, seemed to Roz more intense, focused, never arrived with drink on his breath. His intention seemed structured; it was more than just a quick fuck he wanted.

"Who is that man?" she asked Betty.

"Him? That's Hugo Ash." Seeing no comprehension on Roz's face, Betty added, "From Egton mill."

"Where's that?"

"Upriver a few miles – near Glaisdale. Why do you ask?"

"He's…different."

Betty nodded. "Hm. He hasn't asked after you yet. Don't encourage him. He's a dark sort – bedded his sister, they say. His father used to come here – years ago, soon after I took on this place. Mean bastard – beat the girls. I had him kicked out. He's long dead now; drank himself to Hell."

"So, Hugo – is he mean too?"

"Mean?" (pause) "No, not mean. Cold – he's soulless."

"But he doesn't hurt them?"

Betty's gimlet brown eyes peered at her. "No, he doesn't hurt them. He pays up front, takes them away, brings them back… Bea's his favourite; she's been going with him for years. Why don't you ask her?"

"Hugo?" said thirty-year-old Beatrice Gibson, brushing her hair. "There's not much to tell. It's a ride in the cart – an hour, two if it's rained and the track's shitty. He never says much; it's not a social visit. He's pretty silent – grim even."
"Does he frighten you?"
"Frighten me? No. Why would you think that?"
"Because of the stories."
"You mean about his sister?"
"Mm. And his father."
"Hugo's not violent – not like that anyway. He's…detached."
"What do you do there? At the mill. You're away for days."
Beatrice glanced at the girl, set her brush on the table and shook her head. "What do we do? We do the obvious, the usual stuff. Emma comes sometimes – when he asks for two. He's taken to Jane recently." (Jane Saddley, twenty years old, had joined the troupe only a few months previously.)
"Yes. Jane – I know."
Bea pouted in the mirror. "I'd have thought she was too young for him. Hugo's always preferred more seasoned women."
"So, when you go together – you and Emma – what happens then?"
"Use your imagination, girl…"
"Does he have you both? The three of you in bed together?"
"Not so shocking, is it? You must have done that yourself, surely."
Roz cast her eyes down. "No. No-one's asked that yet."
"Oh, listen to you," Bea mocked. "Still the little innocent."
"I'd do it," Roz retorted, irritated. "I do a lot of things…"
"Up the rear?"
"Of course – when that's what they want."
Bea chuckled and continued with her preening. After a few seconds, she said, "He likes to watch as well."

"To watch?"
"Yes, to watch. Me and Emma…"
"What's the mill like?"
"Remote. Damp. Creaky when the machinery's going."
"Sounds interesting. I've never been in a mill."
"The countryside's nice. It's quiet – there's no-one around. It's not noisy like this place. You can hear the wind – and the stillness."
"That sounds nice."
Bea nodded. "Yes, that's nice. There's not much to do though – except wander about and drink gin. Hugo's no companion. He's only interested in getting his cock off. When he's not fucking, he's working. There's no conversation in him – and if you try to start one, he's likely to say shut your mouth."

The years went by. Roz watched Hugo when he visited, curious about this mysterious, taciturn man, brooding like a storm cloud.
"Why do you lurk nearby when he comes?" asked Betty.
"I don't know. There's something about him."
"What?"
"He's…tragic…in a way…"
"What?" Betty smirked. "And you think you might show him some kindness? Be some kind of haven for him?"
Roz felt foolish.
"He's not interested in you," said Betty. "He don't even look at you."
It was true; Hugo never shot her a glance, didn't show the least awareness she existed.

But Roz was a favourite with the fishermen, sailors, tradesmen, and several town worthies. There was even a stupid boy, Arthur Blake, four years younger than she, who claimed to have fallen in love with her. He made a scene, insisted he'd take her away. But Betty sent for his mother, who arrived red-faced and blazing with fury, hitherto unaware that her son had been firing his seed in a whore house. Agnes Blake boxed her offspring's ears and dragged him home screaming. Betty never allowed the youth inside again. And Roz was glad to see the back of him.

Years passed. Hugo went round and round the cycle of his favourites. He seemed to like the older ones, the women in their thirties, forties, but now and then he took Jane Saddley, just a little older than Roz.
Am I invisible to him? she thought. *Maybe I'm dead. I don't feel anything – maybe I'm dead.*
Then, one day in August 1752, about to leave with Emma Brown, he paused and looked at Roz, having sensed her eyes on him.
"You," he said, voice quiet, a rumble.
"Roz," she murmured.
Hugo stared at her, his gaze penetrating. "Hm." He shook his head. "Not this time."

One Saturday evening in November, following a sweaty afternoon in which she'd simultaneously entertained two young apprentices of a well-to-do tailor, Betty stopped Roz on the staircase.
"Hugo Ash was here today. You missed him."
"And?"
"He was asking after you."
"Me?" Roz felt a thrill of anticipation, peculiar, dark. "Why?"
Betty nodded. "I think, next time…"
The girl's heart was fluttering; she was oddly breathless.
"What did he say?"
"Asked your name – your age."
"What did you tell him?"
"What do you think I told him, stupid girl? I told him your name and your age!"
"So I'm not too young?"
"Seems not. He says…" Betty paused, smirked.
"What?"
"He asked after *the dark-haired girl with intelligent eyes.*" The old

woman snorted. "I'm as surprised as you."

"So, after all these years, he wants you," said Bea, pipe cradled in her hand.

They sat in a group, five of them, on the jetty wall, watching the reddening sky at sunset, the boats, ignoring the men's whistles and suggestive cries: Roz, Beatrice, Emma, Jane, and the new one – May Wilkinson, barely fourteen.

"You don't mind, do you?" Roz replied. "You're his favourite."

"He's big – down there," said Bea. "Just so you know – so you're not surprised."

Emma and Jane mumbled confirmation.

Bea took a pull on her pipe, blew out the smoke, and added, "You won't wear anything while you're there. It's one of his rules. Clothes come off the second you're in the door and stay off till he takes you home."

"You said it was damp," said Roz. "Isn't it cold, going round with nothing on?"

"He lets you wear a blanket if you're cold," Emma told her. "But most of the time you're in bed anyway, either with him or with a gin bottle. Or both."

The sky's blood deepened; water lapped against the jetty.

"It's quiet there," Jane mused. "The quietest place I've ever been. Peaceful. I love it."

"Peaceful," Bea muttered. "Maybe – for some."

"What do you mean?" asked Roz.

Bea flicked her a glance, shook her head slightly. "Never mind."

Christmas came and went, the New year grew, days lengthened. Whitby lay for weeks shrouded in heavy snow. Roz waited, wondering if the miller would come again. Perhaps he'd died. She thought he must be in his middle forties; people died in their middle forties.

"It's been longer than usual," said Betty. "Four months since he was last here. He could come any day – or maybe never. Who knows? Men come and go."

Easter arrived – and Roz found herself on her knees in church, praying she wouldn't be forgotten.

Wednesday, April 25th, noon – three days after her prayer.
"Roz!" Betty called up the stairs. "Get your coat. You're going to Egton."
Her heart pounded. She was almost blind with excitement, flitting about her room, gathering things.
Why, why, why? Why do I feel like this?
She checked her dress in the mirror (a modest pink garment with white frills), donned her coat, picked up her bag, and came charging downstairs like a stupid girl.
There was Hugo Ash, unsmiling, waiting for her, Betty at his side, arms folded, equally cold, slowly shaking her head at the idiot child.
"Slow down, you fool. Get some dignity about you."
Roz halted, took control of herself as best she could.
"Sorry..."
"I should think so," growled Betty. "If the gentleman wanted a riotous street urchin, he'd have picked one from the gutter."
"I'm sorry sir," Roz murmured, descending the last few steps. "Forgive me."
Mr Ash inclined his head, acknowledging her plea.
"Away with you, girl," Betty commanded. "Give a good account of yourself."

It was a bright day, warm, and the harbour was busy. Hugo took her bag and led her uphill.
"My horse is at The Bull. It's eight miles to where I live, and I didn't want to make him climb the hill from the waterfront. He's tired enough already, what with the journey here."
Roz trotted to keep up. "What's his name?"
Hugo turned and glanced at her. "My horse?"
She nodded.
"He's called Horse." He turned away and strode on, lightly swinging her bag in his right hand.

The cart was a simple two-wheeled affair. Hugo paid the stable boy, helped Roz up to the box, then mounted, sat next to her, and clicked the horse out into the street. Roz couldn't help smiling as they re-emerged into the sunlight, riding above the throngs of people, through the smells of the town, the scents of life – fresh bread, coffee, horse dung. She was full of joy, wanted to laugh with happiness. In all these years, she'd rarely been further than two or three miles north or south along the coast, or up to the abbey ruins. She and Bea had once walked as far as Goathland, hid themselves in the church overnight, and struggled home in the wind next day. So this – this riding out of town like a lady, with a handsome man – this felt like a real adventure. She slid her arm through his, and he didn't throw it off.
"I've watched you come and go," she ventured, but he didn't reply, didn't look at her. She swallowed, worried she'd made her first mistake by daring to speak.
The town fell behind them. After a while, he said, "I've seen you there. You've been with Mrs Drabb a long time, I think."
"Since I was a girl," she replied. "Most of my life."
"How old are you?"
"Twenty-four next month," she answered. "I'm Roz."
"I know who you are."
"Should I...What should I call you...if anything...sir?"
"You can call me Hugo. It's my name."
"Hugo..." she breathed.
They lurched along in silence for a minute or two, he staring ahead, she nursing the smile she couldn't shake out.
"Is Roz your real name?"
"Yes," she answered straight away. "Well, not quite. It's Rosepetal."
"Rosepetal," Hugo chuckled, glancing sideways at her, smiling. *They said he never smiles!* thought Roz. *But he is smiling! He's smiling at me!*
"Rosepetal Epplewith," she admitted. "I hate it – I gave it up."
"Hmm..." he mused, nodding. "I like it."

"You do?"
"I do."
"You can use it if you like," she said.
"Roz is shorter," he commented. "But I think I might use Rosepetal now and then…"
She studied his profile against the early afternoon light and realised she was excited, looking forward to being…with him.
"I thought you must like only older women," she said.
"Why did you think that?"
"Bea's your favourite, isn't she? You choose her mostly. She's thirty-eight."
"I like Bea," he replied. "But I like the others too."
"They said you didn't speak," she ventured.
Hugo looked at her again. "The others are not as talkative as you."
Roz hung her head. "Sorry."

They drove through Egton, not a soul in sight, then turned right and followed a path by the river. Shortly thereafter, Hugo branched off, again to the right, and guided the horse down a shallow incline into a meadow.
"Is this it?" asked Roz, scanning ahead, eyes on the overgrown track.
"Soon," he murmured. "You'll see – a few minutes."
Moments later, she caught sight of what she took to be the watermill – dark, tall, forbidding.
"That's where you live?"
"That's it."
She nodded. *Very soon now, he and I…*
"What's that?" she asked, indicating a substantial ruin away to the right, ancient, in complete decay. "Is it a castle?"
"It's the old mill," he answered. "At least, so they say. It's been abandoned for centuries."
The crumbling pile was open to the sky, windows gaping eyes in its broken face. It looked cold, soulless, a corpse left to rot.
"It's frightening," Roz muttered.

"Don't go there," he advised. "It isn't safe."

"Oh, I won't," she assured him.

Turning her eyes ahead, she saw the millpond, its various streams and channels, and a stone building, overcome with moss and lichen, set a few yards from the mill itself. Hugo pointed it out as they approached.

"Stable and turf shed. And the shit-house – just so you know."

He drew up next to the structure, dropped to the ground and helped his visitor down. "Your bag..." (handing it to her, shaking his head, the ghost of a grin on his features). "You know, there was no need for you to bring anything at all."

"I know," she mumbled. "I know the rules."

Hugo freed his horse from the traces and released the animal into a fenced paddock by the stable. Then he took Roz's bag from her, smiled, and gestured towards the mill. "Shall we?"

"Mm," Roz replied, heart hammering.

The mill looked even more forbidding than the ruin they'd passed – tall, dark, damp-looking – and the enormous oaken wheel fixed to its side, black, weathered, water flowing at its base, looked like a machine used for torture, for ripping women to pieces.

Hugo led Roz across a little wooden bridge over the leat stream, turned right, and shepherded her to the cottage, a small two-storey house attached to the mill's north wall.

"Here we are," he said, opening the door. "Your home for the next day or two – or three."

Roz tried to smile, to look pleased, but found she couldn't.

"It's quite safe," he invited, voice low. "I've never killed anyone."

She met his eyes but remained silent as she passed inside. Hugo followed her and shut the door behind him.

"Are you hungry?"

"No."

"Thirsty then?" (leading her forward into the kitchen). "There's gin, ale too. I can boil some water if you like. No tea, I'm afraid. Can't stand the stuff."

"I'm fine. Thanks," she answered, looking round the room

(flagged floor, beamed ceiling, pale walls, two large windows, fireplace unlit, pot hanging on a chain above it, oven to the side, a dresser, table and chairs, cupboards, pans and various utensils on hooks).

Hugo nodded. "Good. I'll make the place comfortable – it's a bit damp. Give me a moment – I'll be back shortly."

Then he was gone, and Roz was alone. She shivered, took a few deep breaths, tried to blink away her sense of unease. Her head was thrumming – a soft whispering she took to be her own nervous blood rushing in her ears.

It's a test. I have to behave as he expects.

With no further thought, she removed all her clothes, dropped them folded on the table, and slid her footwear tidily out of sight beneath a chair.

There. Now wait...

She stood straight, fists clenched into balls, nipples erect in the chill, tiny hairs all over her body sprung to life by the cold. Her breath was visible in the air, like a phantom – the spirit of the mill.

"My God! You must be freezing!"

There he was, sweeping his eyes over her. She'd been concentrating so hard she hadn't heard his steps returning. She unclenched her fists, fingers stretching rigid, gasped, and squeaked, "I... Bea said we weren't allowed to wear anything."

Hugo guffawed at length, rocking, slapping his thighs. Roz reddened with embarrassment.

"Well, that's true," he said, calming, grinning broadly. "But only if the place is warm. I don't expect you to die of exposure in here." He shook his head, profoundly amused. "Let me get you something."

He disappeared and returned seconds later, clutching a large woollen blanket, which he hung round her shoulders, fingers brushing her skin in the process.

"There, that's better."

Roz pulled the blanket tight, clutching it closed at the front.

Hugo stood very close, gazing down into her eyes. He caressed

her cheek with his right hand, then ran a finger along her lips. "You're pretty," he murmured. "Very, very pretty."
Roz parted her lips, allowed his finger into her mouth and bit it, blood thundering in her ears. Hugo slipped his hand inside the blanket and took possession of that part of her that he desired most of all. Roz threw her arms about his neck, lifted her head and met his kiss, the covering he'd provided just seconds earlier sliding to the floor.

The day was dying, shadows deepening. The fire in the little grate had reduced to embers. Roz lay on her back in Hugo's bed, staring at the cobwebbed ceiling. His bedroom, on the cottage's ground floor, was lit by two small windows through which it was possible to see only when standing. He was asleep, snoring lightly, turned away from her, his naked body concealed beneath the bedclothes.

Bea had told Roz that Hugo rarely spoke; she'd been wrong. According to Bea, Hugo never smiled; she'd been mistaken in that too. But Bea hadn't been wrong about his…thing, which was one of the mightiest Roz had ever seen – like the horn of an animal. Cock, prick – the words seemed inadequate. The man had been like a bull in bed, and she'd come, gasping, after two or three minutes of his onslaught. Orgasm during sex was an extreme rarity for Roz, who could usually achieve climax only when alone, with her fingers. And Hugo's own peak had been brutal – intense and prolonged, his ejaculation like cannon fire inside her. That sensation, too, was unusual for Roz, accustomed to feeling nothing (or almost nothing) when her callers fired their seed in her body.

First time I've fucked in a watermill, she thought, grinning, gazing upwards, pleased with herself. The cobwebs moved as if breathing, enlivened by air currents she didn't feel, huddled beneath the sheets as she was. A single lazy fly fuddled about the room, crashing into the walls, protesting in the windows. That sound was still there beneath the creature's buzzing – the soft rumbling she'd previously taken to be the sound of her own

excited blood, cateracting in her ears.
Water, she thought, *the mill stream. Or the wind – maybe the wind's getting up. God! I'm thirsty. And I need to piss. But it's so warm in here – with him. Can't be bothered to get up...*
She turned on her left side and moved closer to Hugo, stroking his bum with her right hand. He stirred.
"You were good," she murmured.
Hugo turned onto his back, took the girl in his right arm but didn't open his eyes. "Mm," he rumbled, drowsy.
"I need a drink," she whispered.
"Help yourself," he muttered.
"You?" she asked. "Drink?"
"You bring it."
Roz turned once more on her back and again stared at the ceiling, steeling herself for the expedition.
Up with you, she told herself. *The sooner it's done, the sooner you can be back in the warm. Up, up, up!*
Determination engaged, she flung back the covers, swung her feet to the cold stone floor and boosted herself upright. Moving towards the door, she was immediately aware of the stickiness of Hugo's semen between her legs.
"Need to wash," she called.
"Next to the kitchen," he answered. "You'll find it."
The washroom was little more than a cupboard, daylight entering through a single horizontal window, grubby, narrow and elevated, making it impossible to see through – little more than a slot. There was a basin set upon a stand, a chair, towels, sponge, soap, two pitchers of water on the floor. A candle and striker stood ready on a ledge by the door. Roz considered lighting it but decided enough illumination remained to get the task done without the extra bother. She emptied some water into the basin and began to freshen herself, but realised as soon as the cold water touched her just how badly she needed to pee.
Fuck! I mustn't piss myself in here. What would he think of that?
There must be a shitpot somewhere, or a close stool. But where? Should she ask him? Indelicate – might put him off. Roz

hurried to the front door, hesitated, thought briefly of putting something on her feet, then rejected the idea in her haste, opened up and stepped outside.

The wind was getting up, the darkening sky well advanced. Roz scanned round about to make sure no-one was in sight, deeply conscious of her nudity, then hurried across the bridge and along the track to the privy.

It was very dark inside, light penetrating only through a couple of holes in the stonework. Perhaps Hugo's custom was to leave the door open. Roz decided to do the same, lowered herself onto the single wooden seat, relaxed, and channelled her water into the bucket below.

Oh…that's good. She sighed, the sound amplified in the cramped cell. *Bucket's dry. I guess he just shits in the field – or the stream.*

It was deeply peaceful, sitting there in the little shelter, surveying the field, the millpond, the trees beyond. Despite the chill air, Roz felt utterly at ease, as if her life had come to rest, a pause between one chapter and the next.

Oh, I could live here. How wonderful it would be…

She shut her eyes, pushed, and was rewarded with one splash, then another; two dry pieces, a weight dropping away, like shedding her old life. Lightning flashed far off, whitening the sky for an instant. She waited – nearly ten seconds, then the rumble, echoing around heaven's vast dome.

This is only the start – there are two more days, maybe three. If he likes me, he'll have me back. It'll be like coming home every time. And perhaps one day – if he likes me enough – if I make him like me enough…

Roz ran her tongue around her lips, holding the dream in her mind. It was so quiet here – the kiss of wind in the trees, the lightest purl of water in the mill stream, distant animals (lambs and their mums mostly, a few cows). There were no people, no bustle, no hurry, no clock to watch.

This is where I want to be.

She stood, took a handful of straw from the stack arranged for the purpose, cleaned herself and dropped it into the bucket.

She'd intended to pay only the briefest visit to the Jakes before returning to Hugo's bed; but now, emerging, standing free under the evening sky, cool air caressing her skin, she decided to extend her excursion.

Into the field then, the grass up to her knees, Roz wound her way to the far side of the millpond and stopped, looking back at the mill, the time-dried ruin, the incline leading up to the lane, the old stone bridge over the Esk. There was not a soul in sight. But if there had been, they'd have seen her there in the meadow, naked as Eve before the apple – and just as happy.

Re-entering the cottage, Roz was instantly aware of the sound – the subdued rustling, whispering, murmuring that seemed part of the place. She'd assumed it must be air moving in the gutters or the chimneys, perhaps even water running under the house, but now she wasn't so sure. It hadn't been audible outside; it was only in here. She stepped into the little washroom and was instantly struck by how much more present the restlessness was in the confined chamber. It seemed to be all around her – in the walls, the ceiling – fluttering, like a hundred butterflies. It troubled her, not knowing what it was.

Was it here before? Why didn't it strike me then? Maybe I was too desperate for a splash to hear it...

Her feet were filthy from outside, so she cleaned those first, then washed between her legs, her rear, armpits, hands, face. Then she went to the kitchen, hunted till she found two glasses, and filled them from the pin barrel Hugo had pointed out, twisting the wooden tap as she'd seen the barmen do in various Whitby alehouses. The liquid was dark, pungent. Lifting a glass to her lips, she drank at length. It was delicious – rich, complex, invigorating. She emptied the glass, refilled it, and carried both receptacles to the bedroom.

Hugo, lying on his right side, watched her as she entered.

"You were a long time."

"Been outside," she replied, handing him the glass and setting her own on the nightstand. He took a long swig as she got into bed. "It's nice here," she continued, snuggling up to him. "I love your house."

Hugo drained his glass, set it on the little table at his bedside, drew the covers around them, and took her in his arms, fondling her body.

She kissed him, looked into his eyes, and murmured, "Fuck me."

"You on top," he smiled.

Roz drew back the bedclothes and found him ready.

"You're beautiful," she whispered. "Beautiful man. I love your cock." She took it in her hand. "Clean, smooth, hard…" Sitting astride him, she ran it into her body and began to move in rhythm. "I like you. I want to please you."

"You do please me," he breathed. "I'm glad I chose you this time."

Lying with him afterwards. Warm, dark, the daylight entirely gone, running her hand on him, kissing his chest, his arm cradling her.

"You can do anything with me," she murmured. "Anything at all. Tell me – I'll do it."

"Are you hungry?" asked Hugo. "Did you eat when you got up?"

"No," she answered. "Too cosy here with you. Later maybe. You?"

"I graze," he told her. "Don't eat meals as such. Not often anyway. The larder's easy to find. Help yourself – treat the place as your own."

"I like you a lot," she said. "Do you like me?"

"Yes, I like you," he assured her.

"I'm glad." She was quiet for a while, then asked, "Why do you sleep downstairs?"

A minute passed. Hugo didn't answer. Roz listened to him breathing, concerned she'd gone too far. "I'm sorry," she muttered. "I talk too much – too many questions. I'll be good – keep quiet."

"I don't go upstairs much," he told her. Roz waited. After a while, Hugo added, "The past is up there."

She rubbed him more firmly, as if to soothe, to reassure.

"You can go up there if you like," he said. "It's empty; I had the furniture taken away long ago."

Is that where you slept with your sister? Roz thought. *Your parents both died here, so they say. Upstairs? Is that it? You don't go up there because you want to forget. That's it, isn't it?*
The questions tumbled in her mind, but she kept her mouth shut, not daring to voice them.
"That noise…" she began.
He turned his head and looked at her. She could just see his face in the gloom.
"Noise?"
"Yes," she said. "That noise – that…whispering."
"You can hear that?"
"Can't you?"
"Yes, of course. But most people can't."
His words puzzled her. "I don't understand."
"Did Bea tell you?"
"Tell me what?"
"She can hear them too."
A chill crept through Roz's body despite the bed's warmth; her hair seemed to stand on end. She lifted herself on an elbow. "What do you mean?"
"The voices."
"Voices?" Panic was rising; her heart began to thump.
"Ignore them. They can't hurt you."
"But…what…who? You mean…?"
"They've been there all my life. They're in the mill."
She shook her head, rising to a sitting position. "What do you mean – in the mill?"
Hugo sat up and took her arms in his hands. "It's alright – there's no danger."
Roz spoke rapidly. "You mean they're ghosts? Fuck! Are you serious? Is this a joke?"
"Ghosts," Hugo echoed. "Maybe – whatever you want to call them…"
"Who are they?" she demanded, interrupting him. "How many? One, two, three?"
"Calm down," he urged. "I don't know how many – lots, I think."

"Why? Why are they here?"

"I don't know. I've never known. They've always been here. Ignore them. Soon you won't even notice them. They're louder in the mill. Here, in the cottage, they're much further away. I'm amazed you can hear them at all."

She paused, wondering if she was asleep. Was this a dream? "They're louder in the washroom."

He nodded. "That's because the washroom's connected to the north wall of the mill."

"Fuck!" she repeated. "Fuck! Why didn't you tell me?"

"I've had thirty, forty girls here over the years – maybe more. You're only the third who can hear the voices."

Roz paused again, pressed her hand to her breast, feeling her heart, willing it to slow.

"You see them?" she asked.

"No," he answered. "Never seen anything."

"My mother could," said Roz, eyes down, unfocused, shaking her head. "I never believed her – she was always pissed senseless. Said she could see them – walking about like people. She used to talk to them…"

Her voice trailed to silence. She felt dizzy, unreal. Hugo put his arms round her and settled her into the bed again, pulling the bedclothes around them. "Are you alright?"

"Can they see us?" Roz asked. "Can they see me?"

"No," he replied. "I don't think so. Who knows? What does it matter?"

Her breathing slowed. She listened; there they were – the ghosts in the mill.

"I'll take you home if you're frightened," Hugo murmured.

"Do you want me to go?" she asked.

"No," Hugo replied. "I don't want you to go."

Roz slept peacefully in Hugo's arms. At midnight he got up, ate, drank, and lit the kitchen fire, the voices keeping him company. The endless whispering had dropped out of his awareness, he'd lived so long with it, but the girl's fright had refreshed its presence. He pulled a chair before the fire, sat, and stared into the flames for an hour, allowing the flickering glow to blank his mind, to wash out his past.

She was still asleep when he returned to bed in the small hours, but he roused her and took her again. It was her job, after all, and he'd paid for her services. He needed this; while he was fucking, he wasn't thinking. So he fucked a lot.

Hugo rose at first light, and finding Roz still fast asleep, strode out naked to the millpond and swam, as was his daily custom. At nine he woke his new whore with a glass of small beer.

"The day's half gone," he complained, grinning, sitting on the edge of the bed.

"Sorry," she answered between gulps. "I must have been tired."

"How do you feel today?"

"Better," she replied.

"Not upset?"

"No. I don't think so."

"That's good. You should eat. There's fresh stuff sent down from the farm."

"Mm. I need a wee."

"Off you go then," he said, rising. "I'll see you in the kitchen. It's warm. The fire's going." He withdrew to prepare breakfast, allowing the girl to get on with her ablutions.

The kitchen remained unblest by the risen sun, its windows facing west, but the dancing fire lent a certain cheeriness. Roz appeared after a few minutes, dutifully naked, and sat at the table.

"Eat," he commanded. "Keep your strength up."

"Can I go into the mill?" she asked.

"If you like. Curious?"

"Mm. I want to hear them there."

"Alright," he nodded. "It'll be warm inside, particularly in the upper levels. You understand?"

She nodded. "Why just me though? You're dressed. Why?"

He chuckled. "Because I pay you – and you do as I say."

"Suppose someone comes to the mill while I'm there?" she asked.

"They'll see me."

"And?" said Hugo. "If you're worried, you'll hide. If you're not, everyone will see why I've brought you here."

So Hugo took Roz to the mill.

She hated it.

The place was gloomy, stifling, and the voices pressed around her head. She cringed at the sight of the machinery on the ground floor, particularly the huge, menacing pitwheel. The black slot in which it rested appeared to her like the gullet of Hell, probably bottomless.

"Alright?" asked Hugo.

Roz didn't reply, squeezing her eyes shut, holding her terror in check.

"Upstairs?"

She nodded. The staircase creaked under their weight, and Roz imagined it collapsing, the two of them falling, crashing through the earth into the gleeful jaws of unspeakable monsters. She could take no more.

"God! How can you stand it? Listen! You can almost hear words! There are children in here, Hugo! Listen to them! Children, crying in fright!"

"This was a bad idea," he muttered, shepherding her downstairs and out into the sunshine. "They're not alive, Roz. They're only echoes, somehow left behind."

"Hugo, it's awful! How can you live with it?"

"I told you. I grew up with them. They didn't even register till I was in my teenage years. It's never been more or less than this. It's constant – it's the voice of the building." He sighed. "This is too much for you. I think you should go home. Get your things. I'll take you now."

She'd gone too far. Her dreams were about to fall in.

"No! No, no. Please. I don't want to go. I'm sorry." She clutched at him. "I…It was a shock – that's all. Look – I can cope with it. I won't talk about it again. I want to stay. Please…"

He hesitated, studying her face. "You're sure?"

"Yes. Please. Forgive me."

He nodded, waited a few seconds, exhaling. "That's an end of it then. Agree?"

"Yes. Thank you."

Hugo smiled and began to unbutton his breeches. "Can you swim?"

Roz grinned, relief filling her like the grace of God. "I can. How cold is it?"

He pulled his shirt over his head. "It's cold."

Her grin broadened; she was saved. "Too cold for a hot girl?"

Hugo kicked his shoes free and yanked off his breeches and stockings. "We'll see…"

So they raced to the pond and hurled themselves in. The water was freezing, and Roz shrieked, giggling, screaming as her body became accustomed to the chill. Hugo was a far better swimmer than she and teased her in the water, diving, pulling her under.

"You're good at this!" he called. "Some of them can't swim at all."

"You're amazing!" she yelled in response. "No wonder you're so fit!"

Afterwards, they had sex in the grass, and she climaxed again, loudly, thrilling under the open sky. It was one of the happiest days of her life.

That first visit lasted three days, and the return journey to Whitby was conducted in almost complete silence, the firmament grey, overcast, like Roz's mood. At the door of Mrs Drabb's, she gazed sadly at Hugo and asked, "Can I come back? Did I do well?"

He smiled, lifted her hand and kissed it. "You were wonderful. I'll dream about you."

She gasped – hadn't expected him to say anything so emotive. "Oh! Oh really? Oh God! Hugo, I love you!" But realizing instantly the confession's effrontery, she tried to backtrack. "No. Sorry – I didn't mean it like that – not in a grasping clingy way – not in a wifey way…" (eyes squeezed shut, head shaking in frustration) "Oh, this is not coming out right…"

Hugo put a finger to her lips, silencing her immediately. "It's alright. I know what you mean."

"I really like you a lot," she managed. "That's all I meant. I don't say that to many people."

"I know," he reassured her. "Come here." She stepped forward, and he took her in his arms and kissed her on the lips. "You'll stay with me again. I promise."

But the next time, Hugo took Bea. Then he took Jane. Then Emma. Then Daisy Bland – who wasn't even fifteen!

God! What does he see in her?

It was late October before Hugo asked for Roz again.

"It's nice to see you," she said as they drove towards Egton. "I've missed you."

He smiled at her. "You've been on my mind a lot."

"Have I?"

"You have."

She nodded but thought, *Obviously not enough.*

Hugo took her to bed as soon as they arrived at the mill. He was as vigorous as ever, but Roz didn't come. In fact, she never came again with him.

Months flowed on – years. Roz stayed at the mill for a few days every four or five months. Hugo was kind enough but showed Roz no greater affection than he displayed to any of them. Roz, Bea, Jane, Emma, May, Daisy and the others – they were just bodies to Hugo. But the cottage was nice – its remoteness, its calm, the fields, the millpond, trees, the wind. As for the voices, they never changed; they were no more than a meaningless babble at the threshold of audibility. She ignored them (as far as it was possible to ignore such a thing).

Once, Roz suspected she'd become pregnant with Hugo's child. She didn't tell him. Nurse Little poked it bloodily out of her one stormy Thursday afternoon.

The gin bottle became her friend, as it had been her mother's.

The red-haired girl appeared in the spring of 1757, eight years old, sharp as a pin. She'd been spying on Hugo, apparently, during his morning swim in the millpond and hadn't run away in terror when he'd confronted her, cockproud, wet skin sparkling in the sun. He'd been impressed with that. And now they were reading books together. Reading? Hugo? Roz could hardly believe it – she'd been only superficially aware that Hugo could read at all. And now? Reading *books?* At the suggestion of a *child?* It seemed absurd; this wasn't the Hugo Roz knew.

Hugo used Roz as the sun came up that day, then left her in bed and went to work in the mill. She lay alone for a few hours, staring at the ceiling, picking at her teeth, masturbating, painting her eyelids blue, tying up her hair before jumping out of bed and tracking down her booze. Then she padded about the house, nude as he still insisted (he could have returned at any moment, cockstiff and fuckhunting). She peered through the windows of the three dusty, musty, empty, spider-infested rooms on the upper floor, draining the bottle as she went, finally prising open a casement and hurling it out. The front door opened as she descended the stairs. Voices *(fuck!)* – the infant probably – he'd said she might come that day, but Roz hadn't expected him to bring her into the cottage.

Flitting across the narrow hallway, she caught her first glimpse of the girl – a flash of flame-red hair.

She saw me! In the fuck-arse skin!

Gathering her wits in the bedroom, easing her unnecessary panic, Roz refreshed her lip rouge, pouting into the little mirror.

There you go, sweetie. Now you'll know what a real tart looks like.

She draped the blanket around her and calmly padded to the kitchen to join the fun.

There they were – Hugo and the little sex fantasy he'd told her about (at least, that's what Roz imagined the child to be – Hugo's little fuck toy).

"Hello," Roz purred, stepping forward, eyes fixed on the child.

Hugo spoke to his titless plaything. "Kate, this is Roz. Roz, Kate."

"Pretty girl," Roz murmured, lowering herself into a chair close to the creature. She reached out and ran a hand through the

child's shockingly fiery locks, dislodging the blanket as she did so and exposing one of her fine breasts to the innocent's gaze. "Pretty girl," she repeated, emphasising both words. "From the village?"
"From the farm," Kate replied, clearly fascinated by Roz's flesh.
"Roz hears the whispers," said Hugo.
Roz was surprised to hear Hugo speaking openly to a child about the voices. She covered herself and said to Kate, "You can hear them?"
"Yes," the child replied. "Can you hear what they say?"
Roz shook her head. "No. I hate them."
"I've had about fifty girls here since Cristina left," said Hugo. "Roz is only the third to hear the voices."
"They're ghosts," said Roz. "In the mill. They're hateful. I only come here because he pays good money." She indicated Hugo with a gesture of her head but kept her eyes on Kate. "How old are you?"
"Eight," the brat replied.
"Eight?" Roz echoed. "Aren't you frightened? Most children would run all the way to Whitby if they heard noises like that."
"I didn't say I liked them," Kate countered.
There was something odd about the girl – as if she was more than she appeared to be. Roz sensed it even in her semi-drunken state.
Hugo gestured Roz away with his hand. "Kate and I have things to talk about. Go and warm the bed. I'll be there in half an hour."
She stood. "Gin."
He indicated the bottle and warned, "Don't get drunk."
Roz collected the booze and headed for the door, blowing Kate a bright red whore's kiss on the way. "Pretty girl..." she soughed, departing.
Out in the hall, on her way to the bedroom as ordered, Roz caught Hugo's apology to the little worm ("Sorry about that..."). *Dismissive, patronising bastard,* she thought.
The arrival of the girl marked the beginning of the end.

Hugo seemed interested only in the young ones after that. Within a week of Roz's return to Mrs Drabb's establishment, he arrived seeking fifteen-year-old Dapple Graham – or, if she wasn't available, any of the young teenage girls. Polly Scuttle went with him that time, her first visit to Egton, a week before her fourteenth birthday.

"He shouts in the night," she reported on her return, visibly unsettled. "It's scary – like he's mad. He's all sweaty; his eyes are glaring."

"Did he hurt you?" asked Roz.

"No – not really. But he's too big. And he shouts and screams while he's doing it. It frightens me."

The description worried Roz. It didn't sound like Hugo.

"Maybe it's just the way he behaves with the young ones," said Bea. "Men change as they get older. I've seen it a lot. And Hugo's… what? not far off fifty, I think. Don't worry about it. He's done her no harm, brought her back in one piece. She'll be pleased when she gets her money; Hugo pays over the price. Then she'll be keen to go back. You'll see."

Before the end of May, Hugo returned, asking for Polly again, but she didn't want to go.

"What's wrong, child?" asked Mrs Drabb while the customer stood by, watching. "Don't be so disrespectful. The gentleman's asked specially for you."

"I'm frightened," Polly replied, holding back her tears. "It's lonely there."

"Mr Ash is a very good friend of this house," Mrs Drabb pointed out. "As he's requested you, he should have you." Seeing Polly's lips begin to quiver, Mrs Drabb added, "Supposing I send someone with you?" Hugo held up his hand, rejecting the idea, but Mrs Drabb countered the gesture with one of her own. "Don't worry, Mr Ash – it'll be with our compliments. It's the least we can do to show our gratitude…"

"Bea then," Polly cut in. "Or Emma." She clearly hoped for someone old enough to be her mother, but Hugo wouldn't have it.

"No," he said. "Dapple can come – or May."

"May's busy all day," Mrs Drabb told him. "Will you take Roz?"

He shook his head. "No. It must be Dapple. Dapple and Polly together." He smiled at Polly. "There's nothing to fear. And I've bought lots of sweets for you. The two of you together – you'll have a happy time."

But the pair returned four days later, having decided to make a stand.

"It's horrible there," said Dapple. "He runs about in the night, screaming and breaking things. He shouts, *Who are you?* like someone's there."

"But there's no-one?" asked Mr Drabb.

"No-one but us," Polly replied. "He goes mad. It's like he could kill us and not even know he was doing it. We can't go back – please don't send us back."

"Do you hear anything?" Roz muttered, watching them carefully beneath arched brows.

Dapple stared at her. "Like what? You mean like a person?"

"Do you hear voices?"

Polly looked puzzled. "Voices?"

Bea tapped Roz's foot with her own and whispered, "Don't. They don't hear them – and they're scared enough."

Hugo turned up again in the third week of June, demanding the young girls once more, but they refused to go – even at the express orders of their mistress. He became visibly frustrated, speaking rapidly.

"What have I done? I'm good to them, feed them well. They can run, swim. I don't see…"

Roz stopped him. "I'll go with you."

"You?" He scowled.

"I can be a little girl for you," Roz murmured. "You'll see. Trust me."

Hugo stilled, thinking, eyes fixed on hers. "Alright."

He took her to bed the minute they arrived at the cottage, desperate, unable to restrain himself.
"Oh uncle – it's nice," she purred beneath him.
"Does your grandmother know you're here?" he growled.
"No. Nobody knows. I love this – what you do to me."
"Oh, good girl…" (tempo increasing), "good girl…"

He liked her to kneel close to him, naked and silent, wherever they were, whatever he was doing. In the kitchen, in the stable, the field, even in the mill (where she concentrated hard to shut out the tortured souls), she knelt close, obedient, available to please him whenever and however he wished.
"Pretty child," he murmured, running his hand through her hair.
"Thank you, uncle."
Sometimes he liked her to dress in a simple frock and shift, so he could strip her, pretending he was taking her, fresh and virginal, for the first time.
"Let me kiss your bottom."
"Oh, uncle!" (feigning shock) "What would my grandma say?"
"Is that nice?"
"Yes… Do it again."
"Let me put my tongue here…"
"Oh! That's lovely!"
"And here…"
"Oh yes…" (gasping).
"And here…"
"Oh, uncle…"

Roz put on an excellent performance at all times, worried about him, wondering if this was an illness that would pass, a fascination with his little fiery-haired vixen that might eventually fade. He was particularly troubled at night, tossing and turning, muttering incoherently in his sleep. More than once, he got out of bed and seemed to be chasing something around the house, shouting, banging on doors (*"Leave me alone! I don't want to hear it! Fuck off to Hell, where you came from!"*).

It frightened her, but she didn't comment on it, didn't break her little-girl charade. A dream lingered somewhere in her mind – a notion that if she was persistent enough, she might be the instrument that would guide him through his troubles and bring about a recovery. And then, perhaps, despite everything… But the shock she received on her last night at the mill proved terminal for their liaison.

There was a strange smell in the bedroom that night, like something rotting, and the voices seemed louder than usual. She imagined she could hear someone crying out, begging for mercy, and something snarling – an animal…or a demon. She was on all fours, facing the end of the bed, Hugo on his knees, taking her from behind by the light of a single candle, his exertions making the bedframe creak. The shadows seemed alive. Several times she felt a breath of air on her face, as if from the waft of a cloak – or from the nostrils of some dark thing. Terror rose; it was a struggle to maintain her role play. She wanted to end this, to cry out, to stop him. And then she saw it – a figure, just discernible, in the corner of the room, shrouded, tall, pink eyes gleaming dully, reflecting the candle's light.

"What the…!" (breathless). She scrambled to get free, but Hugo yanked on her hair and held her in place. Something giggled – not Hugo – something cruel and damned. Hugo withdrew, flung her on her back, pinned her legs up over his shoulders, and plunged into her again, laughing, ignoring her panic, the blows she rained on him, the scratching of her fingers.

"Juicy tart!" The words came from Hugo but the voice was not his. It echoed strangely, consonants with multiple attacks, as if uttered by more than one mouth.

"Let me go!" she screamed, impaled.

But Hugo slapped her face and chuckled, "Hold still, little slave. It's been years since we've had our meat up a cunt tight as yours." Then she saw the light in his eyes – the same dull pink as in the eyes of the thing she'd imagined in the room seconds before. Her mind broke, reason shattered.

"OH, MY GOD! HUGO! HUGO!"

He was ejaculating. Roz ceased her struggles and waited for him to finish, anticipating a chance to run.
But the vision (if that was what it had been) was over; the smell had vanished; the voices had quietened.
Hugo opened his eyes, the hideous pink glow no longer shining in them. "That was exciting," he murmured.
"What the fuck...?" she mumbled.
He grinned. "Does your grandmother know you behave like that?"
"Fuck off," said Roz. "And get off me. I've had enough of this."
Hugo laughed, rolled away from her, settled himself and pulled the sheets around him.
"In the morning, I want my good little girl back. Understand?"
The nightmare was dispersing like smoke; Roz wasn't sure if she'd imagined it or not. Anger took the place of terror.
"You can fuck right off, Hugo Ash," she spat. "You won't be seeing me here again."
"Calm down," he crooned. "I enjoyed that. You were brilliant. You'll feel better when the sun comes up."
"I can't stand this," she told him. "And I can't stand those fucking voices anymore. No wonder you're mad, living here."
But he didn't answer. Roz lay next to him, not touching, staring up into the dark. He was snoring within minutes.
No more, she thought. *No more.*
So she got up, dressed, left the cottage for the last time, and walked to Whitby in the dawn light.

Roz never saw Hugo again. She expected him to appear at Mrs Drabb's any day, demanding the young ones, but he didn't do so. Polly, Dapple, May and the others breathed a sigh of relief. Months later, they heard he'd killed himself. His body had been found hanging in the mill. Roz felt a pang of sadness; she'd once had a fantasy about the place, about him. It had lasted only one summer, but dreams to her were rare and precious.
Rosepetal Epplewith died in 1768, stabbed through the heart by a drunken infantryman, dissatisfied with her services. She was

thirty-nine. She never knew who Kate was, what she was, or what she became, perishing, as she did, before the great witch returned from France – and long before the chamber beneath the mill was discovered, the grave revealed, and the bodies removed.

FAITHFULNESS

North Yorkshire coast, Summer 1758

Jenny had been gone seventeen years, but she was still in his head, in his heart. Every day, every night: her smile, her voice, hands, her kindness, gentleness. Her love. Still there, undiminished, bright as the blue sky. She'd been twenty-one when she died, and they'd been married less than a year. Blonde, blue-eyed, beautiful Jenny Clifton – the meaning of his life *("Speck, Speck Beckwith, my wonderful, cuddly, gentle man. How I love you…")*.

He'd found ways of bearing the loss as time ground on. First, by caring for her parents in their grief; then, when they'd both passed away, by exchanging his shepherding for droving, distracting himself, shielding himself from the pain. And now, another new life, working on the land as a farmer for an educational institute. He'd grown used to solitude, had even come to treasure it, a defence against the temptation to form new relationships; relationships that ran the risk of new loss, new grief. Solitude was the smooth cantabile of his life – that and the steadfast companionship of an alert, intelligent dog.

"Go on, boy!" He lobbed the stick with all his force and grinned as the animal cannoned along the beach, launching into the surf to retrieve it. "Good boy! Good Bastard!" Perhaps not the most elegant name for a faithful friend, but the creature had been more or less christened thus by his previous owner, and the label had stuck. In any case, Bastard didn't seem to mind, panting, tongue lolling as he dropped the sea-worn length of driftwood at his master's feet, eager to have it flung again.

Speck and his dog had ventured nearly half a mile north from the Lookout, the village of Peak about the same distance ahead.

The summer sun shone; gulls whirled and cried overhead and cackled from their nests on the cliff. The surf crashed and the wind picked up, blowing in from the sea as it often did when clouds built up in the west.
"HELP! HELP!"
A commotion up ahead – screams, panicked voices. Speck hurled Bastard's stick and lurched after it as fast as the shingle allowed, the dog barking, believing it part of the game, delighted to have the man join in. The source of the cries was not immediately visible, the white rollers obscuring anyone who might have been in the water. Speck halted, made a visor with his hand and scanned the shoreline. Nothing – nothing... and then he saw them; white limbs flailing, heads bobbing just a few yards from the beach; two desperate women, helpless in the current's undertow. He sprinted to their aid.
"I'M COMING! IT'S ALRIGHT!"
The rescuer stepped into the sea, holding himself upright and steady against its surge, reached out, grasped a hand, and pulled the first woman to safety; then the next, the same way. Seconds later, he was facing them on the beach, two naked girls, about twenty, one brown-haired, the other blonde. The latter crouched, arms wound tight as a nut, concealing herself, anxiously watching the man; the other stood upright, covering her breasts with her left arm, right hand cupping her pubis. Bastard dropped his stick and sniffed at the newcomers.
"Down boy! Away!" Speck was embarrassed, both for himself and for them, but felt he should explain what had happened. "It was an underset. You know?"
The girls eyed him warily, vulnerable, exposed. "Underset?" the brown-haired frowned.
"Yes," Speck replied, staring fixedly at her face. "The tide – I mean, the surf. When it blows in like that – with force – it turns under and creates a reverse current. You were caught. It would have been nearly impossible to get out by yourselves."
"So, you saved our lives..." said the smaller girl, the brown-haired.

"Well..." Speck began, then realised he knew them. Recognition had been slow because he'd encountered the girls only in their work uniforms before this chance meeting and had exchanged no more than a few brief words with them. "Edie..." he muttered, recalling her name, half lifting a forefinger; then, glancing at the other, "Margaret."

Edie Ashton had arrived at the school only a few months previously to take up her job as one of the new kitchen maids. Margaret York, the blonde girl, a year or so older than her companion, was a chambermaid.

"Oh my God..." Edie murmured, cringing. "Mr Beckwith..."

"Speck – please," he insisted, turning away, shaking his head at his clumsiness. "Forgive me. You're quite safe – I shan't speak of this."

Margaret addressed Speck's back. "Thank you, Mr Beckwith. We owe you our lives. We'll never be able to repay you."

Again, Speck shook his head, tongue-tied. "No, no. It was nothing. I mean, there was no effort... Er...forgive me, I'm sorry. There are two of you, and I have only one jacket..."

"It's alright," said Edie (Speck thought he detected a smile in her tone). "Our clothes are just along the beach."

He nodded to himself, relieved to be excused. "Then...I'll bid you good day."

"Don't let us interrupt your walk," said Edie.

"Not at all," Speck replied. "I was about to head home anyway."

He began to step away, whistling for Bastard, slapping his thigh, but Margaret cried out, halting him, "God bless you, Mr Beckwith."

"Think nothing of it," he called over his shoulder, and lifted his hat as an afterthought. "A very good afternoon to you, ladies."

The incident troubled Speck. He'd been faithful to Jenny since her death, and the intimate encounter with the two young women on the beach stirred up desires long suppressed. He slouched in the kitchen of his little cottage in the early evening, head bowed, glass of whisky on the table before him, Bastard asleep at his feet.

Forgive my weakness, my love. You're the only one – darling wife. Keep me strong…

A thread of sunlight pierced the gloom, setting the amber liquid aglow, an answer perhaps, from beyond: *My man, my steadfast love. I'm always here, watching over you…*

He went about his work as usual the next day, toiling in the fields, passing a few words with the near-silent John Eldenshaw, and smiling at Tranter Tickle's repetitive jokes. They sat smoking together on their customary wall at noon, sweltering in the heat, watching the animals, the sky, the few figures – mostly maids – at work near the school.

"What a life, to be here," Tranter murmured, unusually philosophical for him.

"We're very lucky," Speck agreed.

"It's like the Garden of Eden," Tranter added.

John Eldenshaw grunted – whether in agreement or mockery, Speck couldn't tell.

Pixie Silden (wife of Ned, one of the gardeners), strolling by a few yards distant, bent low so they could peer into her cleavage, and jangled her plentiful breasts at them, grinning.

"Yer saucy vixen!" Tranter drooled, lifting his pipe from his lips.

Pixie snorted and flounced on, hips swaying temptingly.

John Eldenshaw laughed – a rare occurrence. "She's a ray of sunshine."

"Damn right she is," Tranter seconded. "Lucky bastard, Ned – getting his spicket up that every night."

Speck drew hard on his pipe but offered no comment.

"How old is she?" asked John.

Tranter screwed up his eyes and did a quick calculation. "Twenty-five, I think. Three years younger than Ned."

"She's a lively one alright," John commented.

"Your Teresa's a good-looking woman," said Speck to Tranter. "You're settled well."

"Teresa's fair enough, sure she is," Tranter conceded. "Not so young and juicy as that one, though." He tipped his head towards Pixie's receding figure. "Used to be a blinder, Teresa – not so big as she is now." He paused. "She'll be forty-eight next month. Forty-eight. And me, fifty. We been wed nearly thirty years. Still goes though – still squeezes the juice out o' my old rod." He removed his pipe from his mouth, stared into the bowl, and quietly observed, "It's good to have a companion – to have a mate to share your life with – to grow old with. I give thanks for my lot."

That evening, as the sun began to sink, Speck answered a knock at his door and found Edie Ashton smiling nervously up at him. She looked fresh, vital, soft, in a yellow summer dress, hair tied up with a bow. Bastard sniffed at her.
"Made you this," she said, handing him a basket.
Speck took it and lifted the lid. It was a fruit cake. She'd gone to a lot of trouble for him.
"Thank you, Edie." He stumbled over his words. "You don't need to..."
"I wanted to," she interrupted him.
He clutched the basket clumsily and gazed into her eyes but didn't know what to say. She stared back, her smile holding for a few seconds, then fading, awkwardness taking hold.
"Speck..." Her lips quivered, but she couldn't say any more. He had to make the move, *he had to make the move...* She willed him to reach out, needing him to accept her. One touch would have done it.
Speck felt the pull in his heart – a desire for affection, for a way out of solitude? She needed it as much as he – he saw it in her eyes. He wanted to brush her face with his fingers, to caress her, to hold her... But the moment grew, peaked...and passed.
"I..." he managed.
"Mm," she responded, eyes gleaming, stepping back.
"Thank you," he said, trying to smile as he lifted the basket.
Edie smiled sadly in return, nodded, and walked away, glancing over her shoulder to find him watching her.
Speck closed the door before she was out of sight, stepped into

the kitchen and set the basket on the table. He sat, hunched forward, resting on his forearms, and surrendered to his loneliness.

IN HER SLEEP

A cottage on Cappleman Farm near Glaisdale, Yorkshire
Monday, February 12th, 1759. 3.15am

Silence.
Breath.
Girl warmth heating the night-filled room, frost's chill fingers clutching winter's wraiths.
Stay, ice, snow, dark days.
Dark days.
They had names once, the three brothers, the three become one. Names – perhaps even a mother. But the memory of her was hidden from them – from him. The three brothers; the two sisters. How long ago? Thousands of years, tens of thousands.
He, they, occupied a space close to the room's north wall, although their awareness – his awareness – squeezed into every corner, squeezed into her mind; the sleeping girl. She was dreaming, dreaming. A prince, travelled from far away to find her *(the most beautiful girl in the world...)*.
They remained dark, the brothers – darker than the room's darkness, their feet some inches above the floor. Watching. Skin death-white, eyes sulphur-yellow, hairless skull like raw bone, the three brothers, huddling in single form, unseeable, just beyond the veil of perception; long, jagged fingernails runnelling the earthly edge of existence. The three brothers; one.
She was here again, made flesh once more, the hated, the Red, hiding from herself, as she'd done before. Her sister – the pale, the White – remained apart, suffering the rotation of the infinite wheel in solitude. Stay away, till eternity's done.
But the Red; the abhorred one...

They'd offered her to the miller, as they always did, urging him to bind her, to skin her. Failed. Yet there had been a few passes, many cycles distant, in which they'd successfully driven the man to rape the girl. But not this time. Not this time. Even so, his agony never ceased to amuse them.

Soon, he and his brothers would have to look again on their own death; to suffer extinguishment anew. But others must pay first, surrender their lives, their souls, to atone for his death – for their death. It was always so, in the everlasting round, the same. His death, their death, the same.

Yet it *could* change – there *were* changes. He'd witnessed them – it was never quite identical. Their death, in one eternity, might perhaps be reversed, and the child might not summon the power to consume them. Perhaps *this* was the time, *this* cycle. When it came, if it came, it would be worth the passage of a million infinities.

The girl stirred in her sleep, aware she was dreaming *(don't wake up, don't wake up – it's too nice...)*, relishing it, moist for the touch of her handsome nobleman. She gasped, bit her lip in the throes of a love that would never be hers.

Another soul. Another soul for the mill, to join the voices there, trapped in the walls.

Reudh and Kweid, the Red and the White, the two sisters; they had names – many, many names, their spirits dancing through time, skipping generations like young girls leaping steppingstones across a raging torrent, laughing, joyful as they went, particularly the Red, the ever-youthful, age-old, unspoilt. Her existence was an abomination to him. The Red had many names: Wath, Yossel, Corsen, Ealswith, Cassia, Rufina, Julia, Willa, Aisling, Ruby, Astrid, Liv, Anne. More. Now, she sheltered beneath the identity, Catherine. And when Catherine was done, there would be yet one more – the last, shielded from the others, from time, from knowledge; the final embodiment, the perfect one, the modest, ignorant, gentle bud, born more than a century after his own defeat.

She flowered, the Red, perpetually renewed; the White also,

though less vividly: Kweid, Luna, Thyra, Maria. But he, they – they crawled forward, the three brothers, dragging the weight of ages behind them, rolling onwards into endless death. Soon she'd be rutting with the farmer again, shunning herself ever more fully, rejoicing in her fragile carnality, fashioning of it a barrier to shut out the knowledge, the memory, of what she was. It was pathetic, pitiful, disgusting.
The suffering of others soothed his journey, distracted him from his hate. Crowan he watched with pleasure, engineering the exquisite agony of pretty things; ripe, sensual creatures. But it wouldn't last. Even Crowan faltered, doubted, crumbled, contaminated with love. They'd watched the man's path countless times; its peaks and troughs, its cruelties, resolutions, and withdrawals. Crowan was both the beloved and the despised. Ultimately, he was the instrument of revenge. And that moment was eternally delicious, the slow shots tearing her flesh, one after another after another…
But the ignominy followed, always the same – their own destruction, he, his brothers, the three in one, clutching each other, denied escape. Their demise, endured over and over through the eternities, the spinning spheres of intersecting time that fashioned the everlasting nothing into the perception idiot man called *real* and *unreal.* Their death was commanded by a child. *Why?* A child! A child whose frame did not even harbour the spirit of the Red, of the great one – or rather, no more than the tiniest insignificant sliver of it. Yet the child saw him – saw him even though others could not; saw them cowering together, the three cursed brothers. Their annihilation was achieved with the mere utterance of a number, understated, laced with loathing – and they were cast into the abyss. Until time began.
Wind licked at the window.
The sleeping girl, the girl in the warm bed, delighted in her nocturnal fantasy, gasping at the touch of her dream prince – this girl had a name. He looked beyond her, at her birth, at her mother's love, and found it:
Holly.

Twenty-three, cherished, beloved daughter. The brothers extended a hand, vast, unseen, above the bed and lifted her soul from its shell. It was done silently, without effort, life's bright spark separating from the dust of flesh, like a pea from its pod, connection broken, return impossible.
Frail breath, so easily snatched away.
Away.
Silence.
Silence.
No movement.
The bed grew cold.

TERREL'S WOMEN

Saturday, May 17th, 1760, 1.30pm
Weather: sunny, warm

Two men sit opposite each other at a table outside The Eagle Inn at Peak, Yorkshire, each nursing a flagon of ale:
Terrel Nisbet, dashing, 30 years old; mathematics tutor at The Lookout.
Egerton "Ben" Badger, 39, not so fortunate in appearance, somewhat worn, an odd, off-white streak through his hair; literature tutor at The Lookout.
Both are slightly worse for drink.

Ben: Told anyone else about this?
Terrel: No. Only you.
Ben *(pause):* Not sure whether I envy you or not.
Terrel: I didn't think I'd feel quite…such a bastard.
Ben: Poor boy.
Terrel *(glancing up from his ale):* Mock if you wish. It's a pretty complex situation. I have to keep quiet about both of them. Can't tell anyone for fear of the ripples widening.
Ben: But they're women. Surely, they natter to their friends? Brag about getting your trousers down?
Terrel *(frowning):* Leafy's not like that. I'm pretty certain she doesn't gossip. *(Pause).* I'm not sure she has *friends* as such anyway.
Ben: Denise then. The housemistresses are all noisy harridans, aren't they?
Terrel *(grinning at Ben):* So unkind! Denise isn't like that at all. She's meek and mild. I mean – I know they're all party girls – specially Eve. Lettice too, I guess. Not so sure about Eleanor. But Denise is…demure. That's why I found her so attractive…

Ben: I don't believe that for a second!

Terrel: I know, I know. It was the more obvious charms as well. But it was her smile that drew me first. *(Throws up a hand in protest).* You don't believe me.

Ben *(smirking, shaking his head)*: They're the best paps in Yorkshire. You know they are.

Terrel *(nodding)*: They are. And I confirm your enthusiasm twelvefold, having had the pleasure of them at close quarters…

Ben: You dog…

Terrel: But Leafy's tits come a very close second. She keeps them well hidden under that modest little dairymaid's uniform, but I can tell you, she makes up in quality what she lacks in quantity…

Ben: Never been one for small jugs, me…

Terrel: Ho-ho! Unfair! Leafy does not have small jugs. She just… doesn't put them on display. No. I would say – of all the women I've known…

Ben: Fucked…

Terrel *(scowling)*: So coarse. And from a literary man too.

Ben: I humbly beg thy pardon, O sensitive soul.

Terrel *(pause)*: Bugger. I've lost my thread…

Ben: You were assuring me that your dairymaid's dugs are as heavenly as those of your eager housemistress.

Terrel: No. Before that… We were talking about gossiping women and the likelihood of my unloading cargo at competing ports becoming common knowledge.

Ben: I bet you Denise hasn't kept quiet. Leafy, I don't know. I've hardly exchanged a word with her. *(Frowns).* She's so taciturn – as if she's keeping a secret. *(Pause).* Perhaps she's a spy.

Terrel: There you go – fanciful again. It's those books you read – they send your imagination firing off all over the place. Leafy's no spy. Who would she spy for?

Ben: It was a flippant remark.

Terrel: She's just modest. That's all. *(Pause).* I sometimes think she's running away from something, some sadness. *(Pauses again, frowning).* There's a desperation in the way she loves…

Ben: The way she loves?

Terrel: I mean physically. There's a kind of agony in it – a desolation, loneliness…Ach! I'm not putting this well…
Ben: Sounds pretty grim.
Terrel: No – I'm misrepresenting her. She's a serious girl, that's what I'm saying. I don't always know what's going on in her head…
Ben: Does any man ever know what's going on in a woman's head?
Terrel: There you go again. How many women have you slept with, Ben?
Ben: Fewer than you, evidently.
Terrel: There we are then. Listen – you might learn something. Leafy's not shallow; that's what I'm saying. You look at her in passing, she's just a milkmaid. But when you're with her – intimately – you get closer. Not in words – I mean, she hasn't told me much about herself. Her mother died when she was very young; she never knew her father. After that, from what I can gather, she's been in service in various places…
Ben: Never wed then? No husband lurking somewhere, planning to knife you in the dark?
Terrel: No. I asked her if she'd ever married, and she answered directly. She's had lovers before – serious relationships, I think – but she won't talk about them.
Ben: Contradictory. How do you know? I mean, how would you know unless she told you?
Terrel: Communication isn't just achieved through vocalisation, you know…
Ben: That's a laugh. Coital transmission of information? I don't think that's posited in any known philosophy.
Terrel: Really? It's not so hilarious, surely? Anyway, she lets things slip here and there – a word, a phrase. She called me Edwin once, when she was…flowering… Don't think she was even aware of it. You put the information together, bit by bit, and you know – you know she's had a life. She's loved before – and been loved too…I think…
Ben *(pause, deep in thought, staring at Terrel):* How old is she?

Terrel: Twenty-nine next month.
Ben: And how did you start with her?
Terrel: It was her eyes, something in her eyes, some longing. It happened a few times. By chance at first. Then we both began to look for it. We'd pass each other, and I'd look at her. There was a kind of question in her eyes – or an answer. I don't know – I can't explain it. Then, one day, we didn't pass, but stopped. And there were her eyes... I touched her – her arm. Hardly a touch at all, but there was this...charge – and I saw how surprised she was – she felt it too. Next second she was in my arms, and we were kissing.
Ben: When was this?
Terrel: March. The sun was shining. The first really shiny day of the year. It was on the first-floor landing, near the staircase, just by the big window. Extraordinary – completely spontaneous. Never felt anything like it. I didn't even stop to worry if anyone was watching. *(Pause).* "I'll come to you," she said. And I said, "Five o'clock."
Ben *(long pause):* And...?
Terrel: She came to my room at five. Said nothing. I locked the door, kissed her. *(Pause).* Then she undressed...
Ben: You love her.
Terrel: Do I? Maybe. *(Pause).* She's in command in this relationship. I think the physical act is important to her – I think it gives her some kind of relief. I... *(pause)* I was going to say it makes her forget – something. But I'm not sure that's true. I don't know; I *can't* know. Whatever her motivation, it's somewhere I can't go. Perhaps the screwing makes her forget – or perhaps it makes her remember. But what it *is* she needs to forget – or remember – I don't know. *(Pause).* She's good; she has a lovely body. You'd never know under that bland, shapeless uniform. *(Pause)* She's very confident in bed, experienced, exciting. She's alive – flowing – like a wave...
Ben *(eyebrows raised):* Like a wave...
Terrel: Yes, she is. Of all the women I've known, she's the most... the most...quickening.
Ben: Sounds a bit intimidating.

Terrel: Some might find it so (*grins*) – lesser men.
Ben: You've been with Denise since before Christmas. Do you keep a timetable of appointments?
Terrel: There you go, mocking again. But you're right – it *is* something like that. Keeping them secret from each other...
Ben: It'll all end in tears.
Terrel: I know. It's precarious. I wish I were stronger. Leafy does things in bed that would horrify Denise.
Ben: Such as?
Terrel: You can imagine. I don't need to spell it out.
Ben: You take precautions, I presume?
Terrel: Leafy won't have the cundom. We tried it once; she hated it.
Ben: Risky.
Terrel: Doesn't seem to worry her. I don't think she can have children. I've never asked her specifically – always been worried the question might upset her. She knows best. I always thought, if she's so sure it's safe, just go along with it.
Ben: What about Denise?
Terrel: You mean, with the sheath? (*Ben nods*). Almost always, yes. We've done it a few times without – just after she's bled.

Ben waves at the serving maid and wags his finger between their two flagons, signalling the desire for more ale. The maid smiles and raises her eyebrows in acknowledgement.

Ben: So, where's this going, Terry?
Terrel: I'm fond of them both, God help me. I'm reluctant to give up either. They're so different from each other. They complement two contrasting aspects of my character. Denise is like a clergyman's daughter...
Ben: She *is* a clergyman's daughter, isn't she?
Terrel: Yes, yes, of course. But she *behaves* like one – that's what I mean. If there were a Platonic Idea of a clergyman's daughter, Denise would be it. She's beautiful, kind, smiles all the time; she's softly spoken, modest, has a face like sunshine...

Ben: …and the best bubbies in Yorkshire…

Terrel: And in bed… In bed, she lays there, smiling at me like a saint and lets me get on with it.

Ben: Whereas Leafy…

Terrel: Leafy is an enigma. She may not be quite as fair of face as Denise, but she's a thrilling lover. She's the most exciting woman I know – the most exciting I've *ever* known.

Ben: You should marry her then.

Terrel: Marry her? I can't do that. She's just a dairymaid.

DILLY AND EMILY

Saturday afternoon, March 12th, 1763

BANG! SWOOSH!
Emily giggled. She loved to stand close and watch while Toby let Jonah work the shuttle. The lime-washed room was alive with mechanical sounds, the weaver's encouragement, and the boy's delighted laughter. It made Emily happy; she bobbed up and down, knees bending, dancing with the unique excitement of a two-year-old.
CLICK-CLACK! Toby working the pedals. *BANG-SWOOSH!* Jonah firing the shuttle.
Toby Lightwell, sixty, tall and grey, loved entertaining the children while he worked. He and Mary had never managed to produce any of their own despite decades of trying. Now she was gone, dead two years. Toby still grieved for her but was pleased to have bonded so well with young Dilly Sollett, Emily's mother. It was as if a granddaughter had suddenly appeared out of nowhere one night in the pouring rain, helpless, homeless, lost, begging shelter, her little girl clutched tight beneath her cape. He'd given them one of the downstairs rooms and they'd stayed, the two of them, Dilly and Emily, and become part of his life. He loved them.
As for Janice Woodcock's seven-year-old Jonah – he was a lively one! Toby held the lad on his knee, arms securing him in place, while the youngster gleefully propelled the weft back and forth. *BANG-SWOOSH!* He had a sharp eye and a firm rhythm. Soon Jonah would be able to work the loom entirely by himself; he was going to be a good weaver.
The weather was surprising; unnaturally warm for mid-March, the sky cloudless, sun kissing the earth as if it were summer.

Toby's workroom sparkled with sunlight and happiness. Emily watched, danced and laughed, a bundle of rapture, her mother's little ball of joy.

"I don't believe this!" Sarah Bennett exclaimed, scanning the azure heavens. "It was so cold two or three days ago, I thought winter was coming back. Now look at it! I can't believe we're sitting outside!"

Dilly agreed, smiling, happy to have half an hour to share with Sarah and enjoy a glass of ale. "Busy?" she asked.

"You mean guests?" asked Sarah, lifting her flagon.

"Mm," Dilly confirmed.

"No," the older woman laughed. "If we were busy, I wouldn't be gossiping in the sun, getting drunk with you!"

Dilly raised her glass and wished her companion good health. She liked Sarah. The woman was a pillar of the community: wife of John, landlady of The White Bull, portly, ruddy-faced, forty-six years old, a beacon of confidence and goodwill.

"And how are you?" asked Sarah, setting down her drink, beaming across the table.

"Oh, so lucky!" breathed the young woman. "So, so lucky!"

Sarah's eyes moistened. Slender, pretty, flaxen-haired Dilly Sollett was like the daughter she'd never had.

Children. She and John had wanted more than the one son they'd managed. Now he was gone. Edward. Long flown the nest; in the military. Always away, fighting in some war or playing his part in some exercise. There was a girl, apparently; he'd written about her a few times in vague terms. Sarah suspected the object of her son's affections was probably a married woman – and that was the reason for the lack of detail.

"Toby fed up with you yet?" she asked, tongue in cheek.

"No," Dilly replied, drawing out the single syllable in a falling inflexion. "You've seen him with Emily. He loves her."

"Everybody loves Emily," Sarah added. "You're so blessed – to have such a sweet child."

"I know," Dilly replied. "I never thought I'd be so happy, so settled."

"Settled," Sarah echoed.

Dilly nodded. "Mm. You know what I mean."

Sarah took a draught of ale. "Toby's not just fond of Emily, you know."

Dilly dropped her gaze to the tabletop. "It's not like that. He's like… He's like my dad used to be – except older…"

She'd been thirteen when her father died, and had never got over the loss. Two years later her mother married Roger Ullswater, an aggressive, stocky farm labourer twenty years her senior. Dilly disliked the man; he was crude, stank of booze and tobacco, and was not averse to cuffing her mother when it suited him. Sensing Dilly's disgust, he adopted a threatening demeanour towards her, manifesting first in scowls, dismissive comments, criticism of her dress, her hair, her "attitude". Later it developed into mild sexual threat, personal remarks; he'd "make a woman" out of her, do her "a favour". She'd thank him afterwards, he said. Dilly sought safety at her mother's side, but Agnes Sollett wouldn't hear her daughter's complaints, instead chastising her for her lies.

Then Leo Kelly came along, striding north from Manchester. He hated his father, he said. "Always putting me down! Nothing ever good enough! I'll show him!"

Leo took work at the Cock Robin alehouse in Catterall, close to where Dilly lived. Each took comfort in the other, mutual dislike of their male parents strengthening their bond.

"We'll go away together, you and me," Leo told her. "That'll teach 'em."

Then, one day in the summer of 1760, seventeen-year-old Dilly realised she was pregnant. Leo had commenced a relationship with one of the alehouse wenches by that time and considered Dilly's predicament an impediment to his desires, so he broke off with her, left his employment at the Cock Robin, and set up home in nearby Garstang with the more recent object of his lust.

"What did I tell you, you stupid doxy?" Dilly's stepfather yelled at her.

The atmosphere in the house, already bad, became increasingly frosty as Dilly expanded, and Agnes Sollett, fearful of her new husband, did nothing to support her daughter.

Emily was born on Friday, January 9th, 1761, at the very moment the winter sun peeped over the eastern horizon. Agnes's heart melted at the sight of her grandchild, and relations between herself and her daughter thawed for a while. Roger took one sneering look at the little girl and hurried off to The Plough in Bowgreave, where he spent the whole day drinking with his mates, claiming the new girl was his.

Dilly's relationship with Leo had been no secret in the tight-knit community, so Roger's boasting was laughed off by most. But Agnes, receiving news of it a week after Emily's birth, found it disturbing. Her husband was not faithful to her – she knew that. Could he have taken advantage of her daughter? It was possible. And Dilly was the kind of girl who might have willingly endured some ghastly arrangement for her mother's sake. She imagined the possibilities ("You do as I say, girl, or your ma will suffer...").

"Mum, it's not true," Dilly insisted. "You know it."

"You wouldn't...?" Agnes asked, uncertain.

"He's horrible, mum. He's a liar. Everybody knows it."

Agnes had long since fallen out of love with her new man, but fear bound her to him, and as the months went on, the bond between mother and daughter steadily broke down. Roger observed its decay, relishing his power over the two women, abusing his wife and cursing his stepdaughter – and her wailing brat.

His fantasy of having fathered the child took root in Roger's mind, and he began to think of Dilly as his property. She lived in his house; he could do as he pleased. There seemed no reason why the next baby shouldn't genuinely be his. Agnes, at the age of forty, wasn't producing any more after all. She still bled every month, but nothing ever took root. So why not make use of the little tart? They weren't blood relatives; there was nothing to prevent it taking place.

Roger engineered opportunities to be alone with Dilly. First he tried tenderness, apologising for his former brutality. But she hated him still, and his unwanted advances became more forceful, his groping hands lunging out to take possession of her, his stinking tobacco lips seeking fusion with hers, his tongue…
"Come on, come on. You'll like it. Let's have a look at you…" (lifting her skirts).
Dilly fought him off every time, but he was not disheartened. He enjoyed the game and knew that sooner or later she'd give up, finding submission less stressful than resistance.
One day in June 1762, Agnes out of the house, Roger attacked Dilly, pinned her against a wall with the weight of his body, unbuttoned himself, and pulled up her clothes. Dilly shouted, screamed, resisted with all her might, craned her head forward while he was fumbling at her, and bit a chunk out of his cheek. Roger was horror-struck, withdrew from the assault, and tested his bloodied face with his fingers.
"Fucking whore!" he spat and would have beaten her, but she was quicker, kneeing him savagely between the legs so he collapsed on the floor, groaning, nursing himself. Dilly hurried to her room, gathered a few things, took up her young daughter, and left the house, tramping south, she knew not where.
Agnes stumbled upon her, passing in the opposite direction.
"What's happened? Where are you going?"
"Away."
"Why?"
"Ask your husband."
"Did he…?"
But Dilly was already gone. "I'll write," she flung over her shoulder.
It was warm, the summer heat kind, easy enough to sleep in the open. She knocked at a few doors, begging food, and people took pity on them. Sometimes they sheltered in barns or churches. They didn't cover much ground. Dilly spent a lot of time mothering Emily, singing to her, playing with her, laughing.
Early July found them approaching Ribchester, just twelve miles

from their point of departure. The sky was black, and lightning flashed not far off, thunder rolling over the land. Rain came on suddenly, and within seconds it was hammering down, soaking Dilly to the skin. Emily was frightened, sheltered beneath her mother's cape, never having experienced such a tempest. They hurried into the village, cottages on the right, the inn on the left, a church tower just visible in the gloom. Lightning cracked overhead like God's whip. The young mother selected a door and knocked...

Pale-skinned, twenty-six-year-old Alex Regan crept up behind his wife, squeezed her bottom, and pressed himself suggestively against her body.
"Filthy beggar!" Helen grinned, turning away from the window and accepting his embrace, kissing him.
Now he had both hands on her bottom; he loved her bottom. "Francis?" he asked, kissing her neck. Their little boy, nine and a half weeks short of his second birthday, was fast asleep in their room on the upper floor of The White Bull.
"Exhausted," Helen whispered. "Snoring – like you."
"Want to make another," Alex breathed. "With you – right now. Come on..."
His left hand was on her breast; his right... Alex was the love of her life, the best thing that had ever happened to her – along with Francis, of course.
"Sarah's outside with Dilly," she replied. "Let me take them another drink. Run upstairs. I'll be there in five minutes."
He pecked her on the lips and hurried away, loosening his clothes.
Helen drew two more flagons of ale. Sarah Bennett was fond of the local drink, as was John, her husband. "Full of sunlight," Sarah described it, and Helen understood what she meant: its paleness, its hoppy odour, the bright, delicate froth, the lively tang on the tongue. It was a joy never to be understood by those who drank only wine.
"Here we are," she said, arriving at the women's table and

presenting the blessed liquid.
"You guessed my thoughts!" Sarah exclaimed. "Sit with us?"
"Bit busy right now," Helen replied. "Alex…"
Sarah raised a hand. "Say no more. Away you go, pair o' rabbits."
Helen smiled and nodded at the younger woman. "Dilly."
"Helen," Dilly returned, lifting a hand in greeting.
Their stories were similar, Helen knew. Like Dilly Sollett, she'd run from an abusive father, although she hadn't confessed it to Emily's mum. Helen was happily settled now with the best man in the world, and with a little son she loved with all her heart. She'd listened to Dilly's story but didn't want to undermine its gravity by revealing her own, which she considered buried in the past. Now the future lay open to her. She would grow old with Alex, joyful and fulfilled.

Dilly and Sarah alone again in the unseasonal sunshine, the latter advanced her thoughts:
"Toby loves you. He's kind, caring, thoughtful. You could do much worse."
Dilly was quiet for a few seconds, eyes fixed on Sarah's. "He's gentle – always kind, like you say. And I know he adores Emily. But…"
"I can see his love – every time he looks at you," Sarah cut in. "Are you worried about his age?"
Dilly scanned the tabletop again, confused. "I don't know. He's fit and strong – and handsome. But he's quite old…"
"He's sixty," Sarah interjected.
"He'd be Emily's dad – but she wouldn't have him for very long."
"And that's what holds you back?"
"Yes, I think so," said Dilly, looking across the table at Sarah. "I'd like her to have a dad for a long time – I think it's important. It was horrible when mine died. I don't want Emily to go through that."
"But isn't Toby already Emily's dad?" asked Sarah. She looked into Dilly's face and found the answer there. "He is, isn't he? You know it. He's already become her dad."

Dilly was quiet, then sighed and said, "Alright. I've thought about it; of course I have. I feel very close to him. He's so tender-hearted. But if I... if I... I mean, *how?* What would he think?"

"Toby Lightwell's love is waiting for you," Sarah said gently. "Let him know – reassure him – a look, a touch. Show him your heart's open."

Dilly stared at her friend, eyes moistening. She was about to reply but suddenly realised that George Fowles, approaching on horseback, was about to stop and speak to them.

Sarah got to her feet and greeted Ribchester's surgeon. "Good day, sir."

Doctor Fowles tipped his hat first at Sarah, then at the younger woman. "Mrs Bennett. Miss Sollett."

"Good afternoon, Doctor Fowles," Dilly replied.

"Emily well?" he asked.

"Very well, sir. Thanks for asking," Dilly smiled.

"Good," the doctor returned. "That's good." He turned to Sarah. "All well at the inn, Mrs Bennett? No-one ill?"

Sarah shook her head, puzzled he should ask. "Everyone's good. What's up?"

Without warning, Helen's ecstasy issued clearly from the circular window on the first floor, as if it were a cry from an orgy in Paradise: *"Oh, Alex, Alex!"*

Doctor Fowles, embarrassed, turned his gaze away from his audience, but Sarah chuckled and told him not to mind. He was silent for a moment, then took a deep breath and said, "There's something coming across the country, an illness, spreading from the coast – Liverpool, it seems. Came in by ship probably – maybe a slave ship – or from Ireland perhaps."

Sarah frowned. "Must be bad if you're worried about it."

"Best to be vigilant," the doctor replied. "There are cases in Preston. I received word yesterday. I'm going to see it for myself. I'll be back tomorrow. Janet's in charge till then."

That was reassuring at least, thought Sarah. The village midwife was more than capable of holding fort for a day.

"We don't want it here, whatever it is," she declared as the surgeon resumed his course.

"Don't worry," he called back. "I shall take every precaution."

Dilly followed the departing man with her eyes for a few seconds, then became aware that Sarah was gazing at her.

"What?"

"Don't wait," said Sarah. "Toby won't make the first move; he's got too much respect for you."

Dilly looked inwards again. It was true; she loved Toby Lightwell and had known it for quite some time. Fear of her own perceived inadequacy had prevented her from acting on it; fear of rejection too. What could he possibly see in her? A stupid, colourless girl, four decades his junior; a girl who'd barely lived, who lacked the wisdom of years. How could her love match his? But now she knew that what she *could* give, she'd give gladly – to aspire to him.

Sarah was nodding, a subtle acknowledgement of what she saw passing across Dilly's countenance. "You're going to be very happy," she whispered.

Dilly saw her future stretching out before her, a future full of love, with lots more children; a blessed life, richer than she could ever have imagined. She felt complete.

"Another drink?" asked Sarah.

"No," Dilly replied. "I'd better keep a clear head."

Sarah reached across the table and took the young woman's hand. "God bless you, Dilly."

DOMINOES

October 1772 – Venice

Four well-to-do but slightly shabby men, mostly elderly, sit around a table outside the Caffè Marco, overlooking the Grand Canal. Two – facing each other – are playing dominoes; the others look on, taking more or less of an interest. It's a tradition with them, stretching back decades.
Tommaso Rossi: seventy, tall, thin, bearded, wearing an aged grey wig; a retired galley captain (a *sopracomito*).
Bernardo Favaro: fifty-seven, slightly rotund but agile; still has all his hair (of which he's proud) and a well-groomed beard and moustache, brown but peppered with silver; a printer, retired, left the business in the capable hands of his three sons.
Padre Girolamo Calvene: seventy-five, clean-shaven, wearing the scant remains of a tonsure; retired, but stands locum when called upon.
William Crowan: eighty-four, bent, arthritis well advanced, somewhat less than average height, hanging onto the wispy vestiges of his hair and beard, unwigged; English, but resident in Venice for a quarter century; a retired London cobbler.
There should have been a fifth – Nicolo Sartori – but he's dead. His burial is today, but these four friends of his are not welcome – by order of his wife, Gabriella. (Ah well – at least they can drink to him. Eighty-six wasn't a bad age.)
"Nicolo!" toasts Tommaso, raising his glass of wine.
"Nicolo!" they echo.

The weather has begun to cool, but it's still comfortable at midday. And it's good to sit here watching the boats, listening to the lap of the water, admiring the fine women, the painted ladies, as they pass with their maids – the young girls. The wine is good, the brandy – the food too. Little snacks, sweetmeats (old Will is particularly fond of the salted sardines). Marco Colussi is a good host – sees their table is kept vacant for them *("My friends! How are we today? Signore Crowan – always a pleasure. How is your beautiful wife?")*.

Alison. Nearly twenty years his junior. She's swallowed Will's life, taken away all his cares, his responsibilities. He hasn't had to work for twenty-five years; she's bought him *("You keep me safe, William – you shelter me. As long as you're here, I can do as I wish. No-one can own me...")*. Will eats, drinks as much as he likes, attends the theatre, the opera, and spends time every day in the company of his friends. They talk to each other in subdued tones about his wife, but Will pretends not to hear. Alison is what they all have in common.

Across the canal, a little to the south, a woman appears on a second-storey balcony. She's completely naked, but they can see her only from the waist up. She stands proudly in the sun, staring ahead, fine large breasts shining in the noon light, nipples like cherries, clearly visible even at this distance – Signora Marianna Barbarigo, Nobildonna, sixty-one, widow of Patrizio Francesco Barbarigo, Nobil Homo.

"There she is again," Tommaso growls, distracted from his game. "I could eat her – I bet she rides like a racehorse."

Will raises his hand, waves to the woman, but she ignores him, ignores them all – doesn't even cast them a glance. But she knows they're there – pathetic old men.

"He's probably in her apartment," Padre Girolamo speculates, "stiff as a pipe."

Signora Barbarigo is the mistress of Padre Jacopo Arcengeli, an elderly priest, retired from Treviso following a scandal involving a married woman. She'd been displaying herself in this way for eighteen months ("He likes to flaunt her," Padre Girolamo had told them. "It's his way of boasting, preening, congratulating himself. Arsehole...").

She cups both her breasts as the men watch, squeezes them, then rests her hands on the balcony and puffs herself up, fruits thrust forward, offerings to Helios.

"She knows we gaze upon her," Will mutters.

"Of course," Bernardo replies. "She's very fine. But she's not lovelier than *your* wife, Will."

It was true. Voluptuous ginger Alison, Will's second wife.

A chance meeting in The Haystack Tavern in Lovat Lane. Will wasn't a womaniser and hadn't expected to find love at all, let alone so easily. But there she was, giggling with her friends, eyeing him, grinning. He'd guessed her age at about thirty and was surprised when she admitted she was thirty-nine.

"You're joking..." he mumbled.

"No, sweet Will," she replied. "I've been around a while..."

Sex with Alison had been wonderful. Beneath him, on top, submissive on all fours, lying on her back with her ankles over his shoulders, she smiled, encouraged him.

"I love you!" he cried at the peak of his passion.

And she stroked his face and chuckled, "Sweet Will..."

"Don't you love me?" he prompted.

"Of course I do."

"Say it then."

"I love you – sweet Will."

The phrase was always offered with a smile, but he wasn't sure if it was true. She lived deep inside herself, and William never felt he opened all her doors; she was down there somewhere, shut away from him, shut away from everyone, concealed in some inner chamber.

He was pretty certain she'd never had an orgasm – at least not with him...

(*"Signora Crowan – such tricks with her tongue – you could never imagine in your wildest dreams..."*

"Her flesh is so firm. She's like a young girl..."

"Such a pull. The most exquisite figa in all Venice...")

Will wasn't sure if they intended him to overhear their comments. They probably thought him too deaf to catch their words – or too old to care. He hadn't slept with Alison for nearly

fifteen years. It wasn't that his affection for her had cooled; it was more as if his lust had simply faded away with time – evaporated.
("Sweet Will." Lying beside him one night, caressing his genitals.
"I'm tired," he answered. "Sorry. Tired and old."
"You're not old."
"Older than you."
"Not too old."
"Maybe tomorrow...")
But Alison had all her other men; only God knew how many there were. Admirers, lovers – they couldn't stay away. They'd sneak away from their wives and come calling. *("I have a visitor today,"* she'd say. *"Go down to Marco's; play your little game. I'll send for you...")*
It had been the same in London. He'd guessed, never asked. Realisation had developed slowly, acceptance simultaneously. As long as she was happy... It was her money that had brought them here to Venice, where she'd always wanted to be; her money that bought his life, made it possible to live without labour. The word *prostitute* sometimes knocked about in his head. But she wasn't that; she cultivated her men, nurtured them like a gardener before allowing them into her inner circle. And once there, they were devoted forever. Even the young men – thirty-year-olds, forty – they'd come, trembling, thrilling with anticipation. Alison was ageless, her sixty-five years chasing her but never catching up.

"Fuck!" (*"Cazzo!"*) exclaims Bernardo. "Bastardo! You win again." Girolamo leans forward, sweeps the dominoes together and begins to shuffle them. "Will – you and me."
Will relights his pipe and watches his opponent prepare the tiles. It's an old set they use – bone pieces, white, black skull and crossbones engraved on the back of each, grinning, sardonic. They belong to Tommaso and live in their walnut box in a cupboard in Caffè Marco.
Signora Barbarigo is no longer in sight. Padre Girolamo flicks his

head towards the good lady's apartment. "They'll be up there right now, banging like Solomon and the Queen of Sheba."
"Maybe he just looks," Bernardo suggests (he's the youngest of their number and wonders if intercourse in old age might prove problematic). "Perhaps he can't manage it."
"Why?" Tommaso shoots back, frowning. "You think he's past it? God keep us all stiff to the end, I say." He himself is two years older than the Nobildonna's lover and has no difficulty in bed, enjoying perfectly healthy sex with both his own wife and with Signora Crowan. Simona still rewards him with her little cries and gasps of pleasure even after more than forty years of marriage (she's always managed to fake convincingly – but he doesn't know that).

Alison told William little of her history. He'd wanted to know of her earlier lovers. Had she been married before?
"That's an old life," she replied. "Don't worry about that."
"But..."
"No," she insisted, stroking his cheek, shaking her head. "It's dropped away. I'm here now – with you."
"But your family – your parents, brothers, sisters?"
"Parents are dead – long ago. Brothers, sisters – all older than me. Never got on with them. Who cares?"
A pause.
"You have children of your own?"
She shook her head again, closed her eyes. "Don't, Will. Life runs from today forward..."

A bell tolls rhythmically from San Apostoli a couple of streets distant. The men gaze at each other.
"That's it then," says Padre Girolamo. "They'll be lifting his coffin."
Tommaso stares at the tabletop and sniffs. "Nico..."
Nicolo Sartori had been the wealthiest of them, running two successful businesses, a merchant in salt and in fabrics. Will had dreaded giving Alison the news of his death; she'd been very

fond of Nico – perhaps even more fond of him than of Will himself.

"Nico," he'd murmured.

"He's dead then…"

"I'm sorry."

She shed more than a few tears.

But Gabriella Sartori, Nico's widow, had *not* been fond of Alison. In fact, she hated her – hated the woman's menagerie of pet men, despised them all, and tolerated her husband's membership of Signora Crowan's bordello only because he was one of the wealthiest men in the city, and she was unwilling to sacrifice her status as his wife. But now he was dead, and she emerged the victor, with all the money, the pride – and the power to shun, to ban Nico's friends from his final rites. She had the power to spit in all their faces – to spit in *her* face – the English whore.

I'm going there too, to that place, thinks Will as the bell mourns. *To death, the final silence. I'm eighty-four; there can't be much left. Too late to set anything right. I've come to nothing, wasted my existence, sitting here, clicking away the days in little bone men, booze and salted sardines. I used to have a life – not much of one, admittedly – but there used to be a purpose. I let her take it away. It didn't seem to matter much at the time – but now it seems a lot. To have had a function and allowed it to die.*

That time in the shop – the day the man visited, bald, wigless, urgent. It was before Jacob was born; Ruby and he had been married only a year; his father had followed his mother into the grave just weeks earlier. William had been alone that afternoon, idle, the shop quiet. Then the door opened, jangling, and this man entered.

"You! Shoemaker?"

"Yes," Will answered. "William Crowan, at your service."

The man strode forward, finger wagging. "You have good name. I ask – people say *you*."

"Me?"

"Mm. Make shoes for me." The visitor located a chair, sat heavily on it and thrust out his feet. "You do it?"

William came forward. "Yes, of course. I'll measure."

"Special shoes," the man said. "For organ playing."

"Organ playing?" Will frowned. "With your feet?"

"Narrow, not too heavy. The heels not too high, not too wide. You can do it?"

"Er..."

The gentleman seemed impatient. "Komm, komm. Sag ja oder nein."

Will nodded. "Yes, of course. I've just...never been asked for such a thing before."

"Hm," the man grunted. "Zey have new pedal keys in Saint Paul's. I can play as I used at home. It would not be polite to besmirch the new woodwork with London shit."

So the measurements were made, and Will suggested his customer return after two days.

"Gut," said the man, standing. "Until then." He turned, about to leave.

"Your name, sir? If I may?"

"Händel," the man nodded, raising his hand in farewell. "I see you again – soon."

William wasn't much interested in the arts but thought he'd heard the name somewhere, perhaps read it in the newspapers. In any case, the shoes were finished on time, and the patron seemed satisfied with the results.

"Ja..." Holding them up, peering at them, then sitting, pulling them on. "Ja, ja, ja! Sehr gut. Diese werden sehr gut tun. You have done a good job, my friend."

The customer was satisfied – delighted even. He settled his bill and shook Will's hand.

Business flourished within hours.

"Mr Crowan?" (Another visitor, younger than Mr Händel, of more delicate build.)

"Yes sir."

"Mr Handel recommends you."

"Let me guess. Shoes for playing the organ?"

The young man laughed. "Well done!"

A string of customers followed, gentlemen and ladies of every age, all on the recommendation of the original client, though few with such a specific, bizarre request. William took on apprentices and was able to pay a reasonable wage. Ruby was impressed with him – for a while. Life got better. Jacob was born, their only child…

"Will!" Tommaso poking him. "Wake up!"
William shakes the daydream out of his head. "Scusa – Ero lontano." *("Sorry – I was far away.")*
Marco has brought them his finest wine to commemorate the passing of their friend. Two of his boys approach the table, bearing platters of tasty things to eat.
"It is a sad day for us," their host declares. "A final farewell to one so dear for so long." He raises a glass and salutes the deceased. "To Signore Sartori – a great man and a true friend."
"Nico!" the comrades respond, elevating their toasts, drinking.
I'm a failure, William muses – *as a husband, as a father, as a craftsman. I've given up on everything and allowed myself to rot, to drift, purposeless. I wonder where Ruby is now; is she even alive? She'd be seventy-three – thirty-four when she left me and Jacob. She walked out on her four-year-old son. What does that say about me? She found her life with me so pointless that she left her own child. Why? How could I have rescued it? Why couldn't I see what was going wrong? I had love as a boy – my mother loved me – at least, I think she did. Why couldn't I pass that on? Maybe Ruby would have stayed – we might all have been happy.*
And my job, my skill. I abandoned it. Making shoes – not exactly an epic calling maybe, but at least there was a purpose in it – and pride, sometimes. Like that time – and after – for a while. Cutting the cloth, the leather, wood, stretching, stitching. There was craftsmanship in it – and I was good – a good teacher too. Remember John, Margaret? They mastered it – particularly John, John Noon. He became a fine cobbler, an artist. What became of him? He'd be…sixty-three now – maybe still working. And Margaret…what was her name…? Southwell, Margaret Southwell. She was younger than John, a year

or two. Good girl, pretty, lived across the bridge. I let them all down, never smiled in the shop, always dull – except in the early days with Alison. Things were brighter then – for a while.
But Jacob... I had a son, and I let him go. Why? What went wrong? We lost each other when he was young – moved apart. Getting closer always seemed too big an effort. I abandoned him – abandoned him in spirit, my own boy. He was eighteen when I saw him last; now he'd be forty-three. No contact. He's probably married; I probably have grandchildren I'll never see.
"I should write to Jacob," he suggested one night a few months after they'd settled in their apartment on the Calle del forno. Alison lay in his arms. The window was open, the sky dark, air warm.
"Let him have his own life," she whispered. "He's a good boy."
"But I'm his father," William replied. "I should make an effort to keep in touch."
"If you like."
"You have his address?"
"Yes."
He felt relieved; if she'd said no...
"That's good," he murmured.
But the days slipped by, the weeks, months, years – and he'd never made the effort.
Failure. You've aborted everything – aborted your whole life.

The silence of his friends brings Will to himself once more. They're staring at the canal – Tommaso, Bernardo, Padre Girolamo – all staring. Will follows their line of sight and discovers the source of their fascination. It's a gondola. Three of the four passengers are men: a young aristocrat, about thirty, effeminate-looking, clean-shaven, dressed to display in a fussy jacket of silver silk, white wig beribboned with pink; the other two are in darker apparel, more worn, probably servants. The older is tall, swarthy, threatening in appearance, four or five days' stubble darkening his face; the other is much younger, perhaps twenty, clean-shaven, bright of eye. But it was the woman reclining in the vessel's rear who'd caught the attention of the domino players – and now that of William.

My God…

He rises to his feet to more clearly see her as the boat continues on its way.

Sweet Jesus…

She appears to be in her middle twenties, but Will senses she's older, ageless; there's a gravity about her, a vortex, as if she's intruding into this world from another. Her beauty is devastating, like a weapon that cannot be resisted. There's something Medusa-like about her flowing, shockingly red hair. It's not just the red of this realm, but of Heaven and Hell also, the red of centuries, a red that could kill, could turn a soul to stone. And she's gazing coldly at him – at William. Not at the others, but at him, her stare like twin lances penetrating through his spirit and on, into his secrets, his essence, the kernel of his flimsy existence.

Will's heart races as the gondola pulls into the distance. The air crackles as if lightning is about to strike. Jacob's image flares into his head. He's falling, smoke blotting his vision…

"Will!"

"Marco! Fetch help!"

CHARACTER LISTS

Dates following the character names indicate year of birth. Dates of death are given in a few cases where the disclosure does not undermine the narrative.

THE ORIGIN OF VIVIANNE STAMPER

Characters arranged into groups

Lostwithiel and London

Cadan Tremayne – 1715. A gentleman, writer, poet, living near Lostwithiel, Cornwall; son of Eseld Tremayne; husband of Isla Kello; father of Olivia Lucy Tremayne.

Isla Kello (later Tremayne) – 1719. Daughter of Chesten Kello; wife of Cadan Tremayne; mother of Olivia Lucy Tremayne.

Olivia Lucy Tremayne – April 15, 1743. Daughter of Cadan and Isla Tremayne.

Eseld Tremayne – 1691. Mother of Cadan Tremayne.

Chesten Kello – 1696. Mother of Isla Kello.

Bessie Graves – 1725. Maid to Cadan and Isla Tremayne in London; Olivia's nurse.

York

Ambrose Stamper – 1712. A wine merchant resident in York.

Cicely Wood (later Stamper) – February 1699. A woman resident in York; wife of Ambrose.

Vivianne Stamper – April 1743. Ambrose and Cicely's acquired daughter.

Joshua Foster – 1677. A York jeweller who for many years kept Cicely Wood as his mistress.

The Heavenly Host

Guy Burrage (the Angel Gabriel) – 1703. A criminal: kidnapper, rapist, murderer.

Robert Dixon (the Archangel Michael) – 1709. A criminal:

kidnapper, rapist, murderer.
Patricia Muir (Mary Magdalene) – 1712. A criminal: kidnapper.

Oulston

Caspar Haggard – 1710. A farmer near Oulston, Yorkshire.
Joan Haggard – 1714. Caspar's wife.
Joel Haggard – 1733. Son of Caspar and Joan.
Bennet Haggard – 1736. Son of Caspar and Joan.
Milo Grimes – 1688. A labourer at Oulston Manor, Yorkshire.
Greta Grimes – 1692. Milo's wife.
Blousy – 1740. A water spaniel owned by Milo and Greta Grimes.

The School Scouts

Daphne Harlan – 1722. A scout for The Lookout and other such establishments; lover of Martin Brixton.
Martin Brixton – 1706. A scout for The Lookout and other such establishments; Daphne Harlan's lover.
Jasper Denholm – 1713. A scout for The Lookout and other such establishments.
Edmund Carlton – 1730. A scout for The Lookout and other such establishments.

Peripheral Characters

Stuart Brown – 1709. York wine merchant; colleague of Ambrose Stamper.
Simon ? – 1700. Manager of a wine warehouse in York; Ambrose Stamper's employer.
Joe ? – 1703. Cicely Stamper's landlord in York.
Jack ? – 1701. Landlord of The Bull alehouse, Oulston, Yorkshire.
Mrs Limb – 1687. Widow resident in Oulston, Yorkshire.
Sir Nicholas Yearsley – 1714. Lord of the Manor at Oulston; husband of Lady Anne.
Lady Anne Yearsley – 1720. Wife of Sir Nicholas Yearsley.
Jacob Crowan – April 20, 1729. Headmaster of The Lookout, a school on the Yorkshire coast.

Jack Archer – 1695. Gatekeeper at The Lookout.

NATTY MILLER

Natty's family

? ? – 1668. Husband of Dorothy Flint; father of Barbara. Disappeared in 1685.
Dorothy Flint – 1661-1700. Warwickshire healer; mother of Barbara Flint; murdered.
Barbara Flint – January 19, 1679-September 30, 1726. Herbalist, healer; keeper of a "house of correction" in Lealholm; Mother of Natty Miller.
Natalia "Natty" Miller (née Flint) – February 23, 1710. Daughter of Barbara Flint; mother of Nicholas and Buffy (Pond Girl), with whom she shares the warrener's cottage at Cappleman Farm.
Bruce Miller – 1704-? Warrener at Cappleman Farm, 1724-28; husband of Natty (married in 1726); father of Nicholas.
Nicholas Miller – July 5, 1726. Assistant warrener at Cappleman Farm from 1739, later promoted to warrener; son of Natty; brother of Buffy (Pond Girl).
Buffy Miller (Pond Girl) – March 7, 1742. Daughter of Natty; sister of Nicholas.

The Fleshers

Timothy Flesher – 1628-1699. Owner of Cappleman Farm; son of William Flesher and Margaret Cappleman; father of Benjamin.
Benjamin Flesher – 1663-November 1744. Owner of Cappleman Farm. Son of Timothy Flesher; husband of Emmeline Flesher (née Carrol); father of Hugh.
Emmeline Flesher (née Carrol) – 1678-December 1757. Wife of Benjamin; mother of Hugh.
Hugh Flesher – 1701. Son of Benjamin and Emmeline. Later

owner of Cappleman Farm.
Amelia Flesher (née Barker) – 1713. Wife of Hugh; mother of Louise and Henry.
Louise Flesher – 1737. Daughter of Hugh and Amelia; sister of Henry.
Henry Flesher – 1739. Son of Hugh and Amelia; brother of Louise.

Hazel Priestly's family

John Sykes – 1657-1733. Husband of Scarlet (née Marshall); father of Hazel.
Scarlet Sykes (née Marshall) – 1670-1719. Daughter of Slade and Daisy Marshall; wife of John Sykes; mother of Hazel.
Hazel Priestly (née Sykes) – 1695-April 1759. Daughter of John and Scarlet; wife of Oswin; mother of Adam, William and Nara; grandmother of Kate Swithenbank.
Oswin Priestly – 1690-August 1741. Son of Eleanor; husband of Hazel (née Sykes); father of Adam, William and Nara.
Adam Priestly – 1720. Worker at Cappleman Farm; son of Oswin and Hazel; brother of William and Nara; Kate Swithenbank's uncle.
William Priestly – 1724. Worker at Cappleman Farm; son of Oswin and hazel; brother of Adam and Nara; Kate Swithenbank's uncle.
Nara Priestly (later Nara Swithenbank) – May 18, 1733. Daughter of Oswin and Hazel; sister of Adam and William Priestly; wife of Alder Swithenbank; mother of Kate.
Alder Swithenbank – April 2, 1703. Labourer at Cappleman Farm; son of William and Heather; husband of Nara Priestly; father of Kate.
Catherine (Kate) Swithenbank – March 29, 1749. Daughter of Alder and Nara Swithenbank; granddaughter of Hazel Priestly.
Eleanor Priestly – 1656-March 1742. Mother of Oswin Priestly, resident in Northallerton.

The Buckleys and the Swifts, in service to the Fleshers

Douglas Buckley – 1685-1740. Husband of Maria; father of Elys.
Maria Buckley (née Cox) – 1694-1756. Wife of Douglas; mother of Elys.
Elys Buckley – 1716. Son of Douglas and Maria.
Bernard Swift – 1697-1762. Husband of Florence; father of Richard.
Florence Swift (née Wheatley) – 1705. Wife of Bernard; mother of Richard.
Richard Swift – 1724. Son of Bernard and Florence; husband of Emma; father of Amy and Beatrice.
Emma Swift (née Barnaby) – 1721. Wife of Richard; mother of Amy and Beatrice.
Amy Swift – 1744. Daughter of Richard and Emma; sister of Beatrice.
Beatrice Swift – 1746. Daughter of Richard and Emma; sister of Amy.

Various Cappleman Farm worthies

Miriam Exley – 1725. Lives at Cappleman Farm.
Zachary Foley – 1701. Labourer on Cappleman Farm; husband of Prudence; father of Alice.
Prudence Foley – 1707. Wife of Zachary; mother of Alice.
Alice Foley – 1726. Daughter of Zachary and Prudence.
Tudor Green – 1719. A carpenter on Cappleman Farm. Betrothed to Hazel Robinson.
Bridie Lyle – 1697. Landlady of a rooming house on Cappleman Farm.
Tozer Robinson – 1705. A labourer on Cappleman Farm; husband of Apple; father of Willow, Hazel, Cedar and Holly.
Apple Robinson (née Barrow) – 1708. Wife of Tozer Robinson; mother of Willow, Hazel, Cedar and Holly.
Willow Robinson – 1725. Eldest child of Tozer and Apple Robinson; sister of Hazel, Cedar and Holly.
Hazel Robinson (later Hazel Green) – 1729. Daughter of Tozer and Apple Robinson; sister of Willow, Cedar and Holly;

betrothed to Tudor Green.
Cedar Robinson – 1731. Worker on Cappleman Farm; son of Tozer and Apple Robinson; brother of Willow, Hazel and Holly.
Holly Robinson – 1736. Youngest daughter of Tozer and Apple Robinson; sister of Willow, Cedar and Hazel.

Parsons

Revd Cornelius East – September 12, 1700. Parson of Glaisdale from 1724.
Revd Robert Forest – 1727. Parson of Easington from 1752.
Revd Henry Swallow – 1675-1738. Parson of St. Peter's church, Lealholm.

Various folk from Lealholm, Glaisdale, Easington, Thimbleby and Whitby

Tom Britton – 1691. A Whitby dockhand.
Doctor William Clover – 1679-September 1741. Medical practitioner based in Easington, 1708-1741; friend of Oswin and Hazel Priestly.
Charles Davies – 1684. A Lealholm gentleman.
Miles Forley – 1691. A Lealholm thatcher.
Toby Hauxwell – 1679-1747. Resident of Glaisdale; warrener at Cappleman Farm 1728-43.
Doctor Neil Levinson – 1710. Medical practitioner at Easington from 1741.
John Miller – 1683. Father of Bruce Miller; husband of Mary. Resident in Thimbleby.
Mary Miller – 1681-1715. Mother of Bruce Miller; wife of John.
Clifford Noble – 1668. Lealholm undertaker; husband of Doris Noble.
Diane Noble – 1681. Wife of Clifford Noble, Lealholm undertaker.
Meadow Reid – February 2, 1737. Friend of Louise Flesher.
Joan Shepherd – 1656. A Lealholm matron – ran a small part-time "school" in her house.

Peggy Silkin – 1708. Lealholm friend of Natty.
William Taggart – 1695. A Lealholm chandler

POOR NANCY

Raymond Harding – 1693. A gentleman of independent means, resident in Bath; husband of Nancy.

Nancy Harding – 1697. Wife of Raymond Harding.

Tom Cox – 1688. A gentleman of independent means; husband of Brenda; friend of Raymond.

Brenda Cox – 1696. Wife of Tom Cox; Nancy's best friend.

An unnamed elderly man, possibly of Cornish origin.

A young woman, his companion, fifty-three years his junior.

A second elderly man, who sought to quell the argument in the theatre.

Fanny Harris – 1728. Raymond's mistress; Formerly Nancy's maid.

A coachman.

SECRET GIRL

Characters arranged into groups

The Ottershaw household

Jerome Ottershaw, Revd – 1711. Rector of St. John's Church, Halifax; husband of Celia.
Celia Ottershaw – 1720. Wife of Revd. Jerome Ottershaw.
Sam Dunn – 1697. The Ottershaws' butler.
Muriel Pratt – 1722. A maid at the Ottershaws' house.
Carl Lipscombe – 1696. Jerome Ottershaw's lawyer in Halifax.

The Stavely Household

Alasdair Stavely – 1705. A Halifax gentleman, in the partial employ of his father-in-law, Sir Percival Finch; husband of Lady Ivy Stavely.
Ivy Stavely – 1726. Daughter of Sir Percival and Lady Anne Finch; wife of Alasdair Stavely.
Anne – September 21, 1749. Daughter born to Ivy Stavely.
Frank Sullivan – 1684. The Stavelys' butler.
Linda Drewitt – 1690. The Stavelys' housekeeper.
Kenneth Drewitt – 1687. The Stavelys' head gardener.
Bronagh Duffy – 1729. Daughter of Maeve; Ivy Stavely's maid.
Jane Stephenson – 1705. Midwife hired by Alasdair Stavely.

Secondary Characters

Celestine Pringle – 1699-1754. Nurse at the Halifax workhouse.
Mo Grayson – 1695. A farmer.
Daniel Morris – 1726. A labourer on Mo Grayson's farm, south of Halifax.
Victor Entwhistle – 1703. A labourer on Mo Grayson's farm.

Crafty – 1746. Dan Morris's foxhound.

Peripheral Characters, arranged alphabetically by last name

Doll ? – 1714. A maid at the Halifax workhouse.
Albert Bridewell – 1688. Jane Stephenson's landlord in Leeds.
Peter Creston – 1700. Halifax constable. Owner of a linen shop on Petticoat Lane.
Revd Claudius Daubuz – 1704-1760. Vicar of St Peter's Church, Huddersfield.
Maeve Duffy – 1701-1750. Bronagh Duffy's mother, living in Belfast.
Desmond Ellerby – 1726. A single man; Lorraine Philips's lover.
Agnes Fairchild – 1696. A Halifax matron.
Sir George Finch – 1660-1732. Sir Percival's father.
Lady Sophia Finch – 1670-1729. Sir Percival's mother.
Sir Percival Finch – 1692. Son of Sir George and Lady Sophia Finch; Lady Ivy's father; a tobacco farmer in the Chesapeake Bay.
Lady Anne Finch – 1700-1738. Sir Percival's first wife; Ivy's mother.
Lady Rebecca Finch – 1712-1745. Sir Percival's second wife.
Dyani Finch – 1727. Sir Percival's third wife, a native American woman.
Kosumi Finch – 1746. Son of Sir Percival and Dyani.
Mrs Fulham – 1686. One of Jerome Ottershaw's parishioners in Halifax.
Pamela (Pammy) Heron – 1749. A girl at the Halifax workhouse.
Dominic Lowell – 1730. Jerome Ottershaw's curate in Halifax.
Giles Ottershaw – May 10, 1762. Son of Revd Jerome and Cecilia Ottershaw.
Lorraine Philips – 1700. An attractive Halifax widow.
Agnes Pickering – 1701. A Skipton woman; Jerome Ottershaw's first love.
Portia Ralston – 1701. A Halifax matron.
George Ralston – 1693. Portia's husband.
Maude Risby – 1718. An enigmatic woman, supposedly

bisexual, encountered by Jerome Ottershaw in Westmoreland. His third love.

Caroline Thackley – 1709. Choirmistress in Jerome Ottershaw's first parish in Todmorden; wife of the town clerk; Jerome's second love.

STALKER

Daniel Higgins – 1714. Constable at Falmouth.
Grace Higgins – 1722. His wife.
Vincent Higgins – 1741. His son.
Jennifer Higgins – 1744. His daughter.
Timothy Higgins – 1748. His youngest son.
Jason Matthews – 1702. Constable at Penzance.
Hal Brown – 1700-1751. Coachman killed by Felix Poole immediately before Poole's capture.
Zachary Stannard – 1729. Coach guard.
Nathaniel Humphreys – 1720. Highwayman.
Isaiah Collins – 1711-1749. Friend of Daniel Higgins, killed by Felix Poole.
Deborah Collins – 1722. Wife of Isaiah. Raped by Felix Poole.
Felix Poole – 1701. Highwayman.
Unnamed young woman – 1731. Daniel Higgins' prey.

THE APOSTATE

James Bevington I – 1603-1678. Violinist. Father of James Bevington II.

James Bevington II – 1644-1723. Violinist. Father of James Bevington III.

Margaret Bevington – 1659-1751. Portrait painter. Wife of James Bevington II; mother of James Bevington III.

James Bevington III – 1683. Violinist.

Mary Bevington – 1685. His wife.

Matthew Bevington – 1710. Violinist. Eldest son of James and Mary.

John Bevington – 1713. Violinist. Youngest son of James and Mary.

James Nares – 1715-1783. Organist of York Minster.

THE MILL

Roz – 1729. See Rosepetal Epplewith.
Kate – 1749. See Catherine Swithenbank.
Hugo Ash – 1709. Miller at Egton watermill; brother of Cristina.
Cristina Ash – 1714. Estranged sister of Hugo.
Agnes Blake – 1706. Arthur Blake's mother.
Arthur Blake – 1734. A boy, charmed to distraction by Roz Epplewith; son of Agnes.
Frank Butterworth ("Doctor" Butterworth) – 1704. Whitby abortionist and unlicensed backstreet medic.
Annabel Epplewith – 1714-43. Mother of Rosepetal; a prostitute, sold at the age of eleven by her mother to work as a prostitute in Betty Drabb's Whitby bawdy house.
Rosepetal Epplewith (Roz) – 1729. Daughter of Annabel; a Whitby prostitute; acquaintance of Hugo Ash.
Matilda Little ("Nurse" Little) – 1699. Whitby abortionist; mistress of Frank Butterworth.
Will Pratt – 1690. Secretary to the Lord Mayor of Whitby.
Catherine Swithenbank (Kate) – March 29, 1749. A girl from Cappleman Farm; friend of Hugo Ash.

The troop at Betty Drabb's house of ill repute, in descending vintage

Betty Drabb – 1680. Madam of a brothel in Whitby harbour.
Annabel Epplewith – 1714-43. Prostitute; mother of Rosepetal.
Beatrice Gibson (Bea) – 1714. Prostitute.
Emma Brown – 1720. Prostitute.
Jane Saddley – 1725. Prostitute.
Rosepetal Epplewith (Roz) – 1729. Prostitute; daughter of Annabel.
May Wilkinson – 1738. Prostitute.

Daisy Bland – 1739. Prostitute.
Dapple Graham – 1742. Prostitute.
Polly Scuttle – May 2, 1743. Prostitute.

FAITHFULNESS

Speck Beckwith – July 7, 1719. Farmer at the Lookout.
Jenny Beckwith (née Clifton) – 1720-April 4th, 1741. Wife of Speck Beckwith.
Edie Ashton – 1740. Kitchen maid at the Lookout.
Margaret York – 1739. Chambermaid at the Lookout.
Tranter Tickle – 1708. Farmer at the Lookout; husband of Teresa.
Teresa Tickle – September 1710. Wife of Tranter Tickle.
John Eldenshaw – 1716. Farmer at the Lookout.
Ned Silden – 1730. Gardener at the Lookout; husband of Pixie Silden.
Pixie Silden – 1733. Wife of Ned Silden.

IN HER SLEEP

A malevolent unnamed entity, the remnant of three brothers.
An unnamed child, the brothers' nemesis.
Reudh. A spirit with many names passing through successive incarnations (Wath, Yossel, Corsen, Ealswith, Cassia, Rufina, Julia, Willa, Aisling, Ruby, Astrid, Liv, Anne, Catherine, Rose, etc.); sister of Kweid.
Kweid. A spirit with many names passing through successive incarnations (Luna, Thyra, Maria, etc.); sister of Reudh.
Hugo Ash – 1709. Miller at Egton watermill.
Jacob Crowan – April 20, 1729. Headmaster of the Lookout.
Holly Robinson – 1736-59. Youngest daughter of Tozer and Apple Robinson.

TERREL'S WOMEN

Terrel Nisbet – 1730. Mathematics tutor at the Lookout.
Ben (Egerton) Badger – 1721. Literature tutor at the Lookout.
Leafy Crosthwaite – June 6, 1731. Dairymaid at the Lookout.
Denise Trent – 1734. Housemistress at the Lookout.
Eve Miller – 1732. Housemistress at the Lookout.
Lettice Shelley – 1733. Housemistress at the Lookout.
Eleanor Rodman – 1735. Housemistress at the Lookout.
Edwin ? – an unknown man, possibly a former lover (or fantasy) of Leafy Crosthwaite.

DILLY AND EMILY

Dilly Sollett – 1743. A young woman from Catterall, resident in Ribchester, Lancashire; mother of Emily.
Emily Sollett – January 9, 1761. Dilly's daughter.
Agnes Sollett – 1721. Dilly's mother; wife of Peter, later of Roger Ullswater.
Peter Sollett – 1719-1756. Brewer; Dilly's father; husband of Agnes.
Roger Ullswater – 1701. Farm labourer; Agnes Sollett's second husband; Dilly's stepfather.
Leo Kelly – 1739. Alehouse worker; left his father's house in Manchester; lover of Dilly Sollett.
Toby Lightwell – 1703. Weaver; a Ribchester widower.
Mary Lightwell – 1698-1760. Toby's wife.
Jonah Woodcock – 1756. A Ribchester boy; son of Janice.
Janice Woodcock – 1733. Jonah's mother.
John Bennett – 1715. Landlord of the White Bull, Ribchester; husband of Sarah; employer and friend of Alexander Regan and Helen Shaw.
Sarah Bennett – 1717. Landlady of the White Bull, Ribchester; wife of John; friend of Dilly, and of Alexander Regan and Helen Shaw.
Alexander Regan – January 10, 1735. Irishman; barman at The White Bull, Ribchester; husband of Helen Shaw.
Helen Shaw (Helen Regan) – 1736. Maid at The White Bull Inn, Ribchester; wife of Alexander Regan.
Francis Regan – May 18, 1761. Son of Alexander Regan and Helen Shaw.
George Fowles, Doctor – 1712. Ribchester Surgeon.
Janet ? – 1720. Ribchester midwife.

DOMINOES

Characters are listed in alphabetical order of last name.

Padre Jacopo Arcangeli – 1704. A retired priest from Treviso. Lover of Signora Marianna Barbarigo.
Patrizio Francesco Barbarigo, N.H. Nobil Homo – 1672-1768. A Venetian nobleman. Husband of Marianna Barbarigo, Nobildonna.
Marianna Barbarigo, Nobildonna – 1711. Widow of Patrizio Francesco Barbarigo.
Padre Girolamo Calvene – 1697. A retired priest. Lover of Alison Crowan.
Marco Colussi – 1726. Proprietor of the Caffè Marco, overlooking the Grand Canal in Venice.
William Crowan – 1688. A retired London cobbler, resident in Venice for 25 years. Husband of Alison Crowan; father of Jacob Crowan.
Ruby Crowan – 1699. William Crowan's first wife; mother of Jacob.
Jacob Crowan – 1729. Son of William and Ruby Crowan.
Alison Crowan – 1707. Wife of William Crowan. A celebrated courtesan, first in London, then in Venice.
Bernardo Favaro – 1715. A retired printer; father of three sons. Lover of Alison Crowan.
George Frederick Handel – February 23, 1685-April 14, 1759. Composer, resident in London.
John Noon – 1709. Cobbler. Once apprentice to William Crown.
Tommaso Rossi – 1702. Retired galley captain (a *sopracomito*). Husband of Simona; lover of Alison Crowan.
Simona Rossi – 1704. Tomasso's wife.
Nicolo Sartori – 1686-1772. A merchant in salt and fabrics.

Husband of Gabriela Sartori; lover of Alison Crowan.
Gabriela Sartori – 1686. Wife of Nicolo Sartori.
Margaret Southwell – 1711. Cobbler. Once apprentice to William Crown.

The occupants of the gondola

The red-headed woman – March 29, 1749.
The aristocratic man – June 2, 1740-December 2, 1814.
The tall, swarthy servant – 1737.
The younger, bright-eyed servant – 1753.

THE AUTHOR

Kevin Corby Bowyer was born in Southend-on-Sea in 1961. He spent most of his life as a professional musician, travelling the world, playing solo concerts, making commercial recordings and trying to teach others how to play. He always imagined his musical performances acts of storytelling. He is the author of *The House on Boulby Cliff*, *In the Silence of Time* (2 vols.), *Close to the Silence*, *Babylon House*, *Cadmun Gale*, and *Splinters of Silence*. Kevin lives in Scotland with his wife Sandra.

Printed in Great Britain
by Amazon